SLEEPING W

Catherine's head fel... pain was that unbearable and the pressure that intense. The heavy drapes were drawn tightly shut, and the room was still so dark that she had no idea where she was or even what time it was.

There was a cramp in her leg, her wrist felt like it was on fire, and she was starving. Though drifting toward consciousness, she was not fully awake yet and remained completely unaware that she was at Nowell's house. Despite her misery, she was grateful at least to be cuddled up with her husband. She burrowed her backside a little closer in to him, hoping that maybe she would go back to sleep that way, but her headache wouldn't surrender. Then, suddenly, a slow realization began to settle in.

"This cannot be Michael!" she said to herself as she opened her eyes all the way and saw that she was not in her own bed. The man beside her was Nowell! And, to her utter astonishment, he was smiling at her as though nothing were out of the ordinary. She was almost too alarmed to move.

Catherine stared at him with dark, hardened eyes, unable or unwilling to comprehend fully what was happening. . . .

Immaculate Deception

———✦———

by

Stacey Sauter

AN ONYX BOOK

ONYX
Published by the Penguin Group
Penguin Books USA Inc., 375 Hudson Street,
New York, New York 10014, U.S.A.
Penguin Books Ltd, 27 Wrights Lane,
London W8 5TZ, England
Penguin Books Australia Ltd, Ringwood,
Victoria, Australia
Penguin Books Canada Ltd, 10 Alcorn Avenue,
Toronto, Ontario, Canada M4V 3B2
Penguin Books (N.Z.) Ltd, 182–190 Wairau Road,
Auckland 10, New Zealand

Penguin Books Ltd, Registered Offices:
Harmondsworth, Middlesex, England

Published by Onyx, an imprint of Dutton Signet,
a division of Penguin Books USA Inc.

First Printing, September, 1997
10 9 8 7 6 5 4 3 2 1

 REGISTERED TRADEMARK—MARCA REGISTRADA

Printed in the United States of America

PUBLISHER'S NOTE
This is a work of fiction. Names, characters, places, and incidents either are the product of the author's imagination or are used fictitiously, and any resemblance to actual persons, living or dead, events, or locales is entirely coincidental.

PART ONE

Chapter One

Catherine Harrison examined herself closely in the mirror and, for the moment at least, liked what she saw. She'd spent considerable time working her natural blond hair into a chignon, artfully arranging wisps to fall on the nape of her neck. The effect was quite sexy, she thought as she applied her lipstick: a full-bodied red that belied her growing nervousness. She'd never needed a lot of makeup; nature had blessed her that way. But tonight was different. It had to be.

Where is Michael? she wondered anxiously, glancing at the small clock radio in their bathroom. It was 6:00 P.M. The cocktail reception started in less than an hour, and she had no desire to be late. Her tension over his absence changed to anger. "This is absurd," she muttered grimly. "He still has to take a shower, get dressed . . . he knows how important this event is to me, dammit." She moved into the bedroom and sat on the edge of the bed while pulling silky black stockings up her long, lean legs.

The fact that they couldn't afford tickets to the American Federation of Arts black-tie dinner dance might have made Michael an unwilling date, but it hadn't deterred her. Catherine considered attending the gala at Manhattan's famed Rainbow Room one of her best chances for landing a position at a prestigious interior design firm—something that had eluded her since joining Michael in New York as he studied for the Episcopal priesthood at General Theological Seminary.

They'd been married nearly eighteen months—eighteen of what seemed like the longest months in Catherine's life. She simply hadn't foreseen that the transition into marriage or life in New York would be this rough. She'd felt certain that by now she'd have it all—a decent income from a decorating career and the man she loved. Living in the Big Apple had struck envy among her more cosmopolitan friends back in North Carolina, and her move here had elevated her to near-celebrity status among them. If they could only see her now—nearly broke and living in a shabby brownstone building.

We should have waited until he finished school to get married, Catherine admitted to herself while continuing to dress for the evening's event, but quickly vanquished the thought as she heard Michael's keys in the door.

"Oh, thank God," she hollered with forced cheerfulness. "Honey, please hurry, we've *got* to leave in fifteen minutes."

Expecting him to pop immediately into the bedroom and begin undressing, Catherine unzipped the plastic bag that contained her gown. The apartment remained quiet for a few moments longer until Michael finally moved toward her—but without the intensity of someone late for a black-tie affair. She felt her chest tighten with renewed frustration. Without a word Michael walked past her and over to the closet, where instead of stripping down he began fishing for something.

"Your tux and shoes are out in the living room," Catherine offered sweetly, hoping to nudge him along.

"I noticed," he replied sharply, pulling his favorite sweatshirt from the laundry pile.

"What are you doing?" she started to snap but caught herself, hoping to conceal her anger. She wanted tonight to be special and needed Michael's full cooperation to make it a success. It was important not to set the tone of the evening with another fight.

"I'm not going," he announced, tugging the well-worn garment over his black hair. His usually soft, soulful eyes looked unsympathetic as he pulled the sweatshirt over his muscular torso.

"What do you mean, you're not going?" she snapped. "You can't do this to me now!"

"I never said for sure I would go. I said I would think about it."

Tears filled her brown eyes and she blinked them back; less out of vanity and more because she didn't want Michael to see how badly he was getting to her.

"Did you hear me?" he asked, as though somehow her silence meant she'd missed the point.

"What do you want me to say, Michael," Catherine said chokingly, then moved toward the living room where she wouldn't have to look at him. The sight of his tuxedo all perfectly laid out on the sofa made her flinch. She bit hard on her lower lip and looked up at the ceiling. Behind her, Michael entered the room, his demeanor softening.

"Catherine, look, I'm sorry," he offered. "But you've gotta understand. First, I have an exam the day after tomorrow, and secondly, I'm not going to know anybody there. It's an absolute waste of my time."

Catherine clutched at her robe, drawing it more closely around her body. What had started out as a well-laid plan was turning into a disaster. Michael had no idea that she'd spent five hundred dollars apiece on the tickets, leaving only one hundred fifteen dollars in their savings account. But a close, wealthy friend of her family—someone considered trustworthy on these matters—had assured Catherine this gala was a must for meeting the right people. Catherine had never gone to an event like this alone, and the prospect of attending such an affair by herself and without knowing a single person seemed unimaginable.

"Why did you have to wait until the last minute to do this to me?" she finally blurted without looking at him, her voice tinged with bitterness.

"Catherine, you make it sound like I'm doing this to hurt you."

Catherine mumbled a response.

"I'm sorry, I didn't hear you," replied Michael. His remark was met with thick silence, irritating him greatly.

"Do you have something to say?" he asked. "Otherwise I'm going back to the seminary to study."

"We should have waited to get married!" she blurted, her back still toward him. She knew her comment would cut to the quick and it did. Michael didn't say another word. Instead he gathered his coat and keys and within seconds was gone.

Unable to hold back tears any longer, Catherine slumped onto the sofa, crushing Michael's tuxedo beneath her, then laid her head in her hands and sobbed.

Compounding her fury was a sharp sense of guilt over her rash statement.

It wasn't Michael's fault that she didn't have a job. If anything, he'd encouraged her to stay the course and not settle for anything that wouldn't make her happy. He said the bills would always be there, and so would mediocre jobs. But the chance to work in Manhattan with some of the finest designers in the world would not. He felt that she should take full advantage of it, even if it took longer than usual to get the right position. But neither of them had realized just how long it would take. It was particularly frustrating for Catherine who until marrying Michael never had a financial worry in her life.

"Oh, why," she cried, wiping away tears with the back of her hand. "Why does it have to be this way?"

Catherine looked down at the wet streak of mascara on her hand, then began slowly turning her gold wedding band. She remembered telling her father she was in love with Michael and wanted to marry him, and how hurt she'd been by his response. Though Edwin Howard claimed to admire Michael's lofty goals, he never shared Catherine's enthusiasm for him, making it clear he wanted her to marry someone with more money or greater financial potential.

"Be smart, girl," he replied condescendingly, "love doesn't pay the bills."

When it became clear Catherine was serious about Michael, her father badgered her repeatedly to rethink her relationship, even threatening not to pay for a wedding. But Catherine genuinely loved Michael. And more than that, she respected him, which was something she didn't feel for her philandering father. And so, a year after their first meeting, she and Michael secretly eloped.

After the ceremony Michael moved on to school in New York alone, while Catherine remained in North Carolina, and their families had not suspected a thing. In fact, Catherine's father thought the long-distance relationship was winding down and felt grateful that his daughter had finally put things into perspective. Until Catherine nearly died.

A month after their elopement, Catherine discovered she was pregnant. It was a thrilling but frightening development in their lives, one which she and Michael didn't know how to handle. Tragically it ended up taking care of itself. One night, eight weeks into the pregnancy, Catherine awoke with debilitating pain radiating throughout her abdomen. Shortly after arriving at the hospital she was told the pregnancy was ectopic and that the fallopian tube where the embryo had mistakenly lodged was about to burst open. Emergency surgery saved her life, but there was no way to save the baby or the fallopian tube. It was a sad and traumatic event for her and Michael—especially since the doctor informed them that future pregnancies might be difficult, if not impossible, and they both longed for children.

Even more shocking was her parents' reaction: they were livid over not having the chance to give her a proper wedding, at first showing more concern over the missed social event than her health. She could barely wait to get away from them afterward, and remained in North Carolina just long enough to finish school at their expense, then promptly joined Michael in New York. But her move brought none of the positive changes she dreamed of.

Michael was often gone for long stretches of time to study or participate in charitable activities, always leaving Catherine alone. In addition to her loneliness, she'd had no luck finding a job. The interior design market was tight and she was repeatedly told she didn't have the level of experience to penetrate it.

And now, tonight, feeling angry and remorseful, she realized what she must do and began pulling herself together. This was no time to get choked up on pride, she decided. Regardless of how self-conscious she felt going alone, it was imperative that she make it to that gala and not come home empty-handed.

Chapter Two

For the first time that evening a sense of ease returned to Catherine, in spite of the high-profile company beside her. She smiled warmly at the waiter filling her wineglass for the second time, then at her dinner companion. It was Lucas Sloane, the world-famous fashion designer. He and his wife, Candace, seated opposite them at the round table, had been business and marital partners for over thirty years. Together they had built a multimillion-dollar empire through their line of quality, classic clothing for men and women. And within the past decade the couple had launched a home furnishings division that had come to define American taste in its most simple, yet elegant form. Catherine couldn't believe her stroke of luck at being seated beside Lucas Sloane, and in spite of his overbearingly bad breath, she clung to every word he said. As for Sloane, he was also unable to believe his own good fortune at being seated beside this sumptuous Southern dish, and couldn't stop himself from flirting with her despite his wife's quiet wrath.

"Truth or dare?" he said with a chuckle, his eyes aglow with mischief.

"Hmmm," Catherine mused back coquettishly, "what if I don't want to play?"

Though still stylish and sophisticated in appearance, up close Sloane looked every bit of his sixty-nine years—liver spots showing where his thick white hair had receded and sagging jowls under a once taut and attractive face. Catherine thought she detected a slight Brooklyn accent in the man's voice, something he probably worked hard to suppress since it defied his aristocratic image. Catherine glanced over at Candace, as though somehow expecting to gain permission from her to engage in this silliness with her husband. Candace, sitting beside Michael's vacant seat, had her own distraction however, appearing to be happily locked into conversation with the man seated on her other side. Catherine could understand why; he was, quite simply, strikingly handsome.

"Trust me, this is harmless," he said, chortling.

"Truth," Catherine stated playfully to Lucas Sloane while stealing another glance across the table at the man chatting with Candace. She had never seen him before. And unlike the Sloanes' overexposed faces, she couldn't recall him being featured in any of her style magazines.

"Okay," Sloane began, drawing her back into his game, "and mind you, I'm pretty good at this. In other words, I'll know if you're bluffing."

"Then why do you even have to ask me the question?" Catherine asked with a mixture of deference and amusement. Sloane thought he might just melt at the sight of her, but the sound of her soft, measured drawl drove him nearly mad. She seemed genuinely engaged by him, which made her even more alluring. He was usually stuck sitting beside some stuffy dowager at these events. And though his present antic would be deemed highly inappropriate with any of them, it seemed just the thing to retain this young woman's attention.

"Well," Sloane stated, "how about this. I say it's an original, and you just tell me honestly if it is or isn't?"

"If what's an original?" Catherine laughed, sipping her wine.

"Your dress," he said, leaning into her, his face breaking into a broad grin revealing very straight but yellow teeth. His breath was so bad that Catherine fought a natural impulse to tilt as far as possible away from him. The combination of his breath and musky cologne reminded Catherine of being in a stable where the sweet smell of leather and hay would suddenly be overcome by the stench of horse urine with the slightest shift in wind. Despite her years in the stalls, she never got used to it and often held her breath to avoid the smell. She was doing the same tonight.

"You're absolutely right, it is an original," said Catherine, more grateful than ever for her mother's castoff. It was a black velvet, form-fitting bustier gown by Yves Saint Laurent, made more dramatic by a revealing slit

Catherine had cut up the right leg. With the exception
of one-carat diamond stud earrings, a graduation gift
from her parents, she wore no other jewelry except her
wedding ring—which was concealed by black elbow-
length gloves.

"Now, let me guess who did this number for you,"
Sloane said with authority. "I believe it is a creation
by my friend Yves, from his fall collection about four
years ago."

Catherine blushed at the thought that he could identify the make and year of her dress like an auto buff
knew cars.

"Don't worry," he offered reassuringly, "people aren't
looking at you like a secondhand rose. This is just a
particular knack *I* have."

"Thank goodness," Catherine said demurely, taking a
large sip of her wine. Dinner was being set before them,
for which she felt grateful, and not just for the chance
to fill her empty stomach. A quick but steely glance from
Candace said it was time to break up the frivolity. However, Sloane persisted. Catherine only half listened to
him, though, because for the first time she caught the
man across the table looking at her. It was a kindred
look, as if he also felt somewhat trapped by social circumstances. Catherine's mouth curled into a soft smile,
and surprisingly he smiled back, while never ceasing to
listen to Candace Sloane. It had been a long time since
Catherine had looked at another man with interest, but
she simply couldn't help herself from peering at this
rather intriguing fellow.

Though his face was a bit long, even thin, his jaw was
well set and his ruddy cheeks high. His hair was dark
brown, slightly long and wavy, and his nose was perfectly
proportioned to his face—not too long or thin—leading
down to perfectly proportioned lips. He seemed to smile
easily and when he did it revealed a somewhat crooked,
yet very charming and boyish grin that betrayed his aristocratic demeanor. None of that, however, compared to
his eyes, which were deep blue and wide-set under dark,
even brows. There was an intensity, a magnetism, in
those eyes that transcended the rest of his good looks
and drew Catherine in like an undertow.

Catherine turned her attention to Lucas momentarily,

then stole another glance across the table, only this time at the other woman seated beside Candace's dinner companion. She noticed that the man had spoken to her a few times, even leaning in closely toward her as he did. Catherine assumed she was his date, though it wasn't all that clear since he spent most of his time carrying on with Candace Sloane.

Catherine thought her more handsome than attractive, as she had a square jaw and a fairly high forehead giving her something of a horsy look. But her low-cut dress revealed a striking figure, and its deep magenta color offset her raven hair rather nicely. Catherine glanced once more at the man beside her, and unexpectedly caught him looking at her again. She quickly looked away.

"You don't suppose they'd ever have the nerve to serve meat loaf at one of these events?" grumbled Lucas Sloane, unaware of Catherine's growing curiosity in the man across the table. Catherine chuckled, agreeing that a hearty bite of meat loaf would be far more pleasing at the moment than the cornish hens at which they were picking.

"Hey," she interjected with levity, "I believe it's my turn."

"Your turn?" Lucas Sloane asked with an arched brow while slicing a petite carrot in half.

"Well, you asked for the truth and got it. Now I'm going to dare you into doing something."

"This ought to be good, go on," he guffawed, drawing a threatening look from Candace. Emboldened by the wine, Catherine pressed on.

"Well, actually, I dare you to hire me."

"Okay," Sloane said without missing a bite.

Catherine snickered in amusement. "You mean just like that, okay? You don't even know what it is I do!"

"It doesn't matter. I'd be honored just to have your charming presence near me each day. Do you know how to type?"

Catherine's spirits immediately sank. She wasn't sure who'd stepped out-of-bounds first. But feeling he wasn't taking her seriously, she remained silent wondering how she could have blown such a chance with one of the biggest figures in the fashion and design industry. Her worries, though, were short-lived.

"You know, that really was rude of me, and I apologize. You weren't joking about a job, were you?"

"Actually, no. And to tell you the truth, oops, we gotta stop this game." She laughed, feeling relief that perhaps Lucas Sloane, a trendsetter for blue bloods and social climbers, wasn't so crude after all. "Anyway, one of the primary reasons I came here tonight was to meet folks like yourself who could help me get a job. I'm an interior designer."

Sloane proceeded to inquire about her credentials in a more businesslike manner, nodding politely as she shared her education and background. Not wanting to appear desperate, Catherine paced herself, explaining the recent gap in her employment only in terms of taking time to get married and resettle in Manhattan. As she finished, Sloane reached inside his tuxedo and produced a business card.

"You busy tomorrow?" he asked.

"Well, I . . . I don't think so. I mean I'm not really sure." Catherine blushed, still trying not to appear too eager. "Why?"

"If you have some free time tomorrow morning, say around ten-thirty, perhaps you could stop by my office. I'd be happy to take a look at your portfolio. I can't promise you anything, you understand," he stated, still sounding all business. "But I'm always on the lookout for new design talent. You never know." As Catherine reached for his card he winked at her, which annihilated any remaining faith she had of being taken seriously or that Lucas Sloane wasn't a lecher.

"Well, thank you, Mr. Sloane," she said with a smile masking her deep annoyance, "I'll meet you tomorrow at ten-thirty."

As she reached down toward the floor for her handbag she was startled to see someone's feet planted next to her. Looking up, she was surprised to see the man from across the table now standing between her and Lucas Sloane. Catherine uneasily looked across the table and noticed his date staring curiously at them.

"Pardon me," he said in a rich baritone voice made even more distinct by a British accent. Catherine had no idea how long he'd been there, and blushed as she straightened up. "I hope I'm not interrupting something . . ." He cleared his throat and smirked at Lucas as though catching him at an indiscretion.

"Oh, Nowell, bug off," Lucas said with a laugh, then grabbed the man's hand in a hearty shake.

"How are you, old chap?"

"Not bad, not bad. And yourself?" said Lucas good-naturedly, now slapping his arm.

"Quite well, thank you. I enjoyed talking with your wife, though she suddenly abandoned me when someone a bit younger and perhaps a tad more handsome passed by."

His remark prompted a soft chuckle from Catherine, who thought this elusive stranger even more adorable up close.

"Can't say that I blame her," said Lucas. "I see, however, that your date . . . is it Lydia tonight?" he jested.

Nowell said nothing, he only smiled slightly, then arched his brow as if to say yes.

"Well it appears that at least *she* is holding out for your company." Lucas flashed a smile and waved at the young woman who smiled warmly and waved back. Her behavior reminded Catherine of an obedient dog—watchful and eagerly waiting for her master to return. Nowell remained aloof, making Catherine feel somewhat sorry for Lydia.

"Oh, forgive me, Nowell. Have you two met?" Lucas said while placing a sweaty hand on Catherine's bare shoulder.

"Can't say that we have," Nowell answered and took a small step backward as Catherine rose for the formal introduction. Their eyes, having met briefly over dinner, engaged at length as they shook hands. "Nowell Stuart," he offered.

"Catherine," she said, offering her hand but not her last name. Being coy was something that came naturally to her from her single days. She was a masterful flirt, capable of stringing men along just enough to hold their undivided interest, but not so long as to thoroughly frustrate them. Marriage and her recent social isolation made Catherine appreciative of the male attention this evening, and momentarily happy that Michael had de-

cided not to join her. And though she was at the gala
to make job contacts, with Nowell Stuart she slipped
unconsciously into her old habit of drawing male attention for no other reason than the attention itself.

"Catherine," he said with a hint of condescension,
while grinning in his handsome way. Catherine could tell
he was accustomed to having his way with women, and
that asking for her last name would signal defeat.

"Yes, nice to meet you," she replied.

"Are you a patron of the Federation?"

"I am tonight," she continued, smiling.

"To tell you the truth," Lucas interjected, "she's here
job hunting. Better than husband hunting, I suppose,
which is why most young women your age come to these
things—though they'd never admit it!"

Catherine felt a stinging humiliation setting in. She
didn't know why it bothered her that Nowell Stuart
should know she was out of a job, when in fact job
hunting was precisely her mission.

"Any luck?" Nowell asked genuinely, still not asking
her full name or what sort of work she was looking for.

Catherine smiled at Lucas. "A little."

Lucas didn't hesitate to brag. "She may be coming to
work for me. Catherine is a designer."

Catherine's annoyance toward Lucas deepened for
sharing information about her so casually.

"A fashion designer?" Nowell inquired.

"No, interior designer. Are you in the business?"

For some reason her remark made both men laugh,
causing Catherine to blush again.

"I'm sorry, did I say something wrong?" she asked
timidly.

A good-natured sneer crossed Nowell's face. "No, no.
And don't take this personally. It's just that my friend
Lucas knows in what regard I hold most designers. I'd
say arrogant bloodsuckers describes most of the lot."

Lucas let out a coarse laugh, which Nowell joined in.
There was a wonderful rapport between them, as though
they'd known each other a lifetime.

"You know," Nowell proceeded, "I do know from
chatting with him earlier this evening that Wilton Dresden is looking for another interior designer. Have you
heard of him?"

Of course Catherine had heard of Wilton Dresden. He was a big league designer, most notable for his work in the private quarters at the Reagan White House and for his tasteful makeovers of several luxury hotels.

"Yes, indeed," she remarked earnestly.

"Well, I'd be happy to introduce the two of you," said Nowell. "He's seated just a few tables over." He slightly nodded his head in Dresden's direction.

"That would be . . ." Catherine paused from saying "really great," with wide-eyed enthusiasm. "Wonderful," she said gently, "I would appreciate it."

"Lovely. Lucas, do you mind?" he stated.

"Well, as a matter of fact I do," he answered light-heartedly. "Don't forget, ten-thirty tomorrow morning."

"Absolutely." Catherine smiled sweetly. "I'll be there."

Nowell paused briefly to tell Lydia he would be back shortly, then without waiting for her response slid his arm through Catherine's and began guiding her over to where Wilton Dresden was sitting.

Even from behind Catherine could see Dresden was an animated man, as he wildly gesticulated while recounting a story to some rapt table guests. They all laughed in harmony at his punch line. Catherine drew in a deep breath as she prepared to face Dresden. Most of the guests at his table had finished dinner. And some began streaming out to the dance floor, swirling to the tunes of the Lester Lanin orchestra while the lights of Manhattan sparkled brightly outside from their top-floor perch at Rockefeller Center. Nowell waited for an appropriate break in the conversation before tapping Dresden on the shoulder.

"Wilton, if I may steal a moment of your time, I'd like to introduce you to someone."

Dresden's reaction to Nowell, though polite, had none of the warmth displayed by Lucas Sloane. He placed his dinner napkin on the table and rose to greet them, making Catherine feel—yet again that evening—momentarily dumb struck. She'd long read about these famous people. To be in the same room, let alone talking with them, left her feeling giddy.

"Wilton, I was recalling for my friend Catherine our

conversation earlier when I believe you mentioned you're looking for another designer. It just so happens Catherine is a designer and is currently in the market for a new job. I thought you two should meet."

Catherine seized the moment. "First, let me say I'm very honored to meet you. I've been following your career for some time now and I love your work."

Dresden's face broke into a more cordial grin. He was notoriously gay and well known for his bitchy temper. And though he might not be affected by Catherine's sex appeal, he certainly warmed to her flattery.

"Thank you. Anything in particular that you liked?"

Catherine immediately realized he was testing her, and despite her slightly drunken state easily recited several of his projects that struck her fancy. He reminisced about each of the renovations in return, even dropping a few famous names as he did, then finally stuck out his hand to shake hers.

"I'm sorry, I don't believe I caught your last name, Catherine."

"Harrison," she said, now glancing over at Nowell, who'd remained quiet but intensely interested in their exchange. Catherine saw that he registered her last name with a slight grin. She could also see he had a naturally winning way with women, because if she were single he would certainly be getting the best of her. Realizing he might have helped her only because he believed she *was* single, Catherine was in no hurry to ruin the ruse.

"Well, Ms. Harrison. The fact is, I am looking for another designer. And I would love to talk with you further. The problem is, the day after tomorrow I'm heading to Europe for a month. My schedule is packed tomorrow, but I am going to be in the office and would like to move ahead on filling this position. Could you stop by at ten-fifteen?"

"Perfect," Catherine responded warmly. "Only if you're positive it won't be too much trouble."

"Darling, my life is nothing but trouble, as I'm sure your friend Mr. Stuart can attest."

Both men laughed, only not with any fraternal spirit.

"Well, it was a pleasure meeting you, sir. And I'll look forward to seeing you tomorrow," said Catherine. Dresden acknowledged her remark, then just as quickly walked away. Catherine was about to thank Nowell when he gently grasped her arm, guiding her out to the dance floor as the band began their rendition of Dave Brubeck's "Take Five."

"Would you care to dance?" he asked, though her response didn't seem to matter. He'd already placed his hand around her waist, gripped her right hand in his, and begun moving her with light grace around the floor.

"What if I said no," she said with a smirk.

Nowell met her eyes after spinning her once around. "Oh, but you see, you wouldn't. At least you shouldn't. I believe you're in a bit of a jam, Ms. Harrison, and I'm only prepared to help you out of it if you finish this dance with me."

Catherine threw her head back and laughed. Not only was he adorable, he was cocky too. "Oh, you're pitiful," she gibbered. "I would have been perfectly happy to dance with you without some silly excuse."

"I'm touched by your charity," he said mockingly. By now they were moving with such fluidity that Catherine felt her feet were barely touching the floor. Occasionally she glanced at his brilliant blue eyes, and then quickly looked away again. At one point she leaned in a little more closely and caught the mixed scent of tobacco and a musky, yet subtle cologne. It reminded Catherine of her father, a dapper and charming man who'd made a tidy fortune in North Carolina's tobacco industry. No matter how freshly scrubbed, he always seemed to smell like cigarettes—lit and unlit. And tonight, she found the same mixture of cologne and tobacco mildly intoxicating on Nowell Stuart.

Their dance seemed to end too soon, and Catherine was quietly hoping to go another round when Nowell escorted her off the floor.

"Thank you," he said politely. For a moment Catherine was worried he would abandon her, leaving her alone with no one to talk to. What happened next was even worse.

"Well, how do you feel about your meeting with the one-and-only Wilton Dresden tomorrow?"

"You know, I can't thank you enough for your help with that. It was really sweet of you."

"Yes, I suppose. And would you say it was sweet of

me to bring to your attention that you booked an interview with Wilton Dresden at ten-fifteen and another one with Lucas Sloane at ten-thirty?"

Catherine turned ashen over being made such a fool by Nowell Stuart. While flirting with him and trying to impress Wilton Dresden, she had completely forgotten the time of her prior commitment. Relief briefly settled in, since she felt certain that Lucas Sloane wasn't someone she'd want to work for anyway. But she couldn't kid herself. He was a powerful man, and perhaps the key to what she needed most in her life right now—a decent job.

"Oh, my God," she nearly shrieked. "What am I going to do? Wilton Dresden will think I'm an idiot if I suddenly ask to reschedule."

Nowell remained unruffled by her outburst.

"Why didn't you say something earlier?" Catherine asked defiantly. "Especially since you knew all along what was happening."

"Oh, did I now?" he responded devilishly.

"Excuse me, please. I've got to find Lucas Sloane. With any luck *he'll* reschedule a later time."

"Before you go, I may be of some assistance, you know. You see Lucas and I are old chums. I'd be more than happy to smooth the way for you." His expression was smug and vain.

Knowing he was having some fun at her expense, she shrugged off his offer when the thought crossed her mind that she deserved this mishap. Instead of being mildly flirtatious and coy with him, she should have behaved like a married woman out on her own for the evening to do some professional networking. She moved quickly through the crowd to the table which she'd shared with Lucas, but there was no sign of him about. Even Lydia was gone.

"At least my purse is still here," she muttered as she collected it. Scanning the room once again for Lucas Sloane, she gratefully saw him in a far corner chatting with a small group of people. Not anxious to barge in on their conversation, Catherine decided to head to the ladies' room and freshen up first.

As she left one of the stalls, Catherine was surprised to find Candace Sloane washing her hands at one of the sinks. She was a trim and elegant woman, wearing rings heavy with diamonds. Up close, the skin on her face appeared more youthful than that on her hands, suggesting to Catherine that she'd had a face lift—perhaps even two. She wore her brown hair in a classic page style, though it was teased just enough to camouflage the apparent thinning on the crown of her head. Her beaded beige chiffon gown was not too youthful or too matronly, contributing effectively to her sophisticated image.

But despite her reputation for class and social graces, Candace Sloane deliberately ignored Catherine. She did glance at her once while applying fresh lipstick, but when Catherine smiled in response Candace threw her lipstick in her purse, clicked it shut, and began to leave.

"Mrs. Sloane," Catherine said quickly, viewing this as a chance to resolve the schedule.

The woman stopped and as if in slow-motion turned around. There was no warmth or animation in her face. Catherine, however, knew there was no stopping now.

"Mrs. Sloane, hi," she proceeded, tension gripping her voice. "My name is Catherine Harrison. I sat next to Mr. Sloane at dinner this evening, but I never got a chance to meet you." Catherine stuck out her hand which the woman ignored.

"Yes," she said flatly. Candace Sloane clearly didn't want to be bothered by Catherine.

"Well, I just wanted to let you know that I considered it an honor to be seated beside him, as I feel about this chance to meet you."

"Thank you."

"And I also wanted to let you know I'm looking forward to meeting Mr. Sloane tomorrow. I'm an interior designer, or rather an unemployed interior designer . . ." she said, taking a stab at some self-deprecation. Candace Sloane's eyes darkened and narrowed, making Catherine realize that rescheduling her appointment was out of the question. "Anyway," she went on, "Mr. Sloane offered to take a look at my portfolio tomorrow, and I thought if you were free . . ."

"Young lady," Candace interjected sharply. "I can assure you of two things. First, our schedule doesn't permit us the luxury of interviewing people, especially people

I've never heard of, on such impossibly short notice. And secondly, even if it did, we have no job openings. I apologize for my husband's . . . enthusiasm, if you will, about looking at your portfolio. But it really would be nothing more than a huge waste of his valuable time. Consider your appointment canceled."

She turned and walked away, passing an acquaintance on the way and smiling warmly as she did.

The force of Candace Sloane's pronouncement left Catherine feeling like someone who'd crashed a party only to be forcibly thrown out by the hostess. In all her life she'd never experienced such rejection. Catherine stood fixed in the same spot—unable to determine how anyone could be so incredibly rude and catty, and also unable to determine what her next move should be.

What is it with these people? she asked herself, over and over. *Who do they think they are?* It wasn't as if she'd grown up in rags or without privilege. Catherine was a well-bred, well-educated woman. And though she might have been out of her league financially, she certainly wasn't without class. An overwhelming sense of failure and sadness began gripping her. She wasn't sure if having Michael there at all this evening would have made a difference, but she was sure of one thing—she was glad he wasn't there to see her be made into such a fool. And while fighting to retain her composure she moved to the coat check, then on toward the elevator.

Chapter Three

Nowell removed a silver-plated cigarette case from his breast pocket, tapped a Marlboro on the outside cover, then lit it with his monogrammed lighter. Though most everything he owned had a European flair, he loved American cigarettes, and inhaled with deep satisfaction.

Lydia, grateful for Nowell's attention again, smiled affectionately at him as he casually slipped his arm around her waist. He smiled back, mostly because her company served as a mild diversion from the endless prattle of "yammering Yanks," as he often put it, chattering on around him about which pieces of art they'd recently acquired. It seemed clear to him they were mostly trying to impress him, partly because social-climbing Americans loved nothing more than being publicly well received by British aristocrats like himself. And more specifically, because he owned one of the most prestigious collections of fine arts and antique furniture in England and perhaps the United States. Collecting was not only his hobby, he was also a part-time dealer, and a very successful one at that. Lately his business brought him from London to Manhattan so frequently that he'd recently acquired a spacious Upper East Side town house to use as a residence and gallery—the purchase and renovation of which cost him nearly four million dollars.

"That mahogany breakfront bookcase from the Cartwright estate is going up for auction at Sotheby's," said one thirtyish woman, directing her gaze at Nowell while continuing her numbingly chatty discourse on British antiques. "It's expected to sell for . . ."

Where is she? Nowell thought to himself while tuning out the woman's prattle. He took another drag off his cigarette, his eyes scanning the room for her. It was un-

like him to feel remorse for a prank like the one he'd
pulled with Catherine Harrison. He was accustomed to
having women suffer through his antics, and then return
for more. But there was something different about her—
an innocence; a vulnerability that betrayed her apparent confidence.

It was bloody careless of her, he thought, his eyes still
searching but seeing no sign of her. He caught a glimpse
of Lucas and Candace in a far corner, then promptly
excused himself from Lydia and headed their way.

"Ah, Lucas, I see Candace didn't have much luck with
the young gent who stole her away from me," Nowell
jested. Candace laughed heartily, happy to be in Nowell
Stuart's charming company once again.

"I say, do you know what happened to the young lady
seated beside you at dinner?"

Candace's upbeat countenance suddenly shifted, and
for the moment she remained quiet.

"Not since you whisked her away earlier, I haven't,"
said Lucas.

"Hmmmm. Well, if you should see her . . ."

"Oh, Nowell, thank you for reminding me," Candace
interrupted. "Darling," she started, and turned to Lucas.
"I ran into her outside the ladies' room a short while
ago. And she asked me to tell you she was sorry about
some interview tomorrow. She said she can't make it
after all."

"Why the hell didn't she tell me herself?" blurted
Lucas, sore that he wouldn't have a chance to see Catherine's pretty face again.

"I don't know, darling. She didn't say."

"Well, did she at least say she'd like to reschedule? I
wonder where she is?" He looked quickly around, but
didn't see Catherine anywhere.

"Actually, I think she left. I saw her head to the coat
check shortly after we talked. Come now, Lucas, you
promised me a dance," she offered with a pout.

"Kids," sputtered Lucas, believing Catherine had
made a rash decision. "They have no damned values or
sense of business anymore. C'mon, let's do it, Mrs.
Sloane."

Nowell was immeasurably grateful for their departure.
Hoping he could catch Catherine, he bolted for the coat

check and not seeing her in the line anxiously boarded
an elevator for the sixty-five-floor trip down to street
level. He didn't see her amid any of the departing party-
goers on the ground floor of Rockefeller Center, and
feeling somewhat dejected dashed outside, only to find
himself in an unexpected downpour.

"Dammit," he said aloud, frustrated that Catherine
had slipped so easily from his grip.

"Oh, this blasted weather," he muttered, now regretting that he'd left his overcoat behind. He looked at his
watch that read 10:35 P.M., and realized he had no desire
to go back to the gala. Instead of returning to the party
and collecting both Lydia and his coat, he hurried into
the warmth of his waiting limo, which was parked half
a block away.

"Would you like to go home, sir?" inquired the driver.

"Yes," Nowell said, disheartened. "Actually the answer is no, but I've no better plans for the moment."

"And what about your date, sir?"

"What about her?" Nowell responded with cool detachment. It wouldn't be the first time he'd left Lydia
behind.

The driver, a regular hire of Nowell's, was accustomed
to his moodiness and knew better than to push the issue.
Instead he turned on the windshield wipers and pulled
out into the traffic. Nowell settled into the plush backseat, produced a handkerchief and wiped off his brow,
then reached into the bar and pulled out a bottle of
Courvoisier. He was just about to pour himself a snifter
full of the potent cognac when the sight of a woman in
a ball gown trying to flag down a taxi on Fifth Avenue
caught his attention. Though she had her coat pulled
over her head as protection from the rain, it didn't take
him long to recognize that it was Catherine. She was
having no luck.

"Pull up slowly, then stop beside that woman, please."

The driver did as instructed, obstructing Catherine's
ability to spot oncoming taxis. She looked at the driver
with deep frustration etched in her face, beckoning with
her hand for the limo to move on.

"What shall I do, sir?"

"Stay put," said Nowell, then took a long sip of his

drink. He edged over to the window and lowered it with a button on the door.

"Do you mind?" she shouted at him. "It's a little wet out here and I'm trying to catch a taxi!"

"It's quite dry, in here. May I offer you a lift?"

She ignored him and tried to move around the car.

"Don't let her get away," said Nowell firmly. The driver inched forward, once again blocking Catherine's access to the road.

"I say," Nowell said engagingly, this time leaning slightly out the window, "it is rather dry and comfortable in here."

Catherine turned around, moving in for a closer look. "Oh, it's you," she said with a mixture of disgust and relief. She was happy that it wasn't some total stranger, yet Nowell Stuart was the last person she wanted to see.

"Really, may I offer you a lift?"

"I'd rather walk home."

"Don't be ridiculous, Ms. Harrison. In case you haven't noticed, it's about fifty degrees and raining. I can have you home, warm and dry, in no time." He paused, then added with sincerity, "Besides, I feel like it's the least I can do considering how I screwed up your day tomorrow. I hope you'll accept my apologies even if you won't accept the ride."

Catherine let out a deep sigh from within her tented coat, her mouth twisting into a grimace. "How do I know you won't dump me in the East River or something?"

"Well, now, that all depends. Do you like to swim?" he said with deadpan humor.

"Oh, my God, you are impossible," she said with an unwilling laugh. Nowell took advantage of her brief change in mood by opening the door and sliding over on the seat. Catherine climbed in but ignored his gesture, occupying the jump seat across from him instead. She placed her wet coat on the floor and still wearing her elbow-length gloves patted at her damp hair, some of which was falling loose from the confines of her chignon.

"Where's Lydia?" she asked flatly.

"She decided to go home with someone else. Would you care for a drink?" Nowell asked politely, proffering the bottle of Courvoisier.

"Can't say that I blame her," Catherine said while examining the bottom of her rain-soaked dress, her shapely leg prominently displayed through the slit. "And no I don't want a drink, thank you." She continued inspecting her clothing, not once looking up at Nowell who was watching her in bewildered amusement. "I had no idea it was supposed to rain tonight," she nonchalantly rambled on. "Did you?"

"Not really." Nowell smiled. "Though I came prepared nonetheless."

Catherine rolled her eyes, then finally looked at him. "Oh, excuse me for not packing a tote-sized limo in my handbag."

"Are you always this rude?" he taunted, increasingly attracted by her sauciness.

"Only with people I don't care to impress."

Nowell let out a cynical laugh. "You are a smart aleck, aren't you?"

"Only with people I'm not trying to impress *and* that I hold a grudge against."

"Oh, I see. And because of your faulty—shall we say—scheduling practices, you feel entitled to hold a grudge against me?"

Catherine didn't answer him. Instead she looked out the window, seeing nothing more than the driving rain, refusing to meet his gaze.

"Actually, I have to be honest with you. I feel really stupid about tonight and I only have myself to blame." She leaned back into the seat, offering something of a conciliatory grin but no formal apology. "You know, I think I may have a drink after all."

"Splendid," said Nowell, happy to see she was warming up to his company. "You can have some of this Courvoisier. Or better yet, I believe there's a bottle of champagne here in the fridge. Let's have a look." He opened up a hidden minifridge, which indeed contained a chilled bottle and two glasses.

"Look at this," he boasted. "I'd be delighted to share some with you."

"What the heck," replied Catherine, the combination of soft lights and warmth inducing her to indulge. As Nowell opened the bottle, Catherine took a moment to inventory his features once again. His thick hair was a bit mussed up from the weather, and even in the dim light she could see fine lines in his face where it creased as he smiled.

"Here," he said, catching her curious gaze. "And may I propose a toast."

"By all means," Catherine agreed, reaching for the glass.

"Here's champagne to your real friends, and real pain to your sham friends." He paused momentarily, "And which category do you choose for me?"

"Neither," said Catherine, clinking her glass against his. "Since I really don't consider you my friend."

"That's rather harsh, don't you think, toward someone who did introduce you to Wilton Dresden, though I am sorry about the fact you had to cancel your appointment with Lucas Sloane."

"I didn't cancel my appointment with him," said Catherine, her voice edged with surprise.

"No? That's not what I heard."

"Really? And what exactly did you hear?"

"Candace Sloane told us that you approached her and abruptly canceled the interview, without any apologies I might add."

Catherine rolled her eyes heavenward. "That's atrocious. I did no such thing. In fact, it was the exact opposite. I tried talking to her, and she made it clear to me that I was not wanted. She said it would be a huge waste of their time to interview me."

"I'm sorry to hear that, though it doesn't surprise me coming from her. She's rather jealous of other women. As you can imagine, most of the ladies that work for him are either fat, ugly, or both. Please forgive me"— he paused, arching an eyebrow in amusement—"but it's obvious to me you lack certain job qualifications."

Catherine chuckled. "I suppose if that's your way of dishing out a compliment, then thank you. But you know what? Lucas Sloane can go to hell."

Nowell let out a throaty laugh at her unexpected expletive. "You can't be serious. I thought he was the pinnacle of American class and fashion. I can't imagine you wouldn't love a chance to work for him."

"The guy is crass and I'd be miserable working for him."

Nowell smiled in a wry, yet understanding way, finished his first glass of champagne, and then poured himself another.

"Say, listen," he said, adroitly changing the subject. "I don't want you to get all jittery about this suggestion—considering your remark about being tossed into the river and all. But we do have a fair amount of champagne left, and presumably a full tank of gas. How would you like a first-class tour of Manhattan? I suspect in the same amount of time it takes us to finish the bubbly we could travel from one end of the island to the other. What do you say?"

Very tempting, thought Catherine, believing it would serve Michael right if she came home later than he probably expected. "What time is it?" she inquired.

Nowell glanced at his wristwatch. "It's ten to eleven. The night is young."

"What the hell," she said, clinking her glass against his once more. "To my sham friend," she mused.

"To my real friend," he said, smiling back.

When Catherine finally awoke the next morning, it wasn't to turn off the alarm clock or say good-bye to Michael as he left for the day—she'd already slept through both. It was to answer the incessantly ringing phone. Grappling with the cord, she pulled the receiver from off its hook and finally placed it near her mouth.

"Hello," she managed, her voice dry and coarse. The other party hung up without saying a word. "I love you too," she muttered while fumbling to hang up the phone from her prone position.

"Oh, dear God, what have I done?" she asked herself, suddenly realizing that she hadn't gotten to bed till nearly 2:00 A.M. Her legs felt like blocks of steel and her head pounded like a ringing anvil. Trying to decide if she was hungover or still drunk, her mind began racing over the previous night's events when it suddenly occurred to her where she was supposed to be that morning. She glanced over at the clock. It read 9:25.

"Oh, no," she shrieked, quickly turning over and throwing back the covers. "I'm screwed." She had no idea how she was going to get showered, make herself look presentable, and arrive at Wilton Dresden's office in fifty minutes. Despite nausea and a fierce headache, Catherine promptly jumped out of bed and into the shower, feeling grateful for the phantom wake-up call.

I wonder if it was Michael, she thought to herself, realizing she'd missed the chance to tell him about her big interview today. She climbed out of the shower, frantically combing her long, wet hair. If she only dried the top, then pulled the rest of it into a French braid she could probably make it on time.

Grabbing a suit out of the closet, Catherine was about to get dressed when the phone started ringing again. She didn't have a minute to waste—regardless of whether it was Michael or not, and so she deliberately ignored it. After about a dozen rings it stopped, only to start all over again seconds later.

"What?" she shrieked with exasperation as she finally picked up the receiver. The caller, however anxious to get through before, promptly hung up again.

"Oh, the hell with you!" she fumed, slamming down the phone.

She finished getting dressed with no further interruptions, and with seconds to spare grabbed her portfolio and coat. While fussing with the multiple locks on their apartment door, down the hall a neighbor graciously held the elevator assuming she wanted a lift. Catherine usually preferred the stairs, but took the offer, only to regret it somewhere between the second and third floors.

They were stuck. And with no building superintendent around to help them. Neither of them could get the doors open wide enough to attempt climbing out, and it seemed as if she and this other person were the only ones left in the building that morning. They screamed for help until they were both hoarse, and repeatedly rang the alarm. But assistance was long coming, and Catherine realized that this would have never happened if not for Nowell Stuart. If she'd gotten home at a reasonable hour as she'd planned, she would have woken up a long time ago and would probably be sitting in the waiting area of Wilton Dresden's office by now.

To my sham friend, she thought as she slumped to the floor with her portfolio in hand.

What she didn't realize was that if not for Nowell she would still be asleep.

Chapter Four

Michael watched one of the faculty priests bless the remaining wine in the sacramental chalice, then gulp it down in one quick swallow. Though he felt the Holy Eucharist was beautiful and sacred, he disliked this portion of the ceremony. It was like drinking swill to him, downing the remaining wine after the congregation had all received communion from the same cup. The distaste was even greater to him due to his educated palate—he loved a fine bottle of wine—and the wine used for communion was always cheap and tart. He felt such a meaningful ceremony deserved a better vintage.

Michael usually enjoyed sharing the daily Eucharist with his fellow seminarians, but that day his thoughts were elsewhere. He couldn't get his mind off Catherine, especially after what had happened last night and particularly after she poured herself into bed around 2:00 A.M. reeking of cigarettes and alcohol.

He felt more frustrated with Catherine than ever before in the two and a half years they'd known each other. His decision not to join her last night was admittedly selfish and impatient. But he'd had it with her outbursts. He realized she'd suffered a lot lately, but she didn't seem to understand that he suffered too: that her prolonged unemployment was his financial loss and responsibility too; that he'd also lost a baby.

He felt convinced that beneath her edginess was a deep sadness over the fact that she might never bear children. While she'd recovered physically from the ectopic pregnancy, he knew that emotionally she remained wounded and vulnerable. But still, he'd just about had enough.

By nature, and now by calling, Michael was a forgiving and patient man. But he felt ever since their marriage as if his patience, perhaps even his faith, was being tested. He regretted giving into his frustration last night, but for some reason he couldn't help himself.

He wished he could make it like it used to be, thinking of the spur of the moment fun they used to have when he was a graduate philosophy student at Duke and she pursued her decorating education in Raleigh. Sometimes they'd cut classes and sneak in a movie matinee and then a burger at one of Duke's local pubs. He decided that what they both needed now was a spontaneous infusion of fun and quickly made a plan.

"Excuse me, Reverend Whitlock," said Michael, catching up with one of his instructors outside the campus chapel. "May I have a word with you, sir?"

"Michael, hello." Jack Whitlock smiled, pausing along the main walkway in The Close, the seminary's walled-in garden sanctuary. Reverend Whitlock reached into his well-worn corduroy jacket for his pipe, a bag of sweet-smelling tobacco, and some matches. He prepared his pipe while Michael began chatting.

"Thank goodness the rain finally let up," stated Michael, making prerequisite small talk before asking for what he really wanted. The professor smiled at him, agreeing with his point on the weather, and happy to have a word with the young man. Michael not only enjoyed Reverend Whitlock's respect as a seminarian, but also as a student of fine wines. The professor, as it turned out, was a reliable source on where the best vintages could be found in New York City.

The Reverend lit up his pipe and inhaled deeply. His pipe smoking was a nuisance to most people near him, but for the moment Michael enjoyed the pungent aroma of the slow-burning tobacco combined with the damp autumn air.

"Hmmm." The Reverend nodded while taking another satisfying drag off his pipe. "What can I do for you, son?"

"Well, sir. I know this is not an exceptional reason for missing your exam tomorrow. But I really need to spend some time with my wife. And I was wondering if . . . well"—he paused, trying to gather himself for the punch—"would it be okay for me to miss class tomorrow and take a makeup exam? Trust me, it's not a matter of being unprepared. In fact, if anything I'm prepared to take a more difficult exam if that's what it requires. It's just that . . ."

Reverend Whitlock took another deep drag off his pipe. "Michael," he intoned seriously, "you need to learn to keep your priorities in life straight."

Michael immediately felt embarrassed for asking. "I'm sorry I even brought it up, sir. I'll see you in class tomorrow."

"Son, I don't think you heard correctly. You need to keep your priorities straight. I'd say spending time with your family is one of the most important."

Michael closed his eyes and smiled at the gentle ruse. "Thank you, I appreciate it, sir. You have no idea what this means to me—and Catherine. It could be my furlough out of the doghouse. Things have been kind of crazy lately, and we could really use a day off together."

"That bad, huh?" Reverend Whitlock chuckled. Michael knew the professor had been married for almost thirty-five years, and no doubt realized what he was going through.

"Only one thing, son. Don't get used to it," he warned playfully.

"Listen, thanks again. I really appreciate it. And I'll see you the day after tomorrow."

Michael quickly moved across the campus, telling his other professors he planned on being out the next day, then bolted off campus for Times Square to buy tickets to *Les Misérables*—something he knew Catherine wanted to see. The tickets weren't cheap, they would cost at least sixty-five dollars apiece, but Michael decided it was a purchase he could happily justify on their MasterCard. He felt great about his snap decision and couldn't wait to surprise Catherine.

Nowell fidgeted with his wrist watch. It was 10:40 A.M. and Catherine still hadn't left her building, despite her apparent eagerness over today's interview with Wilton Dresden. Nowell had not shared her enthusiasm about it the night before, since in reality he despised the man. Still, he simply couldn't believe she'd blow it by being late. He tapped at the cellular phone in his pocket, wondering if perhaps he shouldn't call her again to make certain she was on her way.

He had a perfectly protected view of her building from inside General Theological Seminary's cloistered garden across the street, and had watched and waited for her departure since before 9:30 A.M.

He had never met anyone like Catherine Harrison before. Normally Nowell could intoxicate nearly any woman with his good looks and wealth. And a snifter of fine cognac or a flute of champagne often served as an easy pass to a hotel suite or the backseat of the limo for an evening of gratuitous sex. But Catherine made no advances on him and, worse, told him in no uncertain terms when he dropped her off that she wouldn't see him again. Just like that. Through a playful smirk and in her saucy Southern voice she thanked him for a "wonderful tour, some decent champagne, and your surprisingly civil company."

Nowell could not remember a single time in his life when he'd been so blatantly rejected by a woman from the start. When he asked for her phone number she refused, stating she simply wasn't interested in seeing him again.

The only Harrison in the phone directory at her address was listed under "M." Knowing that most women preferred not to use their full name in public phone directories, Nowell wondered if she'd lied about her first name. Or perhaps, he thought disconcertingly, she's married. Either way, he decided, it wouldn't deter him from trying to see her again.

Plus, that morning, he knew he had dialed the right number. Though her voice sounded a bit rough, he recognized her sweet drawl. Nowell decided there was only one way to approach her while limiting his chance of rejection—to follow her until the best opportunity presented itself to bump into her, treating the encounter as coincidence.

Maybe I missed her, he thought, but reassured himself that would have been difficult. Though keeping an open book in his hands, he'd managed to keep a steady watch on the front door of her building. He glanced at his watch again, his impatience mounting. Perhaps she'd changed her mind about Wilton Dresden. Or worse, what if she'd fallen back asleep? Tugged by the thought that he was partially to blame for her tardiness, another idea occurred to him as to how he might approach her.

Suppose I just go over, ring her doorbell, then suggest I was worried she'd miss her morning interview on account of my keeping her out so late. I'll explain that I wanted to make sure she made it.

Leaving the protection of the sanctuary's garden, he moved swiftly across the street. Pausing for a moment while facing her brownstone, he took a deep breath to brace himself for possible humiliation, then dashed up the steps and began scanning the names on the outside intercom for Harrison. That's when he first heard the alarm bell from within. It wasn't as urgent as a fire alarm, it was more sporadic than that. And it didn't take him long to recognize it as an emergency bell on an elevator.

"I wonder if she's stuck on the blasted lift?" he said, then tried opening the double doors to the building. They were locked. He frantically buzzed every apartment, but no one answered. Thinking of only one other thing to do, he quickly grabbed his cell phone and dialed 911.

"Police, fire, or rescue?" asked the operator.

"Damned if I know," said Nowell. "Which one of them responds to stuck elevators?"

"Is this an emergency, sir?"

"Well, yes, I'd say so."

"What is the nature of the emergency, sir?"

"My friend, I believe she's stuck on the elevator in her apartment building."

"I'm sorry, but unless it's an emergency, there is nothing we can do. I suggest you get in touch with the building's super or call an elevator repair company."

"Oh, bugger," he said, then hung up the phone. The ringing from inside persisted, and his own anxiousness on Catherine's behalf grew. He recalled Wilton's schedule being frighteningly tight, and knew the man well enough to know he'd be unsympathetic with Catherine's plight if indeed she was stuck. He dialed 911 once more, and in the best Hispanic accent he could muster, asked for help.

"Police, fire, or rescue?" asked the dispatcher.

"Fire, there's a fire," he blurted.

"Calm down, calm down. Give me an address please."

For a moment Nowell drew a blank, trying to remember if he was on Nineteenth or Twentieth Street.

"I need an address, please," came the man's firm, steady voice on the other end. Nowell recalled Catherine telling the driver which street to turn on last night.

"Four-twenty West Twentieth," he finally barked into the phone, then hung up. He wanted to get out of there before the fire engines arrived, and hustled for refuge behind the seminary's walls again.

It didn't take long for two fire trucks plus two engines and the battalion chief in his car to show up. With all the commotion, several onlookers quickly gathered to catch the action, creating quite a scene.

It also didn't take long for the firemen to determine the real nature of the emergency. After forcing their way into the building with an ax, they quickly conducted a fruitless search for smoke and fire, only taking time to set Catherine and her neighbor free once they were satisfied there was no blaze. Nowell kept a close eye on his watch the whole time. By now it was a quarter past eleven, and Catherine was an hour late for her appointment with Wilton.

Frustrated and consumed by dread over missing her job interview, Catherine barely acknowledged the firemen who rescued them. Instead she rushed back into her apartment to phone Mr. Dresden, afraid he wouldn't have the time or inclination to reschedule another meeting with her, especially given what Nowell had told her the previous evening about his hot temper and flair for drama.

"He should hire an electrician before he hires another decorator, he short-circuits so much," Nowell had said snidely as they discussed what she might expect at her forthcoming interview.

Catherine frantically dialed his number, feeling relieved if a bit nervous when Dresden finally accepted her call. Her confidence dwindled rapidly, however, as she hastily explained why she'd missed the interview. "It happens," was his cool response. He wasn't happy about it, but said that one of his afternoon appointments had canceled anyway, so he'd see her "very briefly" at one-thirty.

Grateful for a little time to pull herself together, Catherine set about fixing herself a late breakfast. A poached egg on an English muffin, half of a grapefruit, and some strong, black coffee was what she felt would help cure her nagging hangover. She was just about to eat when the phone began ringing.

"Hello," she said more cheerfully than when she'd answered the phone earlier in the morning. But just as before, the caller hung up.

"What is going on here?" she asked out loud, still clinging to the receiver. For a moment the thought of Nowell Stuart flashed through her mind, but she quickly dismissed it. She couldn't imagine him wasting his time this way, or why he wouldn't talk to her anyway. They'd parted amicably last night, even if she had refused to see him again. No, she convinced herself, it couldn't be Nowell.

Chapter Five

Oh, God, this is ridiculous, Catherine thought while suppressing a heavy sigh. The urge to walk out the door and bring the job interview to an abrupt close almost consumed her. It was near torture for her to watch Wilton Dresden's static face as he perused the pages of her decorating portfolio. He turned the pages with the speed of a seven-year-old boy looking through a Christmas catalog for toys. But unlike the eager child, he didn't seem to want anything.

"You definitely have a look," he finally offered clinically, without even glancing up. He zipped her portfolio shut, then pushed it toward her across his gleaming, empty desktop. He gently straightened his olive-colored, double-breasted jacket, then adjusted a cuff link on his royal blue-and-white pin-striped shirt, obviously showing more interest in the proper alignment of his attire than for her.

Dresden folded his hands neatly in front of him, and finally looked straight at her with a sneer—his way of saying the interview was over. His snappy Italian suit did nothing to hide his age, and Catherine wondered how a man with such an obviously bad toupee could take himself so seriously or be regarded so highly by the fashion elite.

"I see you have a flair for the conservative Southern influence."

"Well I *am* from the South," she said with feigned warmth.

"I noticed," he replied with equally shallow politeness. "It's just that there's not much of a market for your look here. I hate to say this." He faintly snickered, then became quite blunt. "But New York is a *little more* cosmopolitan than Raleigh-Durham. My clients are versatile and demanding. Your work is nice, but I don't see enough diversity in your portfolio to make me believe you can meet the range of demands on our firm. I need a decorator with greater depth and adaptability right now, and I'm afraid I won't be able to use you."

Catherine felt a heavy pall slip over her. In a strange way it was comforting to have such an honest assessment of her work from one of the premier decorators in the world, painful as it was. In truth, her portfolio probably did seem mundane, filled primarily with sample swatches and pictures of similarly decorated homes in the Raleigh-Durham area. Unfortunately her clients had little vision beyond the traditional, neo-colonial theme so popular in that area, made unique for each of them only by slight variations in fabrics and wallpapers.

Catherine grabbed the handle of her portfolio and pulled it into an upright position on her lap. "Hmmm," was all she could manage to force out, afraid she might cry. Looking up at him, she detected a slight but surprising flicker of sympathy in his eyes. Knowing she couldn't leave empty-handed, she decided to swallow her pride.

"Mr. Dresden, first, thank you for agreeing to see me not once, but twice. I'm really sorry about what happened this morning. Wouldn't you know it, I usually never take the elevator."

He impatiently raised his eyebrows, and Catherine pressed on.

"However, I have to tell you something. I've been job hunting for almost six months now, and my husband and I are nearly flat broke. I attended the gala last night hoping to make connections with people like you, and I don't want to waste this opportunity. If you can't employ me as a designer, could you possibly place me in some other position so that I can at least prove to you what I can do?"

Dresden shifted in his chair though his composure remained the same.

"What about your friend, Nowell?"

"What about him?"

"Certainly he must know other people you can talk to."

"First of all," she promptly but politely shot back.

"he's not really my friend. I'd just met him last night when he took it upon himself to introduce me to you."

"How kind of him," Dresden said snidely. It was obvious Dresden felt animosity toward Nowell, making Catherine wonder why he'd even bothered with her. She moved back to the point.

"Again, is there any chance, sir, that you'd consider hiring me for any other job, even an entry-level position?"

"No," he said flatly. "I need an experienced designer right now, and that's it. However, the designer that just left is opening his own business. I'll forward your résumé to him, how's that?"

"Well, thank you for your time," said Catherine, feeling certain she'd never hear from his former colleague. She gathered her belongings, shook his hand, then headed toward the door.

"If you should happen to see our friend Nowell again, please send him my warmest regards, would you?" he said from behind in a patronizing, almost mocking manner.

Catherine paused and turned around to see a clearly derisive look on his face.

"I doubt I'll ever see him again," she said defensively. "But if I do, I'll be sure to let him know."

Feeling dejected and with nothing better to do, Catherine began walking casually around midtown Manhattan. In her favorite Donna Karan suit, she at least appeared to belong; to be a part of something. No one would have to know how desperate she was for a job.

To them she could confidently walk into any store and purchase whatever she wanted—something she'd been accustomed to doing with her father's money before she married Michael.

She strolled past the windows of Bergdorf Goodman's, then paused to look at some avant-garde mannequins displaying the latest fashions. It's ironic, she thought to herself, that the last time she'd been shopping in Bergdorf's was with her father as part of their annual Christmas pilgrimage. For a long weekend each December they would fly up together and binge on shows and shopping. Just like her father, she loved fine quality things, and some of her fondest memories were of those spending sprees together.

It was during their last trip up here, nearly ten years ago, that Catherine discovered a third party had joined them. Her father, claiming to have back pain, decided to stay in the hotel while Catherine shopped. He told her to take his wallet and to help herself to whatever she wanted.

It wasn't until she'd gotten to Saks Fifth Avenue just a few blocks away that she realized she'd left his wallet on the dresser and promptly returned to the hotel to get it. That's when she found him in bed with Suzy Fitzgerald, one of the bouncy, young secretaries in his company. The trips to New York with her father stopped after that, but not his profligate spending on her behalf. She knew it was hush money, even though she suspected her mother already knew of his affairs.

And today, feeling sorry for herself, she knew that nothing would pick up her mood faster than a shopping spree in one of her favorite stores.

"To hell with poverty," she said as if speaking to the mannequin, "I'll just use the MasterCard."

She knew Michael would be furious, since they'd promised to use the shared card only for planned expenses or in emergencies. But she couldn't help feeling a sense of entitlement—as if she'd earned an impulsive shopping trip after all the hardship endured over the past six months. She breezed through several designer salons with the same lighthearted flair as though shopping with her father's money, then headed to the second-floor shoe department, where by pure serendipity there was a major sale in progress. Catherine eagerly joined the ranks of fussy socialites clamoring for the best bargains in designer footwear and left with two pairs of shoes "on sale." The total: two hundred eighty-five dollars.

But her spree didn't end there. She picked up a silk blouse and a pair of linen slacks, for a combined purchase of over three hundred fifty dollars, not at all concerned about the limit on her MasterCard.

When it appeared she was getting ready to leave the store, Nowell carefully paced himself behind her and exited onto West Fifty-seventh Street just after she did, following her across the street and back to Fifth Avenue. When she paused to look at a Liz Claiborne window display, he slid quietly up beside her.

"I don't believe that's your color," he whispered in her ear. Catherine jumped.

"Oh, my God, Nowell, you nearly scared me to death. What are you doing here?"

"Well, I could ask you the same question, I suppose. But the fact is, I forgot my coat last night and I'm heading back to the Rainbow Room to retrieve it. It's just around the corner, care to join me?"

"I suppose that's one downside to always having a limo at your beck and call—you forget that you need or even had a coat?" she replied sarcastically.

"Do you see a limo waiting for me?" he asked, looking around with obvious good humor. "Let me know if you do, I would love the lift. Oh, say, by the way, how did your interview with Dresden go?"

"Basically the story of my day is Lions, one; Christians, nothing."

"That bad, huh? I'm terribly sorry. What did Dresden have to say for himself."

"You know what, I really don't want to talk about it right now. Though he did ask me to send you his warmest regards. But it was more like this . . ." she went on, mimicking Dresden's condescending delivery.

"Oh, he did, did he? That coldhearted bastard," Nowell muttered softly.

"What is it with you two?"

"Just a business deal that went awry. I'd be delighted to share the whole story with you over a spot of tea. Would you care to follow me while I get my coat, and then join me at the Pierre?"

All the animosity she'd felt toward Nowell earlier in the day seemed to evaporate with his presence. Catherine felt it was a nice coincidence to run into him on the street. She pulled her left hand out from underneath the garment bag she carried and glanced at her watch. That was when Nowell first saw her wedding band, and suddenly felt his spirits dash.

He'd had liaisons with married women before—their marital status always bothering them more than him. Those women were usually quite easy, and he typically felt little regard for them afterward. But not before taking full sexual advantage of them. Afterward he would stake false claims to the moral high ground, lamenting: "We just can't carry on like this, it's not right." Some women took it harder than others, but it was always the same for him, he simply didn't care and never came close to them again. But already he sensed Catherine was different, that she would not be easy to overcome. *A delightful challenge,* he decided.

"Let's see, it's three-thirty," she said. "I've got a little time. Of course the last time I decided to join you I came home drunk. I had quite a hangover this morning; thank you."

"Well, it wasn't as if I had to pry open your mouth and pour the liquor on down," he said, mildly reproaching her.

"No, but you are a rotten influence."

"I would say my powers of influence are only as strong as one wants to be swayed. Now, do you care to join me?"

Catherine laughed. "Could it be," she asked, "that you simply don't know how to take no for an answer?"

Chapter Six

Though the air was damp and chilly, Michael decided to stroll to Times Square. He could use the exercise, he told himself, and besides, it felt good to be alone for a while and not studying or thinking about school.

However, he couldn't get his mind off Catherine. And as his mind wandered, he thought back to their first meeting at his employer's seventy-five-acre estate outside Durham.

One hot summer afternoon Catherine and another interior decorator with whom she was doing an apprenticeship arrived unexpectedly to take room measurements at the Gardners' home where Michael received free room and board in exchange for caretaking services. At the time, Michael was sitting comfortably in an old rocker under the shade of the sprawling front porch wearing his usual attire—crumpled khaki pants, a cotton golf shirt, and Weejun loafers with no socks. He was drinking a Mountain Dew out of a long-necked bottle while reading the Bible.

"Hey, how y'all doin'?" he inquired politely as they climbed out of the car.

"Just fine, thank you. I'm LisBeth Carter and this is my associate Catherine Howard."

Catherine smiled at him but didn't say a word.

"Nice to meet you. I'm Michael Harrison," he said while standing up. "What can I do for you ladies?"

"Well, Mrs. Gardner asked us to come over today and take room measurements," said LisBeth blithely. "Is she here?"

"No, I'm sorry. They're not home right now."

"You wouldn't mind, would ya, if we just went on in and got this done? I mean since we're already here and all?" LisBeth queried in her saccharine-sweet drawl.

"Not today," Michael insisted, explaining he never allowed anyone in without explicit instructions from the Gardners to do so. Seeing her charm went nowhere with him, LisBeth's composure suddenly snapped. "Oh, give me a break," she responded. "Like we're going to steal something. Just who are you anyway?" Michael ignored her question.

"Is there any way we can reach her or Mr. Gardner by phone?" Catherine quietly piped in.

"Naw, not right now. But if you ladies want to leave me some kind of business card I'll be sure to let them know that y'all stopped by."

LisBeth lost all ladylike pretension at this point. "God dammit!" she shouted at Michael. "I just talked with her yesterday. She was expecting us."

"Yeah, but I'm not." With that Michael went back to his rocking chair, swigged his Mountain Dew, and resumed his reading. LisBeth climbed into her late-model BMW and slammed the door shut. Catherine, however, calmly dug into her purse and produced a business card.

"I'm sorry about the confusion. Will Mrs. Gardner be home later today?" she asked courteously.

"Naw. Her daddy died unexpectedly last night and they flew out of here in a hurry. They're in Atlanta right now."

"Oh, gosh, I had no idea, I'm so sorry."

"I hope you understand," Michael said. "It's just that I've given them my word, and I have studying to do right now so I can't take the time to follow y'all around."

"What are you studying?" asked Catherine sincerely, finding herself curiously drawn to this man.

"Specifically, prophecies revealed in the Old Testament compared to what happened in the New. Generally, I'm working on my Master's in philosophy over at Duke."

"Are you a minister?" He shook his head no, but the smile on his face revealed some pride in being asked. Catherine went to hand him the business card once again.

"Listen, I'm sorry about the intrusion. Why don't you call me directly and let me know what we can work out about coming back. I'd appreciate it. And please tell Mrs. Gardner I'm so sorry about her father."

"You sure are sorry about a lot of things," he said warmly, accepting the card.

"Well, really I'm just sorry that we put you in this spot."

"There you go again," he said with a laugh.

"Jesus Christ." She laughed back, then grimaced over her blasphemous remark.

"Thanks for the card," he finally said, tucking it into his shirt pocket.

"See ya." Catherine smiled self-consciously. LisBeth chastised her the moment she shut the door.

"Why did you waste your time with that hick?"

"LisBeth, the Gardners are in Atlanta. Her father died last night."

"Oh, God," was all she could say. "Oh, God."

The following day Michael called Catherine. He'd spoken with Mrs. Gardner, who was extremely apologetic about forgetting their appointment. Michael wanted to make it up to Catherine, inviting her personally to come over and take measurements while he fixed her some dinner. There was no mention of LisBeth. And while Catherine rejected the chance to do measuring alone, she easily accepted the dinner invitation.

He turned out to be a charming, romantic, and funny man, though not much of a cook. He'd draped a round table on the front porch with a heavy, white linen tablecloth, placing fresh-cut flowers and candles in the center—then set it with paper plates and plastic cutlery, which thoroughly amused Catherine.

And though it seemed somewhat awkward at first, Catherine felt warmth and admiration for Michael as he tenderly took hold of her hands and asked that she join him in prayer before they commenced eating his burnt barbecued chicken.

"Lord, in the name of Your Son, Jesus Christ, we give You thanks not only for this daily bread, but more importantly for the daily bread of life. We thank You for Your mercy, for the special gift of friendship and Your presence among us. Amen."

Catherine couldn't help but stare at him as he kept his head bowed in silent meditation for just a moment longer. Her hands were warmly molded inside his tender grip, and she couldn't bring herself to remove them until he'd gently squeezed and released them while casting a warm, satisfied smile in her direction. Never had a date shown such respect for the Lord by initiating a prayer of thanks over a simple meal. She saw strength and uncommon humility at once in him, feeling moved by the depth of his convictions.

They sat outside from twilight into late evening, finishing off a vintage bottle of wine, talking endlessly about religion and philosophy, life and death, and then mostly life—specifically about each other's.

Michael was a rapt listener, and when appropriate, he would enlighten her with his knowledge of philosophy and religion, but never condescendingly. Catherine felt impressed by his confidence and intellect, but more so with his gentle, yet humorous manner. She'd never met anyone like Michael in all her life, and before the night was over she felt a deep desire for him.

Michael told Catherine all about himself. How he was twenty-eight years old, had been raised on a tobacco farm in Tarboro, was the third of six children, and had made it to Duke University on a basketball scholarship where he played out first-string hopes on a second-string status. He claimed not to be bitter about it, since he considered sitting on Duke's bench an honor after the team went on to become the national champions his junior year.

He told her his teetotaling Baptist father had been killed by a drunk driver when he was fourteen, forcing him, his mother, and his siblings to take responsibility for the farm. But the workload combined with school had been too much for them all, so his mother eventually sold the farm and bought a house closer to town.

"We were so darned poor," he said through his gentle grin. "For thirteen years she worked two jobs. Had to, to make ends meet. One as a waitress and the other as a secretary at the local funeral home. She finally retired from the funeral home last year. We always teased her that it was a 'dead-end' job anyway. She used to laugh and say there were more stiffs at the restaurant."

Catherine laughed heartily, imagining a woman like Michael—patient, yet strong-willed with a good wit to match. Michael's self-effacing manner was a refreshing change from the typical men she dated who, by comparison, were self-absorbed and cynical with none of Michael's gentle passion for life.

Catherine wanted to know how he knew so much about the fine wine they were drinking, especially considering his Baptist upbringing and the tragic consequences surrounding his father's death.

"Well, first," he began humorously, "I like the stuff. And secondly," he continued more philosophically, "I've never thought of myself as a Baptist. I was a typical rebellious kid, and resented being forced to go to church three times a week with my mom and dad, then having what I considered hogwash jammed down my throat for every indiscretion I committed. I was an average red-blooded farm boy out there shucking tobacco. And if I wasn't chewing it, I was smoking it. Or else sipping someone's beer followed by a peek at a *Penthouse* at the local Zip-Mart.

"According to the Baptist church I was on a toboggan ride into hell, though I wasn't doing anything my friends and older brothers weren't doing. After my father's funeral I never set foot in another Baptist church."

"Well then how did you come to find religion, and what church do you belong to now?" asked Catherine, intrigued.

"Well, to answer the second question first, I'm a member of the Episcopal church. Regarding the first question, I think religion found me. Aside from my father's death, there was nothing dark or serious that happened to me which made me see the light. In fact, it was quite the opposite. I was totally happy. I was having a great time at Duke, I loved playing basketball, I had a three point nine grade point average and a real nice girlfriend that was about a nine an' a half outta ten. Kinda like you," he mused.

"What? Only a nine point five!" Catherine pretended soreness.

"Well, no one's perfect, you know. And just for whining about it, you lose ground. Now you're a nine point oh."

"That's not fair!"

"Eight point five."

Catherine zipped her mouth shut while trying hard not to laugh. Michael just kept right on chatting.

"Anyway, as I was saying, one day I got to thinking about life. Sometimes it seems so chaotic, and often sad. Tragic things happen and you can't explain why." He paused and took a deliberately long sip of his wine.

"But then," he continued while pouring them each a little more Bordeaux, "when you think about the beautiful order of nature, and how things relate in so many subtle, yet harmonious but critical ways, you can't help but believe there is a power, both good and great, more intelligent than we can imagine, behind it all. Whether it's a medical cure, the effect of the moon on the tides, you name it—it's all so miraculous. Thinking about it made me start to take a closer look at myself, and wonder what I was going to do with my life to contribute to the good of the order."

Catherine sat fixated by his simple, yet compelling sermonette, then cracked up laughing. "So," she asked, "whatever happened to the girlfriend?"

"Well, like I said, she was nine point five outta ten. But that was pretty much in looks. She turned out to be pretty shallow, with a low level of tolerance for my newfound spirituality. I think she's married and living in Charlotte now."

"That's where I'm from," boasted Catherine, begging to know who she was. Michael insisted it didn't matter anymore and refused to identify his former girlfriend. Instead he asked that Catherine tell him about her own past. She told him they had at least one thing in common—their fathers had both earned a living off tobacco.

Her father was a prominent tobacco executive in Charlotte, she explained. Her mother was a housewife and country club enthusiast, with two sons and one daughter. Catherine was the oldest of the kids. She'd grown up Episcopalian, made her debut at one of North Carolina's most prestigious debutante balls, went to the University of North Carolina, where she'd joined a sorority, and was now back in school studying to become an interior designer.

"On paper you would appear to be just the kind of woman I would avoid like the plague," said Michael.

"What do you mean, I'm an Episcopalian?"

"Believe me, not that. It's the cookie-cutter type. Perfect family. Little interest in anything beyond material things, a pedigree husband, and perfect-looking children."

Catherine seemed somewhat startled by how serious he sounded, then took a sip of wine. "You know," she said, her demeanor softening. "It may seem that way on paper. But there's a less-than-perfect story between the lines." She looked away from him as she spoke.

"Hmmm," Michael responded, realizing he'd touched a nerve. He didn't press her, and she offered nothing more on the sore subject of her father's infidelities, instead moving on to something else.

"You still didn't answer my question about your knowledge of good wine. I've seen my father break open a bottle or two of this stuff over the years."

"Well, I suppose you could say I'm interested in more than just one Holy Spirit," he said, laughing. Catherine groaned at the pun.

"What? Just because I'm a religious man doesn't mean I can't appreciate some of the better things in life. I happen to think that a fine wine is just another part of nature's beautiful order. Besides," he added more seriously, "I consider this a special occasion." He raised his glass in a toast while Catherine demurely responded in kind.

Yes, it had been special, Michael concluded, still lost in memory while walking toward the Times Square box office. Actually it turned out to be momentous. They fell deeply in love with each other. A year later they eloped, with Michael moving to New York soon afterward. He knew all that had happened since had been extremely tough for Catherine, yet he never lost faith that things would work out.

"Two tickets for tomorrow evening's performance of *Les Mis*," he said, finally reaching the ticket office. He handed his MasterCard over to the box office clerk. The guy punched several keys on a computer keyboard, then ran Michael's card through a credit card scanner.

"This card's been rejected," he said with no sense of apology.

"I'm sorry," said Michael, surprised. "There must be some mistake. Please try it again." He couldn't imagine why it wasn't working, and watched closely as the clerk tried once more.

"Like I said, it's not working. You wanna pay in cash?"

"Does your computer say what's wrong?" Michael inquired. He felt ashamed, as though the clerk might take him for a deadbeat.

"No, you gotta call your credit card company and find out yourself. Do you want to pay in cash?"

"Well, I'll have to come back to do that," said Michael. He stepped out of line, then headed to the nearest automatic teller a block away, deciding to withdraw money from their savings account, but then encountered his second shock of the day—there wasn't enough money in their account to cover the cost of their two tickets!

"What the hell is going on here?" he asked out loud. He was furious. There could be several reasons why the credit card hadn't worked, but only one explanation for why there was barely any money left in the savings account—Catherine spent it behind his back. It was then he suspected she'd rung up purchases exceeding the $2500 limit on their credit card. And it made him both furious and perplexed.

And as Michael stood quietly trying to sort out his emotions, his wife slipped into the posh Café Pierre on the arm of a man who would soon make their money troubles disappear.

Chapter Seven

The maître d' at the Pierre's Rotunda restaurant smiled warmly when he spotted Nowell, whisking him and Catherine past several waiting patrons toward the only vacant table in the room. This was definitely a place to see and be seen, thought Catherine, finding herself grateful now that she'd accepted Nowell's offer. She loved the luxurious feel of the hotel, basking in the attention of the maître d' and the looks of the other guests as they passed to the head of the line.

"Claude, thank you for taking such good care of us. But dare I ask," said Nowell in a practiced manner, "could we possibly be seated in the Café Pierre?"

"Sorry, Mr. Stuart, but we're not serving in there right now," Claude replied. Nowell cast him a disapproving look, which didn't seem to bring the man any closer to moving them into the empty, adjacent restaurant.

"Claude," Nowell began and then completely startled Catherine by speaking in rapid French. Claude's face creased deeply as he smiled.

"Ahh, *mais bien sûr*." Claude nodded, gesturing for the two of them to follow. Catherine couldn't imagine what Nowell said to make the man change his mind, but he promptly escorted them past the artful opulence of the Rotunda, with its soaring muraled ceiling and haute couture crowd, and led them directly to a choice window table in the adjacent Café Pierre. Their view looked out at Sixty-first Street, where she and Nowell could see pedestrians scurrying for shelter from sudden drops of rain.

"Madame," said Claude, offering to take her coat. Catherine handed it to him, then sat down as he pulled out her chair.

Nowell spoke again in fluent French to Claude, who smiled respectfully, then left them alone together in the quiet, comfortable elegance of the Café. Catherine caught the impish look in Nowell's eyes and began to laugh.

"What did you just say to him?"

"I told him to bring us tea service and finger sandwiches for two," he answered with a radiant but cunning smile.

"How kind of you. Oh, and thanks for asking me what I wanted," she said tartly while rolling her eyes. "You know that's not what I meant. What did you say to him in the Rotunda to make him usher us in here like he did?"

"You're sure you want to hear this?"

"Why not?"

"I told him you are a married woman whose husband doesn't know your whereabouts and that we would appreciate the privacy."

This first reference from Nowell about her "husband" caught her so completely off-guard that she felt herself blush deeply. She now wished she'd mentioned something about Michael herself. Instead she felt guilty, as though she'd been deliberately hiding him.

"Well, I'd say only half of that is true," she quickly retorted. "I am a married woman, but I don't see the need for privacy."

Oh, you think you are so clever, he thought. *I wonder how long you would have waited to admit you were married had I not said something.*

"Actually, I'm the one who prefers privacy. The tables are a bit too close for my taste. You don't mind, do you?" Nowell stated just as a waiter arrived with their order. He carefully laid everything out on the table, then unfolded a napkin and gingerly placed it on Catherine's lap as Nowell unfurled his own. The waiter went quietly about his duties pouring tea and arranging the table setting, which included two votive candles flanking a small crystal vase of lavender roses. He lit the candles, asked Nowell if there would be anything more, then politely departed.

"So, you didn't answer my question," said Nowell, taking a short sip of tea.

"No, I don't mind the privacy. What I do mind, however, is that you may have given that man the wrong idea about us."

Nowell felt surprised but impressed by her bluntness. "Oh. And in what way is that?"

"Your implication that we're having an affair."

Would that be so bad were it true? he wanted to say. "I'm sorry. Perhaps that was a poor excuse. But it at least got the job done."

His remark hit Catherine with a surprising sting, as though somehow she wasn't worthy of an affair with him.

"You know what," she began, "let's change the subject. In fact, you still haven't answered a question that *I* asked you earlier. What is it between you and Wilton Dresden?"

"Wilton Dresden, Wilton Dresden," he said mockingly, his eyes glowering. "I can't stand the bloody bastard, that's what's between us."

"Then why help me get a job with someone you can't stand?"

"He owes me, that's why, and I'll extract any favors out of him that I damn well can. And since at the moment you seemed genuinely interested in meeting him, I thought perhaps the two of you might hit it off," he said sarcastically. Nowell briefly glanced out the window, then turned his attention back to Catherine.

"The fact is, he owes me money. Several months ago he badgered the hell out of me on behalf of one of his clients to come down in price on a Chippendale giltwood mirror I possessed. It was a beautiful piece—about two hundred and thirty years old and in near-perfect condition. It was actually something that had belonged to my parents who both died in a plane crash a few years ago. I decided to part with the mirror only to help settle some of the taxes.

"I had some other clients, a rather charming couple from Connecticut, who had already made me an offer on it. But Dresden had brought me a fair bit of business over the years, and I gave in to him, reducing the price at that. And wouldn't you know I've yet to see the first farthing from him. He claims his client is now in bankruptcy and to 'take a number.' According to him there are so many creditors ahead of me that I shall be lucky to ever see any money, let alone ever lay eyes on my mirror again." He paused as a calculating look crossed his face. "Believe me," he said, his voice low and tightly drawn, "I will see that mirror again or I will have my money. No one has ever cheated me and gotten away with it."

Catherine sat momentarily speechless. It seemed obvious that Nowell could afford the loss. So why couldn't he just let go and forget about it. Yet she also found herself feeling sympathetic—sad that someone had taken advantage of him following a time of grief.

"Gosh, Nowell, I'm so sorry." Catherine delicately sipped her tea, glancing outside. The rain was now a downpour, making her grateful for being inside the cozy Café Pierre rather than struggling for a taxi or waiting for the bus. She looked back at Nowell.

"If it makes a difference, I think Dresden is a pompous jerk," she said, sighing. "He claims I don't have the right level of experience, that he needs someone with greater depth and adaptability."

"Oh, balderdash. In other words, some young man he can shag in the you-know-what. And I mean that literally and figuratively."

Catherine snickered at his candid and derisive remark, then just as suddenly gasped.

"OH, MY GOD," she cried, looking frantically under the Bergdorf's shopping bag on the seat beside her. She jumped up and pulled out her chair, searching madly underneath the table.

"Oh, no. Oh, no!" she continued crying.

"My God, woman. Are you choking? Should I summon help?" asked Nowell urgently.

"My portfolio," she barely whispered. "I must have left my portfolio in Bergdorf's. Oh, my God, what have I done. It's all I've got. I will *never* get a job without it now." She slumped down in her seat, fighting off huge tears.

"Calm down, not to worry. Let's just give them a ring, someone is sure to have noticed it."

Nowell reached into his overcoat pocket and produced his cellular phone, dialing directory assistance. He got Bergdorf's number and promptly called the store.

"Yes, I'd like the ladies' shoe department, please."

Catherine looked at him quizzically. *How in the world did he know to call the shoe department,* she thought.

"Hello," said Nowell with authority. "A young woman, an attractive blond-haired woman wearing a brown suit," he added, "was in your shoe department this afternoon and perhaps left behind a portfolio. Uh-hmmm. It's an average-sized portfolio, black. Have you seen it?

"Yes, I see. Well could you kindly check around. Perhaps some other clerk there might have picked it up and put it in the back. Uh-hmmm. Yes, I can hold. Thank you."

It was then that Nowell saw that the look of panic on Catherine's face had been replaced by one of puzzlement. At first he thought she was impressed by his efficiency when he suddenly realized his blunder. He leaned slightly across the table and put his hand over the receiver as though not wanting to be heard by the other party, then stated: "I'm presuming it's black, isn't it? That's what most professionals use. I am right, aren't I?"

Catherine nodded her head yes as he went on. "I saw your shoe bag there, and also presumed that you must have done some shopping in that department."

Catherine nodded her head again, believing his story and now feeling grateful for his help.

It seemed like an interminable wait until someone picked up.

"Splendid," said Nowell, offering Catherine a hearty thumbs-up. Catherine slumped even farther in her seat, leaned back, and ran a hand through her thick hair, then began to cry. She'd come so close to yet another disaster, and had braced herself so hard for the blow, that the sense of relief was overwhelming.

Now it was Nowell's turn to look quizzical. He wrapped up the conversation with instructions about what to do with the portfolio, then hung up.

"Catherine, it's okay. They have it. We can walk right over there when we leave here and retrieve it." He reached into the breast pocket of his double-breasted, pin-striped suit and produced a handkerchief, which he handed over to her. He was completely struck by the beautiful but vulnerable vision before him. Her tears magnified her sensuous brown eyes, and he wanted so much to touch her soft skin and wipe away the tears. Instead, he politely excused himself, brazenly stepped behind the restaurant bar, and helped himself to two snifters of brandy.

Catherine willingly accepted one from him and took a long sip. It burned her throat but immediately began to calm her rattled nerves.

"I'm sorry," she said, quickly glancing around to see if anyone was watching, grateful to see they still had the room to themselves.

"I don't even know where those tears came from," Catherine continued, then immediately corrected herself. "Actually, I suppose I do," she confessed through a deep sigh, then took another hearty sip of the brandy.

And then she opened up her heart. For the next half hour she talked, and drank, as Nowell sympathetically listened. She talked to him like an old friend, sharing details of her move from a bright, cheerful town house in North Carolina into the small, dark apartment next to Michael's school. She talked about her deep sadness over losing the baby, about her futile job search, about getting stuck in the elevator that morning, and even her anger at Nowell for bringing her home drunk.

And then she began talking, softly and sweetly, about Michael. Nowell was moved by her sincerity. It was obvious that despite all her troubles, she was deeply devoted to the man. Nowell was further struck by the irony that Michael was studying to be a priest at General Theological Seminary, thinking how close he was to him that morning while waiting for a glimpse of his wife.

"You know, I love my husband more than anyone or anything in the whole world. He's trying as hard as he can, and I know he wants the best for me. It's just that living in New York has been really difficult, to say the least." Catherine sniffled, then looked earnestly at Nowell through her watery eyes. "I'm so hard on him. But that's not fair, it's not his fault." The tears started falling again. "I love him so much."

Nowell couldn't escape a sudden sense of envy toward Michael. In all his life, Nowell had never known the kind of love from a woman that Catherine had just described for Michael—pure, loyal, and constant. Sadly, he'd come to discover in his own life that most women were attracted to him for his money and status. And here before him was a woman who by looks alone could probably have any man she wanted, yet she'd settled for a penniless, would-be priest.

The waiter quietly appeared and asked Nowell if there would be anything else. He tipped his glass and nodded his head toward Catherine, indicating he wanted two more. "Courvoisier, V.S.O.P.," he instructed.

Catherine accepted her second drink, then reached over, putting a hand on top of Nowell's. "Thank you for listening to me. I didn't mean to burden you with all my problems."

Her slight touch caused a soft wave of sexual tension to ripple through his body, moving him to place his hand on top of hers. The combination of her sadness, beauty, and honesty thoroughly captivated him, and he found himself wishing he could hold her; offer her the promise that with him nothing bad would ever happen to her again.

But he withdrew his hand instead. In his personal affairs, as in business, Nowell possessed an impeccable sense of timing. And he knew that now was the perfect time to strike without coming across as taking advantage of her.

Calmly clasping his hands in front of him, he cast her a self-possessed look.

"Catherine," he began in a measured tone, "I need to ask you something."

Chapter Eight

Nowell climbed the steps to his town house thinking back on the first day he'd met Pamela Wainwright—his assistant and sometime love interest of over two years. He knew from the moment they had met that he'd hire her. She had just the right skills to keep his professional life in order and was attractive enough to keep his personal life interesting. She had not disappointed him in either way.

He was hoping Catherine Harrison would turn out the same. Entering the two-story foyer of his plush residence and gallery, and thinking of Catherine's startled yet happy reaction to his job offer, Nowell smiled. It didn't take her long to accept the position as his assistant. She was as eager to work for him as Pamela had been back in London when he'd first hired her.

The trouble with Pamela, Nowell thought while removing his damp overcoat, *is that she now expects too much of me.* At Nowell's insistence, and less than eight weeks ago, Pamela had moved from London to help run his stateside operation. She was doing a fine job too, which made what he was about to do slightly more complicated.

But she'd become needy, he'd convinced himself, expecting more of his personal time than ever before. He had no desire for a committed relationship with the woman—despite the fact that she was a lively companion in bed and in many ways a good friend.

Nowell thought of Catherine again as he opened the double doors leading toward Pamela's office. She might have readily accepted his job offer today, but he knew she was not someone easily conquered. Catherine possessed a rare and attractive spirit to him: innocent and refined, yet irreverent and slightly stubborn. And the fact that she proclaimed such love and devotion for her husband made her even more enticing. *This one,* he thought, *really will be a sweet challenge.*

Nowell walked quietly through the main gallery and paused as he heard Pamela carrying on a lighthearted conversation with Gwendolyn Hatcher—one of his most trusted and knowledgeable staffers. A former executive of Sotheby's in London, he first met Gwendolyn when she appraised his parents' estate following their deaths. She was one of the most respected authorities in the world on British antiques, and someone who had done a considerable amount of appraisal work for the Royals.

Though her style was quiet and disarming, she was one of the shrewdest negotiators he'd ever known. Nowell did not know how he could function in the business without her, and though he had to pay her a king's ransom in wages, she was undeniably worth it to him.

Nowell drew in a deep breath as the two women broke into easy laughter. They were good chums, and he hated breaking up the pair. But he knew their friendship would endure—unlike the opportunity to have Catherine Harrison close at hand.

"I say," he said, entering the room smiling. "I'm paying quite handsomely for all this frivolity. Care to let me in on the joke?"

His surprise appearance caused the two women to laugh even harder.

"We were laughing about you, actually," Pamela said, smiling affectionately.

"Oh, do tell."

"It's nothing, really," said Pamela sheepishly, trying to suppress her laughter.

"I had no idea you asked that poor woman who came in yesterday when her baby was due!" Gwendolyn confessed for them both. The two women cracked up laughing again, as Nowell rolled his eyes, then plopped down in a cushiony wing-backed chair.

"Oh, mercy," he said, "that was rather embarrassing, especially since it seemed so obvious. And I didn't ask her when the baby was due. I asked her when she was expecting."

Nowell joined in the laughter over his own humiliation. "You cannot imagine my horror when she said, 'Expecting what?' " he went on. "I thought I should die. I then tried to rephrase the question, such as 'What are you expecting?' You know, such as what it might be she'd like to buy. But she'd heard me clearly the first time. Oh, I shall never ask another woman as long as I live such a question, regardless of how obviously pregnant she is!"

The three of them enjoyed a short, but good-natured conversation with regard to pregnancy etiquette, until Nowell suddenly turned serious on them.

"Gwendolyn," he said sweetly, "I'd like to have a word alone with Pamela, if you don't mind."

"Oh, dear God, Gwendolyn. Don't leave me now," the young woman playfully begged. "He's probably going to fire me for sharing that story with you!"

"I rather doubt it." Gwendolyn smiled back. "I'll be in my office if you should need me," she said while winking at Pamela.

Nowell grinned at her as she promptly left the room, then turned his body toward Pamela and placed his folded hands atop his crossed knee.

"I hope you aren't mad at me for sharing that with her," Pamela offered sincerely.

"No, don't be silly." He half smiled back. He looked down for a moment, and then up into her soft green eyes. He would miss her pretty face and curvy body.

"Listen, Pamela. I've been doing some thinking lately. And there's something I want to discuss with you."

Pamela sat utterly still in her seat, and her heart began racing. She adored Nowell, and had been hoping for some time to move their relationship in a more serious direction. Things between them seemed to be going so well, especially since her move to Manhattan. It had been wonderful making love with him just a few nights ago, and she prayed that he was finally going to make the commitment with her she so longed for.

"Yes, Nowell. What is it?"

"I'm not quite sure how to go about this," he said with forced reluctance. "But I'm afraid having brought you here is a mistake."

She could feel her body go cold with shock. "What on earth are you talking about?" she barely whispered.

"I don't think it requires much explanation," he said with cool detachment. "I think you expect far more from me than I'm willing to give, and quite frankly I find it a bit uncomfortable working side by side with you each day."

"Nowell, I don't believe this. You really are firing me, aren't you?"

"Well, I wouldn't exactly call it that," he said. "I'm willing to pay all your expenses to relocate you back in London, or wherever else it is you might want to go. Plus provide you with a reasonable severance. And you know, don't you, darling, that we'll always be friends?"

Pamela looked for a moment as though she might faint, then slowly rose out of her seat.

"You bloody, fucking bastard," she said. "You can't do this to me. You begged and cajoled me to move over here. Said you couldn't imagine a more perfect arrangement than having me here in Manhattan since you spend so much time here. And now, less than two months after I move, you're planning on packing me up and shipping me off like one of your sold antiques. No thank you. I'm not leaving."

"Well, I suppose I could just fire you without severance and moving costs."

"You wouldn't dare."

"Oh, really?"

"Oh, my God," she cried, "you're serious. You're bloody, fucking serious about this."

Nowell sat emotionless as Pamela started pacing the room, heavy tears streaming down her face.

"What is it I've done?" she cried. "I've put no demands on you whatsoever. I've been a faithful employee—and a good one at that! And this is the thanks I get. Well no thank you you son of a bitch. I'm not a charity case and I will bloody well pay my own way back to England!"

Nowell laughed inside, thinking that perhaps he could let her get away with that. But he was prepared to smooth her transition back home with as much money as it would reasonably take.

"I don't know what it is you expect to do without me," Pamela cried as she moved toward the door. "But

I can promise you one thing, you will never lay eyes on me again!"

Nowell smiled as she walked out the door.

Michael lay wide awake as Catherine slept soundly beside him. It had been ages since they'd made love like that, since Catherine had behaved with such abandon.

Following a simple, but elegant meal of linguine with white wine clam sauce, a crisp salad, fresh bread, and Michael's favorite chardonnay, she'd drifted happily off to sleep. But only after seducing him right on the living-room floor.

Who is this Nowell Stuart? Michael wondered, feeling an unusual pang of jealousy over the man's sudden intrusion into their lives—as well as hurt that it was Nowell and not he who seemed to have inspired Catherine's current happiness and perhaps sexual invigoration. Michael learned the details of her job during dinner.

"His assistant? Catherine, have you lost your mind?" Michael had responded to the news of her employment. "You didn't spend all your time and money training to be an interior designer so that you could be a clerical worker!"

"No," she said reassuringly. "But neither would an interior designer's position at my level pay me sixty thousand dollars a year."

"You're joking!"

"I'm not. Trust me, Michael. Going to this gala paid off. I'm only sorry you weren't there." Catherine blushed at her lie, as she believed Nowell would have never bothered with her had Michael been present.

"Well, it's a good thing there's a payoff because some-one has to be responsible for our overdrawn credit card and near-empty savings account."

Catherine blushed even deeper, thinking of her recent excesses, but then smiled as Michael explained how he'd discovered those facts while trying to purchase tickets to *Les Misérables*. She felt sincerely touched by his efforts.

"Well, it's probably just as well that it didn't work out," Catherine said, "since I have to start work tomor-row morning anyway."

"Tomorrow morning?" said Michael incredulously, thinking what a waste it had been to beg his professors for a day off. "who is this guy and what exactly will you be doing for him?"

Beyond telling him that he was an international arts and antiques dealer, Catherine mentioned nothing about her limo ride around Manhattan or of joining him for tea at the Pierre.

"I know I won't be working as an interior designer, Michael. But think about it. Our bills will be paid." She smiled, trying to soften any hard edges left about the money she'd impulsively spent. "And," she added sweetly, "maybe now we could try to have a baby."

Michael chuckled as the truth came out. He knew she'd love to work as a designer, but that more than anything she wanted to be a mother. A job that paid this well would give them a chance to afford that possibility.

Michael decided his uneasy thoughts over Stuart were better left to himself. He didn't want to be responsible for dashing Catherine's high spirits and enthusiasm for her new job. Besides, she didn't need his permission or approval—only his support.

"Catherine, this is really exciting news. I hope it turns out well for you."

"Why wouldn't it, Michael? I'll be in a position to network with some well-established designers, learn more about art and antiques, and make good money besides. What could possibly go wrong?"

Chapter Nine

Catherine left Michael asleep under their down comforter, grabbing an overcoat on her way out. Though chilly, it was a sunny morning with the promise of warmer temperatures in the afternoon. It was the beginning of October and the trees had turned into bright bursts of yellow, red, and orange, which Catherine loved. Strangely, the dying trees always filled her with a sense of renewal, like the start of a new school year, as well as a feeling of romance. She was full of anticipation and knew as she closed their door that her life was about to change. This, Catherine believed, was the new beginning she'd yearned for.

She hailed a taxi, then read the driver Nowell's address from the back of a Café Pierre cocktail napkin. She knew that even with her new income she wouldn't have the luxury of taking a taxi to work every day, but she didn't have the time or inclination this morning to wrestle with a bus or the subway. Besides, she wanted to look her absolute best when she arrived, and the hassles of public transportation in New York had a way of stripping away one's freshly polished veneer.

The taxi let her out in front of an immaculate four-story, double-wide town house on one of the Upper East Side's more exclusive streets. It was just steps away from Central Park and certainly a prime piece of Manhattan property.

The building was an elegant Beaux Arts structure, its exterior crafted from ornately carved and polished limestone. Two oversized bay windows graced each side of double, raised-panel front doors painted a bright, cheerful red. The multipaned windows were accented by uniquely carved pediments, while flower boxes overflowing with ivy and yellow mums brightened the windowsills.

Marble stairs led up to the entrance, and with the exception of a brass plate on the door reading STUART AND COMPANY, there was no other evidence that it was a commercial establishment.

Catherine tried not to act overimpressed by the size and beauty of the place, and moved gracefully up the steps and pressed the doorbell. It was answered through an intercom by the thin but crisp voice of a British woman. Catherine noticed a small camera monitor mounted above the door and looked self-consciously at it as she spoke.

"May I help you?" the woman inquired.

"Yes, I'm Catherine Harrison. Mr. Stuart is expecting me today."

Her comments produced a buzzing sound from the door, an electronic invitation to enter. She slowly turned the polished brass handle on the right-side door, then moved inside, only to find herself alone in a massive, dimly lit, two-story-high foyer. The interior was distinctively Italian by design, but quite British in its furnishings. Semicircular stairs on either side of the room led up to a musicians' balcony that was graced by a beautiful balustrade, and an ornate crystal chandelier hung gracefully between the two floors.

The walls were covered in a raised-panel mahogany, which served well as a backdrop for various ancestral oil paintings. Beautiful antique furniture tastefully filled the sunken foyer, while a luxurious Persian rug, probably twenty feet by thirty feet, covered the gleaming inlaid parquet floor. Dead center beneath the chandelier stood an elegant round claw-footed table bearing an exquisite and fragrant arrangement of fresh flowers. Potted palms in Chinese urns stood sentry amid the furniture, and a highly polished suit of plated armor whimsically guarded the front door.

Catherine could barely move, the place so captured her with its museum-quality proportions, and she stood soaking up every detail possible. She couldn't help but wonder how much it was all worth, and remained entranced until a set of arched double doors opened at the far side of the room. A gray-haired, thin, and handsome woman emerged and moved with a steady gait toward Catherine. She was smartly dressed in a green shirtdress accessorized with a multicolored silk scarf.

"I'm Mrs. Hatcher," she stated. "May I please take your coat?"

"Thank you," Catherine replied while slipping out of it and handing it to her. Mrs. Hatcher took a few steps to her right, tapped gently on a mahogany panel, forcing a hidden door to pop open. A light switched on, revealing a large walk-in closet situated underneath one set of stairs. Catherine tried not to act too impressed, but Mrs. Hatcher didn't miss her startled reaction.

"He's big on surprises," she revealed tersely. "Please follow me."

Catherine kept pace with the woman while making small talk about the beautiful autumn weather. Mrs. Hatcher's composed demeanor implied she was someone unaccustomed to being crossed, so Catherine was careful not to ask anything that might seem even remotely inappropriate. They passed through the double doors, then past several high-ceilinged rooms filled with furniture, paintings, silver tea settings, and clocks. Mrs. Hatcher directed Catherine into her office, a small but bright chamber off one of the galleries, with French doors leading to a sunny courtyard garden beyond.

"Have a seat," instructed Mrs. Hatcher. "You need to fill out some paperwork."

Despite her nervousness, Catherine settled into one of the wing-backed chairs beside a gently burning fire, then attempted to make more small talk.

"Have you worked for Nowell very long?" asked Catherine cheerfully.

"Long enough," was the woman's cool response.

"I love your office," Catherine went on. "It's really cozy and . . ." She was going to say pleasant but Mrs. Hatcher's demeanor made it anything but. Catherine felt distinctly ill at ease, and wished strongly that Nowell were there. She simply couldn't understand why the woman was so curt with her and decided not to say another word unless Mrs. Hatcher spoke first.

The woman handed her a clipboard along with some tax forms, asked her to fill them out, then left the room.

Catherine did as instructed, then waited politely for

Mrs. Hatcher to return. But she never did. Over an hour passed, during which the phone rang at least four times. Catherine let it go the first three times, but finally feeling worried that something was amiss, picked it up as it rang again.

"Stuart and Company," she answered politely.

"Catherine? My word, Gwendolyn has you answering the phones already?" said Nowell, sounding surprised.

"Well, sort of. I haven't seen or heard from her in over an hour, so I just took it upon myself to answer it," replied Catherine. "I'm glad it's you. I wouldn't know what to do otherwise."

"How odd. Did she say where she was going?"

"No. She just asked me to fill out some paperwork, then left."

"Well, she must be somewhere nearby. Perhaps you can put me on hold for a moment and find her."

Catherine did as he asked, moving out toward the various galleries calling Mrs. Hatcher's name. But there was no response. She went to the main entrance hall where she spotted an envelope on the center table, something she hadn't noticed before. It was a letter addressed to Nowell, so she picked it up, then headed back toward the phone.

"She doesn't answer me, and there is no sign of her, at least on this floor. But I did find an envelope on the front table addressed to you. Should I open it?"

Nowell hesitated. "No," he finally answered. "I'll be there shortly. Just make yourself at home and leave the letter on her desk."

"Do you mind if I look around some till you get here?"

"Not at all," he said, "but please don't go up to the fourth floor. It's my living quarters and it looks every bit the bachelor pad. Also, if you wouldn't mind answering the phones till I return. I presume Mrs. Hatcher has left."

"My gosh, Nowell. Is it something *I* said or did?" asked Catherine earnestly.

"No, no, don't trouble yourself over it. It doesn't concern you at all. Just hang tight and I'll see you in approximately twenty minutes."

                    *   *   *

Nowell hung up the phone, then grimaced at his attorney.

"Gwendolyn is rather ticked off at me," said Nowell to Vincent Gambrielli, counselor-at-law. "I did something foolish in her opinion, and it seems as though she wants me to pay for it."

"I thought no one made you pay," said Vince with a leer. Nowell had been a client of Gambrielli, Brown & Muller for over six years now, and was particularly fond of Vince Gambrielli—an elegant olive-skinned man, and a smooth talker with unbeatable street smarts. He'd grown up in the Bronx, the fifth son of Italian immigrants, and put himself through Fordham University and law school on scholarships and winnings from his gambling bets.

Not only did he have a keen mind, but his connections were incomparable. He could negotiate anything for anyone and always got his client's way—for a price. Few people could afford him, and for those who could he made his services worth their while. Like most highly successful attorneys, he went to the edge for each and every client and Nowell Stuart was no exception. Nowell had unshakable confidence in the man.

"What have you done?" Gambrielli asked. He loved small talk but preferred billable hours and wanted to know what legal work might be in this for him.

"Well, there is this woman," he began, but was jokingly cut off by Gambrielli.

"Isn't there always?"

Nowell briefly chuckled. "As I was saying, there is this woman that I just hired to be my personal assistant."

"What happened to Pamela?" Vincent asked with a bit of incredulity.

"Well, that's what's got Gwendolyn so steamed. You see, I let Pamela go to make room for this other woman. Gwendolyn is outraged over my decision, telling me this morning that it was foolish and irrational. She's wrong, however. It was something I'd been contemplating for a while."

"Oh, really. And just how long have you been contemplating this?" Gambrielli asked insinuatingly.

"Oh, Vincent, what does it matter? I'm providing Pamela with a comfortable severance and a glowing letter of recommendation. I just feel this new hire is better suited to the job. Now, if you don't mind, I'd like to get back to this matter regarding Wilton Dresden and David McGowan."

Gambrielli nodded his head, then leaned back in his black leather chair. His office furniture was contemporary and stark, with the only warmth, in Nowell's opinion, coming from the thick, cream-colored carpet. Gambrielli folded his hands behind his head, looking up briefly at the ceiling and then back at Nowell.

"Tell me again, did your friend Wilton Dresden perform on consignment? In other words, did he claim his agency on behalf of David McGowan?"

"Yes. He brokered the entire deal."

"Do you have the paperwork proving that Dresden represented McGowan on this transaction? If you do, we can file a claim."

Nowell slumped slightly into the Scandinavian chair in which he sat, finding it surprisingly comfortable. It did not, however, help to relieve his deep frustration.

"Vincent, you know me to be a prudent man in my business affairs. But I let the mirror go on good faith that Dresden would provide payment, which he promised to take care of in a timely manner. I did not draw up any paperwork that day simply because I've done business with Dresden before and he always came through. Now it's as though he's mocking me, the bloody bastard."

Vince's brow furrowed and he began nervously tapping his desk with the eraser end of a pencil, stopping only as he spoke.

"As I see it, my friend, right now you have little legal recourse over McGowan. The debtor is in possession, which means essentially the court has power over everything he has right now—whether he's paid for it or not. And . . ."

Nowell suddenly cut him off. "Yes, but can't I go after Dresden for the money? That mirror would fetch over fifteen thousand dollars on the market today."

"You have no paper trail—you have no proof of his agency. There would be no way to prove it in court. Nowell, I'm not going to mislead you. This does not look promising. But you know me, I'll do whatever I can."

"Vincent," said Nowell, now leaning on the man's desk with both hands, "no one, and I repeat no one, has ever cheated me in a business deal and gotten away with it. And I certainly don't want Wilton Dresden, of all people, setting new precedents in my life. I don't care what it costs me to resolve this—I want the mirror back or Dresden publicly bled in court."

Gambrielli leaned back in his chair and smiled at Nowell as if to accept the challenge, neither man imagining that it would be Nowell's new assistant—and not his high-priced attorney—who would prove able to accomplish Nowell's mission.

Chapter Ten

An icy blast of November wind whipped Catherine's face as she turned the corner on Eighth Avenue to catch a bus. The temptation was strong to take a warm taxi ride to work. But in the five weeks she'd been working, she'd forced herself to save money by taking the bus each day and so trudged along in the blistery cold as several vacant cabs passed her by.

Approaching the bus stop she saw a woman huddled inside the Plexiglas shelter. A baby carrier was wrapped around the woman's torso, and inside, Catherine could see an infant about three or four months old. The baby was almost completely bundled in blue clothes, and all that could be seen of the child was its bright green eyes fringed with dark, curled-up lashes.

"My goodness," stated Catherine as she reached the shelter, "this weather must be quite a shock to the poor fellow."

The mother smiled. "Actually," she said, her breath visible in the cold, "it's a girl. We thought we were having a boy—at least that's what they told us after the sonogram—and that explains the blue clothes."

"Speaking of shocks," Catherine said with a laugh. "I hope you weren't disappointed."

The mother softly shook her head no, then tenderly wrapped her arms tighter around the infant. "We waited a long time for this baby," she said candidly, "we were thrilled either way."

"What's her name?"

"Allisa."

"What a beautiful name," cooed Catherine, stepping in for a closer look, "for such a beautiful girl."

"Yup, you're pretty special," said the woman to the

child, gently swaying and then stroking the infant's face. "Do you have any children?" she asked, looking up.

It seemed so simple, just to say no and leave it at that. But it wasn't so easy for Catherine, as her mind suddenly raced over the events of her failed pregnancy after she'd first gotten married.

She hadn't even suspected a pregnancy at the time, just concluding that her sudden fatigue was due to the stress following her elopement. She'd also been extremely busy with school, at first not even noticing that her period was late. But one day while flipping through her appointment book Catherine realized how much time had slipped by, then started counting the days since her last period—she was nine days late. The longest she'd ever been late for a period was two days, and so she panicked.

That night she purchased a home pregnancy test kit, which came out with a whopping positive result. She waited till that weekend to tell Michael when she joined him in New York, and would never forget the look of utter astonishment on his face as she broke the news.

"The Lord works in strange ways," he said, quite dazed. He then told Catherine he felt the best thing would be to come clean with her parents over their marriage and get her up to New York as soon as possible. Catherine insisted otherwise. She'd gone to considerable lengths to get into the Carolina School of Interior Design following graduation from college, and she wanted first to finish school at her parents' expense, then move to Manhattan after the baby was born.

She convinced him that her plan was better, promising that when her situation became obvious she would take it up with her parents. Michael reluctantly consented. In the end it didn't matter whose plan was better. The baby was lost and Catherine's father was angry at learning about their marriage in such a tragic way.

And now, given the doctor's prognosis after the miscarriage, Catherine doubted she'd ever get pregnant again. She looked wistfully at the young woman and her baby, and then finally and quite softly began to speak.

"No, I don't have any children," she said sadly. "I lost one last year, and the doctor said it's unlikely that I'll ever have any."

"Oh, I'm so sorry," the woman replied sincerely. "That happened to me too. I lost one a few years ago when I was about nine weeks along. It's such a tough thing." She seemed to Catherine to hold her baby even tighter, as though jealously guarding it. Catherine fought a well of resentment and anguish, thinking that if her own baby had survived it would be nine months old now. Momentarily absorbing herself in the fantasy, she barely heard the woman's next question.

"I hope you don't mind my asking, but are you sure you can't get pregnant?"

Catherine let out a short sigh. In fact, she did mind being asked. It was a deeply painful subject for her. Contrary to what Michael thought—and even though they couldn't afford a child right now—she hadn't used any birth control since recovering from the ectopic pregnancy, and nothing had happened. On several occasions she thought she might be pregnant again, and each time purchased a home pregnancy test kit.

But it was always the same manic experience, always the same result. She'd watch the window panels on the test stick—one the control, the other to determine the outcome of the test—as both of them turned a bright shade of pink, the color indicating pregnancy. For the few moments it took the true test results to settle in, it always cast the impression of being positive. And for that short, precious time she could happily imagine she was pregnant and dream of how she'd break the news to Michael. But again and again the tests proved negative, as the pink in the results faded to white, leaving no trace of its hopefulness behind.

"The only reason I ask," the woman went on without waiting further for Catherine's reply, "is that that's what they told me too."

"You're kidding," said Catherine, now interested in what the woman had to say. They stopped talking about the subject long enough to board their bus, then sat side by side where Catherine softly resumed the conversation.

"Now I hope you don't mind *my* asking, but what did you finally do?"

"Three little words," she answered, a smug grin crossing her face, "in vitro fertilization."

"Seriously?"

"Absolutely. And if you're serious about having a baby you should look into it. It can sometimes take months to get an appointment at some of these clinics. In fact, one of the best clinics in the world for IVF is right here in New York City—the Manhattan Reproductive Center. Dr. Webster, he's the next best thing to God as far as I'm concerned. Look what he created for us." She sweetly kissed the baby's forehead.

Catherine listened attentively as the woman provided more details about the treatment and the program. It wasn't easy and it wasn't cheap, she confided. She and her husband attempted in vitro twice before she had a successful pregnancy, at a cost of over ten thousand dollars a try. "But third time's a charm," she chirped at the baby.

"You know, it doesn't work for everybody," she added more seriously, looking back at Catherine. "But if you really want a biological child, it's the best alternative to taking no for an answer," she concluded.

"Thank you," said Catherine sincerely, getting up to transfer to her crosstown bus. She reached down and sweetly stroked the infant's head as she spoke. "You've given me something very positive to think about."

As she got off the bus Catherine realized she'd never learned the woman's name. It didn't matter, she told herself. She'd learned everything she needed to know anyway.

Finally reaching the town house that morning and anxious to get out of the cold, Catherine let herself in, then immediately brewed some freshly ground coffee. Nowell was still up in his living quarters.

Settling into her office with a steamy mug, she tried concentrating on some bookkeeping, but her conversation with the woman on the bus began ringing through her head. *Ten thousand dollars a try!* she kept thinking. *And three tries! The cost of making that baby could practically pay for its college education!*

It was disheartening to think about it, but at the same time the thought provided a measure of badly needed hope. Impulsively, Catherine reached for the phone directory and looked up the number for the fertility clinic, then picked up the phone and called.

"Manhattan Reproductive Center," answered a pleasant voice. Catherine abruptly hung up. *What am I doing? What should I say?* she thought. *This is crazy. I better talk to Michael first. No, I can't. Michael would never consent to this. Not right now.*

But Catherine couldn't let go of the urge. If nothing else, she thought, she should make an appointment and at least get an opinion from Dr. Webster. Find out just how bad her situation is and what her options are. Besides, she reasoned, if what the woman said was true—that it could take months to get an appointment—then she had nothing to lose by calling today. She could always cancel. She picked up the phone and redialed.

"Manhattan Reproductive Center," came the pleasant voice again.

"Uhm, good morning. I'd like to make an appointment to see Dr. Webster," said Catherine tentatively.

"Let me transfer you to his assistant."

"Good morning, Dr. Webster's office," said the next woman, sounding professional, but harried.

"Hi, my name is Catherine Harrison, and I'd like to make an appointment to see Dr. Webster."

"Are you a new patient?"

"Well, yes. I've never seen him before.'

"Who is your regular doctor?"

"You mean my OB/GYN?"

"Yes."

"Dr. Collins. Grace Collins."

"Oh, of course, I know Grace," said the woman, her voice softening up a bit. "Did she refer you here?"

"Actually, no. I heard about Dr. Webster from someone else. You see," Catherine said, her voice winding up a bit, "I had an ectopic pregnancy about a year and a half ago, and lost one of my fallopian tubes in emergency surgery. I haven't used any birth control since then, and also haven't gotten pregnant." She said it all in one quick breath—as though at a confessional; finally purging her soul to someone who could make a difference.

"Have you had any workups done? A hysterosalpingo-gram?"

Catherine lightly laughed. "I'm sorry, a hysto-sal-what-o?"

The woman laughed back. "I guess not."

"I was told that it could take months to get in and see the doctor. How long would it take to get me in?"

"You know, you're in luck. Someone just canceled an appointment for two weeks from today. I called two women on the waiting list for that slot, but one is out of town and the other one expects to be out of town. If you'd like, I can schedule you for then. Trust me," she added, "it would be late next year before I could get you on the schedule otherwise."

For a moment Catherine felt like a lottery winner. Of course she would accept, but then just as suddenly she panicked. She didn't want to start something she couldn't finish—what if Michael disapproved?

"I hear Dr. Webster's one of the best," said Catherine, stalling.

"I wouldn't work for him otherwise," said the woman. "He doesn't promise everyone will have a baby. But you've a far better chance through him than just about anyone else in the world."

"Make that appointment," she said enthusiastically, marking the day and time in her appointment book with big, bold letters.

Chapter Eleven

"Judy, good morning," Catherine said sweetly into the phone. Judy Klein was a middle-aged decorator who did a lot of business with Nowell and was one of his favorite "Yanks" besides. She was brash but funny, and harbored a soft spot in her heart for Nowell, always reminding him that if it weren't for some twenty-odd years between them she "coulda had" him.

"Listen, I'm afraid I've got some bad news," said Catherine, "we just got an offer on that desk yesterday."

"Rats!" Judy exclaimed about the particularly fine piece that she'd been eyeballing for a client. "Can you tell me how much?"

"We got the asking price."

"Sixteen thousand! Didn't they negotiate with you at all? They must be from Texas. All my Texas clients have so much friggin' money."

"I can't tell you who they are, really. Do you want to counterbid?"

"You know old tightwad on Park Avenue would kill me if I paid more than thirteen." Judy paused, then added disappointingly, "Catherine, c'mon. Who's buyin'?"

"You know I can't tell you that. If it's any consolation, we have another piece that just arrived from London. It's very similar, but not quite as old, and he's only asking fourteen thousand for it."

"Who else knows about this?"

"No one."

"Then put my name on it as sold. I'll deal with the old biddy myself. By the way, I heard something that may be of interest to your boss."

"Oh, yeah," said Catherine, "what is it?"

"First, tell me who got the desk!"

"Judy! That's not fair. You know Nowell doesn't like me to share that kind of stuff."

"I know, I know. Well, here's the scoop. You know that mirror that Wilton Dresden and David McGowan 'stole' from Nowell?"

Catherine edged up in her seat as excitement grew in her voice. "Yeah?"

"Well it turns out that David is trying to sell it on the sly. The only reason I know is that a friend of mine owns a country house in Connecticut, not far away from David's weekend retreat. She was over at his place the other day and he told her he had a few select pieces of his personal collection he was unloading—which, it turns out, included that gorgeous mirror. What he didn't know is that she'd first seen it in Nowell's gallery a few months ago on a buying trip with me. She felt certain that it was the same mirror, and when she asked David where he had acquired it he told her it was a family heirloom—though, of course, he didn't say whose family! Anyway, he's asking nineteen thousand for it. Can you believe that guy's nerve?"

Catherine sat stone silent on the other end, incredulous over what she'd heard. How dare that man, she thought. She couldn't wait to tell Nowell, when suddenly a better plan came to mind.

"Judy, did your friend buy it?"

"No. As far as I know he's still trying to hawk it."

"Let me ask you something. Any chance you can get her to arrange a meeting between me and him? Just have her say I'm a friend of a friend, and don't mention anything about Nowell."

"Well, let me call her and I'll get back with you as soon as I know."

"I look forward to hearing from you." Catherine hung up the phone and was startled to find Nowell staring at her.

Nowell, true to Mrs. Hatcher's word, was big on surprises. Not until she started the job did Catherine learn that he also owned a textile manufacturing plant, Sutthington Mills, as well as a substantial shipping business. Both were located in England, in addition to a London-based gallery brimming with his antiques. He was an extremely busy man. And though he had plenty of staff

at each business to handle his many affairs, he relied
solely on Catherine in the United States for scheduling,
gallery bookkeeping—and since the abrupt departure of
Mrs. Hatcher—occasionally selling to his clients.

Catherine surprised Nowell with her ability at the last.
She was a quick study and within just a few weeks came
to know almost all of his New York inventory and the
significant selling points of each. Catherine's gracious
business manner and understanding of the needs of interior designers made her a favorite with even Nowell's
toughest clients.

Nowell certainly got his money's worth out of Catherine since she often put in twelve-hour days. And even
though she was almost always in the gallery, Nowell insisted on providing her with a cellular phone so that he
could stay in constant touch with her. His demanding
schedule made it imperative that he be able to reach her
at all times, he claimed. And he did, often calling her at
home late at night or early in the morning, even on
weekends, to go over business matters.

At first Catherine felt flattered to be needed so badly.
But she slowly realized there were things on his agenda
that could have easily waited until she was in the office.

One night in particular she and Michael were making
love when her cellular phone began ringing. She ignored
Nowell's first two intrusions, but during his third attempt, and having lost all concentration on Michael, she
finally jumped out of bed and grabbed her purse with
the ringing phone in it.

"STOP! JUST STOP!" Michael said with uncharacteristic hostility.

"Michael, he's not going to give up."

"Just turn the damn thing off!"

"Michael, it's not that easy."

"Oh, yes it is. Just hit the off button."

"But he'll know."

"He'll know what? That you have a life of your own?"

Catherine's whole body went tense as she stood between Michael and the incessantly ringing phone.

"He'll know that I deliberately turned off the phone,
and it pisses him off."

"You mean you'd rather have me pissed off at you
than him?"

"Come on, Michael, be fair. I'll talk with him about it tomorrow."

Michael's look turned hard and cold as he left the bed, grabbed his robe, and headed for the living room.

"Michael, please. I promise this won't take long." He ignored her.

Though Catherine wished many times she could be frank with Nowell about respecting their privacy, she knew she never would. Despite his cellular interruptions and her heavy workload, Catherine was deeply grateful for the opportunity he'd provided her and didn't want to offend him. Just like she didn't want to tell him at that moment, as he stood watching her in the doorway of her office, that she disliked it when he snuck up on her.

"Say, listen," he said sweetly. "Would you care to join me today for lunch? I have to head over to the Met later this morning, and thought I'd grab a bite at the Stanhope afterward."

"Thanks for the offer. But I'm afraid I'll have to beg out. I have a lot to do today."

"Business with Judy?" he inquired.

"Well, yeah, kind of," Catherine replied, feeling excited but smiling calmly as the phone rang again.

"Hi, it's me, Judy. You're in luck. My friend, Charlotte, she's heading out to Connecticut this afternoon to run a quick errand and would love your company. She called David and told him she knew someone who might be interested in the mirror. She can pick you up at two o'clock. Sound okay?"

"Great."

"Catherine, what are you up to? You're not going to buy that mirror, are you?" Judy asked.

"No, no, not exactly." Catherine smiled into the phone. "Judy, can you hold for just a second?" She pressed the hold button, then looked confidently up at Nowell. "Judy has a lead that may bring you, shall we say, a significant piece of business. She wants me to go take a look at a client's estate with her this afternoon. Do you mind if I go?"

"What does the appointment book look like this afternoon?"

"Not too bad. Nothing you can't handle on your own," she joked.

"Whose estate is it?"

"Oh, I'm not really sure. But if Judy says it's worth taking a look at, then you know it probably is."

"Well, perhaps I should go with her. What are they looking to sell?"

"Nowell," Catherine intoned more seriously, "she asked *me* to go along. Don't you trust me?"

"Quite frankly, not entirely. But I suppose I have to start somewhere."

If nothing else, Catherine felt grateful for the chance to get out of the city and join Charlotte Prowly on her way to Westport, Connecticut, about an hour's drive north of Manhattan. It turned out to be a charming seaside community, with beautiful countryside just beyond the shore featuring many century-old homes on acres of gently rolling land. David McGowan owned such a place, not far from the Prowlys' house.

"Charlotte, you're sure now, this is the same mirror you saw at Nowell's gallery?" Catherine asked nervously as they pulled up to his house. It was a tastefully refurbished carriage house on exquisitely landscaped property.

"Absolutely. My husband and I had actually offered to buy it from Nowell several months ago after I first saw it with Judy. I thought we had a deal on it, then Nowell called and profusely apologized saying he had forgotten he'd promised it to some designer. It's a very rare mirror, in mint condition too. And we were prepared to pay full price for it."

"I can't believe this. Nowell told me about you all. He felt awful about the whole thing. He said there was a really lovely couple from Connecticut who wanted it, but he gave in to the pressure from that designer, Wilton Dresden. Let me ask you something. Why didn't you just buy it from David?"

"What, are you kidding? For nineteen thousand dollars! Nowell was only asking fifteen. Besides, we found another mirror. And you know what? It looks great in our entrance hall. Well," she said, turning off the motor to her Mercedes-Benz, "shall we?"

Catherine drew in a deep breath, then opened the car door. She hadn't explained to Charlotte what she intended to do. Charlotte rang the doorbell, and a small bevy of dogs within immediately responded with a chorus of yelps and barks.

"Oh, hush down, hush down," she could hear a man's voice. Clearing a path through the animals, David McGowan answered the door. He was a pleasant-looking man, with a disarming smile. Not too tall, he was slight of build, and despite a receding hairline had thick, reddish hair. And in his corduroy pants, cashmere pullover sweater, and loafers he appeared perfectly respectable to Catherine. She had second thoughts over her mission the moment he extended his hand toward her.

"Oh, please don't mind my menagerie," he said of the four King Charles spaniels jumping excitedly around him.

"Not at all." Catherine smiled, then laughed. "How can you tell one from the other?"

"Believe me, I *do* get them confused sometimes. But not usually. This is Lucky," he said, bending down and patting one affectionately on the muzzle. "Then Richie; Bon Appétit—she eats everything, and believe me I mean *everything*!" he said, laughing. "And, of course, we can't forget Pitty-Pat."

"What a crew," Catherine said with a laugh, wishing so badly that Nowell, with his sardonic sense of humor, could see this.

"Well, listen," David said. "I was just getting ready for some tea. Would you ladies care to join me?"

"Actually," Charlotte spoke up for them, "I have to be back in the city by six-thirty, so I haven't much time. Perhaps you could show Catherine the mirror?"

"My pleasure."

He led them down the stylishly decorated entrance hall toward a study at the far end. As he opened the door, Catherine immediately spotted the giltwood mirror—and gasped at the sight of it. It was an exquisite piece and beautifully displayed over a mantelpiece against the backdrop of vermilion-colored walls. Catherine knew from Nowell's description of it that there could only be one like it. It had an oval-shaped mirror plate, surrounded by an intricately carved frame of foliage, flowers, and fruit.

"Isn't it lovely," he exclaimed from behind her. "I just love it. It's been in my family for generations."

"I hope you don't mind my asking," replied Catherine politely, "but why are you selling it then?"

"Well, I've decided to retire and move to Florida. And quite frankly, to me, the only real reason you hang on to a piece like this is so that it will appreciate in value. And when the time is right, you sell it. This is a very handsome mirror, as you can see. Built in the last quarter of the eighteenth century. Not a nick on it—and it hasn't been refurbished either—which makes it even more valuable. Trust me, I have a trained eye for these things. I would know."

Catherine stepped up to the mirror for a closer inspection. Everything about it was exactly as Nowell had described.

"I have several people interested in it," he added.

I'll bet, thought Catherine, thinking of agents from the IRS who would love to know his shenanigans. She delicately touched it.

"How much are you asking for it?"

"Nineteen thousand dollars," he said without hesitation.

Catherine turned and smiled at him. "I'll take it."

"You're kidding!" he said, his face caught in a half smile.

"No, I'm not kidding at all. In fact, I'll take it right now," she said.

"For nineteen?" he asked, needing reassurance he was closing the deal.

"I said," she repeated with a cunning smile, "I'll take it." With that Catherine reached over the mantelpiece, carefully removed the mirror from the wall, and proceeded to walk out of the room with it.

"Hey, wait just a minute. What are you doing?" he queried from behind.

"Charlotte, are you ready to leave?" Catherine asked. David McGowan rushed toward her, uncertain still what was going on—whether he should help her to the car or snatch it away.

"Are you going to buy it or not?"

"I said, I'll take it, and I meant it. Just like *you* took it from Nowell Stuart."

"You can't do that," he shrieked, his face turning beet-red. He went to put his hands on the mirror but Catherine pulled a quick retreat. "I'm calling the police," he threatened and dashed for the phone on his desk.

"Fine," said Catherine. "I'll be more than happy to talk to them after I finish telling the IRS how you're raising cash."

With every nervous breath she had left Catherine made her way out of his house. Charlotte, startled and nervous herself, was quick on her heels. Catherine could hear McGowan screaming at her as she climbed into the backseat, holding fast to the mirror.

"You little bitch," he screamed. "I'll get you for this!"

Charlotte climbed into the driver's seat and pulled away fast. It wasn't until they were at least a mile away that Charlotte slowed down, then started to laugh.

"In all my life, I have never!" she gasped. It was obvious she'd enjoyed the surprise, and would be talking about this escapade at countless cocktail parties to come.

"Me either," said Catherine, still choked with nervous breathlessness. "Charlotte, please accept my apologies. I'm really sorry I put you through this!"

"Oh, no. Not at all, honey, not at all. I can't stand that little arrogant son of a bitch! But I suppose for all my troubles," she said with a laugh, "you can just leave that mirror right in the backseat!"

"Wish I could, Charlotte. Wish I could," said Catherine. She held the mirror in her arms just as tightly as the woman seemed to hold her baby at the bus stop that morning. And with nearly the excitement of an expectant mother, she couldn't wait to deliver it to Nowell.

Nowell relaxed in his study on the fourth floor of his town house, gazing into a crackling fire while nurturing a glass of brandy. It was nearly six o'clock and he hadn't heard back yet from Catherine. He thought to call her on the cellular phone, as he normally would, but as long as she was with Judy he didn't want to bother her. At least not for another half hour or so.

He glanced over at the security monitor screens and noticed a Mercedes-Benz had pulled up outside. Though it wasn't Judy's car, it appeared to be Catherine climbing out of the backseat carrying a painting or such. Nightfall made it difficult to discern. He watched as Catherine waved good-bye, then mounted the steps to the town house, opening the front door with her own key.

Nowell swallowed the rest of his brandy and headed downstairs in the elevator. As it reached the ground floor the doors opened and to Nowell's surprise he found Catherine standing immediately outside, a broad smile consuming her pretty face.

"Close your eyes," she said confidently, "and take my hand."

Nowell, usually the instigator of such pranks, found it difficult to close his eyes but eagerly reached for her hand. Her touch was soft and pleasing.

"I said, close your eyes," she repeated.

"Oh, Catherine, come now. What could you possibly be up to? Did you purchase a Rembrandt or something?"

"Even better," she said, gently leading the way toward her office. "Are your eyes closed?"

"Yes, yes. They're closed, for God's sake."

"Okay, keep them closed until I say so."

"Oh, dear. What nonsense have I allowed?"

"Are your ready? Open!" she said gleefully, having guided him to just the right spot.

Nowell opened his eyes, then stared in amazement at his reflection.

"Oh, dear God," he exclaimed. "It's my mirror. It's my bloody mirror! How on earth did you manage to get your hands on it?" he asked, tenderly touching the frame.

"Are you surprised?"

"Surprised? I'm utterly astonished. Did Vince Gambrielli have something to do with this?"

"Not a thing," she said, beaming.

"You did this on your own, for me? Oh, pray tell, what happened?"

Nowell listened attentively as Catherine relayed every last detail, and though a seething rage burned inside him over David McGowan's gall, and most likely Wilton Dresden's complicity in the matter, he concealed his anger well. Instead he went over to Catherine as she finished her story, impulsively cupping her face in his hands, then kissed her very sweetly on the forehead. Catherine started slightly, but didn't move.

"You are, unquestionably, the most wonderful employee I could have ever hoped for, and a true friend besides," he said, then kissed her on the forehead yet again.

Catherine did not resist him as he leaned in toward her, surprised by the flush of excitement she felt by his nearness and his touch. Suddenly, though, Nowell was drawing himself in for another kiss—only this time he was pulling himself in toward her mouth, causing Catherine to quickly jerk herself away from him.

"What are you doing?" she sharply reproached him, alarmed by the look of malicious joy in his deep blue eyes.

"What do you mean? I was simply trying to let you know how much I appreciate what you did for me."

"A *simple* thank you would have sufficed," she said, then began walking toward the door.

"Where are you going?" he asked incredulously. "Catherine, please, don't go. I'm sorry."

"It's late, Nowell. I'm going home," she answered softly, but severely while gathering her coat and purse.

Nowell stood fixed in place long after he'd heard the front door click shut behind her, succumbing to something deeply contrary to his nature—remorse. He had never seen Catherine so infuriated. And though he usually never considered his behavior, especially with women, worthy of an apology, with her it seemed different. He felt worried that he might have permanently offended her, and angry with himself for being so inappropriately forward.

And while grappling with his uneasy feelings, Nowell realized that he had never been afraid of losing anyone—until today.

Chapter Twelve

"Good morning," said Dr. Stan Webster pleasantly. He was a tall, older man with gentle manners and thick, pepper-colored hair. His eyes were dark but shined bright behind his half glasses, his smile broad and bright against a nice tan. He picked up a folder from his desk and began reading the questionnaire Catherine had filled out.

"Good morning, sir." She smiled back nervously, sitting across the desk from him. Michael still had no idea about her appointment to see Dr. Webster, and she felt slightly awkward being there alone. Arriving at the Manhattan Reproductive Center that morning, Catherine was struck by the number of couples—young and middle-aged alike, all presumably with the same problem, the same desire—awaiting their turn to see this modern-day wizard with an expensive bag of tricks.

"So," he said, "Mr. and Mrs. Harrison want to have a baby? Is Michael here today?"

"No, he couldn't make it. But I thought it wouldn't hurt for me to get started, since I know I'm the one with the problem."

"Are you sure about that?" he said with a half grin.

"What do you mean?"

"Has Michael's sperm ever been tested?"

"Well, no, actually. It hasn't. We just assumed he was all right because I got pregnant the first time."

"Well, this is a joint venture," he said good-humoredly, then added, "you might be surprised to know that in at least thirty percent of the infertility cases we treat the problem is with the man." Catherine blushed, wondering how she was going to explain all this to Michael.

"Let's see," Dr. Webster went on. "An ectopic pregnancy twenty months ago. I'm sorry about that," he engaged her sympathetically. "That's always a tough loss. Which hospital did you go to for treatment?"

"It happened while I was living in North Carolina. I went to Northern General in Raleigh."

"Please arrange to have your previous doctor send me your charts," he stated, then continued reading her paperwork. "You say here that you lost a fallopian tube?"

"Yes."

"And you've been having unprotected sex since then?"

"Yes."

"Hmmm. How are your periods? Pretty regular?"

"Not always. I mean I always have one, but they're not every twenty-eight days. Sometimes they're a bit later."

"You could be on a thirty-two-day cycle. Any irregular bleeding?"

"No."

"Any abortions?"

"No," she said, beginning to feel as though he had taken a potato peeler to her privacy.

He next told her to head down the hall to an examining room and he would be in to see her momentarily.

Catherine did as instructed, stripping down and dressing in a flimsy gown, then began an interminable wait for Dr. Webster to get back to her. As she sat on the edge of the examining table, swinging her legs in boredom, her cellular phone began to ring.

"Oh, Nowell," she said with exasperation. *"Give me a break!"* She jumped off the table and dug into her purse for the phone and flipped down the mouthpiece.

"Hello," she said tersely.

"And good morning to you too," Nowell chirped into the phone. "It's not like you to be this late. I figured being Monday after the long Thanksgiving weekend that you might have forgotten you had a job."

"I'm sorry," Catherine replied in a hushed tone. "I forgot to tell you that I had a doctor's appointment this morning."

"I hope everything's all right," he said with a note of genuine concern.

"Oh, you know, one of those regular checkups."
There came a knock on the other side of the examining-
room door, and Dr. Webster entered followed by his
nurse.

"Listen, I have to go now. Is there anything urgent?
Otherwise I'll see you in the office in about an hour."

"No, no. Would you care to have lunch today?"

"Fine," Catherine replied impatiently, feeling awkward with the doctor and nurse both listening. "I'll see
you soon." She hung up the cellular phone and clung to
the device as she hoisted herself back up on the examining table.

"You know," said Dr. Webster wryly, "it's a known
fact that stress can play a factor in infertility. Always on
the job, you gals."

Catherine laughed but offered no comment. With Nowell that was certainly true—she was always on the job.

Dr. Webster conducted a thorough pelvic examination
on Catherine, looking for odd lumps or growths, checking the size of her uterus, then taking a pap smear. The
nurse concluded by drawing multiple blood samples. He
made several notes on her chart, told her to go ahead
and get dressed, then meet him back in his office. Fortunately she didn't have to wait long this time.

"Catherine, I need to go over a few things with you,"
he said, pulling his chair up closer to his desk. Beneath
his casual demeanor Catherine detected a man of deep
intelligence and passion for his work. She felt far less
intimidated now than when first arriving at the clinic.

"Assuming that your husband's sperm is up to the job,
we need to look closer at what's happening with you.
Our success rate with patients like you, women in their
late twenties who've had an ectopic pregnancy that is, is
better than average. Typically the patient doesn't have
difficulty getting pregnant. The problem instead is that
the embryo doesn't know exactly where to call home.
But you say you've been having unprotected sex for over
a year and a half now and nothing has happened. How
often do you and Michael have sex?"

It felt like he was wielding the potato peeler again.
"Oh, at least twice a week, sometimes more. Occasionally less." The doctor made a note on her chart.

"Well, I'd say the first thing we'd have to do is a

hysterosalpingogram, which we like to perform between days six and eleven of the next cycle."

"What does it involve?" Catherine asked, still hesitant over how far to proceed without Michael's approval.

"Well, it's an outpatient procedure, pretty simple. Basically we inject a dye solution into your uterus and use radiology to examine the structure of the reproductive organs. It's one way to determine tubal patency—to make sure that your existing fallopian tube isn't blocked and that there aren't any other abnormalities. We can learn a lot from this. And it's far less expensive or invasive than laparoscopic surgery; that's another procedure you might need down the line, where we slice a small hole in your belly button, then feed a tube into your abdomen with an 'eye' on the end of it. Basically that allows us to see up close how the organs look and determine if there are any lesions or other problems that may be inhibiting your ability to get pregnant." He picked up her chart and began perusing it. "Let's see, when did you have your last period?"

"Two weeks ago. What happens after the hysterosalpingogram?"

"Well, in your case, assuming everything seems okay, we would try a few inseminations. Occasionally that's all that's needed. Sometimes the sperm simply cannot get past a certain point in the woman's body, and insemination provides them with a jump over those barriers."

Catherine released a nervous sigh. "How much does this cost?"

"The hysterosalpingogram, combined with the radiology, is about five hundred dollars. The inseminations aren't that expensive. The labwork and procedure probably cost about the same."

"Well, what happens if the inseminations don't work?"

"Then we move on to in vitro fertilization where we surgically remove your ripened eggs and place them in a petri dish with your husband's sperm. We then place several fertilized eggs right into your uterus and hope that your body knows what to do from there, with a little hormone help from us, of course."

"Several eggs? Is that why you hear about so many twins and triplets from in vitro?"

"Precisely. As long as we're at it we might as well increase our chances of success by planting as many eggs as possible. It could be as many as five or six."

Catherine threw her head back in incredulity and laughed, imagining for the moment what it would be like to learn you were going to be the mother of sextuplets.

"How many inseminations would you try first?"

"At least two."

Catherine sat silently for a moment, trying to piece together all that this meant. This was serious business, and she began wondering if maybe she shouldn't wait a little longer before jumping into it.

"Is anything wrong?" asked Dr. Webster.

"Is there any chance I could start this after the first of the year?"

"Actually, no. Once we take a patient on, we expect that the patient is prepared to move forward. Otherwise we'd like to make room for someone who is ready. Unless of course there were other extenuating health circumstances. But you seem to be in fine health. I'd like to schedule you for the hysterosalpingogram as soon as possible, and get your husband's sperm sample as well. Can you bring him in with you on the next visit?"

"Yes," said Catherine, unsure if that was possible, but certain that she didn't want to wait a year or longer for another chance to see this doctor.

"Great," said Dr. Webster. "Now, just talk with Mary out front, and we'll set a target date for the hysterosalpingogram in December. And I'll see you then. Oh, and don't forget to have your former doctor send me your medical reports."

With that he rose and shook her hand while smiling warmly. Though Catherine was still full of curiosity, she knew he was probably anxious to get on to other patients and thanked him for his time, then gathered her belongings and was out the door behind him. As instructed, she made a tentative appointment with Mary, contingent upon when her next period started, then handed over a check for three hundred dollars—Dr. Webster's initial consultation fee.

What am I doing? Catherine kept thinking to herself. *Michael is going to have a fit.*

But exiting the clinic she thought of the young mother

on the bus two weeks ago, and the beautiful baby she carried.

"She was right," Catherine said softly, feeling a restored sense of hope about starting a family. "I will not take no for an answer."

Chapter Thirteen

Michael smiled while watching the young boy and his sister charge excitedly among the Christmas trees, neither child able to decide which one to bring home. Knowing what sadness existed beneath the surface of their current glee, Michael had decided to indulge the young pair by taking them to a Harlem Christmas tree lot and then telling them to pick out whichever tree they wanted.

"This one," finally shouted seven-year-old Kayla, pointing to a short Douglas fir dusted like confectioner's sugar with a light December snow.

"No way!" rebuked her eight-year-old brother, Gordon. "It's too fat!"

"Nu-uh!"

"Uh-huh!"

"Nu-uh!" she demanded again, tears filling her sweet brown eyes. Michael quickly stepped in for the mediation, wishing Catherine were here to help comfort the child. The girl's mother had recently been incarcerated for drug dealing, and from what Michael knew neither Kayla nor Gordon ever knew their father—he'd abandoned the family when they were young babies. They currently lived in a dingy Harlem apartment with their great-uncle, Victor, a man Michael knew through one of the seminary's soup kitchens.

Though Victor wasn't destitute, stopping in at the soup kitchen a couple times each week helped to stretch his meager budget—now strained even further by agreeing to care for his niece's children for an indefinite period of time. Michael's fondness for the quiet, hardworking man, and his own love of children, inspired this spree with Kayla and Gordon.

"Gordon," Michael said softly while squatting down

to the boy's level. "Have you found another tree that you like better?"

"Yes," Gordon replied, quickly scanning the horizon for his phantom pick.

"Can you show me which one."

"That one." The child pointed over Michael's shoulder. Michael turned around only to see a small army of short, fat Douglas firs.

"Hmmm," said Michael thoughtfully. "That's a good one too. Well, the way I see it, you've both picked good ones. The problem is you can only have one tree."

"Mine," Kayla interjected.

"Not so fast, Kayla. I think we should go over and take a look at Gordon's pick. Come on, Gordon, can you show us which one." Gordon nodded, and Michael grabbed Kayla by the hand as they followed her determined brother. The boy stopped proudly beside a tree that seemed a bookend match to Kayla's.

"This one," Gordon said with conviction.

"I see," said Michael. "Kayla, what do you think of this one?"

"Mine is better," the girl whimpered.

"What makes yours better?"

"I found it first." Michael laughed over her seven-year-old logic.

"Listen," he said, now taking Gordon's mittened hand. "From what I can tell, they're both pretty much the same kind of tree—and both are just as special."

"Nu-huh," said Gordon, "mine is better."

"Why?"

"Because."

Michael laughed again, realizing that eight-year-old logic wasn't any more sophisticated. Deciding there was only one civil way to resolve this dilemma, Michael resorted to an old-fashioned remedy by removing a quarter from the pocket of his jeans.

"I have an idea," he said. "Why don't we toss a coin. Kayla, if it's heads we take home your tree. And if it's tails, Gordon, we take home yours. Deal?"

The children agreed and watched in eager anticipation as Michael tossed the coin high into the air, then slapped it atop his hand.

"Tails," he said. "Gordon, it looks like you're the winner."

His proclamation prompted large tears to begin streaming down Kayla's face.

"Kayla, Kayla. What's the matter?" asked Michael. "Gordon won fair and square."

"He always wins," she said softly, then began sobbing uncontrollably. From inside her oversized, hand-me-down parka Michael could see that her tiny body was shaking. Knowing it had less to do with the near-freezing temperature than over feeling genuinely slighted, Michael quickly bent down, then scooped her up. Kayla's sobs continued as she buried her face in Michael's shoulder.

"I want my mommy," the girl cried.

"Oh, honey," said Michael, cupping his hand around the back of her head. He wondered what Catherine, who seemed to have such a knack with children, would say to make Kayla feel better. He wished she were with him now.

Instead, she was off with Nowell Stuart—hostessing a grand Christmas party that held no interest for Michael, particularly given his feelings of skepticism toward Nowell. Which is why Michael turned down the invitation to join his wife. In spite of having never met Nowell Stuart, Michael was fed up with the man.

In the beginning Catherine couldn't stop telling Michael all about Nowell—about his fabulous antiques, the famous people who shopped at the gallery, and about Nowell's amusing ways. At first Michael listened patiently, but his interest quickly waned, which was so unlike him since he usually supported everything Catherine did. When she finally asked him about his indifference, he confessed: he felt like Catherine was increasingly obsessed with the material aspects of her job.

"Catherine, Nowell Stuart offered you a job, not a life. And I'm worried that you're becoming far too impressed with his way of living. And it makes me wonder if you're really prepared to be the wife of a low-paid priest. You're living in Nowell Stuart's fantasy world, Catherine, and I feel sometimes like you're getting lost in there."

"Oh, Michael, you're being ridiculous." She tried defending herself, but then immediately clammed up and began brooding. About an hour later, her demeanor somewhat softened and apologetic, she approached him.

"You're right, Michael, you're right," she conceded. "I have been pretty wrapped up in it all. I mean, you have to admit, his wealth is pretty impressive."

"No, Catherine, it's not impressive. It's just that *you're* impressed by it."

She tenderly took his hands and looked him straight in the eyes. "Michael, I love you more than anyone or anything in this whole world. My job with Nowell means nothing compared to what we have. And you know, in all honesty, I don't think Nowell Stuart is a very happy man. He has no one to share his life with. And if he had just a fraction of the happiness we have together, then he would truly be the wealthiest man on earth."

Michael knew Catherine had spoken from her heart. But still, he worried. And as he stood in the inner-city Christmas tree lot that evening trying to comfort a stricken Kayla, he wondered if his wife would be just as happy comforting an unfortunate and brokenhearted child as she was creating the perfect holiday atmosphere for some overly spoiled people.

Nowell forced himself to chat with Onyx Orwell, one of Manhattan's "society" designers, while keeping a steady eye on Catherine, who was busy entertaining their other guests. Ms. Orwell was one of more than a hundred people attending Stuart and Company's first annual Christmas party—an idea hatched and beautifully executed by Catherine. She thought it would be a good way to say thanks to the people who'd done business with Nowell, and a chance to draw in new clients. Nowell thought it was also a fine way to show her off.

Though she'd only been on the job a couple of months, Catherine had far exceeded his expectations; she not only kept him well organized, but in the past week alone had sold two expensive pieces from his collection to a designer desperately needing "the right look" for his client's Southampton summer estate. The combined sale of a George II mahogany wing armchair and a William and Mary chest of drawers brought Nowell over twenty thousand dollars.

"It wasn't his money anyway," she joked to Nowell after the transaction. Nowell was suitably impressed with her business acumen, believing he couldn't have done better himself.

He watched her work the black-tie crowd that night with her usual grace and Southern hospitality. And while she was always beautiful to him, that evening she appeared absolutely ravishing. She wore a dark green gown with a full taffeta skirt, complemented by a velvet bodice that revealed her creamy skin and soft, graceful shoulders. During his conversation with Onyx, he watched and absorbed all that Catherine did, simply unable to take his eyes or mind off her, feeling as if the night belonged to them.

He watched in amusement as Wilton Dresden, in his Armani tuxedo and stylish white silk scarf, approached Catherine and began chattering in his usual pompous fashion. Catherine smiled and nodded politely at what he said. Though Nowell despised the man and resisted inviting him, Catherine convinced him that it would be a painless way to let Dresden know his business was still welcome—despite the antics of his con artist client, David McGowan.

"Onyx, will you excuse me please. I need to speak to my assistant."

"Of course, darling," she answered in her stuffy, affected manner, then offered a stilted smile. She loved to put on airs, and was particularly adept at it when speaking to anyone with money.

"Enjoy the party." Nowell smiled at her, then began making his way across the foyer toward Catherine and Wilton. His goal was not to speak with Catherine directly, rather to eavesdrop on their conversation. The chamber music played by the small orchestra on the musicians' balcony made it difficult to hear without getting right next to them, which he managed to do by stopping to talk with Mr. and Mrs. Fitzgerald who stood nearby.

"Really, I'm quite happy working for Nowell," was all he could hear Catherine say, and nothing more. The Fitzgeralds began droning on about some Bavarian antiques they thought might be of interest to Nowell. He nodded his head in feigned interest, while straining to hear Wilton.

"Well, just so you understand . . ." responded Wilton. Mrs. Fitzgerald began talking more loudly, forcing Nowell to miss the rest of Wilton's statement to Catherine, who had just managed to break free of his company.

"Mr. and Mrs. Fitzgerald, have you met my assistant Catherine Harrison?" Nowell interjected, quickly corralling Catherine as she began to pass by. She stopped and smiled warmly at Nowell, happy to be by his side.

"No," gushed Mr. Fitzgerald, "I rarely forget a pretty face and I would have never forgotten one as beautiful as yours." He gazed at her cleavage—which was quite enticing—as he spoke. His elderly wife ignored his behavior, offering her own answer.

"No, we haven't met Ms. Harrison in person, but we did speak on the phone. You're the one from North Carolina, right?"

"Yes, ma'am," Catherine pleasantly replied. "I'm so glad y'all could join us this evening. Are you having a good time?" She could beguile even the most cynical New Yorker with her Southern charm, thought Nowell, beaming inside.

"Yes, very much," replied Mrs. Fitzgerald, "I love how this place is decorated for the holidays, it's delightful. Who did it for you?" she asked, assuming the work had been hired out.

"Well," said Catherine with a slight blush, casting a demure look at Nowell.

"Catherine is too modest to admit she did most of it herself," Nowell offered proudly.

"My heavens," exclaimed Mrs. Fitzgerald, then began commenting on the various decorations, a theme developed by Catherine to reflect a Christmas hunt scene at an English manor. A magnificent tree, fully laden with plaid moiré ribbons and bows, glittering Victorian ornaments, and small, glowing white candles adorned the center hall. Oversized cornucopias filled with nuts, berries, and feathers from wild game sat perched on tabletops amid fragrant pine and hemlock boughs, while a garland wrapped with red satin ribbon, gilded magnolia, and sweet gum leaves was festively wrapped around the banister. Every door was decked with a large evergreen wreath featuring brass hunting horns, holly, and bright red bows. Even the suit of armor captured the spirit, as

Catherine had placed a red plaid kilt on it and put jingle bells on the visor.

After thanking the Fitzgeralds for the compliments, and for coming to the party, Nowell politely asked if he and Catherine could be excused. "Of course," the Fitzgeralds said in unison, a habit acquired after forty-two years of marriage.

"Catherine," he began, then took a huge, nervous swallow of his champagne. "I can't begin to tell you how grateful I am to you for making this happen. The party is brilliant . . ." He stopped, and at that moment could no longer resist his impulses. He bent down and gently kissed her cheek, then softly finished his sentence in her ear, ". . . because of you."

Catherine's cheeks flushed. Unlike a few weeks ago when she reproached him for kissing her, she smiled up at him.

"Nowell," she began, but instead of finishing her sentence she unexpectedly reached up and kissed him back on his cheek. "There's something I've been meaning to tell you." She paused very coyly, then took a long sip of her champagne. He appeared strikingly handsome to her that evening in his designer tuxedo, red plaid cummerbund, and patent leather slippers. His hair was stylishly slicked back and there was an utterly incandescent look in his eyes.

"Yes," he answered playfully.

"It's just that, well, I can't tell you how much I appreciate all *you've* done for *me*. You've rewritten the ending to one of the worst years of my life, making it one of the happiest. I love my job and I love working for you."

She grabbed his hand, giving it a small squeeze. Nowell's heart raced in anticipation at what was next to come.

"Really, Michael and I just don't know how to thank you," she started, but Nowell couldn't bear to hear the rest. His fleeting hopes suddenly came crashing down with the mention of Michael's name. He felt slapped by discouragement, but managed an affectionate smile nonetheless.

"Catherine, darling, don't mention it. It makes me happy that you're happy. Speaking of the old chap, where is he? I thought he was going to join you this evening."

"He was. But his finals are in two days and he decided to study instead."

"Oh, I'm so sorry. I was looking forward to finally meeting him."

"I know, I'm sorry too. Don't worry"—she smiled reassuringly—"I'm sure you two will meet soon."

"Yes, I hope so," said Nowell insincerely. "Incidentally, I saw you speaking to our friend Wilton Dresden. What did he have to say for himself?"

"Are you ready for this? He offered me a job!"

"That bloody bastard," Nowell muttered furiously under his breath.

"What?" asked Catherine, unable to hear him.

"Well, did you accept?"

"Nowell, you've got to be kidding. I just told you how much I love my job. No way."

"What, pray tell, caused his change of heart?"

"You'll love this. First he said anyone with the guts to pull the stunt I did on David McGowan is worthy of his employment. It turns out McGowan owes him money too. And the decorator I sold those two pieces to last week is a good friend of his. He told Wilton what a big help I'd been, especially since his clients really liked the furniture, and I gave him such a good price," she said, winking at Nowell mischievously. "Anyway, Wilton said he realized he'd made a mistake, and anytime I'd like to come work for him the door is open."

"Catherine, I hope you're not even entertaining the notion."

"Well, you know it's always flattering to be wanted," she said teasingly. "But the answer is no. I told you already, I'm happy here."

"Good," Nowell said with a grin, but hot waves of anger burned inside him. "That's very good."

Nowell tried to enjoy the party and put the nagging thought of Dresden's back-stabbing out of his mind. What really concerned him was knowing what a deft needler Wilton Dresden could be, usually getting what he wanted. And if he truly wanted Catherine to work for him, Nowell worried that there might be no stopping him. Despite his calm appearance, Nowell was seething inside. No one, and especially not Wilton Dresden, would take her away from him, he would see to that.

The party lasted till well past midnight, and was a huge success—partly because of Catherine's initiative, but mostly because so many people came to see the elusive Nowell Stuart. It was known that he was a handsome man, of fabulous means, and that he dabbled in his arts and antiques business primarily for the sport of it. But beyond that, very few Americans knew him well.

It was public record that Nowell's great-grandfather, already a wealthy man, had amassed an enormous sum of money as a leading British textile manufacturer, and that his son later developed one of England's largest shipping companies. Their money and the family businesses had been passed on to Nowell's father, who built them up even more. Upon the death of his father, Nowell received full ownership of the family fortune.

It was a part of his life that he rarely discussed or flaunted. Nowell preferred it that way, with all people, believing the less they knew of him the better. And though he was on everyone's "A" list, he remained aloof and detached, especially from the money-hungry New York scene. He made occasional social appearances in London and rarer ones in Manhattan. People loved to speculate about his wealth, his past, and his future. Women fawned over Nowell, but few impressed him. He knew—unlike Catherine—they were mostly after his money and social standing.

The last happy and tipsy guest finally departed after 1:00 A.M. Servants quickly and quietly cleaned up the party's remains, leaving Nowell and Catherine to themselves. They retreated to his study for a drink and a recap of the evening.

"You should have heard her." Catherine laughed while speaking about one of the guests who considered herself an expert on English antiques. "I heard her pointing to your William and Mary slant-front bureau and tell someone it was a George the First period piece. No, correction," she said with a giggle, "*definitely* a George the First period piece. It was hilarious." Catherine plopped casually into one of Nowell's soft, down-filled club chairs, kicked off her shoes, then curled her feet beneath herself. Nowell busied himself with the fire.

"Listen to you, madam," Nowell said, snickering, "sounding as if you're the expert here."

"Oh, I know, I know. It's just that she's such a snob and thinks she knows it all, and for once I knew better. It was amusing to me, that's all."

Nowell refreshed her champagne as she spoke. "What time is it anyway?" Catherine asked. "I really need to get home. In fact, I should call Michael."

"Nonsense, don't disturb him. I'll have my car service pick you up and you'll be home shortly. But first, there's something I want to give you."

He went to his massive Victorian partners desk and produced a small rectangular box from one of its drawers. It was aqua-blue with a white satin bow, the distinctive packaging of Tiffany's.

"Nowell, you shouldn't have," said Catherine, startled and surprised by his gesture.

"I found this to be irresistible," he said and paused, then sheepishly added, "much like you."

Catherine looked at him askance, not certain how to interpret his comment. She put down her glass and slowly opened the box, knowing whatever it was wouldn't disappoint since Nowell had such fabulous taste. Lifting the lid Catherine discovered a small felt pouch inside, and the dazzle of the gems inside the pouch nearly took her breath away. It was a small brooch of multicolored, semiprecious stones in the shape of a pheasant. It was stunningly beautiful.

"Nowell," Catherine gasped.

"I wanted to give you something in keeping with the theme of the evening," he boasted. "It's an original, I had it made just for you. Go ahead, put it on," he said, his eyes twinkling and his voice full of excitement.

Catherine sat in prolonged silence, unable to take her eyes off it. It had been a long time since she'd received valuable jewelry as a gift, something her father used to give each Christmas.

"Do you like it?" he asked.

"It's unbelievable," she whispered.

"I thought you would enjoy it." He grinned broadly. "I'd help you with it, but in that dress it would be a bit personal. Please, put it on."

She sat motionless, staring wide-eyed at the brooch

that she held in the palm of her hand like a delicate
Fabergé egg.

"Go on," he coaxed her. "It goes beautifully with your
dress, don't you think?"

"Nowell, I can't," she said in a barely audible whisper.

"Oh, do. Please, put it on."

"No, I mean, I can't accept this," she said with a mixture of uncertainty and resignation. She thought it was
one of the most gorgeous pieces of jewelry she'd ever
seen, and would have been delighted to accept it. But
she knew Michael would object, as well he should. Michael would probably never be able to afford such a gift,
and would find it extremely disconcerting that Nowell
had done this for her.

*"No, it's not impressive. It's just that you're impressed
by it,"* Michael's words about Nowell's wealth began
ringing in her ear as she studied the glittering brooch
before her, then her mind began racing over what she
should do. She'd deceived Michael over so many things
lately—still not telling him about her visit to Dr. Webster or the upcoming hysterosalpingogram. The doctor
still needed Michael to come in for tests, but Catherine
was unable to muster the courage to bring it up with
him until after he'd finished his final exams.

Despite all that, she didn't want to hurt Nowell's feelings by rejecting something he'd obviously put a lot of
thought in to. But she didn't want to have to account
for it to Michael either, and she knew there was no in
between. She hoped she had the kind of friendship with
Nowell that would allow him to understand her predicament.

"Nowell, I honestly can't begin to tell you how
touched I am by this."

"Well, I thought you'd like it. Merry Christmas." He
smiled, leaning proudly against the mantel, his eyes
still shining.

Catherine bit her lower lip, then gingerly placed the
gift back in its box. "Nowell, please don't get me
wrong," she said slowly. "This is one of the most beautiful and thoughtful gifts anyone has ever given me. But
I'm afraid I won't be able to accept it."

Nowell didn't say anything. Instead he turned his back

to her and began poking the embers in the study's over-sized fireplace.

"Nowell, I feel like I can be honest with you, so please don't be disappointed with me. It's just that Michael wouldn't understand this. In fact, I think it might make him angry."

Catherine felt deeply uncomfortable, as Nowell seemed to be brooding, and she didn't know what to say. He remedied that for her.

"Well, I daresay, Catherine, don't tell him about it. It'll be something just between us. Like that dress you're wearing."

Catherine started at his remark. Even in her slightly drunken state she knew she'd never told him about keeping the dress a secret from Michael. "How did you know about my dress?" she asked slowly.

"Why else would you have Bergdorf's deliver it here and not at home? I would have thought you'd want Michael to see how absolutely radiant you look in it. But then if he wasn't coming to the party, he would never have to know, now would he?" Nowell smiled at her, but it was in such a dark, penetrating way that it made Catherine begin to feel uncomfortable. She took a large swallow of her champagne, then challenged him.

"Well, that's a pretty good guess about the dress, No-well." In fact, he was right on the money. Furthermore, Michael was never going to come to the party. Catherine had invited him, but she knew he wanted little or nothing to do with Nowell Stuart, and when he declined the invitation she didn't push the issue. "But why did you say that about Michael?"

"I just did. He hasn't come around since you've started here, and something tells me he never will. He may even be a bit jealous of me, you know."

How the hell does he know this? she wondered.

"Jealous of what?" she asked.

"My money. He would probably never admit to it either. I'm sure he's a fine man, Catherine. But I imagine he worries about you working for an unattached man with so much money. Make that a good-looking, unattached man with so much money," he said, laughing sarcastically.

"Boy, you're really full of yourself this evening, aren't

you?" She laughed back. She wasn't certain if he was serious, but decided to play to the lighter side of it, continuing to speak candidly to him as her friend. "And you know what," she added, "you're right. He might be kinda jealous. I mean, let's face it, Nowell, you *are* good-looking, you *are* unattached, and you do have *a ton* of money. I saw tonight how women react to you, and I'm sure Michael thinks I'm like all the rest of them. But I'm not. You know as well as I do that we're just friends, and that there's nothing for Michael to worry about. He knows I would *never* cheat on him. I love that man to death."

Nowell seemed indifferent to her remarks, standing still while staring into the fire and listening to the crackling embers. Catherine felt desperate to restore the high-spirited feelings they shared earlier in the evening. She was afraid she'd permanently offended him, and rose from her chair, joining him beside the fireplace.

"Nowell, I'm really sorry about this. I hope I haven't hurt your feelings. You do understand, don't you?"

He shrugged and nodded yes, replacing the poker, then took a hearty swallow from his glass. His countenance changed swiftly as a sudden smile consumed his handsome face.

"Catherine, actually I'm the one who should be sorry. I shouldn't have put you in this position. Listen, I'll make a deal with you. You don't have to accept this gift. But I'd like to do something for you, for both of you, to let you know how appreciated you are. I will make a donation to a charity in your honor. How's that?"

"Oh, Nowell," she said, moving even closer to him. "That is so sweet of you, and I know it's something Michael will approve of." With that she grabbed both of his hands, drew him softly to her, and for the second time that evening gently kissed him on the cheek. And though his face seemed responsive, his body was tight with tension.

"Well, I suppose I should call for your car now," he said, quickly letting her go.

Catherine felt perplexed, even a bit brokenhearted. The night had been such a success up until now, making her wonder if she hadn't permanently damaged her relationship with Nowell.

"I'll wait downstairs," Catherine offered, then gathered her shoes and quietly left the room.

Nowell stood by the window watching as the car carrying Catherine pulled away from his town house, his palm sweaty from turning the brooch over and over again.

How dare you, he thought with disbelief, unable to comprehend how any woman could have rejected such an expensive gift.

His anger mounted with each turn of the brooch, and with each turn of the thought that Catherine was going home to another man. It didn't matter to Nowell that it was her husband. He'd been certain that by now Catherine, seeing all that he had to offer, would do anything to have him. And furthermore, would have not only eagerly accepted his precious gift but might have thanked him in the most unforgettable way—by finally making love to him tonight.

"God damn you," he fumed as he walked toward the mantelpiece to pick up his snifter of brandy. As he reached for the glass he dropped the brooch on the hearth, its brilliant colors sparkling bright beside the fire.

He started to pick it up, but stopped, picking up the fire poker instead. Then impulsively squaring it in the center of the glittering pheasant, he pressed down on the poker with all his weight and listened with unexpected pleasure to the crunch of the fine gems. And then, with abandon he repeatedly stabbed the brooch, vaguely smiling as it fractured into unrecognizable pieces.

Chapter Fourteen

On Monday morning following the Christmas party, Catherine opened up the front door to Nowell's town house and was impressed to find it in perfect order. Though there were no lights on and the heat was turned down low, the tree and all the other decorations offered a warm welcome. Catherine could only hope that Nowell felt that way toward her when she saw him.

She went straight to her office, turning on lights along the way, then made her way to the small galley to brew a fresh pot of coffee. Nowell often didn't appear for an hour or more after her arrival, which today would give her a chance to finish addressing some Stuart and Company Christmas cards. When Catherine finally sat down with a steaming cup of coffee she noticed, dead center on her desk, an envelope addressed to her in Nowell's distinctive handwriting. Considering the tension they'd experienced two nights before, Catherine reached for it with a trembling hand, even wondering if she might be fired.

Dear Catherine,

I received a call over the weekend concerning a problem at Sutthington Mills. It needed immediate attention, so I'm heading to England and will remain there through Christmas and New Year's. I'm leaving it up to you to hold down the fort—something I know you are quite capable of doing.

There is some correspondence that needs tending to on my desk; I think you're familiar with it already. The only other thing that needs attention is to follow up with Sotheby's about when the Reischer collection will be auctioned—I'd like to be there or at least bid by phone. I'll let you know about other business as it arises.

   Once again, you did a brilliant job with the party. I could not be more pleased. I hope you and Michael have a lovely holiday.

Nowell

P.S. I've enclosed your Christmas bonus. Please note that the check is made out to you and Michael, since it is my way of thanking him for his patience.

Enclosed was a check for $2500 made out to Catherine and Michael Harrison. Catherine let out a sigh of relief over his friendly tone and generous check, though she couldn't be more perplexed otherwise. *Why didn't he call me on the cellular phone?* she wondered to herself. *He's never hesitated to do that before.*

She busied herself with miscellaneous tasks for a while, and was just about to leave early when the phone rang.

"Nowell." She smiled into the phone upon hearing his voice. "Is everything all right?"

"Yes, hopefully. There was a small fire, and then of course some water and smoke damage. One section will be temporarily closed, but I don't intend to lay anyone off—especially given that it's Christmas."

Catherine again smiled into the phone—he was a truly generous man. And though he seemed upbeat, Catherine couldn't escape a need for reassurance that he wasn't mad at her.

"Nowell," she said tentatively, "I'm so sorry to bring this up, but about the other night . . . I hope you aren't angry with me."

"Catherine, darling, did you open that letter I left on your desk?"

"Yes."

"Does it indicate in *any* way that I'm angry with you?"

"Well, no, not at all. In fact, thank you. Thank you very much for the check."

"Listen, I need you to know how much I appreciate and value you as an employee. I also wanted Michael to know how much I appreciate his support as well."

"You are too kind."

"Say nothing of it. Catherine, now I have something to ask of you. I was wondering if perhaps you might not want to make a trip abroad right after the holidays. I have some projects going on here that could use your attention, more in the decorating scheme of things. I thought right after New Year's you could join me here, and if Michael doesn't mind, stay through the month of January. What do you think?"

"Nowell," she exclaimed excitedly, "it sounds wonderful. What is it you have going on?"

"Oh, this and that. You'll see when you get here. Call Reliable Travel right away and have them book you on the first flight to London on New Year's Day. Deal?"

"Deal!"

"Oh, and better yet. Ask Betty there to book you on the Concorde. If you've never flown it you'll love it."

"Well it sounds great. But, Nowell," she added more seriously, "who will run the gallery in New York?"

"Trust me. It won't hurt us to close shop for a month."

Catherine enthusiastically listened to his brief description of travel on the Concorde, and promised to call Reliable Travel right away. She hung up the phone smiling with anticipation, then immediately slumped in her chair as she found the travel agent's number in her Rolodex. How would Michael feel about a month-long separation, and could she possibly reschedule Dr. Webster's infertility treatment despite his admonition that once he accepted her as a patient she had to stick with the program's schedule? She sat in quiet conflict, wondering for quite some time whether she should go. She decided she'd feel much better discussing it all with Michael, and would do so while treating him to dinner at Tavern on the Green with her bonus money.

On the other side of the Atlantic, Nowell was also sitting quietly, but for a different reason. Finally, he thought triumphantly, he would have Catherine to himself, with no distractions from Michael.

"Do what you want with it," Michael snapped, then buried his head back into a book.

"I can't believe you," Catherine charged back. "How

can you act so pious over a simple bonus check. I mean, you don't *really* believe it's inappropriate for me to accept it, do you? It's a common practice in the business world to give year-end bonuses to employees. Why can't you just be grateful over Nowell's generosity for a change?"

"You haven't even worked for him a year yet. Why is he being so generous?"

Catherine drew in a breath and closed her eyes. It was bad enough that Michael didn't appreciate the twenty-five-hundred-dollar bonus check. But worse, she had no idea how to break the news that Nowell wanted her in England for a month, perhaps even longer. Telling him about her treatment at the Manhattan Reproductive Center was completely out of the question right now.

Thank God I didn't accept the brooch, Catherine thought, realizing that the discovery of an expensive gift of jewelry from Nowell would have probably sent Michael right over the edge. She'd thought he'd be delighted over the bonus money. But his reaction had startled her.

"Merry Christmas," she'd said joyfully while presenting the check to him during dinner at Tavern on the Green. Michael took one look at the signature, then dropped the check on the table, barely saying another word the rest of the meal. Catherine felt crushed by his behavior. Especially since he refused her long-declared wish to snuggle up close in a horse-drawn carriage ride through Central Park after dinner.

Though always slightly contemptuous of Nowell, Michael had never been this obvious with his feelings before. The minute they got home from dinner he changed his clothes, flopped on the bed, and began reading, deliberately ignoring Catherine until she finally burst into tears from hurt and frustration.

"You were the one who said we had to make it on our own," she blurted. "I haven't taken one penny from my parents. I got the best job that I could—and this is the thanks I get. For God's sake, Michael, cut me some slack."

A scowl consumed Michael's face, but he said nothing, instead keeping his nose in his book.

"Fine, dammit. Have it your way," Catherine snapped,

then left the room. Certain Michael would come after her, she paused in the living room for a moment. But he didn't budge. Angrily she threw on her coat, grabbed her purse, then slammed the door shut and left the building, not knowing where she was going or why. The arctic December wind whipped through her long blond hair and numbed her face and hands. But she didn't care, she was so steamed over Michael's behavior.

What the hell is the matter with him? she wondered. *It's only twenty-five hundred dollars.* But as she continued her brisk pace to nowhere, she realized that twenty-five hundred dollars had a vastly different meaning for herself, Michael, and Nowell. To Michael, who'd grown up with nothing, it was a huge sum of money to be saved or carefully spent. For her—prior to marriage—it was about how much she'd spend a month on new clothes and frivolous entertainment. For Nowell, it was pocket change.

Still, why can't Michael just appreciate it for what it is: Nowell's way of saying thanks, Catherine thought. But it wasn't that simple, and she knew it. Michael had been forced to listen to all her excited stories about Nowell's pampered lifestyle, and about all the famous people who strolled into his gallery and dropped vast sums of money without blinking. It was a world Michael knew of only through her, and one he believed was perilous with temptation, making her covet things they couldn't afford.

By now Catherine was near the Ginger Garden, one of their favorite Chinese restaurants. Deciding she wasn't ready to go home, she slipped inside for a hot cup of tea and was cheerfully greeted by Eddie Huang, the owner.

"Why you out tonight?" he asked in his chopped English. "Too cold out. We happy to deliver." He looked at her sad face, and the dark, informative stream of mascara down her right cheek. He also noticed Michael wasn't behind her.

"Everything okay?" he asked sympathetically.

"Thank you, Eddie. Everything is fine. Listen, if it's not a problem, may I just sit in the back and have a cup of tea?"

"Sure, sure. No problem. You sure everything okay?"

"Positive, Eddie. I just need something to warm me up."

He offered to take her coat, which Catherine decided to keep wearing for the moment. Eddie escorted her to a quiet booth in the back, the one she and Michael preferred when they ate in the restaurant, and she slid into it with the comfortable ease of someone plopping into their favorite living-room chair. Eddie disappeared, only to return moments later with a pot of steaming tea. Catherine took one sip of the mild green brew, then realized she needed something stronger.

"Eddie," she asked as he passed by her table a short while later. "Do you have any cognac behind the bar?"

He looked amused. "What kind of class place you think this is?" he teased. Eddie disappeared momentarily, coming back with a snifter brimming with Hennesey.

"This one on The Ginger Garden," he offered as he set the drink down. He could see the sadness etched beneath her smile, and hoped his gesture would help relieve her hurt. Catherine thanked him warmly, then took a swift swallow, followed by another. And as the brandy coursed its way down her throat, it gave sudden rise to thoughts of Nowell.

She reflected on their trip to the Pierre, remembering how he inhaled with style the satisfying bouquet of his cognac before taking a sip. Unconsciously, Catherine brought the snifter of Hennesey before her nose and did the same—the pungent smell of the heavy drink bringing an unexpected longing for Nowell's carefree company.

She downed the drink then, still feeling sorry for herself, and without hesitation she asked Eddie for another one.

In between the first and second drinks, she relaxed enough to sort out in her mind what was happening with Michael. It was clear to her she'd done nothing wrong. If anything, she believed, Michael owed her an apology for ruining the special evening she'd planned. His problem, she concluded quite simply, was a jealousy he couldn't admit.

Michael had always displayed a low level of tolerance for Nowell Stuart—despite the fact that he'd never even met the man. True, Nowell could be something of a pest with his telephone calls at inconvenient hours, commanding Catherine's attention and prompting her to action at his whim. But still, he'd been something of a savior to them, offering Catherine an incredibly well-paying job when they'd hit rock bottom financially, then providing her an opportunity for greater responsibility and growth, even offering commissions on sales she made.

Catherine polished off her second drink and was fishing in her handbag for some money when she spotted her keys to Nowell's town house. She pulled them out and smiled at them like an old friend.

I could always go there, she thought. *With Nowell gone, it won't matter if I spend the night,* Catherine told herself resolutely. It would show Michael, she convinced herself, that he couldn't get away with treating her as he did.

She paid Eddie for her second drink, then faced the windy cold on Eighth Avenue where she hailed a taxi, confidently giving Nowell's address to the cabbie.

The mixture of alcohol and the car's hot, dry air forced Catherine to fight a wave of drowsiness. She tilted her head against the backseat and closed her eyes, only to startle awake as the driver announced they were at the designated address.

"Oh, gosh," she exclaimed, "that was fast." She glanced at the meter, which read $7.25, then handed the man a ten-dollar bill and told him to keep the change. She'd never tipped a cabdriver that much before. But embarrassed at falling asleep and feeling grateful over being safely delivered, she easily parted with the money.

Catherine grasped her keys, then moved eagerly up the steps. Unlocking the large front door, she moved swiftly over the entrance hall's plush Persian rug with its rich red and blue hues, and into her office where she quickly disarmed the alarm system. *The last thing I need is the police swarming around this place and me needing to explain that I'm camping out here because of a domestic dispute,* she thought.

Feeling slightly woozy, Catherine moved to the plump, Chintz-covered sofa in the adjoining room, the one where clients often sat for tea when they came to the gallery. She removed her shoes, then lay down on the

soft cushions, resting her head on one of the many
down-stuffed pillows. Placing her coat over the top of
herself, she thought she'd drift right to sleep, but found
the darkness and eerie silence in the massive town house
unnerving. She'd never felt unsafe in the gallery before.
But with the alarm system turned off she felt vulnerable
and uneasy, yet afraid that she might accidentally trip
one of many security beams around the house should
she turn it back on.

Maybe I should just go home, she thought plaintively,
but her anger over Michael's behavior remained strong.
Catherine sat up and began considering what to do. She
could call Michael and try to discuss things with him
over the phone. But she wanted him to worry and to
think about how unfairly he'd treated her. No, talking
with him and going home was not an option. Then she
thought of the charming, cozy guest room upstairs and
its large canopied brass bed. Certain that Nowell
wouldn't mind if she used it, Catherine gathered her
belongings and rode the elevator up to the fourth floor,
happy with her decision to make herself right at home.

Just being near Nowell's private quarters made Catherine feel immeasurably safer. Turning on the hall lights
as she made her way toward the guest room, the first
thing she noticed was an oil portrait of Nowell's great-
great-grandfather. The family resemblance was striking,
making her smile sheepishly as though being caught by
the long-dead man at an indiscretion.

Placing her hand on the doorknob of the guest room,
Catherine paused as it occurred to her that there was
only one room in the entire town house in which she
had never been—Nowell's bedroom. Tugged by an overwhelming sense of curiosity, her better sense dulled by
the drinks she'd had, Catherine boldly walked across the
hall and entered his master suite.

But immediately after clicking on the lights she stood
frozen at the room's threshold, struck by the sudden
realization that her relationship with Nowell would
never be the same. She was doing something he would
never expect from her, or for that matter accept—stealing into his privacy.

But the warmth of the room and the lure of access to

forbidden quarters drew her in like a moth to a flame. Though quite masculine, the room was posh and warm in texture and color, done in varying shades of green, with soft, celery-colored carpet covering the floor. A darker green bedspread covered the massive king-sized bed with its rolled-fabric headboard, while the walls were papered in a raised pattern of jade. Dark but stylish pieces of antique furniture filled the room. Beautiful floral vase lamps with box-pleated shades sat on tables, and creamy-colored pillows accented the bed and various chairs. It was tasteful, elegant, and, Catherine thought—very Nowell.

It wasn't enough for Catherine to just take a peek—she now felt a need to become intimately acquainted with the room. Moving from item to item, she examined each piece of furniture, running her hand over the drapes and even the bedspread. *Expensive* was all that rang through her mind. She moved into the bathroom, with its heavy, white marble floor and countertops—realizing with amusement that there was absolutely none of Nowell's personal effects in sight. No toothbrush, bathrobe, or even dirty socks on the floor—it was immaculate.

Catherine automatically opened the double doors to his large walk-in closet, where her amusement continued at the sight of his clothes and the precise order of the garments. Suits hung in perfect unison; same-colored shirts on open shelves were folded in well-defined stacks; and even his underwear—boxer shorts in light blue and white only—were geometrically folded inside a wall-built drawer that she impulsively opened. Catherine couldn't help but laugh at the sight of the precisely aligned shorts, or over her gumption for snooping in his underwear drawer.

"What the heck." She laughed and picked up a pair, peering inside the waistband to see what size they were.

"Thirty-four: same as Michael." She laughed again, carefully refolding the pair and replacing it exactly as discovered.

Subconsciously she'd noticed the lingering scent of Nowell's favorite cologne and distinct undercurrent of tobacco smoke, and slowly realized how happy she felt to be greeted by the familiar smell. She stood there for a moment just soaking it up, then nonchalantly ran her hand across his hand-tailored suits. She'd never known anyone, including her own father, who owned so many expensive suits with the same basic look—dark, double-breasted with the occasional stripe or subtle check pattern.

Suddenly a slight feeling of empowerment came over her, the same kind of feeling she'd had growing up when she'd snoop through the closets and drawers of her brothers. Outside of a *Playboy* magazine here and there and an occasional stash of candy, she never found anything truly incriminating. Yet the act of snooping alone always provided her with a sense of control. She felt that way about Nowell at the moment—as though she had finally gained some advantage over him, even if only knowing the size of his underwear.

Looking around the bedroom for what she thought was the last time, she stopped to peer inside the drawer of a bedside table, then startled at the unexpected discovery. The drawer contained dozens of mutilated photographs all torn in half. Nervous about disturbing their scattered order, Catherine sat down on the bed and began carefully extricating the pieces. Several halves featured a smiling and debonair Nowell looking a few years younger than now, while the other halves were of a woman, apparently around Catherine's age.

Catherine sat astonished, trying to put together the pieces, both literally and figuratively. The woman was quite attractive and appeared very vivacious. In several photos she and Nowell were smiling candidly and affectionately at one another, while in others they were handsomely posed for the camera.

Catherine put three of the photographs she could piece together on the tabletop and began studying them, unable to believe that Nowell could have been so intimately involved with any woman—at any time in his life—without her having heard of it. But he had never mentioned this woman, or any other for that matter, which deeply confounded her as she soaked up the details of the pictures. Unable to put them away, and looking even more closely, Catherine gasped.

"My God," she said aloud, "they're wearing matching

wedding rings! Could he have possibly been married to this woman? But why wouldn't he have told me?"

Catherine had to laugh at her own gullibility, as though Nowell's life could have possibly begun the moment she'd entered into it. Of course he'd had a life before her, she thought, and she threw herself back into the pillows while staring at an assembled picture, wondering at the complex outcome of the relationship that would make Nowell so violently tear up all these photos, only to then keep the pieces.

Catherine leaned over and replaced the pictures, her curiosity submerged by a growing fatigue. And while she had every intention of sleeping in the guest room, Catherine gradually sunk into the softness of his bed, burying her head into one of Nowell's many pillows. The comfort felt like absolute heaven, and her body defied any common sense she had left about vacating his bedroom. Instead of getting up, straightening the covers, and moving on, she pulled her coat up about herself and settled down, noticing that even the pillows contained his mildly intoxicating scent. And before she knew it, Catherine was fast asleep, without a thought about Michael, feeling quite safe and very warm in Nowell Stuart's bed.

Chapter Fifteen

Michael heard Catherine enter the apartment, rolled over, and shut his eyes as though he'd been asleep the whole night. It was almost 7:30 A.M. and he'd barely slept a minute. But he wasn't about to let her know that.

Instead of coming over to wake him as he'd hoped she would, Catherine jumped into the shower. Fifteen minutes later, wrapped in a worn terry-cloth robe and combing her dripping wet hair, she emerged from the bathroom.

"You can stop pretending to be asleep," she said matter-of-factly. "I'm not going to set the bed on fire."

"Any concealed weapons?" Michael asked sarcastically, his back still toward her. Catherine looked down at her well-manicured fingernails. "Not unless these count," she said, then went over and ran her nails gently but firmly down his back. Michael didn't budge.

"Fine, have it your way," she said, then went back into the bathroom. Michael finally released a big sigh and rolled over.

"Where in the hell have you been?"

"Oh, you know, out partying with the girls. How 'bout you? Did you have fun last night?"

"C'mon, Catherine. I hardly think this is funny."

"Funny? Neither do I. But I tried to talk with you last night and got nowhere."

Michael let out another sigh. "I'm sorry," he said.

"Excuse me," Catherine said with a snicker, "I didn't hear you."

"I said I was sorry. Okay?"

"Thank you. Now, sorry about what?"

"Everything. I'm sorry I ruined your evening and I'm sorry I let you out the door last night. I've been worried sick about you."

"Yeah, I noticed you put out an all-points-bulletin to find me."

"Oh, c'mon. What did you expect me to do? I figured once you finished stewing you'd come home. I had no idea you'd stay away all night. I'm grateful you're home safe and sound." He paused, not really wanting to ask but still needing to know. "Did you spend the night at Nowell's?"

"Where else am I going to go? And don't worry, he wasn't there," Catherine replied tartly. "I don't know exactly what got into you last night, but I do know this. You might be jealous of Nowell Stuart, but the real message I get is that you don't trust me."

"That's not true. I trust you completely."

"Then why are you so bugged about him? I mean, first of all, the guy has no romantic interest in me. And second, even if he did, I wouldn't do anything about it. I'm in love with you, Michael," she said, her voice softening and cracking. "I would never cheat on you."

Michael sat up, pensively looking down at a pillow propped on his lap, but didn't say anything.

"Hello," said Catherine, "anybody home?"

"I'm sorry," said Michael. "You're right. And I do trust you. I guess my problem is that I don't trust him."

"But how can you say that? You've never even met him."

"It doesn't matter. It's what you've told me, and . . ."

"And what?"

"Oh, Catherine, face it. I'll never be able to compete with someone like Nowell Stuart. And quite frankly, I worry. I worry that despite the fact you love me, you get frustrated because I can't provide you with the lifestyle to which you were so accustomed. And I never will. But someone like Nowell—well, he can not only provide it, he can considerably enhance it."

"So are you admitting that you're jealous?"

"Why do you have to put it like that?" Michael snapped, then let out another deep sigh. "Catherine, what I'm trying to say is that I love you more than anyone in this whole world. I thank God every single day that you are in my life. But sometimes I can't help myself. I worry that I don't have what it will take to hold on to you. That eventually you'll need more, and that you'll find it in someone like Nowell Stuart."

Catherine sat down on the edge of the bed, then leaned over and grabbed Michael's hand. He gently squeezed back, then looked her straight in the eye. "I'm afraid of losing you," he said, his voice a hoarse whisper. He had never exposed his vulnerability to her before, and Catherine suddenly found herself flooded with emotion and a desire to protect him and crawled over beside him. Michael wrapped his tightly muscled arm around her and drew her in as close as possible. For several moments they sat quietly together, grateful for the restored calm and happy to be next to each other's warmth.

"Michael," Catherine said in her soft, sweet drawl. "I did not go into this marriage with blinders on. I knew exactly what I was getting myself into. I'll admit, the money situation frustrates the heck out of me sometimes. But then *you* have to admit, since I've been working for Nowell, we simply don't have the same problems we had a few months ago. And for a change, I'm happy to be living in New York. So look at the blessings that have come out of this job and stop worrying about something that's never going to happen."

Michael chuckled. "Usually it's me telling you not to worry, that everything will work out okay."

"I'm telling you," Catherine said as she reached up and lightly kissed his neck, "I love *you* more than anyone in the whole world. And I have no regrets. I promise."

"Michael," said Catherine later that Saturday afternoon as they walked home from a nearby movie theater. "There's something I need to tell you. I just hope you won't get all pushed out of shape over it."

"What, now you're going to tell me you're quitting your job," he said teasingly.

"Hardly." She laughed back, but her stomach began to clutch at what she was about to reveal. "It is job related, though. Nowell wants me to work in England all of next month."

Michael remained silent, though still holding her hand.

"What do you think?" she asked.

"What does it matter what I think?" he finally replied, picking up the pace a bit.

"It matters a lot."

"No it doesn't. You're going to do what you have to do, and ultimately what you want to do."

"Michael, I thought we resolved everything this morning. It's part of my job. He wants me there to work on some projects, and I'll only be gone a month." He didn't respond.

"Michael?" Catherine said, fighting a renewed sense of frustration.

"Fine," he replied, then stopped on the sidewalk and faced her while placing his hands squarely on her shoulders. "Then I suggest *we* make the most out of the rest of this month *we* have together. Deal?"

"Deal," she answered, though something in Catherine's heart told her it wasn't as easy as that. "Michael, a month will go by like this," she said, snapping her fingers.

"You know, Catherine. Let's put things into perspective here. You found a job that pays incredibly well for what you do. That's good. But it's not what you want to do for the rest of your life, and we both know it."

Catherine, oblivious to the passersby, nodded her head while staring directly into Michael's eyes.

"In fact, though I know you want to work as an interior designer, one of the reasons I married you is because you want to have children. You want to be a mother. And you know how much I want to have a family."

Again Catherine nodded her head, but this time while looking down, thinking of the other news she'd yet to share with Michael about her infertility treatment.

"So, honey, my point is this. Think of the job as a means to an end. We'll only be here for another year and a half. During that time you can focus on three things—check, make that four. First, make as many contacts as possible so that eventually you can do what you want professionally—work as an interior designer. Second, while you're working for Nowell save as much money as possible so that when we start a family we'll have built a nest egg. And third"—he paused, then brought her in close for a hug—"I think we should start working on making you a mother as soon as possible."

Catherine gasped slightly. "Michael, are you serious?"

"Catherine, as far as I'm concerned, we'll be together for all time. And we're going to have our family, one way or another. I think the sooner we make that possible, the better. It will help us to focus on what's most important in our lives. Aside from God, there's nothing more important than each other."

Catherine grabbed both of Michael's hands and let out a deep, grateful sigh. And though she knew this was as good a time as any, she struggled to find the words to tell him about her visits to Dr. Webster and the results of her recent hysterosalpingogram.

"Catherine?" Michael asked. "What is it? You have such a funny look on your face."

"Michael, there's been something I've been needing to tell you."

"My gosh, baby, what is it," he said, somewhat nervously.

"First of all," she replied, giving both his hands a little squeeze, "I couldn't agree with you more about having a baby."

Michael's concerned expression gave way to a grin. "Are you trying to tell me something?"

"Yes," she said, slightly laughing, "but it's not what you think. I'm not pregnant, but I've been working on it."

"What?" he stated with incredulity.

Catherine laughed again. "Michael, a few weeks ago I went to see a physician, Dr. Stan Webster, at the Manhattan Reproductive Center. He's one of the leading infertility specialists in the country, perhaps even the world. Anyway, I wanted to get a clear opinion from someone like him about my real chances of getting pregnant."

"Catherine, why didn't you tell me about this before?"

"Oh, for a number of reasons, I guess. Mostly because I didn't think you were ready to try getting pregnant again. And also because of the cost. None of this is covered by insurance, and it's not cheap."

"We'll talk about the money later. First tell me what the doctor said."

"Well, the first thing he said is that he needs a sperm sample from you!"

"What, oh, come on!" Michael said with mock machismo, then laughed.

"Come on, babe, this is serious. He said it's important to determine whether or not your sperm is viable. Even though I'm the one with the obvious problem, sometimes it's the man as well. They need to check what he called the morphology of your sperm—make sure there's enough, that they're the right shape and can swim fast enough—all that kind of stuff."

Michael guffawed. "We didn't have any problem before, when . . ." He stopped, then squeezed her hand. Catherine gave him a knowing glance, then continued the conversation.

"I know, honey. I know. When I got pregnant before. But still, it's part of their infertility investigation. It's something that all spouses have to do. Anyway, I did go in for a procedure myself, just a few days ago, where the doctor injected a dye into my reproductive organs, then looked at them through an X-ray procedure."

"And what happened?"

"Oh, Michael. Aside from when I lost the baby, it was some of the worst pain I have ever experienced in my life."

"Why didn't you tell me any of this before?"

"I feel really bad and a little stupid about it now. It's just that I couldn't figure out the right time to tell you. Anyway, the doctor confirmed that my uterus looks good and the remaining fallopian tube appears to be open and should be functioning okay. Still, the test isn't very specific, because he said there could be scar tissue in the tube which has prevented me from becoming pregnant."

"What do you mean, 'prevented' you from becoming pregnant. Aren't you on the pill?"

"Oh, Michael, please don't be mad at me."

"Catherine, this is a little exasperating. How long have you not been taking it?"

She hung her head down and spoke in a near whisper. "I never took it."

"You what?"

"I never took it," she said, and as she looked up and

met his eyes she unexpectedly began to cry. "I thought 'why bother' since they told me it was unlikely I'd ever get pregnant again. But Dr. Webster says there's definitely hope. Oh, Michael," she cried, placing her head on his shoulder, "I want to have a baby so badly. I can't believe this has happened to me—to us. You know, you think as a single person that the worst thing that could happen would be an unwanted pregnancy. But now I know, there is nothing worse than not being able to conceive. Not being able to have a family with the man you love."

"Oh, Catherine," Michael said, then tenderly wrapped his arms around her. Still ignoring the pedestrians pushing by them, they stood embracing each other on the sidewalk as Catherine cried softly and Michael stroked her hair.

"You know," Michael said, "I suspected this baby thing was bothering you. But you never talk about it anymore, and so I didn't say anything for fear of stirring up bad feelings. I have to tell you, Catherine, I wished you had said something sooner. I hate the thought that you've been silently living with this anguish. It's my problem too, you know."

"I know," she said through a sniffle. "And I'm sorry. It's just that I wanted to get a job first and make some money before I made this a priority for us. And now, now that I have this job working for Nowell, we have the money to cover the expenses of the treatment."

"No wonder you're so enthusiastic about that job," he said, then kissed her forehead.

"Listen," he went on, "if you want to go through with this, then by all means I'll do whatever is necessary—specimen collections and all!"

"I love you, Michael," Catherine responded, then softly kissed his lips. "Oh, and guess what else the doctor told me," she said, perking up. "He said that for some reason or another patients often get pregnant after having the hysterosalpingogram. Cleans out the plumbing a little, or something," she said with a little more levity in her voice. "So who knows, maybe this will be our month!"

"Oh, yeah," he said through a crooked grin, his brown eyes twinkling.

"Well, sometime next week maybe you can go into his office and do your duty. They need to analyze your sperm before they proceed with anything else. And," she added playfully, "you might as well get used to it since they plan on trying to get me pregnant through inseminations over the next few months. Dr. Webster said if that doesn't do the trick, then we can move right on to the in vitro fertilization."

"Whoa! Whoa!" Michael exclaimed as consternation quickly crossed his face. "Catherine, do you realize what you're talking about? People made in petri dishes. I didn't understand the full extent of this, and I'm not sure from an ethical point of view I'm prepared to go through with it. Aside from the moral implications of lab technicians playing God, if indeed we are faced with in vitro fertilization, don't you think our money would be better spent adopting a child in need?"

Catherine's face went blank. In her anguish over when to tell Michael what she was doing, she had not given the morality issue a single thought. Mostly because it didn't bother her. While she shared Michael's basic Christian values, her religious concerns did not reach the same depth as his. She stood speechless, trying to generate an argument that would lessen his concerns, but nothing came to mind other than the intense desire to have a baby of their own.

"Michael," she said calmly, desperately trying not to fall apart, "I have always thought of adoption as an option."

"Well, then why waste the time or money on in vitro fertilization? Look," he added, "I would like to have a biological child too. But maybe that's not what God has destined for us. Perhaps it's going to be our role in life to adopt and nurture a child who would otherwise suffer in poverty or from neglect."

"So what are you telling me? That you're not willing to go through with this?"

Michael looked away from her, then nervously scratched his head.

"No," he finally said. "I didn't say I wasn't willing to go through with it. Only that I want to find out with full understanding where our church stands on this issue."

Catherine knew it would be foolish to argue he was

putting the church over her. Of course he was, he always did. She had long accepted it too, believing it was a far better mistress than the kind most women had to suffer with.

And then, she wasn't sure why, a fleeting thought of Nowell came to her mind. She was certain that if he were in Michael's position, he wouldn't give the ethics of in vitro fertilization a second thought.

"Look, Michael. I'm sorry if I've put you in an awkward position, and I understand your need to think this through. But promise me two things, will you?"

Michael's eyebrows furrowed together, as he was unwilling to commit without hearing her proposals.

"First," she went on, not waiting for his guarantees, "that you'll at least have your sperm checked to make sure there's no problem in that department."

"That's a promise," he said reassuringly.

"And second, that you won't waste any time deciding where you stand on this matter. I was extremely fortunate to get an appointment with Dr. Webster. Most people wait over a year to get in, and it was pure serendipity that I got to see him when I did. There happened to be a cancellation that his assistant was trying to fill with names from the waiting list when I called. For some crazy reason she gave the appointment to me. He's the best, Michael. And I have absolute faith that if he can't get us pregnant, no one can."

"And one more thing," Catherine added. "You said there were four things I should be focused on right now: making job contacts, making money, and making a baby. What's number four?"

"Making me happy!"

"Michael William Harrison, *you* exasperate *me*!"

"Careful. That doesn't make me happy."

Catherine let out a long groan, then grabbed him by the hand as they continued their walk home.

"So, you promise you'll look into the ethics issue right away?"

"Yes, I promise," he said, smiling.

"And you're okay with me going to England for a month?" she brought up with some reserve, but still needing to conclude the matter.

"Put it this way. I'm not excited about it. But as far

as the bigger picture is concerned, if you have to do it to keep your boss happy . . . oh, wait a minute," he said, laughing. "You're supposed to keep me happy, and your boss minimally satisfied."

Catherine let out another long groan.

"Anyway, where were we? The big picture, right. Just do what you have to do, Catherine. But focus on the big picture. And make sure I'm in it," he said with a laugh. "Please, just make sure I'm in it."

PART TWO

Chapter Sixteen

"Here, allow me," offered an attractive British Airways flight attendant, gently taking Catherine's carry-on bag, then stowing it in an overhead bin. Catherine smiled, realizing she'd entered into a class of service designed to meet every need of a very privileged clientele. She thanked the woman, then settled into her seat feeling somewhat like an impostor.

The plane was surprisingly narrow and compact, but sleek in style. The familiar strains of Vivaldi's Mandoline Concerto played softly on a cabin stereo, while a bevy of flight attendants moved swiftly to prepare for takeoff. There were some frequent fliers on board, judging by the flight crew's familiar reaction to certain passengers, making Catherine marvel at the thought of being a regular on this round trip, which cost more than seven thousand dollars plus taxes and a tip to the Queen of England. She then chuckled, thinking it was Nowell's preferred method of traveling between London and the U.S.

Suddenly remembering the novel she'd stashed in her carry-on bag, Catherine stood up to retrieve it from the overhead bin when she recognized Tom Cruise and his wife Nicole Kidman sitting a few rows back. Feeling like a giddy schoolgirl, she quickly sat back down so as not to embarrass herself by staring. She'd seen movie stars before, but never this close and certainly never while sharing the same compartment aboard a plane. Gathering her wits, once more she finally stood up and got her book without looking at either of them. Instead, she glanced at the woman sitting next to her. She didn't appear to be much older than Catherine, but had an air of spoiled stuffiness about her, seeming to deliberately ignore Catherine by remaining absorbed in *The New York Times*.

As the flight attendants began instructing the passengers what to do in the event of an emergency, Catherine began feeling slightly jittery as she always did when flying. Her well-tailored neighbor, along with practically everyone else, casually ignored their directions, as though owning stock in invincibility.

She thought of Nowell. Nothing seemed to rattle him. He was not easily intimidated, it seemed to her, as many times she'd watched him deftly negotiate with hard-core bargainers, never flinching and always seeming to get what he wanted.

The Concorde jet began its takeoff, racing quickly past other planes stacked up on JFK's tarmac and lifting off at what seemed like a forty-five-degree angle. Unlike regular commercial jets, which normally reached a cruising peak of thirty-five thousand feet, the Concorde performed best in the higher and thinner air and would soon level off at fifty-five thousand feet. Feeling more relaxed than expected, Catherine now regretted not taking the window seat, since she'd learned that when the weather was clear while traveling aboard this supersonic jet, you could actually see the curvature of the earth.

A flight attendant soon appeared, presenting a menu followed by a hot, steaming towel to clean her hands and another one for her face. Feeling indulgent, Catherine accepted both towels and began rubbing her hands inside one when she noticed the woman beside her watching inconspicuously. Self-consciously, Catherine placed the towel down on the tray in front of her, then began perusing the menu. A brief while later an attendant appeared to take both their brunch orders. Catherine went first, ordering fresh fruit and the salmon Florentine. Following her own order, the woman beside her briefly resumed reading the paper, but soon put it down, glanced outside the window, then turned to face Catherine.

"Is this your first trip?" she asked bluntly in her clipped British accent. Catherine resented the note of sarcasm in the woman's voice, but tried to dismiss it. She smiled warmly at the woman.

"Is it that obvious?" Catherine quipped back.

"Not necessarily"—the woman finally grinned—"it's

just that the grilled salmon Florentine is not one of their best entrees, though I have to admit it's decent. Once you've done this route a few times you learn which items are more desirable."

"Well, *now* you tell me!" said Catherine jokingly, then introduced herself.

"Theodora Willis," the woman responded while extending her hand. "But please, call me Dubs."

"Nice to meet you, Dubs," Catherine responded while shaking her hand. In defiance of the woman's refined appearance and even her delicate shake, her hand felt surprisingly callused. "I hope you don't mind my asking," Catherine added, "but how did your nickname come about?"

Dubs laughed. "I suppose it is rather peculiar. Well, to start with, my parents gave me that god-awful first name, which my older brothers refused to acknowledge, calling me only by my initials, T.W. They later condensed it to T. Dubs, and finally Dubs. It just stuck, and eventually everyone began calling me Dubs, though when I went to university I was frequently called Dubbers. And so it is." The more she revealed of herself the more friendly and animated she became.

"What part of the South are you from?" Dubs asked, turning the tables. "Wait, don't tell me, let me guess. Say something, perhaps something about the weather."

Catherine laughed, then offered up a brief weather report. "It's cold and windy today, with morning temperatures near freezing. Expected cloudiness in the late afternoon, followed by a possible shower which could turn to snow or freezing rain by night."

"Quite good. You must be a weather girl!" They both laughed.

"Let's see," Dubs went on. "There's not enough twang to be from Texas, and it's not rural-sounding enough for Arkansas." She paused while thinking. "Hmmm, and not drawn out enough for Alabama or those other Deep South states. I'd say your accent is also more refined, putting you in a larger city, someplace like Atlanta, or even Charlotte."

Catherine was quite amused by Dubs's unique skill. It reminded her of when Lucas Sloane accurately guessed who designed her dress, making her wonder if this sort of game was a common diversion among the super-rich.

"God knows, you're good," said Catherine laughingly, "I'm from Charlotte, originally. But I live in New York now. Can you guess which borough?"

"No need to guess, your clothes say Manhattan. I saw that sweater at Saks Fifth Avenue just a few weeks ago. It's quite lovely."

"Thanks. My gosh, I'm glad my husband doesn't have your skill, I'd really be in trouble. He has no idea how much I spent on this sweater, and I hope he never finds out." Catherine unconsciously tugged at the sleeve of the garment, a cashmere pullover with a pastel-colored, argyle pattern. She'd picked it up at a Saks post-Christmas sale for a hundred twenty-five dollars; quite a bargain, she thought, compared to the original asking price of three hundred fifty. The sweater went beautifully with her cream-colored, woolen slacks.

"Now how do you know so much about Southern accents?" she asked Dubs.

"Well, most of my business in America is in the South, so I can readily pick out the Crackers, if you'll pardon the phrase. And you're certainly not one of them."

"What is it you do, if you don't mind my asking?"

"Not at all. Horses. I'm a breeder and trainer."

"My gosh," said Catherine excitedly, "what fun!" Then immediately she understood how Dubs must have acquired her callused hands.

"Oh, I suppose," Dubs responded. "I become a bit travel weary during certain times of the year. One of my prize mares in Kentucky just gave birth to a foal, which is promised to a British client. I wanted to be present when the veterinarian gave mother and child a checking over, since Mama is a champion. She placed in the Derby and at Pimlico a few years ago, but wasn't as spiffy at Belmont. She's still a champ though—a strong, beautiful horse, with equally handsome offspring."

"I love horses," Catherine offered, "I had one when I was a girl, it was an Appaloosa."

"Oh, so you wanted to be a cowgirl, heh?"

"Yeah, something like that," she said, feeling no inferiority over the workhorse that she'd loved so much.

"And since you're obviously not a cowgirl, do you mind my asking what it is you do?"

"No, I don't mind at all. And I'm not a 'weather girl' either," she offered with mock sarcasm. "Actually, I work for an arts and antiques dealer who has galleries in New York and in England. I'll be working on one of his London projects for the next month or so."

"Go on," Dubs said with a smile, "for whom do you work?"

"Guy by the name of Nowell Stuart."

"Nowell Stuart!" she startled. "You don't say!"

"Do you know him?"

"I should say I do. They were clients of mine, he and his late wife, Elizabeth. She was quite the horsewoman—loved competitive jumping and hunting." She paused, then added more ruefully, "What a tragedy, died so young, you know. And then losing his parents in the plane crash at the same time."

Though the plane was on a smooth and steady course, by the feeling in Catherine's stomach it may as well have dropped a thousand feet. *Those torn-up pictures in his bedside drawer; they must be of him and Elizabeth,* Catherine thought, then gulped. *Oh, my God, so he was married. I can't believe it. Why didn't he ever tell me? And that she died. I can't believe this!*

Catherine felt her breathing go shallow. Nowell had proven himself to be a man of many surprises, mostly delightful and whimsical ones, however. But this one came as a pure, cold shock, with nothing funny about it. Losing his parents *and* his wife together! *The pain over his loss muct be so profound,* Catherine thought, *that it's no wonder he cannot talk about it.* She felt herself moved to tears, but quickly blinked them back.

"My goodness, you appear quite stricken," said Dubs. "You do know what happened, don't you?"

Not wanting to appear ignorant but at the same time needing to extract every detail possible, Catherine partially acquiesced.

"Actually," Catherine answered, "I don't know all the details."

Dubs became even more chatty, eager to share what she knew. "Oh, it was just awful, bloody awful. And she four months pregnant at the time . . ."

Catherine felt as though she would faint, barely able to listen to anything else the woman said, as the second revelation jolted through her. *A baby; he and his wife were expecting a baby!* He seemed genuinely sympathetic over her own story of losing a baby, and now she knew it to be empathy. Oh, why hadn't he told her? Why did he feel it necessary to protect her from this information? Was it because, like the gentleman she knew him to be, he didn't want to upstage her own tragedy? It now seemed insignificant in scope to his own.

"How is he getting along now?" Catherine finally heard Dubs ask. "I've barely seen him since then. He's become a bit of a recluse on the social scene."

"Well, I wouldn't know about his social life, really. But I do know that he works long hours, mostly because I often have to work with him."

"What do you do for him?" Dubs asked.

"I'm his assistant. I do all of his scheduling and correspondence, along with bookkeeping and an occasional sale."

"Really? Does Nowell spend much time there? In New York?" asked Dubs.

"Well, I only started work in October. And until early December he was there all the time. He left to take care of some emergency business at Sutthington Mills, his textile plant, and I haven't seen him since then. I know he plans on returning to New York in early February because we're booked to travel back together."

Catherine immediately regretted telling Dubs as much as she had, seeing now what a truly private person Nowell was. She felt as though she'd betrayed his trust by sharing even that small amount of information on his business trouble, then quickly sought to amend what she'd revealed.

"The problem at Sutthington was nothing, really. But he just decided to stay in England through Christmas. Where did you spend your holidays?" Catherine asked, attempting to steer the conversation.

"In London, actually. And it's odd, you know. I usually see him at this one party of a mutual friend over the holidays, but I didn't see him at all this year. Is he dating anyone?"

The question came as another, yet milder shock to

Catherine. She'd never really thought of Nowell with any other woman until she saw those torn-up pictures, and then dismissed it from her mind. In fact, she now realized, he rarely discussed any details of his personal life. Even if she knew the answer, she decided it would be wrong to offer any more information.

"I don't know," she replied simply to Dubs's inquiry.

"What a shame. Most of the single women in England would kill for a chance to go out with him. For that matter, a lot of married women would too." Her remark provided some comic relief, prompting Catherine to laugh but also to glance at Dubs's left hand, which bore no wedding band. She wondered if Dubs wasn't one of those desirous women where Nowell was concerned, then suddenly felt an urge to protect him.

"You say you've only worked for him a short while. Do you know much about his family?" Dubs asked.

"A little bit."

"Well, of course you must know he's a modest man, contrary to all his wealth. You would never know he's one of the most affluent men in Great Britain, from one of those ancient families with scads of money and land. They, or rather he now, owns the most incredible manor home in West Yorkshire. But I suppose you already knew that, heh?"

Catherine kept a poker face, while nodding her head in agreement. She knew nothing about his home in West Yorkshire, and found herself excited and amused by Dubs's willingness to talk about him. These Brits, she thought, loved discretion in their own affairs, but were world-class gossipers when it came to anyone else's.

"He was considered to be quite a catch, you know, along with the likes of Prince Charles—before he married that poor Diana, that is." She laughed sarcastically, then added, "At least Nowell had the sense to marry someone whom he truly loved and had much in common with. They were truly happy, those two. Such a pity. Plus he absolutely adored his parents." She let out a deep sigh.

"He never really talks about them, or Elizabeth." It felt strange for Catherine to even mention the woman's name.

"It doesn't surprise me. You must understand, he was

devastated. I've never seen him so brokenhearted. She was quite beautiful, and such a lovely girl. Came from one of those ancient, monied families herself. In fact, I know this may sound rather odd, but you bear a resemblance to her. Something about your eyes, and definitely your hair. He loves blondes," she confided, running a hand through her own dull brown hair. "Shame," she said with a flirty smile. "You say you're married, are you?" she asked boldly.

"Yes," Catherine replied. "My husband's studying to be an Episcopal priest at General Theological Seminary in Manhattan."

"Oh, excellent," was all Dubs said in response. "Excellent." She stared out the window for a moment, creating an uncomfortable pause in the conversation. A flight attendant appeared offering beverage service, and without hesitation Catherine accepted a glass of champagne. Dubs joined her.

Catherine felt extremely grateful for the opportunity to break up the melancholy. Nonetheless, with quiet excitement, she could not believe she was sitting beside someone who knew Nowell. Since first meeting him she sensed he was a well-respected man. And though sad to learn more about the tragedy that had so deeply altered his life, it was reassuring to learn from someone else that he was held in such high regard.

Dubs ordered herself another glass of champagne, and Catherine, deciding that three drinks would be excessive should she be pregnant following her hysterosalpingogram, declined the stewardess's offer to refill her glass. She ordered mineral water instead, then displayed her best manners while eating her grilled salmon Florentine, which—contrary to Dubs's opinion—she considered delicious. Dubs heartily indulged in canapes piled with beluga caviar, mozzarella cheese, sun-dried tomatoes, and smoked salmon.

Not to Catherine's surprise, their meals were served on fine china, the flatware was sterling silver, and their stemware expensive hand-cut crystal. She felt she could become quite used to this class of service, and clearly understood now why Nowell preferred to travel this way.

Finishing her last bite, Catherine dabbed at her mouth with the linen napkin, then placed it on the tray in front of her. No sooner did she lean back in her seat than a smiling flight attendant removed her tray, asking if she cared for anything else. Catherine offered her a satisfied smile while shaking her head no. Dubs, however, opted for more champagne.

"Tell me, Catherine, where will you be staying in London?"

Catherine wasn't quite sure how to answer, since she was staying at Nowell's and didn't want to give Dubs any false impressions about their relationship. "Well, to-night I'll be staying at Nowell's place in Belgravia, then I don't know where he'll put me up after that."

"Indeed. That's quite some accommodation. He has a massive town home; all the passengers on this plane could probably room there," she joked.

"Well, I guess that wouldn't be so bad, since that would mean Tom Cruise and Nicole Kidman are coming over to spend the night!"

"Are they on board?"

"Yeah! About seven seats behind us."

"Indeed! You never know whom you'll run into on these flights."

Catherine laughed at Dubs's casual remark, as though she were an acquaintance, if not friends with the super-celebrity couple, and that traveling with them was commonplace. The two women shared gossipy tabloid stories about the couple for a few moments, then made small talk on a whole range of issues for the better part of an hour before Dubs turned the conversation back on Nowell.

"First, tell him for me that I send my warmest regards and that I'd love to hear directly from him on how he's doing. But more importantly," she added with a twinkle in her eyes, "I want to know how his horses are faring."

"He never talks about any horses," said Catherine. "I wonder if he still has them."

"I can't imagine that he doesn't. He's quite a polo player and has some of the finest horses in all of England at his estate. My goodness, that place is incredible," she digressed blithely. "I suppose you'll have to see it to believe it—the most beautiful old house, one of those incredible baronial estates with something like seventy-five rooms, sitting on acres and acres of parkland. I tell you, those horses live the good life, and if he were to sell them I would certainly hope he'd let me broker the deals. You can tell him that too," she added matter-of-factly.

"Deal," responded Catherine while offering her hand to Dubs who warmly shook it. Catherine settled into her seat and began a quiet inventory of all that she'd just learned about Nowell. First Elizabeth, and her being pregnant when she died; polo and horses; an estate in West Yorkshire. Plus, when he talked about his home in Belgravia—one of the most exclusive neighborhoods in London—he simply referred to it as his "flat." She'd had the impression that it was an apartment, probably a spacious one, but an apartment nonetheless. But according to Dubs it was the size of a small hotel. *Is he modest,* she thought, *or simply that he prefers to be mysterious?*

The flight began its descent into London Heathrow, causing a fresh excitement to build inside Catherine. She hadn't been to London in nearly twelve years, having first traveled there on a class trip during her junior year in high school. But there was also a budding nervousness about seeing Nowell again. Given all that she'd just learned about him, Catherine wondered how she would react when she saw him, and if he would ever share the same information about himself.

By the time the jet touched down it was 5:30 P.M., and night had fallen. There was a light drizzle, something Catherine fully expected as she reached for her raincoat and bag in the overhead bin.

"Listen, if you don't mind, let me give you my business card," offered Dubs. "And please ask Nowell to give me a call sometime, I'd love to hear from him. Especially," she reiterated, "if he's selling his horses!"

"I'd be happy to," replied Catherine, accepting her card.

"You might add," said Dubs, "that I'm throwing a birthday party this Friday night at Annabell's for our mutual friend James Douglas. I'm certain he would be delighted if Nowell came. Have him call me, and I'll give him the details."

"Will do," said Catherine, smiling, quietly wondering about Dubs's romantic intentions. It aroused in her yet again a strong instinct to protect Nowell, to make sure that no one, especially someone with manipulative, feminine designs, could hurt him. She tucked the card inside her handbag, unaware that her chance meeting with this woman had provided another piece of a dangerous jigsaw puzzle silently taking shape in her life.

Chapter Seventeen

Just after passing through Customs, Catherine noticed a thin, dark-skinned man in a navy-blue chauffeur's uniform. He looked directly at her, then grinned slightly, revealing perfectly straight white teeth.

"Mrs. Harrison?" he asked in a thick Pakistani accent.

"Yes," Catherine responded congenially, "you must be Sonny."

"Yes, ma'am."

"Nowell told me to expect you," she said, extending her hand as though greeting an old friend. Sonny shook her hand with reserve. And instead of engaging in idle chitchat, he gathered her bags, then escorted Catherine outside to a shining Rolls-Royce limousine, dark gray in color with a tan leather interior—yet another surprise from the enigmatic Nowell Stuart. He used a car service in New York, mostly preferring an unpretentious Lincoln Town Car sedan. But this car was quite a status symbol; something Nowell felt far more comfortable flaunting at home than abroad. Catherine chuckled as she climbed into the rear passenger seat, feeling as though the day was turning into a crash course on the real Nowell Stuart.

There was a closed partition between the front and backseats, making Catherine somewhat happy for the isolation and the chance to be left alone with her thoughts for a while. Sonny interrupted her only briefly to inquire over the intercom if she needed anything, then proceeded driving toward Nowell's "flat."

Catherine was trying to familiarize herself with the stereo console when suddenly a phone began ringing. She could hear it but fumbled in vain trying to find it. Four rings later Sonny piped in over the intercom to

"Lift up the center seat." She did as instructed and quickly located the cellular phone hidden inside.

"Hello, Nowell," she said with a laugh.

"How utterly presumptuous," said the voice grandly, then laughed back. It was, of course, Nowell.

"Who else would be calling *me* in the back of *your* limousine?" she said, laughing back.

"And what makes you think the call was for you? Suppose someone was trying to reach me?"

"Sorry, you're right. Anyway, hello. I'm here."

"And what did you think of your little trip on the Concorde? It's rather sublime, heh?"

"It was dangerous."

"What do you mean? Did something dreadful happen?" he asked with genuine concern.

"Well, it depends on how you look at it. It's just that now I'm so spoiled by flying on the Concorde I don't think I'll ever be able to fly with the commoners," she said, smiling into the receiver.

"Whew," he whistled. "You had me scared there for a moment."

"Actually, Nowell, it was quite wonderful. Thanks for the opportunity."

"My pleasure. Listen," he said, fortunately changing the subject, "I happen to be holding two tickets to *Les Misérables* for this evening. Would you care to join me?"

Catherine could not believe it. She'd been longing to see the musical in New York with Michael, and knew one day they would attend. Yet she couldn't resist the opportunity to see the play in London.

"Absolutely," she exclaimed.

"Excellent. The show starts at eight p.m. Why don't we have a little pretheater dinner at a place called The Ivy, over on West Street. Just tell Sonny to bring you directly there."

"Nowell, I can't. I'm not dressed properly."

"I find that hard to believe for you, madam."

"Seriously, Nowell. I woke up late this morning and had to sacrifice something to save time. I just threw on casual slacks and a sweater. Would you mind if I went to your place first to change?"

"Not at all. We can grab something to eat afterward. How does that sound to you?"

"Much better. You really don't mind, do you?"

"Not at all. Freshen up at my place, then have Sonny bring you straightaway to the theater. By the way, if you pull down the center armrest you'll discover a built-in refrigerator. Rather petite one, but big enough for champagne. Anyway, there's a bottle of Dom Perignon in there chilled and waiting for you."

"Nowell, are you nuts? Do you think I'm going to risk hosing down the inside of this beautiful car with champagne?"

"Nothing I haven't done from time to time."

"I think I'll let you do the honors then. Thanks for the offer, though. Anyway, I had my quota of Dom Perignon on the Concorde today."

"Oh, I see, drinking on the job again?" he quipped.

"What do you mean, 'drinking on the job'? You just told me to take a drink!" she bantered back.

"Catherine, as far as I'm concerned, I want you to consider this trip to England anything but work. For all I care, you may have champagne for breakfast, lunch, and dinner." He paused, then added, "Well, I suppose I would care—that is if I weren't invited to join you."

Catherine sat silent for a moment, wondering just what he had in store for her this month. If it wasn't work-related, then she couldn't understand his need for keeping her in England an entire month. It was somewhat frustrating given that she had to postpone further treatment with Dr. Webster until February.

"Hello," Nowell said, interrupting her thoughts, "Catherine, are you still there?"

"Yes, Nowell, I'm here."

"I thought I lost you for a moment. Well, I'll see you shortly. Now, would you kindly buzz Sonny on the intercom and tell him to pick up," Nowell asked.

"Sure. See you soon," Catherine said sweetly, got Sonny on the line, then put the phone back. She watched as Sonny chatted briefly with Nowell, then hung up the phone. From thereon they traveled in silence, giving Catherine a chance to soak up the sights. By now they were on King's Road and passing through London's Chelsea. It was a place rich in history and old buildings like Catherine's New York Chelsea, but diametrically opposed in terms of population. Catherine's neighbor-

hood was richly multi-ethnic, while this Chelsea neighborhood was simply rich. It bordered Nowell's even
more exclusive neighborhood of Belgravia.

Thoughts of Michael began seeping in. Through all
the excitement of the Concorde trip, the chauffeur-
driven Rolls-Royce, and now her pending plans to see
Les Misérables, she'd quickly put aside her ache over
their month-long separation.

How can I tell Michael that I saw Les Misérables *with
Nowell, something I know Michael wants so badly to see
with me,* she thought. She began to regret so eagerly
accepting the theater invitation with Nowell, but reassured herself Michael would understand.

Sonny turned onto Sloane Square toward Cadogan
Place and Nowell's London residence. Catherine wished
Sonny would slow down, as she enjoyed the splendor
and graciousness of the homes and embassies they
passed. They were mostly attached town houses, but
striking and impressive in their size and architecture.

Finally Sonny pulled into a semicircular driveway of a
grand home on Cadogan Place. Bathed in soft lights
against the evening darkness, the size and elegance of
the place could have fooled Catherine into believing it
was one of the embassies they had just passed.

"Some flat," she said, laughing to herself while Sonny
opened her door. Simultaneously the front door opened,
and a butler appeared, while an excited dog, seemingly
the size of a small pony, came galloping and whoofing
furiously from behind. Man and dog remained at the
threshold, and for a moment Catherine felt grateful that
Nowell wasn't there to see her looking so pop-eyed over
his digs.

"Nigel will show you where to go," Sonny offered
deferentially, obviously referring to the butler. "I'll be
right behind with your baggage."

"Does the dog have anything against Yanks?" she
asked in jest.

"Not unless they're trying to burgle Mr. Stuart,"
Sonny quipped, without breaking a smile.

"What's his name?"

"Rags."

"Rags?" She chuckled, then moved a bit cautiously

up the steps while gauging the dog's reaction to her presence.

"Welcome, Mrs. Harrison," said Nigel in a parched but polite way. "We've been expecting you. Mr. Stuart says to show you to your room right away, and that you should be ready to depart in one-half hour." Nigel was one of those people who had probably looked exactly the same for the past twenty years, and would for another twenty yet to come, making it impossible to estimate his correct age. He carried himself in a refined and dignified manner, and conveyed such confidence in his affairs that Catherine felt certain he must be one of Nowell's most trusted employees.

"All right," Catherine responded cheerfully to his instructions, then bravely offered her hand for Rags to sniff. "Hello," she said warmly to the animal, which had finally stopped barking. Without haste he began vigorously licking her hand, prompting Nigel to call him off.

"Rags, behave yourself," he said firmly. The dog got in one more satisfying lick, then retreated.

"What kind of dog is he?" Catherine inquired, confidently petting the massive animal on the head.

"He's a mastiff, ma'am."

"I've never seen a dog quite this large. He must weigh a ton."

"Yes, rather close," said Nigel dryly. Rags finally moved out of the way allowing Catherine to enter, where once inside she was taken aback again. The interior was stunning in design, yet she immediately felt comfortable and at home in the rich elegance. The entry hall exuded a warm, welcoming atmosphere, making Catherine certain it had been touched by a woman's loving hand.

The floor was laid with flagstone in a diamond-shaped pattern, complemented by black stone insets. The walls were a warm though vivid yellow, while the woodwork was done in a contrasting glossy white. The furniture was whimsical, though practical, including an antique cradle that served as a planter for a large array of colorful, blooming plants. An open door to her left revealed a cozy and charming study in darker hues and rich tapestries, with a brisk fire and inviting hearth—a spot she felt certain Rags called his own.

The main staircase dominated the hallway, but instead of ascending it, Nigel guided her along to an elevator, much like the one Nowell had installed at his New York residence. Rags joined them as they rode to the third floor, where Catherine was ushered into a guest room that rivaled that of the finest hotels in comfort and elegance.

Decorated in muted shades of pink and cream, the oversized room featured a magnificent four-poster bed. Catherine immediately recognized the expensive Colefax and Fowler chintz material used for the custom-made bedspread and dust-ruffle. Floral-patterned drapes hung from each bedpost featured a solid pink lining, which was also used on the inside of the bed's canopy to form a tented rosette with pleats fanning out to the edge. It was a bed of every girl's dream and every young woman's fantasy. The room had such a welcome feeling to it that Catherine could feel her whole body saying "ahhh," and she barely noticed Sonny deliver her bags, or heard Nigel's explanations over what to do should she need anything, at any time.

"Just use this intercom, here," he instructed. "Maggie has been assigned to help you."

"Thanks, Nigel," she finally said.

He showed her the magnificent private bathroom, then opened an armoire to reveal a television set and stereo.

"Well, that should do it for now. Maggie will be along shortly to unpack your things, Mrs. Harrison," he said respectfully.

"Thank you, Nigel," she said, resisting the urge to tip handsomely for his service. Before he left he opened up a large, walk-in closet with a light that automatically turned on when the door opened. He left the room and was immediately joined by Rags who had eagerly observed everything from the hallway.

In less than twenty minutes Catherine had freshened up, reapplying her makeup and changing into a black, crepe chemise cocktail dress, pearls, and patent leather pumps. Nigel saw her off as she stepped briefly into the damp, chilly air and right into the warm, waiting Rolls-Royce. Sonny headed directly to the Palace Theater on Shaftesbury Avenue, just a few miles from Nowell's. Catherine settled in comfortably, amused by the awkwardness of traveling on the opposite side of the road, and by the people who tried to catch a glimpse of who was riding in this luxurious car.

Without any awareness of it, Catherine slipped into a sense of smugness. Though she'd grown up in prosperity, it was nothing like what had been laid before her all day long—travel on an elite, supersonic jet; private servants and a temporary, though highly enviable London address—and she found herself easily adjusting to being pampered.

Sonny pulled up outside the Palace Theater and quickly jumped out of the car to open her door. Having not seen him as they arrived, Catherine stepped out of the car and ran smack into Nowell. She jumped back in genuine fear as he grabbed her by the arms, then began laughing.

"Well, there you are, my lady," he said warmly, his eyes shining.

"Nowell Stuart, I could smack you. You just scared the daylights out of me!"

"Is that any way to greet an old friend?"

"No, no, it's just that I didn't notice you when we pulled up. It's good to see you. You look great. How are you?" An unexpected quiver went through Catherine as she finally looked him in the eye. He did look great, and it felt surprisingly wonderful to be near him again. She also felt, after all she'd learned today about his heartbreaking losses, a compulsion to hug him. Instead, she began nervously smoothing her coat and then fidgeted with her purse straps.

"Actually, I had a particularly hellish day, but nothing in it for you to worry about. Sonny," he said, turning to his faithful employee, "the show gets out at ten fortyfive, and we're going to have dinner at The Ivy afterward. We'll just walk over there, so why don't you plan on picking us up at around midnight in front of the restaurant."

"Yes, sir," Sonny replied dutifully, then retreated into the car and drove away, leaving the two of them standing alone in front of the theater.

"Well, I trust Nigel took good care of you."

"Oh, yes. And Rags, who gave me a bath."

"Oh, that rascal. I suppose that's rather good. I mean, it sounds as though he likes you."

"Well if that's what it takes to stay on his good side, then I'm happy to oblige. How come you never told me you had a dog? Or horses?"

"Horses! My God, woman, did one of my horses greet you too?" he teased her.

"No, no," Catherine said with a laugh. "I sat next to an old friend of yours on the plane today, Dubs Willis. She told me about your horses. She also told me to mention that if you're selling them to please let her know, she wants to broker the deals."

"Oh, she did, did she?" he said, snickering. "What else did she have to say?" he asked wryly. Catherine knew this was not the appropriate moment to discuss her full conversation with Dubs, and played it down.

"This and that. She mentioned something about a party for your friend James Douglas. Mostly we talked about horses. She was just returning from Kentucky to check up on a broodmare and its colt, and I told her all about the horse I had as a girl."

"You never told me you had a horse!"

"Well, now we're even," she said bluntly, amused at finally having one on him.

"I suppose we are. And I now know you should be delighted with what I have on our agenda. Especially day after tomorrow. I say, it's rather cold out here, and the show starts soon. Shall we?" he asked, looking in the general direction of the beautiful, old Palace Theater.

"Absolutely." Catherine nodded, gathering her black wool coat a little closer about her. "So what are we doing day after tomorrow?"

"You'll see," he said as they walked briskly together. "I think you'll be happily surprised."

Catherine had no reason to doubt him. Her life had become an unending sequence of surprises since she'd met Nowell Stuart, and whatever it was, she was certain she'd be delighted.

Chapter Eighteen

The weather turned blustery while Nowell and Catherine enjoyed *Les Misérables,* though Nowell didn't mind one bit as Catherine was forced to share his umbrella during their walk to the restaurant. Through her excited recap of the show she barely noticed he'd wrapped his arm around her shoulder, allowing herself to be drawn in tight.

"Oh, that was fabulous, I can't thank you enough," she exclaimed.

"Not at all, it was my pleasure."

"The music was phenomenal. Michael will love the CD, I'm sure."

Nowell's face hardened, and through a strained smile he concurred that would probably be true. It was the first time that evening that the mention of Michael had come up. He quickly changed the subject.

"You must be starved," he said.

"I ate pretty well on the Concorde. I still can't thank you enough for providing that opportunity."

"I'm glad you enjoyed it. Here, here we are, this is the place." He proudly escorted Catherine inside The Ivy, one of London's most popular post-theater spots. As usual with Nowell, they were promptly ushered to a choice table where it was possible to enjoy the atmosphere and still have a private conversation. They both slid out of their coats and handed them to the smiling, paunchy maître d'. Nowell had such a way with these types, Catherine thought, observing how the man had seated them at the expense of other waiting customers.

At a nearby table sat a small group of young, stylish women, one of whom shyly waved at Nowell, then joined her head in close conversation with their friends. Quick glances were cast at Catherine making her feel as though she was being sized up. Nowell managed a friendly nod back, but didn't bother to go over and personally greet the woman who had recognized him.

"A fan of yours?" Catherine asked, glancing sideways at the group.

"One of many," he remarked with amusement. "And I suppose they're rather jealous of you right now."

"Oh, come on!" Catherine responded. "Seriously, do you know that woman?"

"Not really. She's the daughter of someone I play polo with. Her old man introduced me to her once, with a wink and a nod, if you know what I mean. I suppose she's sort of cute, but definitely not my type."

"Oh, and just what is your type?" Catherine playfully asked, taking advantage of Nowell's sudden candor.

Nowell flashed an elusive smile. "Oh, I'm not sure that I have a specific type anymore," he sighed.

"What do you mean, 'anymore'?"

Nowell seemed to tense up a bit, then fiddled nervously with the salt and pepper shaker on the table. Catherine wondered if this wouldn't be a good time to tell him that she knew about Elizabeth, and was startled to hear what he said next.

"Catherine, this may come as something of a shock to you, but I was once married. I am a widower now."

For a moment Catherine thought to feign surprise and then offer some contrived remarks of sympathy. She didn't want him to know he'd been the primary subject of her conversation with Dubs Willis, and furthermore, Catherine worried that her guilt over snooping through his personal belongings and discovering the torn pictures might somehow seep out. But she simply could not be disingenuous with him, especially over something so significant.

"Nowell, this may come as a surprise to *you*, but I know about Elizabeth."

The oddest expression consumed Nowell's face. It was neither relief, nor surprise, nor even sadness. Instead it was cold and emotionless. Catherine worried that she'd angered him with her confession, and said nothing while waiting for his further reaction.

"How did you know about her?"

"Actually, I just learned about your tragic loss today.

Dubs told me. Nowell," she said, now reaching across the table and placing her hand atop his, her voice barely a whisper, "I also know about the baby. I cannot tell you how sorry I am for you."

For what seemed like the longest time he clammed up, just staring down into a burning votive candle on the tabletop, his eyes fixed and glazed, and not bothering to move his hand from beneath hers. Catherine waited awhile before speaking again.

"Nowell, are you okay?" she asked.

He looked up at her, some emotion finally breaking through.

"Catherine, I will never entirely escape the agony. You cannot imagine what it is like to lose your whole family in one day. You simply cannot imagine the pain."

Catherine remained quiet and observant, noting that he had now taken her hand in his.

"At first I felt as though I would die; as though I wanted to die, to be right with them. But gradually, and I mean ever so gradually, I regained my strength. And I must now confess, bringing you here today is a part of my healing process."

"I'm not sure I understand," said Catherine.

"I need a fresh start. And I need to make some changes. As I'm sure you've figured out, my home here in London, well, it is the home Elizabeth and I shared together. She decorated it herself, and in many ways it has provided solace and a warm reminder of our past. But that's exactly my problem. I'm ready to move on. And I feel one way to finally let go of the past is to make some creative changes at home. I want you to help me redecorate my house. Will you do that for me?"

"Nowell, I'm flattered. But you're asking a lot of me. How do you even know I'm capable of achieving what you want?"

"I just do. I trust you implicitly. Besides, having worked with you I see you have good taste and an eye for finer things. It will work out fine. If not, I'll just fire you."

"Nowell!"

"As my decorator," he insisted with a grin, "not my assistant." At that point Catherine realized he was still holding her hand, and while it felt awkward to appear so intimate, she felt it would be more awkward to just pull her hand away right now.

"Nowell, are you sure? I mean, I think . . ." She paused, feeling the weight of the blunder she was about to commit by telling him Elizabeth had done a beautiful job; that it was stunning just the way it was. "Are you really certain you want me for the job?"

"Positive. Plus, when you're done in London I thought you may want to take a stab at a few rooms at my country home. I was thinking we could head out to West Yorkshire day after tomorrow for a little R and R anyway, and you could start gathering ideas. My horses are out there, so weather permitting perhaps we could take a jaunt in the countryside. It's quite lovely, you know. By the way, that was the surprise I said earlier I had in store for you," he said proudly.

"Oh, Nowell, it all sounds fabulous!" she enthused. "But," she added more somberly, "it would take far longer than a month. What about my other responsibilities? I mean, who would take care of my duties in the New York gallery?"

"Well, that's not for you to worry about. I'll have one of my gals at Sutthington Mills take over some jobs, plus there are two fellows at my London gallery who are itching to work in Manhattan. They can handle sales over there while we're away."

Catherine looked unconvinced, and Nowell offered every reassurance that she wouldn't have to concern herself over anything else.

"That's not what I'm worried about, to tell you the truth," she conceded.

"Then what bothers you?"

A waiter suddenly appeared, momentarily breaking up the conversation by taking their drink orders. Catherine abstained, while Nowell ordered a vodka martini, then pulled out his silver cigarette case and lit up a Marlboro, for which Catherine felt grateful as he finally released her hand. The waiter returned shortly, delivering Nowell's drink, then proceeded to take their dinner order. When finally left alone again, Nowell took a deep drag, then pressed Catherine again on her concerns.

"First, it's just that this could go on much longer than

one month," she answered matter-of-factly, "and I'm not prepared to stay any longer than that."

"But that's what the Concorde is for." He smiled while blithely popping an olive into his mouth.

"Of course," she said, smiling back. "But it's more than that. Nowell, I don't want to alarm you since it's nothing serious. But I'm going through some treatment for a medical problem, and I need to be in New York on a consistent basis beginning next month." She offered no further details, and watched as a mixture of curiosity and concern consumed Nowell's face.

"Good Lord, Catherine, is everything all right?"

"Really, I'm fine. It's just that I was supposed to have a procedure done this month that I'm postponing until next. I'm happy to do what I can while I'm here, and then coordinate things from the States, if that's possible. But I really need to be in New York."

Nowell would not let up. "You have me a bit scared, Catherine. Really. Are you sure you're okay to even be here now?"

"Oh, Nowell," she said, easily breaking down. "Michael and I are having difficulty getting pregnant. So I'm seeing a specialist in New York. That's all."

The news fell like a bomb on Nowell. It was the last thing he would have expected her to share with him, and the last thing he wanted to hear. He couldn't care less about Michael, though he did care a lot about the two of them trying to have a baby. He'd looked so forward to having her alone for a month, and hoped that by the end of it she would find it difficult to go back to Michael. But now, if they were concentrating on having a baby and seeing a doctor besides, there would be added pressure for her to return to New York as originally planned.

"A baby," he said with a smile. "I love children. I'd hoped to have scads of them."

"I'm sure you will then, someday." She smiled back, but then her face turned serious. She glanced over at him, thinking for a moment how handsome he looked in the soft candlelight, his blue eyes tender and sweet. Like Michael, he'd recently let his hair grow out a bit, and though somewhat ruffled from the weather, it suited his boyish good looks. But there was also a vulnerability about him right now, something Catherine had never seen before. And just like earlier while talking about him with Dubs, she felt an urge to protect him, wishing she could shelter him from any further tragedies.

"Nowell, I'm sorry to bring this up again. And I will say it just once and then close the subject. But I was so brokenhearted for you today when I learned of your loss, and then finally realized why you were so understanding when I told you about losing my baby. I wish I had known, because what I went through seems so insignificant compared to what you experienced."

"Don't worry, don't worry at all," he gently reassured her, "you had no way of knowing."

No way of knowing, he said to himself as he sipped his martini, *that it was another man's baby that wretch Elizabeth was carrying.*

Chapter Nineteen

Michael stretched his long legs before him, then leaned back in his classroom chair. Jack Whitlock's lecture today on materialism and envy were subjects of keen interest to Michael given his persistent and simmering feelings toward Nowell Stuart.

Though he never smoked a pipe in the classroom, one was always present in Reverend Jack Whitlock's hand, filled with fresh tobacco and ready to be lit at the first convenience. He had a habit of holding the pipe in his right hand, while rubbing the side of his nose with his right thumb, and was doing so now while reciting the Tenth Commandment.

" 'Thou shalt not covet thy neighbor's house, thou shalt not covet thy neighbor's wife, nor his manservant, nor his maidservant, nor his ox, nor his ass, nor any thing that is thy neighbor's.' Hmmm, why not? I've seen a few houses in my neighborhood I wouldn't mind living in, occupied by some pretty cute neighbors."

A snicker broke out in the classroom. It was vintage Whitlock, using his wry sense of humor to illustrate a point. "Anyone wish to elaborate?"

A middle-aged woman, someone who'd returned to school after raising her family—and ironically after losing her husband to a much younger woman—raised her hand.

"Jean," Whitlock addressed her.

"Well," she began, "Psalm Fifteen praises the person capable of keeping a promise even when it hurts to do so. And the Ten Commandments, being our contract with God, spell out what promises we are expected to keep. And as part of that sacred contract, the Tenth Commandment implores us to remain faithful, even when temptation is explicitly laid out before us—such as your neighbor's house or," she added emphatically, "his wife." Another chorus of good-natured snickers broke out among her classmates.

"Hmmm, a good start," replied Reverend Whitlock. "But what is it that distinguishes the Tenth Commandment from the nine others, and how does it relate to envy?" The class sat in quiet deliberation for a moment.

"Michael, you have an answer?" Whitlock asked, rubbing his nose once more.

Michael took a deep breath. "Well, sir, the distinction between the last commandment and the first nine is that while the others forbid some type of outward behavior, this one prohibits a type of internal sin—one which can lead to committing any of the other nine."

Reverend Whitlock considered his answer a good one, but wanted to spark further debate. "Anyone disagree?"

Another classmate jumped for the bait. "Well, actually," he began, "I don't necessarily disagree. But if envy is coveting someone else's possessions, then wouldn't the First and Second Commandments be just as applicable? Thou shalt have no other gods before me. Isn't envy akin to placing some material object above your love for God?"

"Well, yes and no," answered Whitlock. "Envy is not just limited to a desire for material possessions. I think we need to take a step back and define envy. Anyone care to try?"

"It's an emotion," offered Jean.

"That's a start, but let's be more specific. Michael, any thoughts?" Reverend Whitlock prodded him, breaking his stream of consciousness.

"Envy is the poor man's greed," Michael responded to Whitlock's request for a better definition of envy. His comment elicited laughter, but, according to Reverend Whitlock, was something worthy of further discourse. He asked Michael to explain.

"What has a rich man got to be envious about?" said Michael. "Not much. Plus, even if he's ugly he usually doesn't have to worry about the affection of women."

Reverend Whitlock gave Michael a penetrating look before proceeding, noting an edge of anger in the young man's voice, and wondered why he focused on the issue of money and women. Over many years of teaching this class, he had come to discover that the topic of ethics was about as personal as any of the subjects got, with the students often providing insight into their lives.

"Well, I would disagree. Many rich men covet things they cannot have, and suffer greatly for it. Regardless of a man's wealth, envy can lead to a spiritual decay." Reverend Whitlock stuck his pipe in his mouth as though preparing to smoke, removed it, then rubbed the bowl in the palm of his hand.

"Let's talk money for a moment, and materialism. Jesus said in Matthew sixteen: twenty-six, 'What is a man profited, if he shall gain the whole world, and lose his own soul?' What happens if a man becomes obsessed with his material possessions, and overlooks the goodness derived from sharing them? In other words, he values the possessions, or his money, more than the rich relationships resulting from sharing. His possessions may deceive him into believing he is happy, living in a rich and comfortable oasis. But in reality, he lives increasingly isolated from people, and therefore from the source of love. He is possessed by his possessions."

Michael leaned forward and listened more carefully, hoping something in Whitlock's lecture might help him cope with his anxiousness about Nowell Stuart.

"What is the cure for envy?" Reverend Whitlock asked rhetorically. The class remained silent, knowing he would answer his own question.

"The cure for envy," he began after a deliberate pause, "is to first identify the root cause of it. Did Joseph's brothers hate him because they envied his fabulous coat of many colors? No. They sought to destroy him because his father favored him the most. Did Cain envy his brother because he received God's blessing? No, he hated him because his own offering to God was unacceptable.

"This demonstrates the destructiveness of envy. But again, what is the cure? The cure, my friends, pure and simple, is love. And through forgiveness and the giving of love, we hope to please God and receive God's grace—the greatest love of all.

"If you look at First Corinthians, chapters twelve and thirteen, it clearly tells us that not all of us will be endowed with the gifts of wisdom, knowledge, prophecy, etc., etc. 'But the manifestation of the Spirit is given to every man to profit withal.'

"In other words, we cannot all be wildly rich or successful, but we are all capable of love. And without love, we are nothing. 'Though I speak with the tongues of men and of angels, and have not charity (or love), I am become as sounding brass, or a tinkling cymbal,' etc., etc. Obviously the richest man may be the poorest in Spirit if he knows not love.

"In conclusion, you may not be blessed with great knowledge or profound wisdom. You may not own the Empire State Building, or even your own humble home. But if you have love, you have the greatest of all God's gifts. Therefore love is the antidote to envy."

Michael sat still and reflective, in contrast to many of his classmates who were furiously scribbling notes. Reverend Whitlock wrapped up the class with a few additional insights, then provided a list of reading material to prepare for the next class. While the students gathered their belongings and left the room, Michael remained seated, still thinking of all that he'd just heard. It wasn't long before he and Jack Whitlock were alone in the classroom together.

"Michael, I'm glad you stuck around. I have something to tell you."

"Sir?" said Michael politely.

"Michael, as you know, I'm chairman of the Endowment Committee. And well, I can't thank you and Catherine enough."

"Thank us for what, sir?" Michael asked, perplexed.

"Well, I know it wasn't your money, but the donation was made in your name."

"You know Reverend Whitlock, I hate to sound stupid. But I really don't know what you're talking about."

"My goodness," the old professor responded, then moved to open a window. He searched his pockets for a matchbook, and despite campus restrictions on smoking in classrooms and freezing weather, he lit up his pipe.

"A sizable donation was made to the scholarship fund in your names."

"What!"

"Twenty-five thousand dollars, in fact. From a gentleman by the name of Nowell Stuart. I presume you know him."

Michael felt a chill, and not from the cold air. What he'd just heard was unthinkable.

"It's earmarked for the scholarship fund, which, of course, you yourself are a partial recipient. It is such a blessing," he said, taking another puff of his pipe, then looking out the window toward the starlit sky. "One of our usual big donors failed to come through this semester, which meant we were going to have to cut scholarship funds considerably next fall."

"Dammit," Michael cursed without apology. "Dammit, dammit, dammit."

"Michael, what is it? What's troubling you?"

Michael cleared his throat, then began to speak softly with his eyes closed. "I think what I got out of your lecture today, sir, is basically to love your enemy. But I'm so confounded by that. I mean, suppose you just don't have it in you to love someone?"

"Is it safe to assume this has something to do with Nowell Stuart?"

"Yes, yes it does. Sir, don't you think it's kinda peculiar that someone would give that much cash to an institution that he has no connections with?"

"Well, aren't you his connection? Odd though, you mean he never mentioned anything about this to you or your wife?"

"No, not that I know of, I mean, at least she never mentioned it to me."

"Tell me what you know about him."

Michael readily opened up, describing how Nowell monopolized Catherine's time and how Catherine couldn't help but be impressed by his vast wealth. And fearing that Catherine missed the material things he could not provide her, she would grow to resent him.

"It is the most vexing thing, for me," Michael concluded. "You know, your life is going along just fine, and you think you've got your priorities just right. You've got your health, a great wife, you're happy with what you've decided to make of your life, and then KABAM! Along comes someone, or something, that's a serious challenge to it all. I always thought I was stronger than this, that I could pray my way out of any situation. But I feel more anger toward him sometimes than the drunken fool who killed my father." He let out a deep sigh. "And you know what's even crazier—*I've* never even met the man!"

Reverend Whitlock grew more pensive. "Why do you suppose Catherine married you?" he asked, taking a turn Michael didn't immediately understand.

"Because she loves me."

"They all say that. Why else?"

"What are you getting at?"

"Michael, in my many years as an Episcopal priest I've probably married some two hundred couples. I always counsel them before they get married. I probe into their lives as much as I can, trying to determine their motivation for getting married. Money never comes up as the first answer, and usually never at all. But to many it is a great concern, which comes out in a more subtle fashion. Most women say they want a good provider and a good protector of their children, which translates into a need for money. But they also need someone who meets their emotional and spiritual needs. Catherine knew going into your marriage what to expect financially. Face it, we don't get rich off our sermons. Plus, she's a very attractive woman, and I imagine with her wealth and good looks she could have had just about anyone she wanted." He paused, then took a deep drag off his pipe, blowing the smoke out the window.

"So why did she pick someone poor and insignificant like me, is that what you're getting at?"

"Well, sort of, though I'm not certain I would have put it quite that way." Reverend Whitlock laughed as he turned to look into Michael's handsome face. "I suppose what I'm getting at is that she saw something unique in you. It obviously wasn't your money. She made a spiritual connection with you that is stronger than any amount of money on the face of this earth. What do you suppose it was?"

"She trusts me. She says she never met anyone as honest as me."

"Yes, probably because with you what you see is what you get. There's nothing devious about you, at least as far as I've observed."

"I still don't know what you're getting at, sir."

"Michael, it takes incredible spiritual strength to be an honest person. She sees that in you, no doubt. But your envy of another man will erode that strength, destroying something she values in you the most. Remain faithful, son, and pray for your strength. You know well enough that God will provide for you. And knowing that, what is there to worry about?" He tapped the side of his pipe, then drew out another match and relit the contents of the bowl.

Michael stood up and leaned against the window ledge beside Jack. "Not to change the subject, but there is something else on my mind as well. Remember my telling you about Catherine's ectopic pregnancy?"

Jack took a drag off his pipe and nodded his head yes.

"Well, we've been unable to conceive since then, and now Catherine's begun making steps toward in vitro fertilization. I know from what I've read that the Episcopal church embraces the procedure for the purpose of providing children in a marriage. But I have mixed feelings about it, and I just wanted to know your personal feelings about it."

The professor, a tall, lanky man, briefly chewed on the end of his pipe before speaking. "Michael, IVF is a very complex ethical issue. As you may already know, the process involves the creation of some embryos that aren't used and may be deliberately destroyed. Or sometimes the woman becomes impregnated with too many embryos, and a reduction process must be rendered to remove one or more of them so as not to jeopardize her health or that of the remaining babies."

"Are you saying you're against it?"

"No, not necessarily. But I worry about the extremes people go to to have children of their own. I suppose in general I support the church's line on this, but only to the extent that it is the ovum and the sperm of the people intending to raise the child. There are a lot of children out there in need of loving parents, and I can't understand this obsession over biological children when becoming parents to one of them would seem just as gratifying."

"I tend to agree with you, sir. Naturally we'd like our own child. But I'm worried about the financial stakes in this. The treatment is very expensive, and not always successful. It's more than ten thousand dollars a try, money which I personally think would be better spent on adoption. And furthermore I'm concerned that if I make this a financial issue, it will drive a wedge between us."

"Pushing her closer to Nowell Stuart?"

"Essentially, yes." Michael silently nodded his head, his eyes cast downward. "Though don't get me wrong, sir. I have legitimate concerns about the in vitro; we can only afford it once. Even if we could afford more attempts, beyond that it seems excessive to me to spend that kind of money."

"I understand. Michael, let's refocus on Nowell for a moment, and address your underlying concerns about him. Did you ever stop to think that maybe, just maybe, Nowell Stuart is nothing more than a very nice, very wealthy man for whom your wife works? Nothing more and nothing less? After all, he gave us money with no strings attached. Did you ever consider he might have been too modest to say anything to you about it?"

Michael knew Reverend Whitlock had a point, and also knew that he was spiritually capable of meeting the challenges before him, and that by doing so he would be a better person, a better Christian, and a better priest for it. He decided that from that moment forward he would not worry about Catherine's relationship with Nowell Stuart—that he would trust Nowell as much as he trusted Catherine, and would place his abiding faith in God.

His resolve would not last, however, as he would soon discover he'd need more than the patience of Job to endure Nowell Stuart's intrusion into his life.

Chapter Twenty

Every once in a great while it is possible to discover a bed that is significantly more comfortable than one's own. Every component of it, from the softness of the mattress to the depth of the down pillows and the perfect warmth of the covers, seems superior to anything you've slept in before or will probably sleep in again. Such was the case with Catherine and the bed she called her own while staying at Nowell's London home. Compounded with the five-hour difference in time, it made getting up a very difficult thing to do.

"Mrs. Harrison," said Maggie, the chambermaid. Catherine didn't budge. She'd asked Maggie to wake her up if she slept past ten, which she'd managed to do for the second morning in a row. Maggie had no luck, and retreated to the kitchen to report her failings to Nowell, who was dressed, had long since eaten breakfast, and was enjoying a second cup of coffee while reading the *Guardian* and waiting for Catherine.

"Sir," she said in her sweet Irish lilt, "it's a bit like she's dead, but I believe I saw her breathe, so not to worry."

Nowell chortled. "Oh, what a relief, Maggie. Well I suppose there is someone else who can get the job done." He glanced down at Rags who was dozing on a stylish, plaid-flannel dog bed, big enough for a ten-year-old boy to sleep on.

"Rags, come here," he commanded. The dog lifted his head, and contrary to his usual rambunctiousness, let out a sigh and lazily buried his head back down in his cozy pad.

"Oh, not you too. My two most loyal subjects are willfully ignoring my demands to get up and get on with the day. Well, we'll just see about that."

With that Nowell folded his paper, went to the refrigerator, and began poking around. "I guess this wouldn't interest you either," he said, turning and then squatting in front of the dog's face while gripping an enormous soup bone, one still pink on the edges with meat. Nigel always kept a stash of them on hand as a special treat for the animal. Rags perked up and began waving his enormous tail, waiting for Nowell to drop it right down in front of him. Instead, his master slowly passed the meaty bone beneath the dog's nose. Rags whined, then attempted to snatch it from Nowell's hand with a snap of his mighty jaw, but his master was too quick.

"Not yet," Nowell mocked the eager animal. "Come, come." Without ado, Rags quickly followed on Nowell's heels toward the elevator.

Together they arrived at the third floor and walked in unison to Catherine's guest room. Nowell placed his ear upon the closed door and, hearing nothing, tapped on the door with the soup bone, which prompted the dog to whine some more. Still no response from Catherine.

"This ought to do the trick," said Nowell as he opened the door and peered inside. He could see Catherine was sound asleep. "You stay here," he said to Rags. Though every muscle in the dog twitched with anticipation, he stayed put, smart enough to know he might never get his bone if he didn't behave.

Nowell tiptoed across the room, grateful to see that her back was to him. He gingerly placed the bone on the pillow beside her head, then retreated for the door where the antsy dog stood slobbering.

"Okay, boy, go and get it!" he commanded, slapping Rags on the rump.

Without hesitation the one-hundred-seventy-five-pound beast bounded across the room, then leaped upon the bed, zealously snatching the bone and then gnawing on it right beside Catherine's head. A long shrill scream followed as Catherine bolted upright, with shock and horror consuming her face.

"RAGS, WHAT THE HELL ARE YOU DOING? OH, DISGUSTING, GET OUT OF HERE. GET OUT!"

Rags looked briefly at Catherine as if to say "mind your own business," then continued devouring his reward. Nowell let out a low, sinister laugh followed by a short, clipped whistle prompting the dog to retreat from the bed, though still gnawing on his bone. "Good dog, good Rags," Nowell continued, laughing.

"Ugh, you are such a jerk!" Catherine snarled, wiping her face with one of the sheets, then pulling it tightly over herself for protection. "What was that all about?"

"It's half past eleven."

"I don't care," she bellowed, with obvious infuriation. "Some host you are! That was nasty. Besides, it's only six-thirty for me. What are you trying to do to me?"

Nowell remained indifferent to her outburst. "Don't you recall we were going to leave for West Yorkshire at eleven a.m.? Today, that is."

"Forgive me," she answered contemptuously. "I must have slept right through the alarm."

"And Maggie."

"Maggie too? Guess that shows how badly I need my sleep." She pulled the sheet up a little closer and ran her hand through her tousled hair. Nowell delighted at an opportunity to soak up her morning essence, which even in her cantankerous mood he considered adorable. Feeling aroused, he wished he could jump right into the bed with her.

"I trust that you slept okay?" he asked, casually leaning in the door frame. He was dressed for their country retreat, and in Catherine's estimation, had overdone it for a day in the sticks. He wore a brown cashmere jacket, matching pants, and a checked cotton shirt with plaid cashmere tie. The only thing that distinguished his attire as country wear was the dark green Wellington boots into which his pant legs were tucked, and the fact that he wore his coat lapels turned upward around his collar. It looked like pure prep-school chic to Catherine, who also thought at the moment that his behavior was on the prep-school level.

"You know, I think that's the problem," she finally answered, throwing herself back down on the pillow. "I've never slept better. This bed is phenomenal."

"Yes, that's the general consensus I've heard. Are you hungry? I can have Maggie bring you something while you get ready."

"That would be great," she responded, hoping he

would finally leave. Instead he boldly entered the room again, heading directly to the intercom beside her bed. "Maggie," he said into the box as he flashed his boyish grin at Catherine.

"Yes, sir," her petite voice answered back.

"Might you please come up to Catherine's room and take her breakfast order?"

"Yes, sir. I'll be right there." The intercom static went dead. Nowell lingered by her bedside a moment longer, making small talk and soaking up more of her delicious morning demeanor.

"Well, what do you say we leave in one hour," Nowell said.

"I think I can handle that," replied Catherine, the bed sheets still pulled up closely around her half-nude body.

"Excellent. We'll see you then," said Nowell. Though Catherine was looking forward to their jaunt in the country, what she really wanted now was privacy. As Nowell left, Maggie entered, and she quickly gave the young woman her breakfast order: a cup of black coffee, a roll of some sort, and any fresh fruit. "Actually, do you have any decaffeinated coffee?" Catherine asked, remembering that she shouldn't be drinking caffeine if she was pregnant.

"Yes, ma'am."

"Make it decaf, would you please?"

"Yes, ma'am," Maggie responded, then quietly departed. At last Catherine had the room to herself and gratefully threw the covers down. But a snap of the chill air against her bare skin forced her back into the warm, downy comfort of the bed, where she remained for about another five minutes. That's when she began to notice an old familiar twinge in her abdomen. "Dammit," she said out loud, "dammit." She knew it was the onset of her period.

She forced herself out of bed and into the bathroom, where indeed she discovered her period had started. It would have been wildly lucky to get pregnant following the hysterosalpingogram, she thought, trying to reassure herself; but still she felt blue. She wished that Michael were with her now. Though they'd only been apart less than two days, she missed him. She looked at the clock, which read 11:45. It was early for him, but she picked up the phone anyway, dialed the international code and then their phone number, listening happily to the familiar ring. It rang once, then twice.

About the fourth ring, Nowell from his study downstairs saw the red light on his phone panel and realized that Catherine was placing a call. He carefully picked up the receiver about the same time as Michael answered.

"Hello," came the drowsy, gravelly voice.

"Hi, baby," she said. Nowell touched the mute button on the phone panel to ensure they wouldn't hear him.

"Hey," Michael drawled in a soft, happy way. "What are you doing?"

"Missing you."

"Yeah, me too. How's it goin'?"

"Okay, I guess. I just started my period."

"Oh, baby, I'm so sorry. You doing okay?"

"Yeah," she sighed heavily.

"Don't worry, it's all gonna work out."

Catherine softly clucked her tongue, then sighed, indicating her sadness. Michael went on gently reassuring her, while Nowell picked up a pencil and briefly pretended to orchestrate their conversation. Their dialogue was always simple, easygoing, and affectionate, as Nowell had learned while listening in on previous conversations between them. From his study in the New York gallery he'd often listened the same way.

"Catherine, did you know you left your address book on the table?" Michael was asking. Nowell already knew that, since she'd mentioned her frustration over doing so to him just the day before. Their conversation stayed on the level of small talk for a short while longer, with Michael asking for details of her trip aboard the Concorde. Catherine became excited and chatty about it, noting she shared her journey with Tom Cruise and Nicole Kidman. *Funny,* Nowell thought, *she hasn't mentioned a word about* Les Misérables *or any of our other activities together.*

Listening to the couple always filled him with a sense of power—an empowerment that aroused strong sexual urges, prompting him to lean back in his chair and begin gently fondling himself as they carried on.

"Michael, I wanted to blanket the South with postcards from abroad. While I've got you on the phone, would you mind getting my book and giving me a few addresses?"

"No problem," said Michael, who proceeded to give her four or five addresses. Nowell lost count while focusing on himself, but rapidly became more alert, to the point of removing his hand from his pants, when he heard what Michael had to say about his first day back at school.

"Catherine, we can talk more about this later. But I gotta ask you somethin'. Did you know anything about a twenty-five-thousand-dollar contribution that Nowell made in our names to General Theological Seminary?"

"WHAT!" she shrieked. Nowell hurriedly turned the volume down on the phone so that anyone passing by his locked study doors wouldn't hear.

"I have no idea what you're talking about, this is news to me!"

"You mean he never said a word to you about it."

"Nothing, nada, zilch! When did he do this?"

Michael seemed to view the donation as a kind and charitable act, wholly trusting Nowell's good intentions—precisely what Nowell wanted.

"Michael, what should I say to him?"

"Thanks would be a good start. The money was earmarked for the scholarship fund, which of course means that you and I are direct beneficiaries of our own gift!"

"This is incredible!" Catherine sounded stupefied.

So, Nowell thought, *the brooch will remain our little secret.* To him, her omission was quite telling.

"Well, babe, I better go. Nowell has some decorating projects he wants me to work on. I'll tell you more about it later. I miss you so much."

"Me too. Catherine, before you go, I just want you to know something."

"Yeah?"

"I thank God every day that you are in my life. And I love you more than I think you'll ever know."

There was a long moment of silence—at least it seemed that way to Nowell—as he waited for Catherine's response.

"Michael, I love you too. More than *you* will ever know. And I miss you. Bye."

"Bye."

Nowell waited until both lines went click before hanging up the phone, and watched as the red light faded on his phone panel. As always, he couldn't wait to talk with her to see what, if anything, she would reveal about her conversation with Michael. Meanwhile, he began stroking himself again, this time without any interruptions.

Chapter Twenty-one

Catherine hustled downstairs with barely a second to spare. Meeting Nowell's demands for punctuality was a challenge for her, but it was an area of her life needing improvement anyway, so she was happy to oblige. The single time she'd been late he became genuinely upset, though his anger was slow-burning, taking him half a day to get over.

"Nigel, where's Nowell?" Catherine inquired breathlessly.

"I believe he's in the study, Mrs. Harrison."

"Should I go in?"

"May I suggest you knock first."

"Oh, of course."

She tapped lightly on the door, and hearing his muffled voice stepped back. She couldn't tell if he had someone in there with him or was on the phone. She waited outside instead of intruding, quickly becoming a friendly target of Rags.

"Oh, no. Not you again. Go away," she repeated playfully, "go away!"

Rags would have none of it, instead hoisting his heavy body up and placing his enormous paws on her shoulders, staring her right in the eye.

"You're incorrigible," she said, sighing, then laughing. At that moment the study doors opened and Nowell, thoroughly amused by the sight, laughed as well.

"Excuse me, am I interrupting something?"

"I wish you would," said Catherine through gritted teeth, now trying hard to avoid a face bath by the dog.

"Rags, down," Nowell commanded tersely. The dog looked at him sheepishly, but didn't budge. Catherine felt she'd be knocked down if the creature moved too fast, so she grabbed hold of his paws, gently lowering him to the floor.

"Now stay," she scolded, pointing a forefinger in his large round face.

"I'm afraid he's in love," said Nowell, adding, "I can't say that I blame him. You look marvelous today."

"Well thanks," said Catherine sincerely, oblivious to any deeper meaning. "But I have to tell you, Nowell, you have me a bit confused. I was fully expecting this to be a day for blue jeans. Am I dressed okay for our trip to Yorkshire?"

"You look splendid," he said, sizing up her attire, which in his estimation was fully appropriate for the day. She wore beige gabardine slacks, a dark green sweater vest over a white, wide-collared shirt, and a silk scarf tucked in at the open neck. On top of it all she wore a dark green wool blazer, along with brown leather, lace-up boots with stacked heels.

"You know, I have a confession to make," said Nowell.

"You mean you've been keeping something from me? Not you," Catherine replied with mock sarcasm, then rolled her eyes. "Well, out with it," she demanded.

"I'm rather embarrassed," he said, self-consciously pinching his chin, "but you may be interested to know that I don't even own a pair of blue jeans."

"Nowell! That's un-American!"

"Precisely."

"What do you mean, 'precisely,' " she said, imitating his refined British accent. "After all, you do spend a fair amount of time there. What could you possibly have against Americans?"

"Oh, I know. Forgive me, I'm not bashing America, really. It's just that I grew up with very conservative parents, and denim, for whatever reason, was frowned upon. I once came home from school wearing a jean jacket, and from my father's reaction I might just as well have been dressed like Boy George. He thought I looked like the son of a Labour Party member. Totally unacceptable."

Catherine eyed him in a coquettish way. "But still, denim is not just an American phenomenon," she said. "I mean, lots of Brits wear jeans too. For that matter, probably more than half the world wears jeans at any given moment."

"Perhaps it also has something to do with the impression that America's middle class lives in blue jeans."

"You are such a snob!" she said, laughing. "Where's a phone book?"

"Why?"

"There must be a Gap in London. I say we make an adventure out of this and buy you your first pair of jeans today."

"Oh, no, no you don't."

"Don't what?"

"Don't change thirty-seven years of tradition like that," he said, snapping his fingers.

"Look," she said, boldly entering his study to look for a phone book. "You brought me here for some make-over projects. I say we start with you. Besides, there's nothing like a well-worn pair of jeans, putting them on is like cozying up to someone you love."

"That so?" he responded.

"Uh-hmmm."

"Well, I suppose I'd be willing to try just about anything once. You're on."

They scanned the phone directory, finding the closest Gap to his Belgravia neighborhood, then promptly hailed Sonny to drive them over. For a change, Catherine felt fully in charge of the mission, finding it gratifying to take control of Nowell for once.

The London Gap wasn't very different from its stateside counterparts—a spacious loftlike store, uncluttered but with a wide variety of styles to choose from.

"This is rather daunting," said Nowell, scanning the shelves labeled by size and cut. "Take a look. You have slim, baggy, loose, and easy. Sounds rather like names of American rappers."

Catherine cracked up. "You're not getting out of this now, Nowell Stuart. Let me go get some help." Moments later she reappeared with a youthful clerk. His hair was very short on the sides but spiked on top with a tri-colored, braided rattail down the back. At least he had on a clean pair of jeans and a decent plaid flannel shirt. Nowell took one look at the three earrings in his left ear and muttered "Boy George" under his breath. Catherine heard the remark and chose to ignore it, while the clerk remained oblivious.

"Could you please explain the differences in these styles to my friend?" Catherine inquired.

"Wha' you want to know?" he responded in a thick cockney accent.

"Well, just like I said. Basically, what's the difference between the loose, easy, etc."

"Easy is the stan'ard jean; slim is narrow; baggy, very loose; and loose somewhere between easy and baggy."

"Oh, now I get it," Nowell guffawed.

"Come on, Nowell, it's easy."

"No, it's loose. Sorry, I take that back, it's baggy."

"Thank you," said Catherine politely to the clerk, indicating they no longer needed his help. "Nowell Stuart, I didn't think you had a rude bone in your body. He was just trying to be helpful," she said, then had to laugh herself realizing how odd it must seem to someone unfamiliar with jean lingo.

"What size are you?" she asked, then blushed, remembering she knew his underwear size.

"Well, before dinner I'm easy, and I suppose after dinner I'm loose. Sounds rather like a few dates I've had once or twice." He couldn't stop smirking, he was really enjoying himself at Catherine's expense, and she began to feel her control over the mission diminish.

"Look, I'm serious," she said. "Do you have any idea what size you might be? Like Michael—he's six feet, weighs one-seventy-five, and he wears a thirty-four by thirty-four. You're about his size, why don't you try these on?" she asked, grabbing a couple pairs, one easy, one slim. "The easy ones are great on him, they make his ass look"—she caught herself, then looked at him with utter embarrassment—"I'm sorry . . ."

"Go on, go on. By all means, they make his ass look . . ." Nowell was really having fun now.

"Good. He looks really good in his jeans."

"Oh, come on. You were about to say, they make his ass look . . . ? What? Just say it."

"All right already, sexy. Really sexy."

"And that's good, right?"

"Oh, Nowell, now you're embarrassing me. Just put it this way. Women love to see men in jeans. That's all."

"You mean they don't like to see them out of their jeans?"

"Would you stop it? Now you're embarrassing *and* exasperating me! Just go try them on."

He smiled smugly at her, took the jeans from her arms, and retreated into the changing room. Moments later he reappeared, clad in easy-style jeans, still wearing his jacket, vest, and tie.

"So, what do you think? Will the women go mad for me?"

"Nowell, I don't mean to be rude, but you need to loosen up a bit."

"Oh. Should I try on the loose jeans?"

"No, no. I mean, get rid of the coat and tie."

"Oh, dear God," he reacted while slipping out of his coat and loosening his tie. "Next you'll have me trying on a T-shirt with a Hells Angels logo on it."

"The vest," she added. "The vest has to go."

"I'm feeling positively naked now." Catherine couldn't believe the transformation. He tucked his checkered shirt into the jeans, then did a mini pirouette in front of her.

"Nowell, I'm not just saying this, but they look great on you. Really. I mean, what do you think? Do you like them?"

"Boy George," he muttered, only this time more loudly.

"That's ridiculous. You don't look a thing like Boy George. Besides, the last I saw of him he was wearing a kimono."

"Oh, dear. I hope you won't be pushing kimonos on me next."

Catherine groaned. "You know, you can be impossible sometimes. Don't worry. I won't be pushing kimonos on you. At least, that is, as long as you don't want me to."

"Well, as you've done a remarkable job selling me these jeans, I wonder what will be next."

"In other words, you're going to buy them?"

"Well, yes, I imagine," he answered while turning to look at his rear end in the mirror. "Do you approve?"

"I already told you, they look great on you."

"Yes, but what I want to know," he began, then lowered his voice to a whisper, "does my arse look as good as Michael's?"

"Ohhhh, me and my big mouth," she said with a sigh. "Yes, yes it does. Are you happy?"

"I have an idea," he said, "why don't I wear these out to the country today. When we get back to my place you can change as well. Then I'll feel like I'm in good company."

"Sounds good to me. Here, you want me to hold your stuff while you get your slacks and boots?"

"That would be very kind of you," he said, dumping his jacket, vest, and tie in her waiting arms. He disappeared long enough for Catherine to catch the scent of the spicy cologne on his clothes. She hadn't been able to identify the brand name yet, but was certain whatever it was, it was expensive. He reappeared while she was still sniffing his clothes.

"Don't tell me, a little vest fetish?"

Catherine laughed. "No, no, it's just that I love the smell of your cologne. It's wonderful. What is it?"

"Truly, you like it? That's nice. Actually, it doesn't have a name. It's a custom blend I have made in Paris."

It figures, Catherine thought. A brand sold at even the best department stores would not be unique or probably expensive enough for him. "Yeah, I really do like it." She smiled at him, then held on to his clothes as they headed for the register. She did it with the same casual ease she would have used with Michael, not thinking twice about how inappropriate or unprofessional it might appear to be handling his personal effects.

Though Nowell had tucked the jeans into his Wellington boots, they still looked charming on him. He paid for them in cash, took his jacket from her, and slipped into it while she held on to the vest and tie. They walked out to the Rolls together, with Nowell taking quiet notice of looks from the clerks and strangers passing by. He assumed people believed he and Catherine belonged together—like husband and wife, boyfriend and girlfriend—no matter, it seemed as if they were a pair. Which reminded him—she'd yet to mention anything about her conversation with Michael.

Sonny opened the door for them and Nowell gestured

for Catherine to climb in ahead of him. It felt so good to be in her company. He felt his blood well in excitement over anticipation of their venture alone in the country today—a day he intended she would never forget.

Chapter Twenty-two

Nigel had already packed Nowell's Range Rover for their trip to West Yorkshire, and Rags, certain he was invited to go along, waited impatiently beside the all-terrain vehicle for his master to come out of the house.

Catherine changed clothes, trading the gabardine slacks for a favorite pair of jeans. She kept on her stacked heel boots in case they went riding, but replaced her blazer and vest for a more comfortable cotton turtle-neck and cashmere sweater. It had proven to be an un-usually mild day for that time of year, sunny and slightly breezy with a temperature in the high fifties. Catherine felt grateful for the improved weather, since it had rained most of the time since her arrival just a few days before. She glanced out her bedroom window to the cir-cular driveway below and laughed at the sight of Nowell ordering Rags out of the car.

"Nigel," she heard Nowell bellow, "get Rags out of the car, would you please?" Nowell, who hadn't planned on bringing the dog that day, had mistakenly opened the car door long enough for Rags to hop in. It was truly a test of wills going on, with Rags the apparent winner. Nigel retreated inside only to reappear moments later with a soup bone, luring the dog out of the car, but not back into the house.

Catherine gathered up the last of her gear for their trip, tossing on a jacket over her outfit, then headed for the elevator. She hit the down button, but decided in-stead to take the stairs—something she hadn't done since arriving. She had also yet to explore the second floor, where Nowell's bedroom was located, and decided to make a quick side trip on her way down. It was, after all, one of the rooms he said needed redecorating.

The double doors to Nowell's bedroom were wide

open and she could hear Maggie inside bustling away. For a moment Catherine thought to continue on downstairs, but her curiosity tugged hard and without further hesitation she walked into the room.

At first glance it appeared truly rich and elegant, and more elaborate in detail than his bedroom in New York. But she barely noticed the trappings, focusing instead on a prominent, yet soft and feminine portrait hanging over the fireplace.

"Goo'afternoon, ma'am," she heard Maggie say from behind her as she walked spellbound toward the painting.

"Hi, Mags," she said vaguely while staring at the portrait. It could only be of one person, she thought: Elizabeth.

Catherine shuddered as an odd mixture of feelings consumed her. It was almost like viewing a corpse in an open casket: unbearable and saddening to look at the lifeless form, at the same time intriguing to see what death looked like on the person. However, instead of being lain flat out as in a coffin, Elizabeth was regally positioned on a chaise lounge; lifeless and haunting, yet beautiful still in her death.

Her face and long honey-blond hair looked brilliant against a muted brown background, with creamy skin showing outside her off-the-shoulder, satin-white gown. Her face was both sweet and beautiful; a look of youthful innocence and come-hither mischievousness combined in the faint smile of her curled upper lip.

And oh, the puppy curled up affectionately at her feet! There was no mistaking Rags. He couldn't have been more than a few months old at the time, the artist having captured a look of innocence and playful mischievousness in the animal as well.

At least Nowell had the sense to marry someone whom he truly loved and had much in common with. They were truly happy, those two. Such a pity. Dubs's words about Elizabeth began ringing in her ears. An aching sadness began welling up in Catherine. She simply couldn't imagine Nowell's heartache, losing this beautiful, young woman, his unborn child, and his parents all so tragically and suddenly.

"Catherine?"

She startled at the sound of Nowell's voice, then slowly turned toward him, unexpected tears brimming in her eyes.

"Oh, Nowell," she whispered, "I'm so sorry. She was so beautiful."

Maggie quickly left the room while Nowell moved slightly toward Catherine, first looking at her, then up at the portrait. He let out a deep sigh, but said nothing.

"I apologize, I didn't mean to intrude. It's just that I saw . . . and I, well . . ." Tears began spilling down Catherine's cheeks, prompting Nowell to move in closer. He hesitated at first, then gently wrapped his arms around Catherine, bringing her close to his chest, shutting his eyes to avoid the image of Elizabeth. He would not let her bitter legacy deprive him of his joy in at last holding this woman so close.

Catherine softly wept over the pain she imagined Nowell had suffered; she cried for the loss of such a beautiful, young woman and for the end of that innocent life within. She even cried for Rags, who she believed must miss Elizabeth terribly. She felt somewhat embarrassed by her sudden display of emotion, but she simply couldn't help herself—it suddenly felt that overwhelming.

Nowell responded by tenderly stroking her hair with one hand, his other arm hugging her close. Catherine, oblivious to his slow-burning passion for her, remained fixed in his embrace. She had no intuition about his motivation to hold her, believing his tenderness had everything to do with the loss of Elizabeth.

No one—except for Elizabeth's impoverished lover, now dead by his own hand—knew that Nowell couldn't care less about her being gone. Nor did they know how badly Elizabeth had betrayed him. How desperate she was to have the other man's child while remaining married to Nowell and taking full advantage of his wealth and position in English society. To the world, Nowell's relationship with Elizabeth had seemed a storybook marriage. But the truth was astoundingly ugly.

She had turned out to be a coldhearted, manipulative bitch, wanting nothing more than Nowell's money, her own family's fortune having diminished while the Stuarts' prosperity and social standing steadily climbed. Unwilling to grant Nowell a divorce, she'd wantonly carried on with the other man, even confessing that she'd made love to him just hours before her wedding to Nowell. Nowell could not have despised two people more if he'd tried.

Worst of all was while vacationing with his parents in Italy, she'd convinced them to come home three days early, unbeknownst to them so she could rendezvous with her lover in London. To Nowell, it was her deceit that ended up killing his beloved parents, their private jet slamming into the Tyrolean mountains during an unexpected storm on that fateful trip. Nowell was only spared an untimely death because he was handling family business back home. But he often wished he had been on board, since losing his mother and father, both of whom he'd adored, made him feel dead inside.

The only reason he had not discarded the portrait of Elizabeth was because it stirred up the only feelings he had left—feelings of hate—which for the longest time seemed the only reminder to him that he was alive. He had not believed himself capable of loving anyone again. He never wanted to love anyone again. Until Catherine.

Gently he spoke. "Catherine, it's all right. Believe me, I'm over her. As I told you over dinner the other night, it's one of the reasons I wanted you here."

She looked up at him sympathetically, while still in his embrace. She didn't say anything, waiting instead for him to proceed.

"I've finally come to terms with it, with Elizabeth being gone," he began, still stroking her hair, shutting his eyes again. "And I realized that part of getting on was letting go, which is why I needed you"—he hesitated, then opened his eyes and met her innocent gaze—"to help me take that vital step."

Catherine's mouth parted into an understanding smile.

"I will always remember her," he continued slowly, "but living with her belongings, her memory . . . it's just, well . . . it's just time. Time to let go. Time to get on with a new life."

Catherine felt deeply moved that it was she he turned to for help in burying the past. Moving back a step, and then taking him by his hands, she addressed him with utmost sincerity.

"Nowell, I'm happy to help you in any way that I can. I simply cannot imagine what you've been through," she said soothingly, her eyes clinging to his. "I'll do whatever it takes, I'll move as quickly or as slowly as you want me to. But I need you to understand something first."

Nowell looked intently back into the beautiful face before him.

"What is that?" he asked affectionately, holding tightly to her hands.

"I want you to know, no matter what, that I'm always here for you. That you should feel you can trust me, and talk with me about anything. I only wish I'd known all about this sooner."

Catherine laid her head down on his shoulder again as a gesture of sympathy, and as she did her pulse quickened and a warm and most unexpected tide of pleasure swept over her.

What is happening to me? she asked herself. But instead of backing away and gaining her bearings, she leaned farther into Nowell, experiencing yet again another hot rush of blood. It was a feeling beyond sympathy or grief, as it was electric and full of sexual tension. She sought weakly to pull herself away, but Nowell resisted, placing his arms around her waist and drawing her in so close she could feel his thigh muscles.

"Catherine," he finally replied, "I know you should have been told about Elizabeth, and all that happened, well before this trip to England. But you must understand something too. I'm a very private and wounded man. It has not been easy for me to share my true feelings. It is only because I have learned through experience I can trust you that I feel even the slightest bit comfortable opening up.

"And," he added, looking deep into her soft brown eyes, "I know that you would never do anything to hurt me, would you?"

Chapter Twenty-three

Rags let out a deep sigh from the back of the Range Rover. They'd been on the road for almost two hours, and he'd been surprisingly quiet and well behaved. At Catherine's insistence he'd been allowed aboard, ecstatic to join his master and a friend on this journey. Catherine was rather subdued herself, trying to sort out all that had happened in Nowell's bedroom. Nowell, also pensive, had just cracked the window and lit up a cigarette.

Catherine couldn't help but wonder what Nowell thought of her outburst. They were truly sad feelings she'd shared with him as she conveyed her honest sympathy. What she hadn't anticipated, however, was this physical craving for his embrace, which continued now some two hours later. Just looking at him gave her that same warm rush she'd felt back in his bedroom and she worried that somehow he might have picked up on her lustful feelings. She felt ashamed.

This can't be, she told herself over and over. *I love Michael. I'm in love with Michael.* Still there was an inescapable attraction toward Nowell. Thinking of Michael made her recall their earlier conversation, and the twenty-five-thousand-dollar contribution.

"Hey, I have a question for you," Catherine started. She glanced at Nowell who smiled at her warmly. If he'd ever doubted his love for her, there was no question of it now. Holding her had been the most satisfying physical and emotional experience he'd had since he could remember, and the warm sensation it created lingered still.

"I can't imagine." He smiled back easily.

"Well, I talked with Michael a little while ago. I guess I should have asked you before I called, I just assumed it would be okay," she said, adding, "I'll be happy to pay for it."

"Don't be silly. Call him all you want," said Nowell, feeling so strengthened by their embrace that the mention of Michael's name barely bothered him. "What's on your mind?" He knew full well where this conversation was headed.

"You know, he could have knocked me over with a feather. He said that you made a twenty-five-thousand-dollar contribution to the General Theological Seminary in our names. Is that true?"

"He told you that?" he said, his smile and tone of voice turning elusive.

"Nowell, come on. Is it true?"

"Well, now, let's think. Why would Michael make something like that up?"

"Oh, Nowell," she said, laughing. "Michael wouldn't make something like that up. You did do it, didn't you? Tell me the truth."

"Now why would *I* do something like that?" he continued, teasing her.

"Because you're rich and you're one of the world's nicest guys, I suppose."

Nowell laughed. "Well, I suppose only half of that is true. Can you guess which half?"

"You know, you exasperate me sometimes."

"Is that good or bad?" he responded, still teasing.

"It's a nicer way of saying that sometimes you frustrate the hell out of me!"

"I can't imagine I have the capacity to do that to anyone," he mused, still avoiding the issue and then stubbing out his cigarette.

"More than you could ever know," she said with a smirk at him. "Now, why did you do it?"

"Why not?"

Catherine let out an exaggerated sigh, prompting Rags to peer over the backseat. Seeing no need for his involvement he quickly settled back down, which made them both laugh.

"Actually, I did make such a contribution in your names. I hope you don't mind. What did your husband have to say about it?"

"He said something like 'Thanks is a good start.' I

can't believe you did it. I mean, I don't want to sound like an ingrate, but really, why did you do it?"

Nowell became slightly frustrated, wondering if Catherine had truly forgotten their agreement.

"Actually, you should know the answer to that."

"I should?"

"Uh-hmmmmm," he answered slowly.

"Let me think." Catherine looked silently out the window for several moments, then slowly turned toward him. "You didn't. You did this in place of the brooch?"

"Are you disappointed?"

"Oh, my God. You didn't spend that much on me for Christmas, did you?"

"I don't know about you Yanks, but I was taught it was poor taste to ask the price of a gift."

"Yeah, but you didn't make an anonymous gift to the seminary. You obviously wanted us to know how much you gave."

"It wasn't a gift *to* you."

"No, ostensibly it was a gift *from* me. I'm just curious. Why didn't you tell me about this before you did it?"

"Because I knew you would object."

"Maybe not. Michael didn't seem to mind. He said the money is earmarked for the scholarship fund." Catherine's tone became softer. "It was awfully generous of you. Thanks."

"Listen, I know Michael relies heavily on scholarships and student loans to get him through, and that it's a burden on the both of you. And furthermore, that you're both too proud to beg." He looked at Catherine to see her reaction. She didn't say anything, instead she shifted in her seat and turned to squarely face him.

"Anyway, you said it yourself just a bit ago, not to hold anything back from you. So you want the truth. Here it is. I was a little surprised and somewhat hurt that you didn't accept my Christmas gift. I didn't mean anything by it other than to let you know how much I appreciate all your hard work, that I value you as my assistant, and," he began more thoughtfully, "as my friend." He turned to look at her again, satisfied to see her blush.

"I suppose if I were Michael I'd have difficulty understanding such a gift to my wife. Incidentally, did you ever tell him about that brooch?"

"Nowell, Michael and I don't keep secrets from each other."

Oh, you cunning woman, he thought, knowing full well that she had not told him.

"Really?" he went on. "That's lovely. Anyway, in keeping with my not holding anything back from you, I thought my contribution to the school would accomplish two things. First, I did say I would make a donation to a charity, but I never said which one and you never specified a preference. Secondly, I was hoping to win Michael's respect."

"Why would you want to do that?"

"Well, I know he's somewhat edgy, if you will, about our working relationship, or for that matter our friendship. And I want him to know that I wish you both to succeed and to be happy. That I have nothing but your best interests at heart. So there you have it. Really, I just thought I was doing Michael, and the school, a big favor."

"Nowell, that's incredibly generous. You're right, you know. Michael is a bit jealous of you. But I think it's mostly because he hasn't met you yet. I know once he does, he won't feel that way anymore."

"What makes you so certain of that?"

"Oh, it's just that I know him," she said. But at that moment she was beginning to feel like she didn't even know herself. Another warm flush of passion crept over her as she looked at Nowell, leaving a disturbing wake of confusion in its course. How could she be so in love with Michael and experience these new feelings for Nowell? But no sooner would she chastise herself for even entertaining such thoughts than the feelings, both strong and sexual, would emerge. And each time the feelings would linger a little longer, allowing her to entertain illicit and passionate thoughts about her and Nowell together. Catherine shifted in her seat again and gazed out the window, unable to look at Nowell for fear he would know what she was thinking.

She tried to focus instead on how stunning the countryside looked. Very large and intensely green tracts of rolling land were surrounded by low stone walls and hedges. The clear blue sky provided a sharp contrast to the rich landscape, punctuated only by a few thin clouds. The sun was still shining bright, giving the false appearance of a new spring day.

Catherine couldn't resist rolling down the window, taking in several gulps of the fresh but chilly air. Her move prompted Rags to awaken and bolt upright from his backseat berth. This time he didn't go back to sleep.

"Now look what you've done," said Nowell jokingly, "you've awakened the baby!"

Catherine chuckled at his remark, but ignored Rags for the moment. "Nowell, it's incredibly beautiful out here. It's just one other thing you've been keeping secret from me."

"Well, quite frankly, it's something we'd like to keep secret from all you Americans."

"My gosh, what is it you have against Americans today?"

"Nothing, really, it's just amusing to provoke your sense of patriotism."

Like a sudden explosion, Rags leaped between them, whining to be let out, looking eagerly first at Nowell and then at Catherine.

"Okay, okay. You win," said Nowell, slowing down the vehicle and pulling over to a gravel side road that wound along a frolicking stream. Nowell parked and opened up the back gate, watching as the big dog bound quickly into the brush.

"Are you ready for a break?" he asked Catherine. Without waiting for her answer he pulled out a picnic basket and a bottle of cabernet, opening the wine without hesitation and pouring them each a glass. He next spread out a cheerful red-and-white-checked gingham cloth across the back gate, and carefully arranged the contents of the basket across it.

"Are you going to sit there all day?" asked Nowell.

"What are you doing?"

"Come and see for yourself."

Catherine climbed out and walked to the back of the vehicle, delighted by the feast laid out before her. There were a variety of cheeses, bread and crackers, some paté, and plump, fresh seedless red grapes. There were even fresh flowers in a vase. Nowell handed her a glass of wine, and before she could say anything proposed a toast.

"To a new chapter in life."

"Here, here." She smiled at him, then took a hearty sip from her glass. It was smooth and delicious, and something she hoped would take the edge off her physical ache. She took another healthy swallow, and then another.

"Nowell Stuart, you never cease to amaze me. This is wonderful, thank you."

"Don't thank me, thank Nigel."

Rags, seeing that there was food on hand, quickly rejoined them and began begging in earnest.

"Rags, you old rascal, you. Here." She tossed him a grape, which he ardently sniffed but rejected. She then tossed him a thick slab of cheese, which he eagerly devoured.

"Hey, what about me?" asked Nowell teasingly.

"What about you? You can fend for yourself," she answered, burying her face into the dog's neck and giving him an affectionate hug.

"Hey, really now, what about me?" Nowell playfully taunted her.

Needing no further provocation, Catherine willingly slipped her arms around Nowell in a playful hug, but her smoldering desire for him made it impossible to let go. They became locked in a way that went beyond mere friendship, neither one willing nor able to step back.

Catherine did not know what had come over her. His incredible warmth against the chilly air, and the even warmer feelings inside that this embrace evoked, made it impossible to move. She buried her head down into his chest, unable to look up at him for fear of what she might read in his face.

Oh, dear God, what is happening to me? she thought, but a feeling of surrender consumed her. She looked up at Nowell's face, his eyes drawing her in even closer until she could feel his warm breath first on her cheek, and then lightly beside her mouth. She turned away, but the magnetism drew even stronger until her lips brushed his, forcing her to turn once more, then to quickly meet them again, this time kissing him with full, searching desire.

She had never felt anything like this before in her life—something so forbidden, something so divine. It was a kiss that sent charges of untold energy and passion searing through her veins, leaving her physically weakened yet strongly craving more. She couldn't stop, she didn't want to stop, so much so that the shock of Nowell suddenly cutting her off took a moment to settle in.

"Oh, Catherine, what are we doing? I'm so sorry." He gently, but deliberately moved her away, placing his hands on her shoulders and staring into her eyes, watching as her lower lip began to tremble. Embarrassed, she broke away from him, grabbing her glass and then hurrying to the front of the vehicle where she quickly gulped her wine.

Catherine was both bewildered by and afraid of the feelings consuming her. She desperately wanted to be held by Nowell again, even to make love to him. Yet her thoughts, her actions, every fiber of her body, felt heavy with guilt, and she knew it couldn't be.

I love you, Michael, I love you, she kept repeating as though seeking absolution. Catherine took a deep breath, and turned, only to find Nowell right behind her.

"Nowell, please don't apologize to me. It's my fault. I got carried away and I promise it will never happen again."

Nowell stood still, his heart thudding, but with no other hint of expression in his face. It was almost more than he could bear. Holding her, kissing her, was more pleasing than he could have ever imagined. Yet he knew that it wasn't the right time to act on his feelings for her. Catherine was just beginning to awaken to her own feelings for him, and soon—but not yet—she would be absolutely unapologetic about her love for him. He knew that by waiting his patience would be rewarded and he would at last possess this woman.

"Catherine, I understand. I fully understand. It never happened. Please, let's pretend it never happened. You are too valuable as my friend, and assistant, to let something like a silly kiss get in the way."

Catherine let out a deep sigh, his words easing away some of her guilt. *He's right,* she thought, *it was just a silly kiss. And why let something like that get in the way?*

*It will never happen again. I have nothing to be
ashamed of.*

Despite forgiving herself, and attributing the kiss to a
momentary lapse of judgment, she couldn't escape the
warm, heavy feeling dancing inside her. She began to
wonder if Michael, with all his misgivings about Nowell,
wasn't right after all. That he couldn't be trusted. No,
she assured herself, it wasn't Nowell. She blamed herself,
and knew that it was her decision to hug, and then to
kiss him.

"You're right, Nowell. It was just a silly kiss. And I
won't let it get in the way. Here," she said, blithely holding her wineglass out in front of him, "fill 'er up."

Nowell did so, then went about repacking the contents
of the picnic basket, playfully throwing large chunks of
bread and cheese at a delighted Rags.

One day, Catherine thought, sighing, *Nowell will find
the love he so richly deserves.* She finished her wine, then
climbed into the front seat. Drowsy from the alcohol,
she settled in, shut her eyes, and drifted off to sleep,
leaving behind what happened.

Nowell finished packing and managed to get Rags inside, then climbed back into the Range Rover himself,
surprised to find Catherine asleep. There was a flush on
her cheeks—a flush that Nowell attributed partly to the
wine, but mostly to unmet desire.

He smiled to himself as he pulled the vehicle back
onto the main road. *Just wait, my love,* he whispered,
just wait.

Chapter Twenty-four

Catherine woke up as Nowell down shifted the Range Rover to make a turn. She didn't say anything to him at first, taking a moment to collect her thoughts instead and to observe all that was around her. She had never seen such tranquil scenery in all her life; the incredibly rich green landscape accentuated by twilight's soft glow gave the impression of being anything but the dead of winter.

The road they were traveling on was paved, but narrow, winding, and hilly. It coursed past small, dense groves of trees, then wide-open patches of rolling land. As the road inclined, Catherine glanced down to her left below and saw a small, enchanting lake emitting an early-evening fog. She had no idea that they'd already entered Nowell's eighteen-thousand-acre estate. Or that they were driving along the private road that led to a very special place for Nowell.

Nowell hadn't noticed that she was awake, and she made no stirrings to alert him, preferring to soak up her new surroundings. It had been such a confusing day for Catherine, and she wished she could turn back time. She regretted terribly now going into his bedroom and discovering the portrait of Elizabeth. She regretted their conversation and embrace; but most of all, she regretted kissing him. It should have never happened, she continued to tell herself, and felt certain that it never would again. Well, almost certain.

There remained in her stomach the faint twitch of a romantic butterfly. She simply couldn't get rid of it, but felt determined not to allow it flight. There was no denying it, Nowell Stuart was an incredibly handsome and charming man. And there was something about them together—a chemistry that exceeded the bounds of a normal friendship.

She reflected back on the lengthy discussions she and Michael had shared about her relationship with Nowell, and what she should expect to get out of this job—which was supposed to be the money and then the contacts. Though Michael wasn't hung up on making a lot of money, he realized this job provided an opportunity for them to build a nest egg and to start a family on. And he trusted Catherine with all his heart to treat it that way too—as a means to an end. Nothing more, nothing less.

Until today she'd been immune to any romantic feelings for Nowell Stuart. And now here she was, an ocean away from Michael and traveling alone with the subject of her newfound ardor. It was very disturbing, but at the same time fascinating and compelling.

Nowell slowed the Range Rover once more, pulling up in front of closed iron gates that were cemented into a high stone wall on either side of the road. The wall ran on as far as could be seen in both eastern and western directions. Nowell hit a remote control device hidden inside his sun visor, and while the car idled the gates opened, as if by magic. Driving slowly through them, he parked at a quaint chapel just beyond. Never bothering to look at Catherine, he climbed out of the vehicle, then disappeared through the wooden gate of another high stone wall. At first she thought he might have stopped to relieve himself, but he was gone much too long for that. Catherine, curious as to where they were, opened the door and wandered to the open gate, gasping slightly at the sight of an ancient graveyard and of Nowell kneeling between two headstones while gently brushing away some debris. He rose slowly, wiping off his kneecaps, then lovingly touched one headstone while more tentatively stroking the other.

Catherine moved quietly beside him. Though it had grown considerably darker outside, she could clearly see the markings on the tombstones: Lady Cornelia Howard Stuart read one; Sir Gerald Arthur Stuart the other; the names of Nowell's late parents. The dates and years of their birthdates, and the times of their deaths—the same for each—was also etched into the stone. Several other

Stuarts were buried there too, some having died in the 1700s.

Catherine simply couldn't bear it. In conversations with Nowell, his parents had seemed nothing more than phantom figures. But now, immediately before her, the physical evidence of their deaths made them quite real. An eeriness crept over her, and while she felt anxious to leave the graveyard, she didn't want to be alone either, and so remained.

Nowell turned and unexpectedly found Catherine standing there, looking both bewildered and awestruck. His face hardened, and the hot, angry look in his eyes frightened and unnerved her even more. Catherine gasped, not knowing what to say as Nowell whisked past her on his way to the Range Rover, leaving her alone in the dark, almost claustrophobic burial site.

She had never seen him behave in such a manner, and wondered what she should do, what she should say. Instinctively she followed him back to the car, but in silence, climbing into the passenger seat and staring straight ahead, afraid even to look at him.

Nowell started the car and began driving in silence along the winding road. It was now completely dark outside, making it difficult to see much of the landscape, and further cementing the strange and frightful feelings Catherine had. She dared not utter a word, Nowell's mood was that somber, until he finally mumbled something under his breath.

"I'm sorry, I couldn't hear you," said Catherine, grateful for a chance at conversation.

"It shouldn't have happened," he said angrily. Catherine was incredulous. He claimed to be over Elizabeth's death, and was prepared to move on. But with his parents it seemed like a completely different story. She began to wonder how she would feel if her parents and Michael were all killed together. The very thought of it frightened her all the more, and she quickly sought to think of something more cheerful. But she couldn't.

"Is Elizabeth buried there as well?"

"No," he answered shortly, offering no other information.

"I'm sorry," she said softly.

"For what?" he snapped back.

Catherine took a deep breath. He was really edgy, and she honestly didn't know what she was dealing with, having never seen him behave even remotely like this before. But she decided to try a little sympathy.

"Nowell, I cannot imagine what you must have gone through."

He said nothing, his eyes staring icily ahead, his hands tightly gripping the wheel. Catherine said nothing either, deciding there was nothing more to offer. Finally Nowell took a deep breath.

"You know, I miss them terribly. You would have loved them. For that matter," he continued, his voice softening up, "they would have loved you too."

"Thank you, Nowell. That's really nice of you to say that."

"I mean it."

"Well, I'm sure they must have been very fond of Elizabeth."

He did not acknowledge her remark. Instead he changed the subject and mood, returning back to the old chatty and witty Nowell.

"Well, you must have figured out by now where we are."

"Rags," she said jokingly to the slumbering animal, "I don't think we're in Kansas anymore."

"There's no place like home," Nowell chanted, "there's no place like home." He turned and smiled at her, all traces of his anger having suddenly vanished.

"Well, now where exactly did you grow up?" asked Catherine, eager to engage him in more lighthearted conversation. "Do you consider London to be your hometown? Or is this really home for you?"

"Indeed, this is home. We spent all of our holidays and summer vacations here. And while I was at public school and university, I used to come here for study breaks. My father and I loved to go hunting and fishing. Mum too. In fact, if you look just over that clearing to your left—that's the spot where I bagged my first deer. I was just a lad of thirteen!" he said proudly.

"Nowell, you killed Bambi?"

"Oh, don't be silly. The place is infested with deer. We have to shoot them or they'll absolutely take over the grounds. They are rather prodigious procreators."

"How big is this place?"

"Eighteen thousand acres, give or take a few. It used to be much larger. But my father sold off part of the land when he wanted to retool Sutthington Mills. It paid off quite handsomely, and he was able to double production at the plant without borrowing a cent to do so."

Now she knew where Nowell acquired his business acumen. She could only imagine what his father must have been like—unflinching and highly successful in business, but a man with a big heart where his family was concerned.

"Nowell, I just want to know one thing," Catherine began playfully, feeling much more at ease.

"Yes?"

"Who cuts the grass?"

"Certainly not I," Nowell said, laughing. "I wouldn't know a hedge clipper from a rake."

Catherine laughed with him, but just moments later her mirth turned to shock as she caught her first glimpse of Stuart Hall—a truly spectacular sight, breathtaking in its proportions and grandeur. There, awash in soft floodlight, was a massive, Gothic revival home that was more impressive, stately, and downright regal than anything she'd ever seen

"Home, sweet home," said Nowell with all sincerity. "God, I love coming back to this place. You shall not be disappointed with your visit, my dear."

And that was precisely what had Catherine concerned.

Chapter Twenty-five

Nowell slowly turned the Range Rover into a wide, circular driveway bordered by neatly trimmed boxwoods, then parked beside a beautiful fountain featuring three bronze figures—a chubby cherub along with a life-sized maiden clinging longingly to a warrior charged for battle. Water sprayed from the top of his helmeted head and into an illuminated, shallow pool filled with dormant lily pads.

Catherine amused herself wondering how many years the warrior had been fixed in place—unable to charge off into the battle he so longed to fight, and how long that woman had suffered at his feet, ignoring the anxious angel. Momentarily absorbed in the fantasy, Catherine barely heard Nowell.

"Like I said," he repeated, "there's no place like home."

Catherine let out a guttural laugh. "Do you suppose that's what she's trying to tell him?"

"If so, he might be well advised to listen. Rumor has it that Sir Arthur Stuart, who built this place and after whom that fountain was supposedly fashioned, can be seen and heard wandering the halls at the most peculiar times, letting out a plaintive wail as he trudges along. Which is apparently the last thing anyone heard from him while he was alive." He paused to see if Catherine appeared frightened by news of such hauntings. She raised a cynical eyebrow in response.

"Anyway, legend has it that he plunged a dagger into his own heart after returning here from war and discovering that his beloved had left him for another man. Apparently she begged him not to go, but he ignored her. This fountain was supposedly erected in his honor—some honor," he added sarcastically, and then even more spitefully: "Typical woman. Wants it, and usually gets it, both ways."

Catherine faced him, her mouth curling up with reproach. "Why do you say that?" she asked defensively, but her stomach clutched. Until today she'd never fully understood the nature of an affair—how people could get trapped into wanting it both ways.

"Trust me, I know," Nowell snarled back with no trace of humor, displaying a perplexing moodiness that Catherine had never witnessed until today. She found it repulsive at the same time alluring—as though she were the only one capable of bringing him out of it.

"Well, enough of this," he said, glancing out the window and nodding pleasantly at a servant just outside the car. "Shall we?"

"Indeed," Catherine answered lightly, but the hidden context of his comment weighed on her heavily, as she believed he was being critical of her. She wished she could take back the afternoon entirely, now regretting terribly their kiss. She sighed in deep frustration, however, as the memory of that embrace remained addictively sweet and fresh.

The male servant, a stern, middle-aged man with tight lips and large forward-tilting ears, opened Catherine's door. Instantly Rags came bounding out of the backseat, and then with considerable agility bounced off Catherine's lap and out the door, nearly knocking the poor man over.

"Good God," the servant muttered as the dog charged past him and up wide, elegant steps toward an unusually large set of front doors. Fortunately the doors were open prompting two domestics to part like synchronized swimmers for the sake of Rags. The dog disappeared, but within seconds returned with an equally impressive companion. The two beasts barked loudly and playfully at each other, then took off in a wild gallop toward the rear of the house. Their antics provided just the comic relief necessary to dissolve the residual tension between Catherine and Nowell, as they both broke out into easy laughter.

"That's Muffin, by the way," remarked Nowell.

"Oh, give me a break," cracked up Catherine. "Rags and Muffin?"

"Don't insult my mother that way. She named them and, I might add, thought them a rather charming duo. Incidentally, Catherine, I'd like you to meet Lawrence. Lawrence, this is Mrs. Catherine Harrison, my assistant in the United States."

"Pleased to meet you," he said, still holding the door while waiting for Catherine to alight. Catherine slid out of the car and was escorted by Lawrence to the front door, where he released her to the attention of the two waiting servants.

"Goo' evening, ma'am," they sounded in unison.

"Good evening," Catherine responded, her tone so serious and self-important she barely recognized her own voice. Her growing pretentiousness was suddenly cut short, however, as she muffled an exclamation at the view inside. While the frescoed ceiling soared to a lofty height, the floors were paved with glistening marble. About twenty feet ahead of the threshold was a double-wide staircase leading to an oversized, ornate landing from which two additional flights of stairs headed east and west. Immediately to her right and left were long, wide hallways filled with various ancestral furnishings and multiple fireplaces. *So this is home, sweet home,* she thought, laughing to herself.

"Should it please, dinner will be served at half past seven, sir. Will you be dining in your usual place?" she suddenly heard Lawrence ask. Catherine turned around to find Nowell quietly staring at her, a bemused look on his handsome face.

"No, I think tonight we'll actually eat in the banquet hall," Nowell said, then addressing Catherine he continued, "I frequently dine in my study. Plenty of time for that, but tonight I'd like you to get a real taste of this place. It's rather cozy, wouldn't you agree?" He winked at her. Catherine laughed, then curtsied. Nowell said nothing about her gesture, but his eyes twinkled at her irreverence.

"Delilah here, more affectionately known as Dee, will escort you to your room, and Conrad, otherwise known as Mr. Dee," he added with another wink, "will bring your bags. Can you think of anything you need right away?"

"A map and a compass," she joked.

"Just don't lose sight of Dee here. That should be direction enough."

Catherine glanced down at her watch, which read six thirty-five. "Nowell, may I have a word with you please?"

"Of course." He nodded, then strode a few paces away with her, gently placing a hand on her shoulder while bending down to listen to her whisper.

"I have to apologize," she began earnestly. "But I'm not sure I know what the appropriate attire for dinner might be, especially since I left my tiara in New York."

"Oh, how could you," he wisecracked. "Actually, I suggest that you wear whatever you want. I for one plan to do something I've never done before: I'm going to have dinner in the most elegant room in the house, with one of the most elegant women I know, drinking some of the most divine wine known to mankind—in my new pair of jeans. Now, if you'd like to join me as such, I'd be delighted. Otherwise, I'm sure we have a spare tiara here somewhere."

Catherine rolled her eyes, then playfully whacked his arm. "You really do know how to exasperate me," she said under heavy breath, "and worst of all, I think you enjoy it."

"Hmmm, it is becoming something of a habit with me, isn't it? Oh, well, carry on. I shall see you in . . ." He paused to glance at his watch, but Catherine beat him to it.

"Fifty-three minutes and forty-eight seconds."

"Now who's exasperating whom?" he piqued.

She turned away from him, grateful that things seemed back to normal between them, and headed up the stairs with Dee and Conrad close behind.

"You know," said Catherine, pausing on the landing, then smiling at the pair, "I haven't the vaguest idea where I'm going."

"Of course, of course," they agreed in cheerful unison, then moved ahead escorting her down a vast hallway with dozens of floor-to-ceiling windows facing out front. Several hearty fires popped and burned in numerous fireplaces along the way, exuding a cozy charm despite the cavernous dimensions. Finally Dee opened a door and invited Catherine to enter, which she did only to stop again with awestruck wonder. The walls were covered in a rich, honey-colored paneling, heavy with molded detail, including a wood-carved floral garland rising above the marble-faced fireplace. But most exciting to Catherine was the massive canopied bed. It was nearly as high as the room, enclosed by a thickly padded tester around the top and heavy, red silken drapes falling from each post. It was truly fit for a queen, she thought.

Conrad placed her belongings near an antique Chinese armoire, as Dee pointed out with her pudgy, yet delicate hand the intercom system and other modern amenities at Catherine's disposal.

"Just buzz us, anytime, for whatever you might want," she offered in her thick Irish brogue. "And Connie here will be happy to get it for you," she jested, prompting a low, but good-natured groan from her husband.

Catherine laughed. "Actually, I can't imagine I'd need much. But it's comforting to know someone's there—especially if Sir Arthur Stuart decides to pay a late-night visit!"

Dee, naturally superstitious, shuddered aloud. "He better bloody well mind his own business!"

Her remark prompted a playful snort from Connie. "Dee, I imagine the poor bloke is more scared of you, knowing what a chatterbox you are!"

Dee shot him a dirty look that made Catherine laugh. "So there really is a ghost?"

"Oh, a number of them," answered Dee emphatically.

"Not a one," Connie quickly dismissed her. "Come on, Dee," he said, "the poor girl doesn't need you scaring the bejesus outta her." Connie, a heavyset Irish man with pasty skin and thick white hair, started toward the door.

Dee frowned at his back, then looked at Catherine. "Really, Mrs. Harrison, if you should need anything, anything at all, don't hesitate to let us know."

"Thank you," said Catherine, truly charmed by the pair. They were just about gone when it occurred to Catherine she didn't know how to find Nowell.

"Oh, please, wait," Catherine quickly spoke. Dee turned, her face creasing into a gentle smile.

"I almost forgot. Where's the banquet hall?"

Dee eagerly provided directions—but some rather

confusing ones, all peppered with suggestions as to which pieces of art Catherine might observe along the way.

"Go back the way you came, turn left at the entrance hall, third door on your left," Connie interjected over his wife's shoulder, his gray eyes narrowing under profusely bushy eyebrows. "I'm sorry, Mrs. Harrison. But if it were left up to Dee you'd be scared *and* lost!"

"Thanks for your help, Connie." Catherine cast him an appreciative grin, then looked at her watch. With any luck she could freshen up, be in the banquet hall at the appointed time, and still have time to look at some of the artwork.

After discovering what appeared to be a ballroom, a billiard room, and even a small family chapel, Catherine finally made her way into the banquet hall—with only seconds to spare.

The room seemed the size of an airplane hangar, and at the center of it sat a magnificatly long table surrounded by at least forty chairs. Oddly, there were two place settings—one at each end of the table. And even more strange, especially considering his penchant for timeliness, there was no Nowell.

Catherine stood in the foyer of the room, eagerly absorbing it all. The architecture, with its gray limestone walls and flagstone floor, could rival a Gothic church in scope and detail. But what distinguished it most were three side-by-side fireplaces; each large enough, it seemed, in which to park the Range Rover. Three finely crafted tapestries, each one telling its own story, hung over the fireplaces. The room was lit exclusively by candles and firelight, giving a warm, romantic feeling to the otherwise drafty hall.

I wonder where he is? she thought of Nowell as she glanced at her watch, then decided to warm herself by the fireplaces while waiting. She started moving slowly into the room when a shadow suddenly and ominously loomed before her, causing her to freeze.

"BOO!" shouted Nowell, jumping directly into her path. Catherine's astonishment and genuine fear did not disappoint him, and he let out an impish laugh.

"I say, you look like you've just seen a ghost!"

"Close to it, since I could just about kill you," she whispered through rattled nerves.

"Oh, how lovely. Murder as a first course."

Catherine let out a long, exasperated sigh. *I am not in the mood for this,* she thought, now remaining silent.

"Oh, good God, must I retrieve a tiara *and* a sense of humor for you?"

"I don't think it's funny," she said, wondering what prompted him to pull this antic, as childish, she thought, as allowing Rags to slobber all over her in bed that morning.

"I'm sorry," he quickly offered, now sensing her frustration. "I thought you'd be amused. Shall we?" He gestured politely toward the table.

"Nowell," Catherine said, looking straight ahead at the table. "I thought you said we'd be dining together."

"Oh, but we are. You must try it this way at least once. It's a rather comical setup and besides, I'll move into your zip code for dessert."

Catherine remained quiet and fixed while gathering her thoughts. She could not recount being more confused about a man or his behavior. She took a deep breath as she pondered it, believing it was his vulnerability more than anything else. He'd opened up a lot with her these past few days, probably more so than with any other woman in a long time. And she suddenly found herself feeling somewhat sorry for him—as though his erratic behavior signaled his need to protect himself from ever being hurt again.

"Nowell," she finally responded, softly touching his arm and then directly meeting his eyes that cast a sweet and curious expression. "I do think it's kind of funny. And perhaps some other time. But you know what? I would really prefer to sit at your end of the table. We've had a long day, a lot has happened, and I'd just like to conclude it in a more civilized manner."

He looked downward. "Of course," he said contritely, "where was my head?"

He smiled appreciatively while taking her hand, then like a gentleman escorted her to the far end of the table, pulling out her seat, then waiting for her to get settled before sitting himself. Within moments, a servant appeared and formally presented a bottle of wine to Nowell.

"Thank you, Stephen," he said, examining the bottle's label. "Just what I wanted."

Stephen uncorked the bottle, then poured a measured amount in Nowell's wineglass. Nowell promptly held up a napkin behind the glass to observe the wine's rich red color, then made a rather loud slurping noise as he tasted it. He did not swallow. Instead, he allowed the wine to linger on his palate while assessing its bouquet. Catherine had witnessed Michael do a similar routine, but there was something far more theatrical, even ritualistic, about Nowell's method.

His eyes closed, his head tilted slightly back, he finally swallowed, then let out a long, satisfied sigh. "Chateau d'Issan, 1961, one of the finest clarets I've ever tasted." Opening his eyes, then holding out his glass for Stephen to fill, he thanked the man, then asked him to make haste fetching Mrs. Harrison's place setting. Stephen quickly and quietly obliged.

Nowell artfully poured Catherine a glass of the wine, while Stephen disappeared through an arched hallway. She picked up her glass, eager for a taste of wine that was older than she, but was stopped by Nowell's proposition of a toast.

"First, I must say it is a privilege to be dining with a friend I consider to be as unique and splendid as this bottle of wine." He leaned into his glass, closed his eyes, then inhaled deeply. "A rich blend of fantastic flavors, soothing, and"—he paused, casting a devilish look at her—"simply irresistible."

Catherine blushed. Normally she would have dismissed such remarks from him as silly, but the double entendre was too strong. His signals were mixed, and she felt certain now that his current behavior stemmed from similarly confused feelings about their relationship. She clinked her glass against his, then took a long sip of the wine, which did not disappoint. But she was at a loss for words. The sensible thing, she thought, would be for them to each address their true feelings, then nip this growing attraction in the bud. After all, Nowell was her employer, and she needed her job as much as she presently desired him.

"What are you thinking?" Nowell asked, his blue eyes suddenly piercing. He placed his wineglass down at the same time reaching for his silver cigarette case.

Catherine chuckled. "You want to know the truth?"

"By all means," he said, placing a cigarette between his teeth and lighting it from a brightly burning flame on the candelabra. He took a deep drag, pushed his chair back, and casually crossed his legs before finally exhaling. Still clad in his jeans and now a heavy fisherman's sweater, his thick mop of dark hair somewhat disheveled, Catherine thought he looked downright adorable.

"I wish you would put that damned cigarette out."

Nowell took another drag before breaking into a throaty smoker's laugh. "You can't be serious?"

"Darned right I am. I hate to see you smoking."

"And why the sudden concern for my health? After all, I thought your father was the tobacco king," he said, taking yet another drag, smiling with satisfaction as he did. She didn't immediately answer. "Out with it," he said in his amiable yet cocky way. "Why the sudden concern?"

"It's not so sudden," she replied calmly but defensively. "I've never liked your smoking. And I'd appreciate your leaving my father out of this."

"Oh, God, women! One kiss and they think they own you!"

His comment provided a perfect opportunity for Catherine to openly address her feelings; to call it quits in their emotional and physical tug-of-war. Yet for reasons beyond her, she couldn't do it.

"Did you ever think that maybe your kiss tasted like an ashtray to me?"

"Oh, and did it now? If it was so vile, as you imply, then why do I recall you seemed to enjoy the taste?"

Their banter was interrupted by Stephen, carrying two dishes each of lobster, turbot, and scallops with a light caviar sauce.

"Shall I bring you the bottle of Semillon, sir?"

"Excellent, Stephen, that would be excellent. We'll save this delightful d'Issan for the lamb. Is that all right with you, Catherine?" She looked at him blankly.

"That will be just fine, Stephen," he said.

"We'll save the d'Issan for the lamb? I thought this

was the main course," she said with a laugh after Stephen left.

"You've a lot to learn about the manor-born."

"That's insulting!"

"Insult you? After you just said kissing me evoked the taste of an ashtray? To show my undying"—he cleared his throat while searching for the appropriate words—"devotion to your politically correct cause, I hereby, this minute, consider myself a nonsmoker. And to prove that I am sincere, I am willing to commit what I would otherwise consider heresy." With that he dropped his burning cigarette right into his glass of vintage wine, producing a loud hiss followed by a suspenseful silence.

"I'm finding it rather hard to believe I did that," he finally said with an astonished look.

"Me too," she said with equal incredulity, and they both cracked up.

The rest of the meal was lighthearted fun, the food delicious, and the remaining wine divine. On one occasion Nowell nervously fingered his cigarette case, then asked Stephen to take it away altogether and bring them dessert.

"I trust," Nowell said smugly, "that you will find the crème brûlée a bit more tasty than one of my kisses."

"Don't be so sure of yourself," she easily flirted back.

"Oh, I see. And now that I've been a nonsmoker"—he looked at his watch—"for the past forty-three minutes, I have a chance of being compared to a sweet and pleasurable dessert as opposed to an offensive ashtray."

"You're putting words in my mouth," Catherine snapped good-naturedly.

"I wouldn't think of it," he said, leaning in toward her. Their eyes locked, and as they did the magnetism they'd both struggled hard to resist drew them in closer and closer until his lips brushed hers ever so tenderly. Catherine shut her eyes.

"I'd say better than the crème brûlée," she whispered, her lips still touching his.

Nowell leaned in even closer, this time placing a kiss full of intention. Catherine tried momentarily to resist, then tentatively kissed him back. His kiss was divine, and she felt weakened by passion at the same time her

body welled with strong desire. Impulsively she drew
herself closer toward him, then stopped, tempering herself by softly stroking his cheek instead of kissing him
again. With his eyes closed, and his mouth curling into
a contented smile, he gently removed her hand from his
cheek and brought it to his mouth, playfully kissing and
sucking her fingertips.

Without constraint, Catherine rose out of her seat and
into his arms, her heart in a frenzy and her mind in a
whirl. And without apology Nowell embraced her, eagerly wrapping his arms around her—this time with no
intention of letting go—all the while distributing sweet
kisses to her forehead, then to her cheeks, followed by
a strong, searching kiss to her mouth.

Her response was equally passionate, as she molded
her body into his and longingly kissed him back. They
were each so racked with desire and both so lost in the
moment that neither of them noticed the young servant
who had entered the room to serve dessert. He stopped
abruptly at the sight before him, unable to control the
dishes that went skidding off his tray. It was only the
resounding crash that caused the new lovers to notice
him and separate. Catherine quickly sat down in her
seat, unable to look at the young man who'd begun
scooping up the spilled contents. Stephen came dashing
up and quietly began assisting him. She felt deeply
pinched by embarrassment and fear at having been
caught. As for Nowell, he was simply infuriated.

"Stephen," Nowell said authoritatively while still
standing. "May I have a word with you, please."

Stephen glanced up and seeing the stern look in Nowell's face dismissed the other servant, then approached
Nowell. Catherine could not bear to look at either of
them.

"I don't believe I know that young man. Is he new?"
Nowell said calmly.

"Yes, sir."

"Good, then he won't regret so terribly losing his
job."

"Sir?"

"I want him gone, Stephen."

"But, sir, if I may, he's my nephew. And I'm certain
that . . ."

Nowell sharply cut him off. "I don't suppose I've made myself clear."

The implied threat that he would lose his job as well was enough for Stephen to nervously shake his head yes.

The abrupt shift in mood and atmosphere now became completely unnerving to Catherine. Just moments before she'd felt such passion, but now she felt the weight of his threat to Stephen and the sudden dismissal of his nephew almost as if they'd been directed at her.

"If you'll excuse me," she said, rising out of her chair, "I'm exhausted and I need to go to bed."

Nowell let out a short, cynical laugh, and Stephen, grateful for the interruption, left them alone. She pushed in her chair and was about halfway out the room when Nowell finally spoke.

"Catherine, please come back. You're making a mistake."

She stopped but didn't turn.

"I'm sorry," he said, "but you don't understand."

"No, I don't," she said, finally facing him.

"Please, sit down."

She reluctantly and stiffly returned, then sat back down.

"You see," he began to reach for her hand but she backed away. He let out an exasperated sigh, then continued in a more businesslike manner.

"It is not uncommon for my overseer to hire the inexperienced relatives of other staff members. Occasionally it is met with success, but I usually find that incidents such as the one that just happened are the norm with such whelps. I do not pay such handsome salaries," he said, casting one of his piercing looks, "for the hand of inexperience to ruin what I would have otherwise considered a perfect meal."

Catherine knew this had far more to do with the young man's poor timing than over spilled dessert. She somewhat understood Nowell's rash behavior, as she couldn't help but feel a bit angry with the young man's indiscretion and over being caught in Nowell's arms.

"Do you understand?" he asked, desperate to put things back on track with her.

"Yes. No. I mean, I don't know. It's not Stephen, or his nephew, really," she stammered, then let out a long nervous sigh. "It's me. It's us. I don't know what's happening here. I feel like . . ."

"Like what?" he asked, tenderly picking up her hand and then gently kissing it. This time she didn't resist.

"Like . . . almost like"—she let out another sigh—"almost like I'm falling in love with you."

Nowell closed his eyes, unable to believe what he'd just heard. "Is there anything so wrong with that?" he asked.

"Nowell, what is happening here?" she whispered. "I'm married. I love my husband. We haven't been married for even two years. But there's something about you, something about us." She cast her eyes downward. "I adore you."

"Oh, Catherine, Catherine," he whispered. "You have no idea," he began, then stopped.

"Idea of what?"

"Could it be?" he began vaguely, though there was a calculating look in his eyes. Catherine studied his handsome face in the soft candlelight, and felt an overwhelming need to stroke it again, but instead kept to herself.

"Could what be, Nowell. What are you talking about?"

Nowell knew he was at a dangerous crossroad. That if he divulged too much of his feelings it might scare her away; giving her the justification she needed to run back to Michael and never lay eyes on himself again. And that if he didn't give her enough, she might well do the same.

"What is it?" she became more demanding.

"Catherine. Perhaps we've been spending too much time together." She felt a nervous lump slide down her throat, as though she were now afraid of being rejected by him. It was so confusing to her—she wanted to escape this budding romance, at the same time she couldn't stand the thought of being denied by him.

"Then again," he continued, observing her saddened doe eyes, "maybe we need to spend more time together. I don't know. I don't know any better than you what is going on. All I know is that I have strong feelings for you too."

He paused, took a long sip of his wine, then poured his glass full again. "But I also would never want to do anything that would hurt you, or Michael, in any way. I believe in the sanctity of marriage with all my heart. But I also know something else my heart is trying to tell me—that there is something extraordinarily special about you. And that I feel like I come alive when I'm with you. It's that simple. It's that complicated."

Catherine sighed with relief when she realized he wasn't rejecting her. She also leaned back in her richly upholstered chair, but offered no response. In her wildest imagination, this was something she would have never expected to happen to her. The loving wife of a devoted Christian, she'd foolishly thought, was immune to this type of dilemma. She tried to be rational.

"Nowell, this must be common for two people who work closely like us. They witness each other's strengths all day long, they work as an effective team and come to appreciate each other that way, and naturally a fondness develops. But I believe in fate, and that if we were meant to be together, you know what I mean—really together—than we would have been.

"You've been through a lot, losing your family and all," she continued. "And I'm sincerely flattered that I bring something positive out in you. But perhaps you're only allowing yourself to feel that way with me because I'm safe. I'm married, and I'm easily accessible to you. But I'm sure there is someone out there who is the perfect person for you; someone who will make you immeasurably happy."

Catherine swallowed hard after sharing her thoughts. There was a selfish part of her wishing that she were the perfect person she'd just projected on him. That she could be the one to bring him that immeasurable happiness.

Nowell quietly absorbed all that she said, offering no hint of expression in his face. He was impressed with her articulate comments, but he knew they were not her true feelings. He believed Catherine was only logical to a degree, acting more often on emotion and impulse, and he simply could not resist the temptation to play with her emotions.

"I suppose you're right. You usually are, you know. That's one of the things I truly appreciate about you— your levelheadedness. It has been a rough couple of years for me, and I've isolated myself from some truly wonderful women. I must admit, perhaps I've misdirected my energies only because with you, as you say, I feel safe. And again, you're right. There is probably someone out there right now whom I am destined to meet and marry. I suppose I shall make it my new New Year's resolution to put myself out there and find her. And please, please accept my apologies. I didn't mean for anything to get out of hand between us. Let's forget anything ever happened. Deal?"

Catherine reluctantly shook her head yes, feeling the lump in her throat become an unexpected ache in her gut. As soon as it started it was over. Could it go on between them as it had before this day—as employer and employee—nothing more, nothing less? She suddenly felt herself missing him, missing what could have been.

"Deal," she said, offering her hand to shake. She wanted him to hold it, to kiss it once more, realizing that the matter of romance between them might be resolved, but that the matter of chemistry would not.

Nowell arose. "Well," he said to her, "if what I hear of the weather tomorrow is true, then I'd like to suggest we begin the morning with a ride. How does that suit you?"

"In the car?" she bantered.

"Oh, dear, some things never change. No," he said, smirking fiendishly. "On one of your dear friend Dubs Willis's ponies."

"Sounds good to me. What time?"

"Oh, say nine a.m. Now, shall I have someone escort you to your room?"

"No, no," she said self-consciously. "I'll manage."

"Good night, then," he said, then suddenly walked out of the room leaving Catherine behind feeling bewildered and lonely. She couldn't believe that Nowell would just walk out on her like that. How he could have moved from such a passionate embrace to a detached departure in such a short period of time. She started to sulk, feeling choked up on pride. It was over, and just as well.

Why then did her heart soar with the possibilities of what might come tomorrow during another day alone with Nowell Stuart?

Chapter Twenty-six

Catherine shut the guest-room door, grateful for the privacy and a chance to sort out her feelings alone. *This is a crush,* she told herself. *What I'm feeling for Nowell is nothing more than a crush. It will go away.*

If only it were that easy. She'd been infatuated with other men, but that was before she'd met Michael. Catherine had naively believed that marriage would make her immune to such feelings for anyone other than her husband. It was especially frustrating to her that something like this should occur so early in her marriage. It made her wonder if Michael had developed similar feelings for other women, and if so, how he'd handled it. Michael would never be untrue. It was just the way he was, and one of the reasons she'd married him—she trusted him absolutely.

But now feeling so utterly helpless about Nowell, she knew she wasn't as strong. Catherine always thought he was attractive, but until today had felt no romantic interest in him. Now she couldn't get him off her mind. Just the thought of his cologne, even the smell of stale cigarettes, aroused her, a feeling intensified by the memory of their last kiss. He was a remarkably good kisser, and she could only imagine what kind of lover he was. Every part of her body now ached with desire.

She slipped out of her clothes and into a bathrobe, preparing to go to bed. But her nerves were near shot. She decided to get a glass of wine to calm herself and buzzed Dee on the intercom.

"Ma'am?" Dee queried.

"Dee, if it's not asking too much, could you please bring me a glass of wine?"

"Would you prefer red or white?"

Catherine could drink rot-gut moonshine at the moment. "Either one, whatever's available."

"Be right up."

"Thanks."

Catherine sat down and gazed at the crackling fire. She wondered what would happen if she did make love with Nowell just to get it out of her system.

Who would know? she asked herself, but knew she could never face Michael again if such a thing happened. And then what she believed to be unthinkable entered her mind—*What would it be like if I were Nowell's wife? For chrissakes,* she immediately chastised herself, *this is insane, absolutely insane.*

But she couldn't help herself. She imagined living as a privileged member of English society. She pictured the wild fun she and Nowell could have traipsing around the world together. She thought of the children she yearned for, and of Nowell as the father. When Dee finally knocked on the door her daydreams were spinning madly out of control.

"Come in," she shouted across the room, her eyes still fixed on the burning fire. Catherine listened as Dee crossed the room and placed a glass on the table beside her.

"Will there be anything else, ma'am?"

Catherine jolted at the sound of Nowell's voice.

"My God," she exclaimed with a laugh, "you scared the hell out of me!"

"So sorry," he said, laughing. "Mind if I join you?"

"No, not at all. How did you know I wanted a glass of wine?"

"I was in the kitchen catching up with some of the crew when you buzzed. I thought you might be able to help me with this bottle I just opened."

Catherine assumed it must be another fabulous selection from his vintage collection. She picked up the glass of red wine he'd placed on the table beside her and took a sip—the taste did not disappoint. Remembering she had nothing on under her robe, Catherine self-consciously gathered it a little closer around herself.

"What is it?" she asked.

"Guess?"

"Nowell, I'm no good at this. You have to educate me."

"I'm sorry I left so abruptly after dinner," he said, failing to answer her question about the wine. "I'm usually never that rude to my dinner guests."

"Usually?" she said with a laugh.

"Oh, you know. There's the occasional guest who drinks too much, then becomes rather boorish. Mostly I endure their company, but sometimes I simply get fed up and head to my study."

She laughed again. "Did it seem to you as if I'd had too much to drink tonight?"

"No, heavens no. In fact, I hope you thoroughly enjoyed the wine. They were two excellent bottles. This one is good, but not nearly as valuable as the others."

"Hmmm," she said, taking another sip, "I wouldn't know. They all taste good to me."

She felt embarrassed, wondering if somehow he could sense the thoughts running through her mind. But now, with him near, the fantasies only began to intensify. She imagined standing before him while opening her robe—allowing him to caress her body and then making love to him. Catherine glanced at Nowell whose bright blue eyes were fixed on her. Her cheeks flushed and she pulled her robe tighter yet, then took another sip of her wine.

"Dinner was delicious," she said.

"I'm glad you liked it. Chauncey, the cook, he was quite a find. He's a Brit, but he trained in San Francisco, can you believe that?" he said, as though it were impossible someone so talented would have learned his trade in the States.

"You've been bashing America a lot today, you know."

Nowell laughed. "I suppose you're right. Funny, I don't have a thing against Americans, either. Especially against you." He reached over and gently stroked her soft blond hair away from her face, tucking it behind her ear. Catherine felt as if she could burst, but didn't respond.

"Listen," he said, "I know what we said over dinner." He was now stroking her cheek. "But do you really believe it?"

Catherine closed her eyes, and let out a sigh, as though somehow that might make him stop. He moved his hand under her chin, then began stroking there, his touch soft yet electric. She began to feel her inhibitions slip away, uncertain whether it was the alcohol or Nowell's affectionate caresses. Perhaps to get away from him, perhaps not—she wasn't even sure—Catherine slowly rose out of her seat. Nowell arose too, only he moved in closer, then kissed her earlobe. "Do you really believe what you said? That fate did not mean for us to be together?"

Catherine didn't know what to believe at the moment. Her sexual desire for him was burning hot and fantasies of them together continued reeling through her mind. She felt close to surrender; it would be so easy to make love to him; it would be so fabulous, she thought, right there in front of the fireplace. No one would ever have to know.

And then in a blinding flash of reality, she caught herself. *What the hell am I doing? I would know. And I would not be able to live with myself or ever face Michael. And it is he I truly love.*

"Stop, Nowell, stop," Catherine said, feeling ashamed she'd allowed him to get this close again. Nowell plopped down in the chair, letting out an exasperated sigh. He bit his lower lip, trying to refrain from telling her to stop acting like a child.

"Nowell, I'm so sorry," she lamented. "This is the worst thing that has ever happened to me."

"Oh, come now," he said sarcastically.

"I'm so sorry," she repeated, oblivious to his cynicism. "This is driving me crazy, I don't know what's gotten into me where you're concerned."

Nowell was nearly mad with his own unmet physical urge. "Catherine, why the sudden crisis of conscience? Don't you think you want me too?"

She picked up her glass of wine and took a sip, her hands trembling as she did. "Nowell, I love Michael."

"Oh? And do you know that you love him, or do you only suppose that you do?"

"Nowell, don't do this to me. Of course I love him." She swallowed more wine, then suddenly became choked up on tears. "There's only one thing for me to do." The fire illuminated her saddened face and watery eyes. She was clearly distraught.

"And what is that?"

She sat silently for several moments, thinking what it would mean to stop working for him. She needed the money and until today had thoroughly enjoyed the job. She would have never guessed there could be an emotional entanglement between them that would make working for him impossible. Then in a barely audible whisper, she finally spoke. "I have to leave. I have to go home to Michael and then find another job."

Nowell realized that her emotions had reached a critical point, and that he must act carefully. There was no way he was going to lose her now.

"Oh, dear God, Catherine," he said, slumping woefully in his chair, trying to gain her sympathy. "This is dreadful. Look what I've done."

But instead of treating him with softheartedness, she became even more detached. Looking up at the ceiling, then rubbing a hand over her forehead and on through her hair, she started to say something, then stopped.

"Catherine, what is it?"

She finally looked at him with a mixture of sadness and resolution.

"Nowell, please don't blame yourself for anything. I hold myself fully responsible for what has happened between us. It was . . ." She paused, trying to gain enough nerve to reveal her honest thoughts. "I think what happened is that I feel sorry for you. After I saw the portrait of Elizabeth, and realizing what a tremendous loss you've suffered, I just, well, I just allowed myself to become too wrapped up in my emotions, somehow believing I could make you happy. But you deserve so much more than this. You deserve someone who can give entirely of themselves to you, to build a new life with." Catherine cast her eyes downward. "I feel like I've taken advantage of your tragedy." She paused again, still looking down at her feet. "The hard part is," she continued in a soft whisper, "is that despite it all, I find you to be a very attractive man."

Nowell slumped even farther in his chair, this time out of genuine chagrin, realizing that his schemes to draw her in had worked—only too well. Elizabeth's death was

the best thing that ever happened to him when it came
to scoring with women. Even married women. The difference was that with Catherine, unlike the others, he
truly wanted her.

"Catherine, I must confess something to you. This has
never happened to me before either. I have worked with
countless women, some who were quite beautiful like
yourself. But nothing ever became of it. I was quite capable of controlling myself, and would never have
thought to cheat on my late wife." He stood up and
thrust his hands in the back pockets of his new jeans,
then began pacing in front of the fireplace.

"But for some reason, with you it's different. I feel
something for you that I've never felt before. And I
realize now that you are as confused as I. What I suggest
is that we take this slowly. Sleep on it tonight, think
about it, then we can talk again during our morning
ride."

Catherine wanted to tell him with conviction that
there was nothing more to discuss. And that there would
be no choice but to leave if anything physical happened
again. But her ambivalence got in the way.

"What do you think?" he asked.

"Fine," she answered firmly, hoping to convey steadfast resolve. "But just understand, my mind is made up.
I will never do anything that would hurt Michael."

There was something, perhaps in her tone of voice or
even the smug look on her face, that suddenly sent Nowell reeling inside. *How convenient for you, and how
utterly naive,* he thought. *Believing you can flash your
wedding band like a crucifix, and think it will ward off
temptation. Oh, you have so much to learn. Your precious Michael has no idea the suffering your love for me
will cause.*

"Well, I suppose that settles it, then. Seeing as how
there isn't anything further to discuss, I for one shall get
a good night's sleep. Would you still care to join me for
a ride in the morning?"

"Absolutely." She smiled warmly. "And thanks for
the wine," she said, tilting her glass in his direction. She
sighed with relief, believing at last she'd gained the
upper hand.

Chapter Twenty-seven

The alarm went off at 7:00 A.M. and Catherine immediately shut it off without her usual early morning crankiness. She'd been wide awake for nearly an hour, full of anticipation about the day ahead.

Despite the bed's remarkable warmth and comfort, she'd slept fitfully, waking throughout the night in bouts of frustration. Regardless of her conviction that nothing further should develop between them, she simply could not get Nowell out of her mind, constantly imagining what kind of lover he was. Her thoughts ran wild, until she would realize, again and again, that what was happening was not just a fantasy. And that the events threatened the end of her marriage.

Impossible, she would repeat over and over to herself. *Michael and I are perfectly happy.* But a physical ache for Nowell would again cloud her judgment, and all reason would begin to fade.

The phone rang, breaking the spell. Catherine waited for it to ring three times before picking up, not wanting to appear overly anxious to receive Nowell's call.

"Hello," she answered with contrived sleepiness.

"Mrs. Harrison?" said the pleasant voice at the other end.

"Yes."

"Goo' morning, ma'am. This is Dee. I received instructions to call and make sure you were up this morning."

"Thank you, Dee."

"Will you be having breakfast in your room. ma'am?"

"Well, I don't know. Will Nowell be joining you all in the kitchen for breakfast?"

"He ate a while ago, ma'am. I believe he's out riding right now."

"Riding! Already?" said Catherine with astonishment. "I guess he'll be back at nine o'clock for me."

She then placed a simple breakfast order, smiling in the belief that she could have asked for and received chilled vichyssoise. Life with Nowell truly was like living in a fairy tale.

Bracing herself for the cold air, she jumped out of bed and made a dash for the warmth of a shower, where she spent twenty minutes letting the steamy jets of water soak her body, less for its comfortable heat, and more because she wanted to look her best for Nowell.

Climbing out of the shower she heard someone bustling about the bedroom. Quickly wrapping a towel on her body she peered out to find Dee stoking a new fire. Catherine's breakfast was laid out on the table.

"Will there be anything else, ma'am?" Dee asked, looking up.

"No, Dee, thanks." Suddenly Catherine remembered she didn't know where to go. "Wait, Dee," she shouted and jumped out of the bathroom, "actually there is something. Nowell didn't tell me where I should meet him this morning. Do you have any idea where I should wait?"

"Heavens, I'm surprised. He's usually so good about those things. Tell you what. Finish up and I'll fetch you in about twenty minutes. Otherwise we may not find you for days! There must be over a mile of corridors in this place."

"Thanks, Dee, I appreciate it," said Catherine, watching the woman leave the room. She felt somewhat confounded by Dee's statement that Nowell was usually so good about those things. Why wasn't he being good about it with her? The thought began to nag at her, but her conscience reminded her that if he was indifferent it was for the better.

She felt determined to show him her resolve on the matter of their affection, but while imagining her fortitude, she couldn't stop looking anxiously in the mirror, adjusting her hair, then applying makeup. Finishing up in the bathroom she was about to eat breakfast, but first opened the heavy drapes. That is when she discovered, even in its winter dormancy, one of the most beautiful courtyard gardens she'd ever seen. It seemed to be an acre or more, completely surrounded by a portico, with dozens of columns and arches. The morning's sun cast an enticing glow on the vision below, and as Catherine observed she also listened to scores of birds dining happily at a well-placed feeder. Their happy chirping made her even more anxious to get on with the day, to get outside with Nowell and enjoy the sights and sounds of nature from the back of a horse.

There was a light tap at the door. And though she was expecting Dee, Catherine couldn't help but wish it were Nowell coming to get her.

"Come in," she said blithely. Dee entered the room and politely inquired if she was ready to go.

"Absolutely," said Catherine, a bit disappointed, but behaving as lighthearted as one of the birds. She took only one bite of her breakfast and a quick swallow of her coffee, then cheerfully headed out the door.

"Any sign of Nowell?" she asked.

"No, ma'am. I heard from one of the stable hands that he went out hunting this morning with Joseph. He's the senior groundskeeper for the estate. Knows this place like the back of his own hand, he does. Been here longer than Nowell's been alive."

"Hunting? He never said anything about hunting today."

"Well, they mighta made up their minds to go at the las' minute, those two. I hear they're in pursuit of some giant stag that's been seen around this way recently. Do you hunt?"

"No, Dee, I can't say that it's ever interested me."

"Oh, now, the missus, or should I say Lady Stuart— Nowell's mother—God rest her soul. She loved to hunt. Quite a sportswoman, she was. Really loved this place."

"I'm sure she was a lovely woman. Did you know her long?"

"Yes, ma'am. Connie and I arrived about a year after Nowell was born. Anyway, the missus preferred this place over London any day, and spent most of her time here. Quite a gal. Loved to entertain, loved parties, loved her husband—but most of all, she loved that boy! She would have done anything for him. And he adored her. He's never really been the same since she died."

"I know it must be incredibly hard for him. Especially losing his father and wife as well."

"Well, he and the old man were close. But they had their differences, if you know what I mean."

"Oh, I'm sure I do. My father and I have locked horns on many occasions. But what about Elizabeth? You must have been fond of her too."

"Yes, I suppose. She was quite beautiful. And God rest her soul too. But that one, she had her moments. Bit of a temper, and rather spoilt, if you ask me." She paused, then whispered next, "Please don't say nothin' to Mr. Stuart 'bout what I just told ya. Those two used to have some doosies, if you know what I mean."

"No, no I won't tell. But what exactly do you mean? That they would fight?"

"Oh, like you wouldn't believe, those two. That boy, if you ask me, he's got a bit of a temper too. And somehow that girl, well, she would bring out the absolute worst in him. I'm not saying he ever hit her, it wasn't nothing like that. But just before she died, there was some real tension between them. Don't know what about, but you could hear them screamin' practically clear acrost the house,"

"My gosh, Dee. I had no idea. What would they argue about?"

"Well, I never really could tell exactly. But one night I heard him in the hallway before he slammed a door, yelling, "Go ahead you little . . ." She lowered her voice to a serious whisper, then spelled it out: "B-I-T-C-H. Go ahead and live with the rotten"—She paused and looked around to make sure no one else was listening——"bastard!""

Catherine was astonished at Dee's candor and wondered why the woman felt so comfortable disclosing this information to her. She had no idea what to make of it and was startled to hear that Nowell and Elizabeth hadn't gotten along. The way she'd figured it from him, they were a match made in heaven.

"What do you suppose he meant, Dee?"

"Hard to tell. Like I said, she was rather spoilt, a real daddy's girl. He mighta been tellin' her to go on back home and live with her da. Oh, there I go again, spilling my guts. Please don't say nothin' to him."

"Promise, Dee. I won't say a word." Catherine smiled, concealing her incredulity over Dee being so garrulous, especially compared to the formality and reserve of the other help. For the moment, however, she was grateful for Dee's indiscretion. The information actually made Catherine feel even more sorry for Nowell. He probably really loved Elizabeth, but she was just a difficult person to get along with. *No wonder he's so shy about getting involved again,* she thought to herself. *I hope he doesn't think all women are like that—especially me. I would never treat him that way. Never.*

"You know, Dee, this morning I looked outside my window and saw that fabulous courtyard for the very first time. I'd love to walk around in there. Why don't I wait out there for Nowell and then you can tell him where to find me when he gets back."

"Oh, lovely, lovely spot. I'd spend all my days out there if I could. In fact," she said, once more lowering her voice to a conspiratorial whisper, "sometimes when Mr. Stuart isn't here, I kind of do."

Catherine softly shook her head wondering why Dee was being so candid. *Most likely,* thought Catherine, *it's because she's the only woman among the dozen or so male staffers and is probably starved for female company.* Nonetheless, Catherine decided she'd better be extremely careful about what she said and did around the maid.

"Well, here you are, Mrs. Harrison. It is Mrs., right?"

"Yes," Catherine smiled politely as they made their way into the garden.

"Well, I must be getting back to the kitchen. Will you be all right here, by yourself?"

Catherine glanced at her watch; it was already 8:50 A.M. "Absolutely, Dee. Nowell will be around shortly if he isn't here already, and I'm looking forward to a few moments of peace and quiet."

Dee cast an offended glance at her, causing Catherine to make amends for the unintended slight. "Of course, it would be really lovely if you could stay here with me," Catherine quickly added, "I've really enjoyed your company."

"Oh, thank you, Mrs. Harrison," she said, relieved to know she would be missed, "but I really must be getting along. I'll be sure to let Mr. Stuart know where you are." She paused, then turned. "Remember, what we talked about is just between us girls."

"Absolutely," said Catherine, offering a reassuring nod. The doors shut, Dee finally gone, Catherine took a long, relaxing breath of fresh air. It was chilly, but remarkably pure, especially compared to the air in London and New York. She tilted her head up toward the sun, closed her eyes, trying to soak up whatever winter warmth it had to offer. The birds, now grown in number, were still busy at work in the feeder and the cacophony of their songs was sweet music to her ears. Momentarily lost in this romantic oasis she could understand why Lady Stuart had preferred the estate over London; Catherine felt the same way.

She glanced down at her watch, which read ten past nine, but there was no sign of Nowell. Catherine continued walking around the perimeter of the garden, anxious to see him, worried about why he wasn't already here. She waited another fifteen minutes, but still there was no sign of him.

That does it, she said to herself, *Dee probably forgot to tell him where I am, and he's inside fuming over my being late.*

Catherine hurried out of the garden and through the corridors until she finally came to the great entrance hall. But it was silent. No sign of Nowell, any of the help, or even the dogs.

"Nowell," she cried out, "I'm here." Her voice only echoed throughout, leaving her feeling eerie and quite alone. She sat down on the staircase, figuring that sooner or later he would pass by this location while trying to find her, when it occurred to her to go back to her room and use the intercom.

"Hello," she said into the box as soon as she reached the room. A man's unfamiliar voice answered back. "Yes."

"This is Catherine Harrison, with whom am I speaking, please?"

"John." Catherine hadn't the faintest idea who he was but proceeded anyway.

"John, I'm supposed to meet Nowell. Have you seen him around?"

"Can't say that I have."

"Oh. Well, what about Dee? Is she anywhere near?"

"No, she and Connie went into town to get some supplies."

Catherine shrugged and sighed, thinking what a foolish woman Dee was for leaving her alone. She was now forty-five minutes late for her rendezvous with Nowell, and hadn't the slightest idea what to do.

"Thanks, John. Incidentally, if you see Nowell, would you please tell him I'm in my room."

"Yes, ma'am."

"Thanks," she said again, then turned the intercom off.

"Why would he do this to me?" she asked out loud. She got off her bed and looked out the window, hoping to see Nowell in the courtyard. But except for a few lingering birds, the garden was empty.

Now convinced she'd been stood up, Catherine began pacing the floor, turned on the stereo as loud as she could tolerate, then paced some more. She felt as if she were going crazy, the whole premise of her trip, and now the prospect of being stuck with him an entire month, beginning to make her mad. She hadn't even wanted to go to England, instead preferring to stay home with Michael and make love, lots of love, as they tried to start a family.

But suddenly here she was—alone in this massive estate, in the middle of the English countryside, waiting desperately for Nowell. *And now this head game—it's ridiculous,* she told herself. *I don't love Nowell. I can't love him. What is he doing to me?*

"What am I doing?" she shouted out loud, thinking of his cavalier entrance into her room the previous night and then his move on her. "He's taking total advantage of me. This is outrageous—all he wants is sex. I'll show him! I'll show him I meant what I said. This is crazy, this whole thing is crazy."

With that she headed out the door, determined to find the stables on her own and to take the horseback ride by herself. Marching furiously down to the great hall, and out through one of the massive front doors, she turned toward the back side of the house, where beautifully landscaped grounds swept down to a serene lake.

But instead of stopping to soak up the scenery, Catherine charged on, certain that because the house was built during the time of horse-drawn carriages, there would be stables nearby. Her hunch proved right, because adjacent to the house on the west side was a large, two-story building with a gigantic packed-dirt courtyard and two carousel horse-walkers.

"Bingo," she exclaimed, entering the stables. "Hello," she hollered. No one answered, but a few horses snorted loudly, and one of them furiously pawed at the ground. She searched the entire building and, surprised to find no one, decided that she would take the horse of her choice for a ride. Examining each of the occupied stalls, Catherine was struck by a chestnut-colored mare with a bright white mark on its nose. A plaque on the door read: OPTIMA.

"It doesn't get much better than that," said Catherine, offering her hand in a friendly gesture through the bars of the stall door. The horse leaned down and nuzzled her hand with its massive head. "Oh, darling, you're definitely the one," responded Catherine with a soft stroke on the horse's nose. She retreated to the tack room, grabbing everything she would need. It had been several years since she'd saddled a horse, but the chore still felt familiar to her.

Optima was already wearing a bridle and offered no resistance as Catherine led her out of the stall. Catherine chatted amiably with the creature, hoping to inspire the animal's confidence. After saddling the horse, she then pulled the girth around the animal's giant belly.

"C'mon, girl," she said, clicking her tongue a couple of times, then heading out to the courtyard. They were ready to go, and Catherine, affectionately patting the horse on the rear after mounting her, noted Optima's increased energy level.

"Oh, my gosh, I forgot what a wonderful feeling this was. Let's go," she boasted, directing a slight kick into the horse's side. Optima briskly and proudly trotted past the house, her behavior reminding Catherine of a powerful sailboat being moved cautiously out of its dock so as not to make waves. She could tell the animal wanted to move at a full tilt, but she responded well to the restraints of the reins and commands of her rider.

They rode over the back lawn and out to the main road that Catherine and Nowell first drove in on. Optima seemed to have a better idea where she was going than Catherine and gently resisted her attempts to travel that route. Catherine conceded, allowing the animal to turn in the opposite direction. And it wasn't long before they were on what was obviously a horse trail.

"Good girl!" cheered Catherine, giving Optima a couple of affectionate strokes on the neck. The horse snorted and jerked her head upward in a friendly manner, letting Catherine know she appreciated the kudos. Simultaneously Catherine's disquietude over Nowell's behavior began to vanish, and her feelings over all that had happened yesterday began falling into perspective. There was nothing Nowell could do for her, or give to her, including a life at this glorious estate, that would ever make her betray Michael.

With fresh resolve, Catherine knew she would never want to lose Michael, and would not do another thing to jeopardize their marriage. And furthermore, if Nowell couldn't respect that, she would leave the job. It was that simple.

Optima kept a steady gait, carrying Catherine up a slight incline and through a small grove of evergreen trees. Just beyond that was a lush field that beckoned them both to abandon all restraint and ride headlong into the wind. Catherine dug her heels hard into Optima and leaned slightly into the mighty creature as they began racing furiously into the emerald-green pasture, kicking up pieces of turf behind them. Unsure of who was getting more delight out of their venture, Catherine encouraged Optima to go faster still.

Optima flew at even greater speed, a speed faster than one Catherine had ever dared experience on horseback, and digging her heels in even harder she hollered in glee. But her joy quickly vanished into an all-consuming wave of terror as Catherine realized she was hopelessly losing her grip.

The saddle began listing to the right, first slightly, then in a more pronounced and uncontrollable way. There was no way to slow the horse. Optima remained oblivious to Catherine's plight, instead charging ahead even faster. There was nothing she could do to regain control, and as Optima's speed increased, Catherine's legs lost all of the remaining grip she'd had on the horse's muscular body.

She grabbed at the horse's mane, but it was hopeless. There was nothing Catherine could do as the saddle slipped even farther, then suddenly flipped under Optima's belly. Catherine was jerked from her last possible grip, then hurled hard and fast to the ground where she received a devastating kick to the head by the horse's swift and mighty hoof—a blow leaving her crumpled and unconscious on the cold, damp grass.

Chapter Twenty-eight

Nowell parked his Range Rover next to Joseph's cottage, about a mile from the main house, so they could unload the freshly killed stag. It had taken them most of the morning to stalk it, and though they started out on horseback, they had returned for the comfort and speed of the all-terrain vehicle. Nowell looked at his face in the rearview mirror, then rubbed a streak of the stag's blood off his right cheek. He knew he was late for his morning ride with Catherine, but he stubbornly refused to give up an opportunity for such a prize kill.

Besides, he had reasoned to himself, she'd asked for it. She had no idea how hard it had been to control himself the previous night as she seduced him over the dinner table, then proceeded to tell him moments later that nothing could happen between them. Then doing the same thing later in her bedroom. *All the better if she has to sit around and stew about it awhile,* he told himself.

He had no second thoughts about his own intentions—he was as committed as ever to taking her. But he wasn't about to tolerate her ridiculous flights of morality; as far as he was concerned, their embraces and kissing was just as adulterous as any other illicit act they would perform, so why was she suddenly so righteous? He knew she wanted to have him, and indeed she would. But only on his terms now.

Joseph brought an ale out of the cottage for each of them, and together they sat on the tailgate of the Range Rover, the bloodied body of the stag planted heavily between them. Joseph proudly rested one of his arms on the rear end of the carcass as he sipped his drink.

"Right between the eyes, I still don't know how you did that. Nothing like it, though, nothing like it, heh?"

"I'll say. Nothing like it, old Joe, nothing like it," and with that Nowell raised his bottle to the old man as they toasted each other's success in bagging the animal. Killing the stag had completely reinvigorated Nowell, and he sat happy and not at all weary from the exercise he'd gained in the process. He didn't know what he loved better—the chase or the kill.

Nowell looked at his watch—it was nearly 11:30—then took a hearty swallow of his ale. *Let her stew,* he kept telling himself, *let her stew.* He couldn't imagine what Catherine was up to, but decided that it didn't matter. By the time he got to her she'd be so happy to have his company once again that she wouldn't let him out of her sight for another minute.

He chatted with Joe for a bit longer, then decided it was about time to unload the dead animal. Joe had agreed to cut it up and provide the kitchen with some venison for the evening's meal, which Nowell couldn't wait to serve up to Catherine—anxious to see her reaction to eating "Bambi" for dinner.

They hauled the stag to the rear of Joe's cottage, cleaned out the back of the Range Rover as best they could, then amiably parted company, both agreeing that they would do it again soon. Driving away over one of many packed-dirt roads on the estate, Nowell contemplated Catherine's reaction over his absence, and what he might say upon seeing her again. He felt determined not to apologize for standing her up; his only concern was in whether he should make her wait even longer.

Nowell turned left onto another dirt road that narrowed considerably until disappearing altogether into an expanse of tall, rough grass. Fortunately the Range Rover allowed for easy travel over the area, and Nowell readily accelerated his pace up a slight incline that led to a pristine valley beyond the brow of the hill. It was the shortcut he always drove when returning from Joe's cottage, and knowing the course so well he could allow his thoughts to wander as he cruised along.

Still pondering what the next step might be with Catherine, Nowell did not notice Optima happily grazing alongside a stream cutting through the valley. It wasn't until the horse raised her head for a curious peek at the vehicle that Nowell caught a glimpse of her. He abruptly slowed down the Range Rover, then came to a full stop to see what was going on with the animal.

"What a curious thing," he said aloud, realizing the animal was wearing an upside-down saddle. Nowell scanned the horizon for her rider, and seeing no one slowly eased the vehicle up toward his champion horse, hoping to determine why she'd been left unattended this far from home. Optima, realizing her freedom was facing foreclosure, dashed off in a playful trot, leaving Nowell to stray from his own course home in pursuit of her. Archie, his chief stable hand, was the only one who ever rode her and he simply couldn't imagine such neglect, when it occurred to Nowell that Archie may have been injured while riding the horse. He picked up his cellular phone and dialed the stable, startling at Archie's voice.

"Archie," Nowell barked into the phone, "what the hell is Optima doing out?"

"I don't believe I follow you, sir."

"Jesus Christ, Archie, *I'm following* Optima in the east meadow and she's fully saddled. Though someone didn't do a very keen job of it since the saddle is dangling upside down from her belly!"

"Bugger!" exclaimed Archie emphatically. "I just returned from town, didn't even notice she was missing. I'll be right out to help."

Nowell slammed down the phone, all the while keeping a short pace behind the animal, who had now shot up over a hill and had taken off into another wide-open pasture. Keeping a steady eye on the animal, Nowell tried imagining how this could have occurred, when the answer appeared to him in a horrifying and lifeless form on the horizon just ahead. Nowell felt his blood chill, as from even one hundred yards away he could tell it was Catherine, her long blond hair whipped around her face, her body prostrate on the ground.

He no longer cared about Optima's welfare—in fact, his adrenaline rushed so furiously at the sight of Catherine he felt he could kill the animal. He pulled the vehicle up close beside Catherine, then jumped out, the motor still running.

"Catherine, CATHERINE!" he shrieked, fearful to the core that she was dead. She didn't respond, she didn't budge. Nowell bent down as far as he could to see if she was still breathing, afraid to touch her, terrified that if she was alive she'd broken her neck.

"Thank God," he said as he heard her shallow breathing, but a fresh wave of panic consumed him as he saw the gash on the right side of her forehead and the puddle of blood beneath it.

Nowell removed his jacket and placed it on the upper part of her body, fearing she was in shock. He wondered what bones she might have broken, then began to consider what the hell had happened. She should have never taken Optima out by herself, he thought. He touched her forehead, anxious for a response, but she did not move.

"Oh, my God, she's dying out here. Catherine, how the hell could you do this to me?" he cursed accusingly. He ran back toward the Range Rover, then grabbed the phone and dialed the emergency number for help, then waited, one ring, two, four, then nearly six rings before someone finally answered. Despite his fury, he managed to speak calmly.

"This is Nowell Stuart, of Stuart Hall in West Yorkshire. We have an unconscious victim of a riding accident in a pasture about a mile east of the main house. She may have a broken neck, there is a gash and some bleeding above her right eye where she was apparently kicked by a horse, and she's in an obvious state of shock. I need her airlifted out of here and taken to Leeds General Infirmary, and I want a physician escort. I will bear any cost if necessary, I just want someone here immediately. Do you understand me?" His composure remained steely as he listened to the response, then very business-like he began giving general landmarks to identify Stuart Hall.

"How long will this take?" he asked. There was another brief pause. "That's not good enough. I told you already I need someone here now, and I am not going to hang up until I see a chopper hovering over my head." He remained stony, listening intently as the dispatcher went about his job. It seemed like an eternity, but within ten minutes the dispatcher confirmed that a helicopter with a physician and rescue team on board was en route and would be there shortly.

"Would you like to continue holding, sir?" asked the dispatcher.

"Yes," said Nowell, never taking his eyes off Catherine. Nowell wondered why in the hell she had gone out without a helmet, then thought that she might be losing a lot of heat through her head.

"I'm still here," he warned the dispatcher, then climbed out of the driver's seat and opened the back gate in search of another blanket. The only one he had was stained with the stag's blood—what the hell, he thought.

He placed it gingerly over her head, first checking her pulse and then softly stroking her hair. It seemed forever before he could discern the distant whine of a helicopter, and it wasn't long before it appeared over the horizon, heading in a direction about a half mile off course. Nowell immediately climbed on top of the Range Rover, frantically waving his arms, but it was to no avail, the chopper seemed to head straight for Stuart Hall, prompting Nowell to jump directly off the top of the vehicle and pick up the phone.

"What the fuck are they doing?" he screamed at the dispatcher, "tell them east, tell them to head east!"

Moments later the chopper soared toward the field, circling once, then landing about twenty yards away. Four people, including the pilot, jumped out, emergency kits and specialized stretcher in tow, each rushing directly toward the victim.

"I'm Dr. Fletcher, Ian Fletcher," said the first man at the scene. He was supremely calm. "Can you tell me what happened?"

"No, not really. I'm Nowell Stuart," offered Nowell. "This is my property. I don't know for certain what happened, only that I found her here about thirty minutes ago. It appears she fell off and got kicked in the head by a horse."

Dr. Fletcher wasted no time kneeling to get a better look, first listening to her breathing, then touching a wrist to check her pulse.

"It's broken," he said matter-of-factly.

"What, what's broken?" demanded Nowell.

"Her wrist, for starters."

"Oh, Jesus Christ," wailed Nowell. "What about her neck or her back? It's all I need, a paraplegic and major lawsuit on my hands."

Dr. Fletcher looked at Nowell harshly. "What is her name?" he asked while proceeding to assess her condition.

"Catherine. Catherine Harrison."

"Catherine," the doctor shouted loudly into her ears. She didn't budge. He clapped his hands together loudly, but still got no response. Neither did a sharp pinch on her cheek. He looked at the cut on her head, then asked one of the medics to provide some rubber gloves and a sterilized gauze pad. Wiping off as much of the excess blood as he could, he moved in for a closer look at the wound. He opened her eyes to check the pupils, which were dilated and unresponsive.

Nowell could barely contain himself. He wanted information, and he wanted it now.

"What do you think?"

"It's hard to say how much brain damage there may be without an MRI or a CAT scan. I'm also quite concerned about the position she is in. At best we're looking at one broken bone, but she may also have a fractured clavicle or broken vertebrae. There is some blood loss here, but the head wound is not terribly deep. Get the neck pack and brace," he instructed a medic, "this is going to be a delicate operation moving her." He turned to Nowell. "The good news is that it's not terribly cold today. She's probably been out here a couple of hours and might have died by now under colder conditions. Are you related to her in any way, Mr. Stuart?"

"No, but she is my employee. I suppose I'm the closest thing she has to a relation here."

"Where is she from? Does she have any family nearby?"

"No, actually. She's American, she's only visiting. May I please accompany you in the chopper?"

"We'll see," was all he said. It was another ten minutes before Catherine was securely packed into the stretcher, the doctor and medics moving her with extraordinary caution. Nowell held his breath as they slowly turned her over, but she never flinched, her unconscious face caked with blood and dirt. She was extremely pale, appearing weak and defenseless.

"I'm going with you," Nowell told Dr. Fletcher. "She'll need me there when she comes around."

"Let's see how much room we have first," the doctor responded coolly. Nowell was infuriated at the doctor's indifference and strode behind him as the team carried Catherine to the helicopter.

At least when his parents died it was over and done without any suffering. But now the quality of Catherine's life, perhaps her life itself, lay in the balance and there was nothing more he could do. He tried to shut the memory of his parents out of his mind, focusing instead on the belief that this accident today would have never happened if not for Catherine's stubborn willfulness. She could just as well have had a warm romp in the bed with him, as opposed to a life-threatening ride on the back of a high-strung thoroughbred.

"I'm coming with you, that's all there is to it," said Nowell to Dr. Fletcher. The doctor turned and with sudden ferocity refused Nowell's demand.

"Mr. Stuart, my primary concern here is the safe transport of this patient. I appreciate your desire to ride along, but we must keep her stable and gauge her condition the whole trip. There is no room on board. I will, however, need you at the hospital to help fill out paperwork and such, and I'm sure she'll want you there later. But for now, you will have to be satisfied that it is best for the patient that you not travel on board."

Nowell let out a clipped laugh. "Sorry," he said, then passed by the doctor and climbed on board.

Dr. Fletcher let out an exasperated sigh. "Just a minute, then," he said, then moved ahead of Nowell to make certain that everything was in order. The rotor on the helicopter started up, moments later soaring toward Leeds General Infirmary, about a forty-five-minute drive north from Nowell's estate, but only a fraction of that time by chopper. Nowell's eyes remained fixated on Catherine as the doctor constantly checked her condition—first her pulse and breathing, next her temperature, then her eyes. He repeated this pattern several times en route to the hospital, creating a twinge of jealousy in Nowell that it wasn't he who was tending to her every need.

Within fifteen minutes they landed at the hospital. Dr. Fletcher had already radioed ahead on the status of her condition, requesting a specialized team of practitioners

be at the ready to do a full evaluation. They were met
on the landing pad by a group of doctors and nurses
with a gurney. The following activities happened in a
rush, leaving Nowell standing alone and uncertain of
what to do in its wake. They practically ran with Catherine off the landing pad and directly into the hospital,
immediately taking her to the emergency room for further treatment and evaluation. Dr. Fletcher deliberately
ignored Nowell, and no one else bothered to ask who
he was or tell him exactly what they were doing.

He ran behind the team until they entered a restricted
area, leaving him dumbfounded and angry on the other
side of the door. If, God forbid, her neck was broken
and she would never walk again, he wanted to be the
first one she turned to for support.

It was the first chance he'd had to sit still and think
about all that was happening. *What if she should die?* he
thought, now regretting the missed opportunity to spend
time with her that morning, and even more that he might
have come on too strong, too soon with her the night
before. His desire for her had not waned since last night,
and for the first time since discovering her unconscious,
he realized how badly he needed her.

But he couldn't change a thing right now, and did the
only thing he could think of at the moment. Reaching
into his breast pocket he pulled out his silver cigarette
case and lit up.

Chapter Twenty-nine

Michael's alarm clock went off at 7:00 A.M. sharp, and by habit he turned off the alarm and rolled over toward Catherine's side of the bed, where he usually cozied up beside her before forcing himself out of bed. It had been three days since he'd talked to Catherine, and as he looked at her empty side of the bed with its still plump pillows, he felt a sense of loneliness. But it was more than that, almost an intuition that something wasn't right.

As he did most every morning, he slipped into his bathrobe and retreated to his favorite chair in the living room to read the Bible and say his personal prayers. Today he turned to the Second Epistle of Paul to the Corinthians, on being comforted by God so that one could comfort others; always a source of inspiration to him.

But the hint that something wasn't right kept surfacing in his feelings. After he finished his reading and prayers, he decided to call Catherine. He looked at the kitchen clock, it was 7:30 A.M. New York time. She'd left the number for Nowell's London residence, which he promptly dialed, hoping that she'd be around for lunch.

"Hello, Stuart Residence," came the austere male voice at the other end. It was Nigel.

"Hello, this is Michael Harrison. My wife, Catherine, is a guest of Nowell Stuart's. Is she there please?"

"No, sir. They've gone out to the country."

"Oh, I see. Are they expected back today?"

"No, sir. They intend to be out there for a couple of days."

"Would you happen to have a phone number there?"

"Actually, sir, I've been instructed not to give that

number out. But I will gladly take your message and provide it to Mrs. Harrison."

"Oh, I see. Just tell her to call home."

"Yes, sir."

"Good-bye," said Michael, "and thank you."

"Yes, good-bye," said Nigel, then hung up. Michael sat listening to the transatlantic static as the line went dead, wondering why Catherine hadn't called. He cradled the phone in his hands for a bit, then finally put it back in the receiver when he realized he was running late for school. Without eating breakfast he went into the bedroom and threw on a pair of jeans, a cotton golf shirt, and his favorite old wool sweater, brushed his hair and teeth and was out the door.

Nowell waited four hours before Dr. Fletcher and another physician finally emerged, both clad in scrubs and head covers. Nowell jumped out of his seat and met them halfway down the hall, studying their faces for any clues of her condition.

"How is she? Is she all right? Please tell me she's not paralyzed, please."

"Good news," Dr. Fletcher said, smiling faintly, "her back and neck are fine. I would say there must have been an angel between her and the ground today. And if that horse had kicked her just the slightest bit lower we would have been looking at some serious brain damage."

"Go on," said Nowell, eager to hear the rest.

"Well, she's not out of the woods yet. The MRI shows that she's got a concussion, but fortunately there is no fracture of the skull. We did have to stitch up her forehead, and at some point down the road she may need some plastic surgery. There was a serious break of the wrist, which we've set, but she remains in a coma and will be hospitalized, of course, until she becomes alert and we are certain there is no swelling of the brain."

Nowell sighed, placing his hands squarely on the doctor's shoulders in a gesture of gratitude.

"How long do you think she'll be out of it? I mean, how long does it take a patient to recover from this sort of thing?"

"It varies," said the other doctor. "That was quite a

blow she suffered. As Dr. Fletcher said, there must have been an angel beneath her today. We've seen far worse in this kind of situation."

"But there are no broken bones anywhere else, and her neck and back are definitely okay?" Nowell asked, needing to hear the good news once more.

"We've checked her over from head to toe. You just got the full report," answered Dr. Fletcher.

"Yes, yes, of course. When can I see her?"

"Well, they're putting her in a room right now up on the B Ward. I suppose as soon as she gets settled in that it should be all right for you to see her. I must warn you, however, such victims typically suffer what is known as retrograde memory loss."

"What exactly do you mean?"

"It's a mild form of amnesia where the victim doesn't remember the trauma. They will remember most events leading up to the accident, but nothing about the accident itself."

"But she'll be okay otherwise, right?"

"Yes, she should be. Though there are sometimes more severe cases of amnesia under such circumstances, which of course is one of the things we'll be watching for. The important thing for you to remember, Mr. Stuart, is that basically Catherine may not know what hit her. It will most likely be a bit confusing for her when she comes around."

"Dr. Fletcher, and Dr., I'm sorry, I never caught your name," said Nowell to the other physician.

"Dr. Potter." The man smiled and extended his hand, which Nowell gratefully shook. "I'd like to thank you both for all you've done. And, Dr. Fletcher," he added, "I appreciate the lift to the hospital."

"Not at all." Dr. Fletcher wanly smiled back.

"Excuse me," said Nowell, "I'd like to find out what room she'll be in." He parted ways with the two men and headed straight for her ward.

"I'm sorry, sir," said the floor nurse rather officiously upon Nowell's request to know Catherine's room number, "but visiting hours aren't for another two hours. Unless you're family, you'll just have to wait."

Despising such bureaucracy, Nowell persisted, but with a twist. "Well, actually," said Nowell, pouring on the charm, but still exuding concern, "we're almost family. Catherine is my fiancée."

Her face broke into a sweet smile. "Oh, you don't say. How lovely. Well, I suppose there are certain exceptions. Room nine-sixty, just around the corner and to the right."

Nowell wasted no further time making his way to Catherine. He knocked tentatively, then softly pushed the door open. The lighting inside was soft and subdued, the room otherwise stark and practical. And there, oblivious to the world or her plight, was Catherine, her head partially bandaged and tubes running out one arm, the other in a cast and sling. Nowell moved to the side of her bed and just stared at her.

My God, she looks like a little girl, he thought. *So fragile, so delicate.* Though the bandage looked ominous, he could see that the pink had returned to her skin, and he lightly touched her cheek to feel the warmth. She still didn't budge, so he stroked her several times, speaking softly as he did.

"Oh, my love, my love. Look at you, I am so sorry."

He bent down and kissed her lips, somewhat parched compared to their sweet moistness last night, then whispered in her ear. "I was afraid I might lose you," he said tenderly.

It was an enormously satisfying feeling to say whatever he wanted to her without consequence, and to touch her lovingly as he did. He pushed a lock of honey-blond hair away from her forehead. "You look like such an angel, my love, such an angel."

A nurse entered the room and dutifully checked Catherine's blood pressure and saw to it that her IV drip was okay. "So you're her fiancé, I understand."

"My, word travels fast around here."

"Indeed. Congratulations. Though I hope the wedding isn't anytime soon."

"Oh, no, no. Plenty of time for recovery."

"Good. Well, I'll be her nurse this evening. Buzz, of course, if she stirs. Otherwise I'll check back in an hour or so."

"Will do," Nowell said, smiling.

Nowell pulled up a chair beside Catherine's bed and proceeded to stare at her, studying every facet of her beautiful features, fantasizing about when they would actually make love. The very thought of it created a strong arousal in him; such that he wondered what it would be like to make love to her right now, and he laughed. Now wouldn't that be just deserts, he thought: *I could give to her now what would have prevented this all along.*

He stood beside the bed, staring at Catherine, while continuing to stroke her, then brazenly lifted her gown, revealing naked skin beneath it. Her body was every bit as beautiful as he'd imagined, and he ran his hand all along her thigh, then around her breasts.

Suddenly she stirred, startling Nowell so terribly that he quickly stepped back. She did not awaken, but alarmed Nowell so badly that he covered her back up, quietly sat down, resuming a more innocent bedside vigil.

Chapter Thirty

When Nowell awoke it was past 7:00 A.M. He'd fallen asleep in the chair beside Catherine's bed sometime after midnight, having otherwise stayed alert in the event Catherine stirred. A morning duty nurse took Catherine's pulse and then checked her IV. She changed the dressing over the cut on her head, adjusted the sling on her right arm, then fluffed up the pillows.

"In your experience, how long does one usually remain unconscious after such an accident?" asked Nowell of the woman, a thin, middle-aged gal with a serious clinical demeanor.

"It varies. One man stayed this way for weeks, despite the fact that his concussion was fairly mild."

"For weeks!" exclaimed Nowell. "Heavens, Catherine, did you hear that? Now that's totally unacceptable—we've got work to do!"

"I wouldn't expect this young lady to be doing much work right away."

"Of course not," Nowell said with feigned respect.

"She'll be needing plenty of rest for a while."

Nowell said nothing else, realizing that the nurse had no sense of humor and was someone who took the issue of her patient's recuperation very seriously. She made some notations to Catherine's chart, told Nowell the doctor would be in, then left the room.

"Catherine, if you knew your care was left entirely up to that bitchy woman you'd wake up and be out of here in a flash." He stroked her hair, then her cheek, noticing that her skin color still looked good, and felt nice and warm to the touch. She looked so peaceful that he almost felt it a shame to wish her awake so soon.

Realizing no one at Stuart Hall knew precisely what had happened, Nowell decided to ring up the stable, hoping to reach Archie, and further hoping to learn that Optima was securely back in place. No one picked up, so he dialed the kitchen at Stuart Hall next. Dee answered.

"Oh, Mary, Mother of Jesus. Where are you? Is the girl all right?" she blurted upon hearing Nowell's voice. Nowell took a deep breath before proceeding—he really couldn't stand the talkative woman. The only reason he kept her around was because Connie was so reliable.

"No, she is not all right. She's got a sizable gash in her head, a broken wrist, and she's in a bloody coma. It's a damned wonder she's alive. Where's Archie?"

All Nowell could hear was the receiver bouncing along the linoleum floor and Dee's broken sobs. Fortunately Connie was nearby and retrieved the phone.

"Sir, we heard about Optima, then saw the medevac fly by. Archie brought your Range Rover back to the house, and Dee's been beside herself ever since. Says if anything happened to the young lass it was her fault, she forgot to tell you Mrs. Harrison was awaitin' for you in the courtyard."

"Well, it was bloody careless of Dee and she should be broken up by it. It might have been much worse, but gratefully I found her in time." Nowell knew there was nothing Dee could have done to prevent the misfortune, but couldn't resist the opportunity to goad her anxiety.

"Sir, we are so terribly, terribly sorry. Is there anything we can do?"

"Was Archie able to round up Optima?"

"Yes, sir."

"Splendid. And tell him if he wants to keep his job that he better bloody well learn how to do it."

"Yes, sir," Connie responded without emotion. He was accustomed to Nowell's tirades, and no longer withered under his pressure. "But the girl, sir. How is the girl?"

"She's in a coma, Connie. Only time will tell how well she is. I must go. I'm at Leeds General Infirmary should anyone need urgently to speak with me."

With that he hung up, and as he tried to quietly replace the receiver he saw that Catherine was trying to focus on him through a squinty gaze.

"My God, my God, Catherine, you're awake, you're

awake. Oh, thank God. How do you feel?'' he said with
nervous excitement.

Catherine's eyes began to blink, but she remained
speechless. She rolled her head slightly back and forth
on the pillow, as though trying to get her bearings, appearing spacy and confused. Nowell promptly and repeatedly hit the call button to summon the nurse, who
arrived moments later. It was the same stiff woman who
had tended to her earlier. She immediately shut off the
light beside Catherine's bed.

"Could you move back, please?" she asked of Nowell,
then began examining Catherine, who moaned. "I'll be
right back with Dr. Potter."

"Water," Catherine murmured weakly. "I need some
water."

Nowell would have happily obliged her, but decided
to wait until the doctor arrived before he did anything.

"Catherine, the doctor will be here shortly. Then you
can have some water. I promise."

"Where am I?" she asked drowsily.

"You are in an infirmary. Do you remember what
happened yesterday?"

"I need some water," she whispered hoarsely. "Nowell? Is that you?"

"Yes, my love, it's me." He breathed a sigh of relief
at the sound of his name, knowing that she wasn't suffering from total amnesia.

"The doctor will be here shortly, then you can have all
the water you want. Do you remember anything about
yesterday? Riding Optima, then having the saddle turn
upside down on you?"

She didn't answer, and was still mostly out of it when
Dr. Potter and the nurse appeared a few minutes later.

Dr. Potter checked her pupils, looked inside her ears,
then began testing certain reflexes—all of which appeared normal.

"Ms. Harrison, do you know what month it is?" Dr.
Potter asked. Catherine moaned. "Can you tell me the
month?" he asked again.

"January?" she murmured.

"Excellent. What year?"

Catherine moaned once more, but answered correctly.

"Excellent," said the doctor. "Suppose you tell me what happened yesterday?"

"Huh?"

"Do you know why you are in the hospital?" he asked.

"Uh-uh," she muttered.

"Is this what you were talking about yesterday, Dr. Potter? That she may not remember the accident?" asked Nowell.

"Exactly. And in all likelihood she will never remember it."

The doctor proceeded to probe a bit more, conducting a series of brain teasers. He asked her to count backward by five, then by seven, and then to spell several words backward and forward.

"Good Lord, Dr. Potter," joked Nowell, "that's difficult for me to do—without a bang on the noggin."

The doctor persisted, however, and the more he engaged Catherine in the exercises the more alert she became.

"My head hurts so badly," she moaned. "And what happened to my wrist?"

"You've been in a riding accident, Ms. Harrison," answered Dr. Potter. "You've got a mild concussion, and you also suffered a broken wrist. The good news is you'll be getting out of the hospital soon and should make a full recovery in six to eight weeks."

"A riding accident?" Catherine asked. "What happened?"

"Well, no one knows for certain because apparently you were alone when it occurred. Your fiancé can explain all the details that he knows."

"My fiancé." She sort of laughed. "You mean my husband. Is Michael here?" she asked with a smile.

Nowell felt a flush of nervousness over the awkward exchange. He glanced at the doctor and winked as if to say "we'll talk."

"No, Catherine, Michael's not here. It's me, Nowell. Boy, you've given us all quite a scare," he said, attempting to change the subject. He reached out and stroked her hand, prompting her to smile at the gesture.

"Nowell," she said softly. "Oh, Nowell, I'm so glad you're here. Where exactly am I?"

"You're in Leeds General Infirmary, about forty miles north of Stuart Hall. We had you airlifted here yesterday after you fell off Optima."

"Airlifted!" she managed with soft astonishment. "Oh, Nowell, what trouble have I put you through? I'm so sorry."

"Don't be ridiculous, it was not your fault. I am just so grateful that you will be all right. You've been unconscious for more than a day and we didn't know when you would come around."

"My head hurts," she groaned.

"I'll prescribe some codeine for the pain in your head and wrist," said Dr. Fletcher. "And if all goes well tonight, you should be going home tomorrow."

"Back to New York?"

"Oh, heavens, no," he exclaimed. "You do have a place to stay here, don't you?"

"Doctor, can we talk?" asked Nowell, nodding toward the doorway.

"Ms. Harrison, I'll be back to see you later in the day. In the meantime, Nurse Sykes will return with your pain medication. You get some rest, all right. And—" he smiled good-naturedly—"welcome back."

"Thanks," Catherine responded warmly.

The doctor walked into the hallway to join Nowell, who immediately began whispering. "Doctor, I know this must sound a bit confusing. You see, Michael is her soon-to-be ex-husband. She and I have been . . . well, you know."

"Ah, yes, I understand," the doctor said, nodding.

"Anyway, we've made plans to marry as soon as her divorce comes through. I think she still must be a bit confused."

"Well, she seems to have all her other facts straight," said the doctor, "I suppose I could allow for one slip-up."

"Yes, you do understand. Anyway, what is her real prognosis? Will she require extended bed rest?"

"I'd say for a few days, at least. She will obviously have to take it very easy, and I would like to see her again next week. Otherwise, avoiding horses for a while should be the quickest road to recovery," Dr. Potter said with a wry grin.

"Absolutely, absolutely. I'm just so grateful she's okay. What a tremendous scare. I cannot thank you enough for all you've done, and," he added, lowering his voice another notch, "for your absolute discretion in our personal matter."

Dr. Potter smiled at him again, then shook his hand. "Absolutely, Mr. Stuart. I fully understand. She's lucky to have you, it's obvious you're quite fond of her."

"Yes, yes, indeed. I'm very fond of her," Nowell stammered.

"Well, best of luck. Now I must go finish my rounds. I will be back to see her later today. Meanwhile, make sure she gets plenty of rest." He patted Nowell in a sportsmanlike way on his arm, one man to another, then moved on down the hall. The nurse left, finally leaving Nowell alone with Catherine again.

"Oh, Nowell. What have I done to myself? This is incredible."

"Tell me about it, woman."

"Nowell, have you called Michael?"

"Yes," Nowell lied.

"What did he say? He must be going crazy."

"I think he's taking it rather well."

"Oh, I need to talk to him. Can we call him right now?"

"Well, I don't think that's a good idea. The doctor and nurse said to keep you quiet. He may try to reach you later, or perhaps when we get back to Stuart Hall you can call him."

"Nothing else? He didn't say anything else?"

"Not really, he knows you're being well cared for, and that there is not much he can do from afar."

"That just doesn't sound like him. Oh, well. Nowell, tell me something," Catherine said as she buried her head back in the pillow, "how bad off am I, really?"

Nowell sat down on her bedside chair and took hold of her good hand. She seemed to hold no ill will against him, and he wondered if it was his good fortune that she forgot being stood up, or that in gratitude over escaping serious injury she held no grudge. He decided not to press his luck by saying anything about what led up to her accident.

"Actually, you're doing quite well. The doctor said he

expects you to make a full recovery, though some physical therapy may be in order to strengthen your wrist. But we'll have you back to normal in no time—trust me."

"Nowell . . ." Catherine smiled, and without finishing her sentence faded back to sleep.

"Sweet dreams, my angel," Nowell said, gently kissing her hand, "sweet dreams."

Chapter Thirty-one

Catherine's progress was impressive enough by the next morning that Dr. Potter agreed to release her that afternoon. He gave Nowell a list of instructions, including a firm directive not to let her return to New York until he'd seen her at least once, and possibly twice, for follow-up consultation.

Nowell consented to all the doctor's orders. In fact, he couldn't have been more pleased since it meant Catherine might have to prolong her stay in England after all.

Nowell had arranged for Dee to pack up some fresh clothes for her, which were delivered by old Joe, who was then to drive them home. As for Nowell, it had been two days since he'd showered and shaved. Regardless, he was delighted to be returning to Stuart Hall with Catherine so soon after what might have been a fatal accident. He'd gotten off easy, he kept telling himself.

The three of them remained fairly quiet during the return trip to West Yorkshire, listening mostly to the rhythm of the wipers clearing away the morning drizzle. Joe made occasional small talk about some of the game he'd seen grazing about the land.

"I can't wait to talk with Michael," Catherine softly piped in from the backseat while staring vacantly out the window.

"Hmmmm," was all Nowell said in response, his face vacant of any expression. *Michael, Michael, Michael,* he thought to himself sarcastically. *Too bad she doesn't have amnesia about Michael, Michael, Michael.*

The staff at Stuart Hall eagerly awaited Catherine's arrival, anxious to tend to her every need. Dee was first out the door, though protocol forced her to wait while Lawrence went down to the car to escort her into the house.

"Good morning, ma'am," Lawrence said politely. "Welcome back to Stuart Hall."

"Well, thank you, Lawrence." She climbed out of the car and despite the light rain stopped to take a deep breath of fresh air—a welcome contrast to the strong antiseptic smell in the hospital.

"Lawrence, will you please help me get Mrs. Harrison up to her room?" asked Nowell.

"Yes, sir."

"Catherine, if the stairs are too much for you, we can accommodate you in my study."

"I'm fine," she snapped, without even looking at him. She'd been somewhat cold and edgy with Nowell all morning. At first he brushed it off as part of her pain, but he sensed her anger and responded cautiously. Perhaps the details were becoming clear.

"Well, just remember what the doctor said about taking it easy. Once we get you up there, you need to stay put for a while."

Catherine started silently mimicking him, reassurance to Nowell of her recovery when she could give as good as she got.

Dee gasped at the sight of the bandage on Catherine's head, and the cast about her wrist, and began gushing the moment Catherine approached the threshold.

"Oh, my, miss. Oh, my. Are you hurtin'? You must be in pain. Don't you worry, we'll be takin' the best care of you ever. I promise. Only if you promise me you won't go off riding any of those old horses," she added jovially.

"Don't worry, Dee. I think my equestrian days are over for a while."

Lawrence and Nowell helped Catherine up the stairs and into her room, which was as welcoming as ever. The bed's crisp white linens were turned down, while the air was filled with the pungent smell of fresh roses and a crackling fire.

Her nightshift was perfectly laid out at the bottom of the bed, while her robe lay across a nearby chair, and her slippers sat at the ready by the bedside.

"Are you hungry, ma'am?" asked Dee.

"Not right now, thank you."

"Are you certain? You'll need to eat well to aid your recovery," piped in Nowell.

"I'm fine. I think I'll just change and get into bed for a while. I'll buzz y'all if I need anything."

"Catherine," Nowell said with a sigh, "we are all here for you, no matter what it is you need."

"Thanks." She smiled faintly.

"Lawrence, thank you for your help," said Nowell, indicating he wanted to be alone with Catherine. The servant immediately obliged him and left.

"Catherine, I must tell you something," said Nowell, shifting nervously. "I hold myself fully accountable for what happened to you. It was my fault that you went riding alone." He studied her face, slightly swollen and bruised outside her bandaged stitches. He could see her expression quicken, and immediately felt he'd tapped into her vein of anger.

"You see," he continued contritely, "Joe and I got so carried away with hunting down a stag the other morning that I completely lost track of time. I had every intention of being here for our nine o'clock ride, I mean, you know me, how prompt I always am." Catherine's unbandaged brow arched in response.

"But the next thing I knew I looked at my watch and it was eleven-thirty a.m. I wanted to shoot myself for keeping you waiting so long. Anyway, as I hurried home to find you, that is when I discovered Optima with an upside-down saddle, and then—oh, God, the memory of it—you, facedown on the ground. I thought I should die."

She looked at him coldly, her mood starkly at odds compared to when she first came out of the coma.

"Anyway, it's a good thing I acted as quickly as I did. The doctor said if I hadn't found you and done the immediate things that I did, well . . . well, we don't need to talk about it. I'm just so glad you're going to be okay. And please, please, if you ever get the notion in the future that you want to go riding alone again—well, just don't!" He laughed. She did not laugh in kind. In fact, she let out an exasperated sigh.

"You know what's odd. I truly don't remember any of the accident. All I can recall"—she paused while glaring at him—"is that I waited a long time for you."

"But certainly you don't believe that was intentional on my part, do you?"

"Nowell, I don't know what to believe. The only thing I know for certain is that my head hurts, and I'd really like to get some sleep. Did you bring my pain medication?"

"Absolutely. And I want you to know, I'm not going anywhere. I've informed my people at Sutthington Mills and everywhere else that if they need me they will have to do business with me from here."

"You don't have to do that, really."

"Catherine, don't be ridiculous. Now," he said, reaching into his coat pocket, "here are your pills. I believe one every six hours as needed is the prescribed dosage. What else can I get you?"

"Nothing, right now, really." She started moving toward the bathroom, then stopped and turned to him. "You know, actually, I hold *myself* responsible for the accident. It was my own stubbornness that got me kicked in the head."

"Well, I suppose we're even then." Nowell gently laughed, then boldly moved to give her a light hug. She did not resist him, but neither did she hug him back. It didn't matter to Nowell, as all he was truly concerned with at the moment was being let off the hook.

"Now I'm going to take a shower and then I'll be in my study. If you should happen to need anything, please use the intercom. Dee will come fetch me and we'll take care of whatever it is you want. You name it—a bison burger from Montana; a soufflé from Paris—whatever, it's yours."

"I just want you out of here," she said, laughing back.

"See you in a little while." He smiled, then headed out the door. Catherine waited for it to click, then immediately picked up the phone and dialed her home number. She looked at the clock which read 4:45 P.M. It rang several times, then stopped, but instead of hearing Michael's voice, she heard her own.

"You've reached the Harrisons. Michael and Catherine aren't home right now . . ."

"Blah, blah, blah; yeah, yeah, yeah," Catherine said back to the machine waiting for the beep, assuming he must be at the library. The tone stopped and she began to speak, but as she did, she also began to cry, suddenly realizing how badly she needed to be home with him.

"Michael," her shaky voice started, "are you home, baby? Please pick up if you are." She sniffled as she waited, but there was no answer. "Honey, I'll try again soon. I'm sorry I haven't called you lately, but I . . ." She stopped, realizing that while Nowell might have already told Michael what happened, it was better he hear the details directly from her. But then a flush of guilt consumed her as Catherine also realized there was no way to reveal the whole truth to him—that she'd willfully saddled up a thoroughbred and took off on her own because, essentially, of a lover's spat. *Oh, God,* she thought, *what have I done?*

"Anyway, I'll try you again later. I love you and I miss you terribly. Bye, baby." She hated to hang up the phone, losing whatever connection, however tentative, she had with him.

Chapter Thirty-two

Catherine slept for so long that Nowell began to worry she had slipped back into unconsciousness. As evening fell, and the air became more damp, he also worried that she might catch a chill if the fire wasn't properly stoked. He closed his book, which he could barely concentrate on anyway, then headed up to her room. He knocked a few times, but there was no answer, so he boldly opened the door.

She was sound asleep, looking sweet and lovely to him in spite of her wounds. He peered a little closer and realized, though nothing was exposed, that she was top-less. She was lying on her left side and had propped her broken wrist atop several pillows.

"Clever girl," he said, then began rejuvenating the fire. He couldn't help but wander over to the bed for a closer look. Her breathing was fine and she appeared absolutely peaceful. Nowell moved around to the oppo-site side of the bed, then sat down, gently stroking her hair and softly calling her name.

"Catherine, can you hear me?"

She didn't stir. He wondered if she shouldn't be awakened in order to eat, then decided she'd certainly let them know when she was hungry. As he watched her and gently stroked her, he was struck not by the same strong sexual temptation that brought him to grope her in the hospital, but by an urge to merely lie beside her. He inched up just slightly, and still she didn't budge.

He had no way of knowing that Catherine, assuming that more than the prescribed dosage of codeine would work better, had taken two pills instead of one. She would sleep deeply and painlessly till the next morning. Nowell could no longer resist, and boldly laid down, positioning himself against her like a spoon in a drawer, then wrapped his arm over top of her. It was an odd feeling that overcame him, something he hadn't experienced in a long, long time. Being in this quaint room, one of his late mother's favorites, and holding the woman he so desired evoked a profound sense of calm. It was an elusive peace, bringing a happiness both deep and enriching, a feeling he recalled only vaguely from his childhood when wrapped in his mother's loving arms. And then, so unexpectedly, yet with such sweet release, he began to cry.

He wept silently, the tears spilling one by one down his ruddy cheeks. From where the tears came, he did not know. Though he mourned for them still, he had not cried at his parents' funeral. Crying would have been an emotional luxury, as his emotions then were so distilled in rage at his wife that he seemed to feel nothing else.

But, Catherine, oh, sweet Catherine, he thought. *Only you could do this to me. Make a man feel so at peace with himself; instill in him such joy that you render him to tears. My darling, Catherine. I will never let you go.*

At last she stirred, and slightly moaned, but she seemed as content as he, nestling her body deeper into his while remaining sound asleep.

She must know it's me, he told himself earnestly, and tenderly stroked her arm. Then like Catherine, he drifted off to sleep—a sleep so deep and satisfying that it would keep him in bed with her all night, rendering him nearly as unconscious as she. So sound asleep was he that he didn't even hear Dee enter the room to see if Catherine needed anything.

"Oh, my word," she said, then immediately hushed herself. And though she felt it was imperative to leave the room at once, she couldn't help but stare, noticing that the nightshift she'd lain out for Catherine was still at the bottom of the bed, and that the young woman appeared naked beside Nowell.

"Oh, my word," she muttered again—half in disbelief, half in joy at having discovered something so lurid going on in the household. *I wonder if the poor girl's husband knows?* she said to herself, then, despite the inches thick carpeting, tiptoed out of the room. She painstakingly opened and shut the door, not wanting to be caught anywhere near without an invitation to enter. "Oh, Connie will never believe this!" she said excitedly as she headed hurriedly down the hall and toward the kitchen. "He will never believe this."

Chapter Thirty-three

Catherine's head felt as if it were in a vise, the pain was that unbearable and the pressure that intense. The heavy drapes were drawn tightly shut and the room was still so dark that she had no idea where she was or even what time it was.

There was a cramp in her leg, her wrist felt like it was on fire, and she was starving. Though drifting toward consciousness, she was not fully awake yet and remained completely unaware that she was at Stuart Hall. Despite her misery, she was grateful at least to be cuddled up in Michael's warmth. She burrowed her backside a little closer in to him, hoping that maybe she would go back to sleep that way, but her headache wouldn't surrender and when she decided to get up and take something to dull the pain, a slow realization began to settle in.

This cannot be Michael! she said to herself as she opened her eyes all the way and saw that she was in bed at Stuart Hall. She was almost too alarmed to move, but as she did and clicked on the bedside light, Nowell awakened. She turned and, to her utter astonishment, found him smiling at her as though nothing was out of the ordinary.

"What the hell are you doing?" she shrieked, bolting upright and fully exposing her naked breasts. "Oh, my God," she cried out, clutching as much of the sheet about herself as best she could. "What are you doing here?" she demanded again, then moaned, her own shouting worsening an intense headache.

"Sleeping." He smiled affectionately.

"But you're *sleeping* with me, in my bed! What are you doing in *my* bed?"

"Relax, woman. I came in here last night to check on you and fell asleep. It's as simple as that."

"As simple as that. You call this simple? I pass out half-naked only to find you cuddled up beside me in the morning, and it's that simple?"

Realizing the precariousness of his situation, yet trying to play it down, Nowell let out a long, low whistle. "Catherine, you don't suppose you're overreacting just a bit, do you? It's not as though we just met each other. Besides," he tried joking with her, "I did a damned good job of keeping you warm."

"I hardly think this is overreacting," she shot back. "Get out of here!"

"Why are you being so hostile?"

"Are you out of your mind? You don't get it, do you? I have never slept with anyone that first, I didn't invite to sleep with me; and second, that I wasn't conscious enough to know that I had invited. And regardless, you would have *never* received an invitation."

"We shared a bed. Is there anything so awful about that?" His calm only furthered her agitation.

"You really don't get it, do you? I want you out of here. Now."

"Catherine, I'm sorry if I startled you. But be reasonable. It's not like we're strangers."

Catherine was so angry and disillusioned that Nowell had insinuated himself upon her this way that she could have almost hurled him out of the room herself; but her head was pounding so fiercely that all she could do was lie back down and groan.

"Where's my medication?" she demanded.

"Here." He stood up and offered her the bottle while opening it for her. She inventoried his attire as he rose; noting that he was still in the same clothes as the day before, only his shirttail hung out over his trousers and he was barefoot. She grabbed the bottle from him, took two pills out, and began to pop them in her mouth when he stopped her.

"Just a minute there. Doctor's orders—only one at a time."

"I took two last night," she fired back, "and obviously felt nothing. Isn't that what you prefer?"

Nowell ignored her surliness. "Listen, I'm only telling you what the doctor told me, and it's my job to make sure you follow his orders."

"There, you happy?" she asked, placing one of the pills back inside the bottle.

"Indeed. Now how about something to eat." His nonchalance only fueled her anger.

"I'll take care of it."

"You promise?"

"Yes. Now leave," Catherine said with infuriation. She couldn't imagine why he'd so brazenly climbed into bed with her—especially given her condition. She'd never felt so used in her entire life.

Nowell slipped into his loafers, then sat down on the edge of the bed.

"I'm very sorry you're so upset. It was a truly innocent thing. I came in here last night to check on you, and settled on the bed for a moment as I did. And well, the next thing I know . . . is that I was being woken by you."

Catherine stared at him with dark, hardened eyes, unable or unwilling to comprehend fully what had happened.

Did we have sex? she thought nervously. She couldn't imagine not knowing it. But then, she'd reasoned, two days before she'd just come out of a coma and couldn't even remember the horse fall. Combined with her drug-induced dopiness, it seemed possible they'd had sex and she couldn't remember. She felt a sickening pit grow in her stomach over the possibility of having broken her marriage vows, and that Nowell might have forced himself on her this way. Catherine felt disgusting inside and out, and was momentarily overcome by raw emotion.

"Get out," she cried.

Nowell shrugged nonchalantly, confident she'd get over it, and headed out of the room.

"Oh, why is this all happening to me?" Catherine lamented and began to quiver as she watched the door slam shut. Pulling herself out of bed she felt bruised and achy all over, and sat down on a chair close to the fireplace and tried to warm herself by the dying embers. She simply couldn't believe how badly this trip was turning out. And she wanted nothing more than to go home, to be with Michael, to surrender herself to his love, and to get on with being his devoted wife. "Oh, Michael, what have I done?" she cried aloud, believing she'd brought all this bad luck on herself by indulging her fantasies with Nowell.

She sobbed a few moments longer, then angrily grabbed her robe and headed into the bathroom, where she drew the hottest water possible before gingerly climbing into the tub. It scorched at first, but soon the heat began to have a calming effect and the pain began to diminish. Only the ache in her heart persisted. She now believed whatever had happened she'd brought on herself. She'd led Nowell on in so many ways. *But still,* she thought, *what gave him the right to get into bed with me. Oh, God, what happened? Why did this happen?*

She remained in the bath until the water turned cold, grateful that the cast on her arm was waterproof, then drained the tub and took a hot shower. The bathroom was steamy and the mirror invisible by the time she dried off. She wrapped herself in her heavy robe—one Michael had given her for Christmas. The warmth of his terry-cloth embrace moved Catherine to cry broken sobs for him—the only man she'd ever truly trusted. And she knew at that moment there was only one thing that would make her feel whole again—she had to go home to Michael and never lay eyes on Nowell Stuart again.

Chapter Thirty-four

It took eight hours for Catherine to get back to London. After calling British Airways and rescheduling a flight home for the next day, she had managed to engage Connie's confidence and help in returning to the city. Connie seemed sympathetic to her plight, fully understanding her need to get home to her husband, regardless of her condition to travel.

Catherine implored him not to tell Dee or Nowell that he knew anything of her departure, to which he willingly agreed. It took extraordinary caution to avoid Dee's supervision and Nowell's watchful eye while sneaking into Connie's car. After telling Dee he was going to the local pub for an ale, nothing out of the ordinary for him, Connie took off for London with Catherine on board—crouched on the backseat. Not until they were clear off the estate and on a main highway did she sit upright. She wasn't fearful; she simply wanted to be well out of Nowell's way before he discovered she was gone. It didn't take him long.

In the early evening when he worried that she might not be getting enough to eat, he tapped lightly on her door. Hearing no response, he let her alone, but wandered down to the kitchen to ask Dee when she'd last eaten.

"I've not heard a peep out of her since she requested some tea this morning." She smiled, thinking of the two of them in bed together the previous night.

"How did she seem? Were her spirits okay?"

"I wouldn't know, sir. She requested Connie's advice on something or other so he ran up with her tea."

"Where's Connie now?"

"At the pub."

"Hmmm. Why don't you buzz her on the intercom

then and see if she needs anything," he suggested impatiently. Dee followed his instructions, but got no response.

"Oh, dear, I hope she hasn't overdone it on the medication again. I'd better check on her," he said with genuine concern. There was no doubt in Dee's mind by the look in his face how much he loved the girl. She wondered if they wouldn't sleep together again tonight.

Nowell rapped on Catherine's door, lightly at first and then with more intensity after receiving no response. In spite of being thrown out earlier in the day, he decided her physical well-being was more important than any anger she harbored toward him and let himself in.

It was perfectly dark—not even one ember glowed in the fireplace. Nowell quickly threw on the lights only to discover an empty bed. He tapped on the bathroom door, and hearing no answer opened it only to discover more darkness. It was now possible to see that all of Catherine's personal possessions were missing from both rooms.

She'd abandoned him. He simply could not understand it, the sudden realization of it bringing forth a dizzying array of emotions; emotions wrapped in the memories of his wretched existence with Elizabeth—a woman who knew no virtue and who stopped at nothing to get her way. How could Catherine, his beloved and trusted Catherine, so willfully betray him? It seemed impossible. Such a callous rejection—especially after all he'd done for her, and all that he had to offer.

No, he told himself, she would not get away with humiliating him like this. And she would not leave him—ever. He would see to that.

Catherine thanked Connie for bringing her bags inside Nowell's London town house. After retrieving the clothes still here she'd head straight to an airport hotel to spend the night, then leave early the next morning. Though Connie offered to drive her to Heathrow, Catherine insisted otherwise, saying she would take a taxi from the Belgravia neighborhood. Pecking Connie lightly on the cheek, she bid him farewell, and promised she would let him know when she'd made it home.

Nigel, deeply surprised by her unannounced arrival

and her physical appearance, escorted her upstairs while strongly encouraging her to stay. Catherine thanked him for his concern, but reassured him she was fine and wanted to overnight near the airport so as not to miss her flight home the next morning.

"There is one thing you can do for me, however. I haven't had much to eat today. Would it be too much to ask for a light snack—fruit, cheese, and crackers, whatever?"

"Of course, Mrs. Harrison. Would you care for some mineral water as well?"

"That would be nice." Catherine smiled faintly. She'd developed a fierce headache on the trip down, but had resisted taking any pain medication for fear she'd fall asleep before making it to the hotel. She tried not to waste time pulling her remaining belongings together, but her head continued throbbing, and she was hamstrung by having only one good hand to do the job. Hungry, exhausted, and in pain, Catherine settled onto the bed, momentarily grateful for its downy comfort.

Contrary to her plans to leave before Nowell could reach her, Catherine unwittingly fell asleep, never hearing Nigel as he delivered a tray laden with snacks and designer water. The man sighed with relief at the sight of her. He didn't know the details of what had happened to her or why Nowell wasn't present. But she seemed highly agitated and in no condition to travel. Hopefully, he thought, he will sleep through the night. He placed a loose blanket on top of her, then turned off the light, wondering if he should ring Nowell at Stuart Hall.

At just about half past four a.m., Catherine awoke. As with the previous morning, it was difficult to gain her bearings and for a moment she had to concentrate on where she was. "Oh, shit," she cried, realizing what she'd done. She turned on the light only to discover a tray with warm, greasy cheese and room temperature fruit on the table. It must have been there for hours. She glanced at the clock—her flight left in two hours. Panic-stricken, she threw off the coverlet. She needed a taxi and wasn't sure how to go about securing one, and certainly didn't want to bother Nigel or other staff members at this hour. Picking up the phone she dialed London's directory assistance.

"Good morning," chirped a young woman's voice. "How may I help you."

"Good morning. Could you help me with the name of a taxi company to call?"

Catherine could hear the woman speak, but another deeper voice, one ominously nearby, overrode her.

"Why don't you just ask Sonny?"

Unexpected fear ripped through Catherine and her heart started racing. "Ma'am," the woman was saying into her ear, "are you still there?"

Catherine clutched the phone tightly but did not immediately answer. "Ma'am," the woman spoke again, "are you there?"

"Yes," said Catherine softly. She dared not turn to face Nowell, and she dared not hang up with this woman either. Where she'd felt absolute confidence in her mission before, she suddenly felt horror that yet again she was awakening to find Nowell, if not in the same bed, then in the same bedroom.

"This is becoming something of a nasty habit with you, isn't it?" Catherine said guardedly.

Hanging up on the operator, Catherine finally turned to find him sitting in a chair across the room, his face darkened by shadows. He was wearing his jeans, their jeans, along with a heavy wool sweater. He was unshaven, and even in the dark Catherine could see he looked haggard. He ran his hand over the stubble on his face before speaking.

"I will consider that comment, as well as your recent behavior, a lapse of your otherwise good judgment."

Catherine nervously snickered. "It takes a lot of gall for *you* to criticize *my* judgment," she stated.

"Oh, and does it now. I think we should get our facts straight, don't you?" Nowell replied, his voice low and steady.

"Absolutely. Like for the second time in a row I wake up to find you've sneaked into my room. At least I had the bed to myself last night."

Nowell chortled. "As I see it, one of my employees decides to take one of my high-strung thoroughbreds out for a jaunt without her employer's permission. Confident though she may be about her riding skills, her ability to saddle a horse is a bit lacking and before long she finds herself cruising upside down on the beast and then nearly dead as a result. Her employer, always looking out for her best interest, bears all expenses to have her airlifted to the nearest medical facility and sees to it that she receives the finest care possible.

"He then provides her physician every assurance that she will be well taken care of outside the hospital. Again, like saddling up the horse, she knows best, and blatantly defies the doctor's orders by doubling up on her pain medication—something which renders her unconscious for the night. Her employer—someone keenly interested in her well-being—mistakenly, and innocently I might add, falls asleep on her bed only while trying to check up on her.

"In spite of his concern he is scorned by the employee. And in spite of her condition and again in defiance of doctor's orders, she leaves—essentially jeopardizing her health and, of course, her job. Do I have my facts straight?"

"This is ridiculous," she shot back contemptuously, prompting a coarse and cynical laugh from Nowell.

"No. Ridiculous is walking out on your job, which is what you are doing, right?"

Catherine sighed. "No. What I'm doing is going home to my husband, which is where I belong. You know damned good and well you would have never let me leave had I asked."

"You're right about that, and you're lying about the job. Do you suppose I would have just welcomed you back to work? Or then even provided a worthy reference?"

He got up from his chair and headed toward the door. "What time is your flight?"

"Six-thirty."

"I'll have Maggie come up and help you finish packing. Sonny will drive you to the airport."

Placing his hand on the doorknob he paused, then turned to face her. The stricken look on her face defied the anger in her voice, and he could tell—or at least he hoped—that she was confused. He decided to adopt a conciliatory tone.

"I will only say this once, so listen carefully. I value our friendship and would never do anything to intentionally hurt you. I am sorry about invading your privacy last night and again tonight—I only acted in what I thought was your best interest.

"But I also highly value you as my employee. And in spite of perhaps my better judgment, I will hold your job open—but not indefinitely. Go home and recuperate, spend time with your husband, and take a few weeks to think about it. Should you return, you have my word that our relationship will remain strictly professional. Because, regardless of what you think, I only want the best for you. Safe travels," he said, then disappeared into the darkened town house.

PART THREE

Chapter Thirty-five

Her first day back at work Catherine listened to her voice mail: two calls from Judy, several calls from various clients and designers, a return call from Wilton Dresden, and another from Dr. Webster's office. She called Dr. Webster first.

After cutting short her trip to England, Catherine had spent three weeks at home recuperating from her physical injuries, though the shock of all that had happened with Nowell remained strong. She tried hard not to believe that Nowell might have forced himself on her in bed that night as she lay in a deep, drug-induced sleep. It was too much to comprehend that he might have taken advantage of her that way.

But even harder to comprehend was how she'd let herself get so carried away with him before the accident. Memories of embracing and kissing him haunted her now—and she was unable to believe how strongly she'd desired him or how dangerously close she'd come to breaking her marriage vows. Catherine felt certain that her current remorse over her lust for him in England was far greater than any fleeting pleasure she might have derived from having sex with him.

Also, she could not have foreseen the difficulty in keeping secret from Michael her short-lived romance with Nowell, and for that Catherine ached with guilt. Yet she knew that in divulging the truth, Michael might leave her, as he truly valued fidelity. If Catherine felt good about anything it was for putting a stop to things when she did. Now if she could only find another decent job, she might finally feel absolved. And though she couldn't imagine leaving the income, she badly wanted to leave Nowell.

She had decided to follow up on the job offer Wilton

Dresden made at Nowell's Christmas party, hoping his offer was still good. She knew he'd probably never provide the same financial opportunities, but at least Wilton would never develop a physical attraction for her.

And then there was the issue of her infertility treatment. Dr. Webster expected her back in his office to begin the pre-insemination workup right after her latest period ended, which was any day now. There would be daily blood and urine workups, coupled with ultrasound scans to determine when she was ovulating. When it was apparent that the egg was on its way out of her ovary, Dr. Webster would inject Michael's sperm in her, and Catherine knew she couldn't postpone the treatment any longer if she wanted to remain a patient of the renowned physician. Based on this expense alone, it was a rotten time to think about switching jobs.

"Manhattan Reproductive Center," said the receptionist as Catherine returned the physician's call.

"Dr. Webster's office, please."

"Just a moment."

"This is Michelle," Dr. Webster's assistant answered.

"Hi, Michelle. This is Catherine Harrison. I called Dr. Webster to let him know my period just started, and I need to make arrangements for blood work, etc."

"Great," said the friendly and supportive woman. "In a couple of days you'll need to start coming to the center each morning, between seven and nine-thirty a.m., for blood work. You can bring a fresh urine sample with you, or provide one here. And when the results show you're close to ovulating, then we'll begin the ultrasounds to see just how ripe the egg is. When the time seems exactly right, then the doctor will proceed with the insemination."

"Would it be cliché to say you have this down to a science?" Catherine said with a laugh.

"Would we be in business, otherwise?" Michelle joked back.

"Michelle, tell me honestly. Just what are my chances?"

"Catherine, that's impossible to say. Our overall statistics for achieving pregnancy are good, actually slightly better than average. But I don't want to mislead you in any way. Each person is different. You may get lucky on the first try, and then again . . ."

"And then again, I may go broke trying to find out if I'll ever have a baby."

"Well, I wouldn't put it like that."

"No," Catherine said, chuckling, "of course you wouldn't. Otherwise you wouldn't be in business!"

"That's right." The woman laughed back.

Catherine hung up with Michelle, then sat thinking about what this meant. She felt nervous about the expenditure, but was more anxious than ever to start a family with Michael.

Wilton Dresden eagerly accepted Catherine's phone call. He was surprised to hear from her, but was happy nonetheless as he hoped she was calling him about a job. After learning how she'd contrived to get that mirror back from David McGowan, Wilton realized she had just the kind of savvy he valued in an employee. McGowan also owed him money, having relied heavily on his expertise for five months, and then never paying one penny for his decorating services before declaring bankruptcy. Wilton knew there was nothing Catherine could do for him in that respect, and even though he couldn't hire her as a decorator, he thought she'd do well as an assistant to some of his established designers. It also gave him great pleasure to think of snatching her away from that cocky son of a bitch, Nowell Stuart.

"Hello, Catherine," he said, picking up her call.

"Well, hey, Wilton. How are you doing? Did you have a nice New Year's?"

"Couldn't have been better. I spent it on the Canary Islands with some close friends. What can I do for you?"

"Wilton," she said, "I wanted to follow up on our conversation during Nowell's Christmas party. Don't get me wrong, I enjoy working for Nowell. But I'm ready to work as a designer. My job is limiting in that respect, so I'm starting to explore other possibilities. I thought if you were still interested that we might get together and discuss the chance of my coming to work for you."

"Catherine, I certainly can't make any promises right now, but we should at least talk."

"Could we meet next week," she asked. "I'd have to

do it during a lunch break, if that's all right with you, since Nowell is unaware that we're talking."

"I understand. How would Thursday at twelve-thirty work for you?"

"Perfect," she said. "I will see you then."

Despite her lingering doubts about him, Catherine's natural response when she first saw Nowell that Monday morning was to smile. He was as witty and affable as ever, two of his most endearing traits as far as Catherine was concerned. Still, she considered returning to work for him risky business and kept him at arm's length.

"I must say, for someone who gave a horse's hoof such a good licking, you look quite well." He grinned in his alluring way.

"Thanks, Nowell. Listen, I got a call from Sotheby's earlier this morning. They just received a complete set of George II dining chairs for auction, and they'd like to know, as a favor, if you'd examine them for authenticity. They think at least one of them is a reproduction, and Hugh Sutherland over there would like your second opinion."

"That's fine. Call and tell him I'll be over later this morning. Anything else?"

"I need you to look over a couple of bills. Here," she said, handing them over, "and this letter also requires your signature."

She was all business, and Nowell suspected it would be a few days more before she let her guard down. He wanted to tell her how he couldn't stop thinking about her, about them, during these past few weeks. But he kept it to himself, instead merely saying he was grateful she seemed well. He then retreated to his study to look over the bills and return a few phone calls.

As he settled in his chair he heard the phone ring. Catherine picked it up from downstairs first, then Nowell hit the conference button. The sound of Wilton Dresden's voice made him bristle.

"Listen, Catherine, about our meeting on Thursday. Something has come up and I'd like to reschedule your interview on Friday, at the same time, if that would work for you."

"Well, sure, Wilton, that's fine. "Oh, wait," she said,

leafing through her calendar, "I promised Nowell I would look at some estate pieces with him that day. It would be difficult to get out of it. Can we meet in the early evening, instead? What about six p.m.?"

"Six o'clock is fine with me. So you say Nowell has no idea you are looking for a new job?"

"We talked about it briefly a few weeks ago, but I don't want to remind him until I have something else to go to. Well, I'm looking forward to seeing you."

"Very good," said Wilton, "I will see you on Friday evening. And don't worry, your secret is safe with me."

"Thank you," replied Catherine, hanging up the phone.

Chapter Thirty-six

It had been a deliberately long time since Nowell Stuart set foot in a crowded bar. He hated the bar scene, mostly because he couldn't stand the pretentiousness displayed by most of the people who convened in them.

It was made all the more difficult this evening since the bar had an over-capacity crowd, and it wasn't the opposite sex that was the feature attraction. He was deep inside Zazabar, a popular Greenwich Village hangout for homosexuals, and a spot frequented by Wilton Dresden.

Nowell set his bourbon and water down on the bar, then reached into his jacket for his cigarettes. As he placed a Marlboro in his mouth, a man slightly older than he and dressed equally conservatively offered a light. Nowell obliged, then smiled as though he truly appreciated the gesture.

"Hi," said the man.

"Hello," said Nowell, uncertain where any conversation under these circumstances would lead. "I'd say it's a bit crowded in here, wouldn't you," Nowell went on, then immediately regretted his statement, believing the man may think it an invitation to leave with him.

"It's especially crowded for a Monday. What brings you out before hump day?"

"Pardon me?" said Nowell incredulously.

"It's not even the middle of the week yet, and here we are. What brought you out on a Monday night?"

"Oh," said Nowell, relieved to know the man was referring to Wednesday and nothing more. "Nothing, really. Just stopped in for a drink."

"George Glenn," the man said, then offered his hand. The more comfortable George Glenn seemed in this milieu, the more uneasy became Nowell.

Nowell half grinned at him. "Phillip. Phillip Stevenson," Nowell said, then tentatively offered his hand to shake. Glenn's grip was firm without being suggestive, not at all what Nowell expected. Nowell took a sip of his drink, then turned and leaned his back against the bar to scan the crowd. He didn't know what to expect when first entering the bar, half anticipating stereotypical gay men clad in tight leather pants and taut T-shirts. But this crowd was quite sophisticated in appearance, mostly dressed in business attire. The atmosphere, not unlike a straight bar, was quite lively. The music was too loud for Nowell's taste, and despite the fact he was a smoker, the thick, smoky air bothered his eyes. Aside from that he was surprised to discover he felt more comfortable in the Zazabar than he expected.

Looking toward the front door, he spotted a bad toupee moving above the heads in the crowd. Knowing that Wilton Dresden had arrived, he turned again, then quickly polished off his drink. He wanted to get out of sight before Dresden spotted him.

"It's getting late for me, George," said Nowell. "Enjoy your evening."

"Thanks, Phillip. I'm sorry you have to leave so soon. Do you live in Manhattan?"

"No, actually, I'm only visiting. Toodle—oo," said Nowell, throwing a ten-dollar bill down on the bar, and without further small talk walked away as quickly as he could, trying hard not to draw any attention to himself on his way out the door. He did not want to be noticed by Dresden, he merely needed to know the man had arrived.

Catherine found out about Wilton Dresden's disappearance two days before it hit the headlines of New York's daily tabloids. The police showed up at Stuart and Company first thing Friday morning, the day of her appointed interview with him.

"Please, come in," Catherine said through the intercom after the two detectives on the door stoop identified themselves. She buzzed them in, then quickly met them in the entrance hall.

"Is something the matter?" she asked nervously.

"Hi, I'm Detective Kahn," the man said, then introduced his female partner, Detective Barlowe. Detective Kahn was a balding, middle-aged man with a friendly face but a "seen it all" cynical demeanor. He had flashed his badge once before at the security monitor, but he did it again while handing Catherine a business card. Detective Barlowe, a young, stylish woman, also seemed cynical, but more from posturing than experience.

"I'm Catherine Harrison, how can I help you?"

"Well, we're following up on a missing persons report. Man by the name of Wilton Dresden. Do you know him?"

Catherine gasped, then caught her breath. "What do you mean *'missing'*?"

"Do you know him?" asked Barlowe in a sharp professional voice.

"Yes, yes I do. This is crazy, I just talked with him the other day. In fact," she gasped again, then turned to see if Nowell had come downstairs yet, "I was planning on seeing him today."

"That's why we're here," Kahn stated, "we saw your name in his appointment book." Catherine had a sick feeling in her stomach.

"How long has he been missing?"

"He hasn't been seen or heard from since Monday night."

"Since Monday?"

"What we want to know," Barlowe began, "is whether Mr. Dresden mentioned anything to you about leaving town?"

"Well, the only thing I can tell you is that I was supposed to meet him yesterday for a job interview. But he called on Monday saying something had come up and he wanted to reschedule for this evening. This is so bizarre."

"Did he mention where he might be going?" asked Detective Kahn, opening his notebook.

"No, I didn't get into that with him. I'm sorry," she said nervously. "Where are my manners? Would you two like to sit down? Can I get you a cup of coffee or tea?"

"No thanks," responded Kahn in his thick Long Island accent, the hint of a smile on his face. He reminded Catherine of a history professor she'd had at Carolina that seemed like a decent guy, but who, it turned out, failed practically everyone due to his exceedingly high standards. She'd scraped by with a "C" and felt eternally grateful for it. Catherine got the same impression from Detective Kahn—he wasn't someone to take lightly.

"We just finished our third cup for the morning," he added, "but thanks anyway."

"I hope you don't mind my asking," said Catherine, "but how do you know for certain Mr. Dresden is missing?"

"He hasn't shown up for work since Monday, and has missed several social engagements besides. His sister actually filed the report, since she said he has joined her every Tuesday night for dinner since she can remember, and he didn't show up or call. She said that's highly unlike him. You sure you can't remember anything else?" asked Detective Kahn. "Did he cancel your appointment because of meeting someone else? Maybe you remember that person's name?"

"No, no. Really. It was just like I said. He told me something came up, and that was it. But what do you think happened? Have you talked with anyone else?" Catherine asked anxiously. This whole affair had her feeling seriously rattled.

"We don't know yet. His sister went over to his apartment yesterday and there was no answer. She had an extra set of keys and let herself in, but nothin' seemed outta place," Kahn said. "His car is in the garage—totally undisturbed, and he didn't have any plans to travel outta the area—at least as far as we know."

Catherine sat down in a chair near the front door, trembling from disbelief. What the cops had just revealed did not sound promising. *I'm sure he's fine,* she began repeating to herself like a reassuring mantra. *I'm sure he's fine.*

"Well, seeing that you have an appointment with him today," said Detective Barlowe, "if you should happen to hear from him, would you kindly give us a call? You've got my number there."

"Absolutely," said Catherine, anxious to share the news with Nowell.

He had already heard the entire conversation from the recesses of the musicians' balcony above the foyer.

There was a door leading to it from the second floor, through which Nowell had carefully entered after observing the presence of the two cops on his security monitor upstairs. He waited till they were long gone before stepping into the elevator and taking it down to the ground floor, behaving oblivious to the encounter.

Catherine looked up at him with a terrible strain on her face as he entered her office.

"Good morning," he said in his usual chipper way.

"Hi," she said. The news was going to be very difficult to break to Nowell, specifically since the cops paid a visit to Catherine knowing she was due to see Dresden later that day. She couldn't lie to Nowell about it, as he was bound to discover the truth one way or another.

"Nowell," she said carefully, "please sit down. I have something to tell you."

"Catherine, you are absolutely white. What is it?" he asked, sinking into a wing-backed chair.

"Wilton Dresden is missing."

"What do you mean, 'Wilton Dresden is missing'?"

"The cops were just here, asking me if I knew anything concerning his whereabouts."

"Is this some kind of a joke?"

She merely shook her head no.

"For God's sake, Catherine. This is quite disturbing. But why on earth would they come here?"

She let out a deep sigh, her hands fidgeting nervously on the desktop before her. "Because I was scheduled to meet with him later today. They saw my name on his calendar."

"You don't say? I hope you don't mind my asking," he said, slightly cocking his head, "but what for?"

"A job interview," she said very matter-of-factly.

"Oh, I see," he said dejectedly.

"Nowell, I'm so sorry," said Catherine. "I certainly didn't expect for you to find out about it this way. But I decided after returning from England that I'd be more comfortable working somewhere else."

"I see. But why would you even bother returning to work here if you weren't planning to stay?"

"I don't know," she answered, looking down at her hands, not wanting to tell the truth, that she simply couldn't let go of the money till she'd found something else. "I guess I just wanted to see how things were between us before I started looking in earnest."

"But aren't things okay?" he asked. "I've behaved like a perfect gentleman, haven't I?"

"Oh, Nowell, it's not you. It's not you at all. It's me. I realized in all that happened what a weak person I am. And I simply cannot afford to have anything like it happen again. That's all."

"Hmmm," he said, then leaned back in his chair, staring out at the courtyard beyond and saying nothing more.

"Nowell," she prodded gently, "I hope you aren't mad at me."

"No, not at all," he responded confidently. "I understand. Have you interviewed elsewhere?"

"No, not yet. Wilton was the first stop."

"Then may I make a suggestion. And please take your time to think about it, because I certainly don't want to come across as putting any undue pressure on you. But I think we have both sufficiently worked the steam out of our systems. Wouldn't you agree?"

Catherine nodded her head yes.

"Well, I want you to understand something. As I previously said, I consider you a valuable employee. As a measure of my appreciation, nothing more, nothing less, mind you, I am offering you a ten-thousand-dollar a year pay raise. The only stipulation is that you agree to finish out the year with me. Following that, you are free to do what you want. Should you choose to stay beyond that, fine. If you want to move on, then I will understand. Though I would find it very difficult, indeed, to replace you. In fact," he said, chuckling, "I would have to hire two people to replace you, so a ten-thousand-dollar increase in pay is certainly worth my while if you will only stay."

Ten thousand dollars a year! thought Catherine. *That would just about cover the cost of the in vitro, if we get that far, and leave the rest of my income untouched.* She was no longer thinking of Wilton Dresden's welfare, instead she was focused strictly on her own. *And a year will pass by in a snap, especially if I'm pregnant,* she continued thinking. *Oh, why does he do this to me. This is so unfair.*

"Nowell," she said, "if you're serious, as I'm sure you are, then you have a deal. But it is only with the following understanding. If things should become even slightly uncomfortable between us again, then I will leave—and won't give it a second thought, no matter what." Catherine studied his face, which had broken into a warm smile.

"Yes, I fully understand."

"Okay," she said, her spirits now a little more upbeat, "then let's get back to work."

"By all means," said Nowell, adding, "and I must say that even though I don't care terribly much for that bugger Wilton Dresden, I certainly hope they find him soon."

Indeed they did. The following day he was discovered bound, gagged, and dead at a hotel in downtown Manhattan, a place frequented by upscale homosexuals searching for quick sex in a luxurious setting. Someone had slashed Dresden's face and throat, then repeatedly stabbed him in the back. It had taken hotel management a while to find him because the maids avoided the room due to the DO NOT DISTURB sign, and also because Dresden was a regular who occasionally checked in for one night, then stayed two without ever leaving his room.

When the hotel manager finally needed Dresden's room he called several times, and when no one answered he went to see if Dresden had just checked himself out. The manager was horrified to find that someone had already checked out Dresden for good. He called the police, asking for discretion. But the story made terrific grist for the tabloid mills—and the coverage of the murder of a high-society designer was extensive.

It hinted that Dresden may have picked up a gay lover at one of the nearby bars, though no one could remember with whom he was last seen on Monday night. He had mentioned to the front desk that he was expecting a guest, but no one paid any attention after that. If someone had visited, he never stopped at the front desk on the way in. Police tried to link Dresden's murder to several recent crimes involving gay men in the hotel's area, but this was one that just didn't tie in.

"Probably a crime of passion," one police lieutenant was quoted as saying. "You hardly ever see something this brutal unless someone goes crazy, like jealous crazy," said another.

Nowell and Catherine attended his funeral together. There was no viewing of the body, since it was reported his face had been pretty badly mutilated. It didn't matter to Nowell, since he was the last to see the man alive anyway, remembering the look in Dresden's eyes as he realized it was Nowell and not his intended lover at the door. *"Don't worry, your secret is safe with me,"* Nowell had taunted Dresden with the words he had spoken to Catherine about their forthcoming interview while slashing him to death. He could not have imagined how good it felt to destroy his old nemesis, at the same time preventing Catherine from leaving him.

Now my *secret is safe with you,* Nowell thought, laughing to himself as the tearful eulogies began.

Chapter Thirty-seven

Catherine climbed out of the cab in front of her brownstone apartment, and instead of heading directly upstairs, she sat down on the stoop in the white winter sun, feeling disenchanted, depressed, and very sorry for herself.

She wasn't pregnant; the second insemination had failed. She didn't even need to know the official results of the pregnancy test taken yesterday at the Manhattan Reproductive Center, as she'd started her period shortly after arriving at work this morning. Unable to keep her chin up, she told Nowell she wasn't feeling well and asked his permission to go home. Naturally, he was concerned about her, even offering to provide a car service to get her there. But she didn't want to wait, and she didn't want Nowell to see her cry, as she felt certain she would. Somehow her tears defied her.

Rather than going upstairs to the quiet, lonely apartment, Catherine decided to head across the street and find Michael. Assuming he was in class, she headed to Reverend Whitlock's classroom, but found it vacant except for the avuncular, older priest.

"Hi," she said softly. Whitlock looked up from some papers he was grading, pushing his glasses onto the top of his head, and removing his unlit pipe from his mouth.

"Catherine, what a pleasant surprise." He could see in her face she wasn't interested in small talk. "I don't suppose you're here to see me. Michael is over in the chapel right now."

"Thanks," she said with a smile. "How's Meredith?" Catherine asked, not wanting to be impolite by rushing off.

"She's doing quite well, thank you. It's been a while,"

Whitlock said, "we're hoping to get you and Michael over for dinner soon."

"That would be nice," Catherine replied, then quite to her surprise began to cry.

"Good Lord." Whitlock moved swiftly to his feet. "Something awful has happened. Are you all right?"

"There's nothing to worry about, really. It's just a personal disappointment."

"Oh, goodness. Well, whatever it is, if there is anything that Meredith and I can do to help you, please don't hesitate to ask," he said with sympathetic eyes.

Catherine thanked him through a muffled sob, then left to find Michael. She found him inside the school's beautiful, old chapel, up at the altar's communion table, alone and seemingly happy in his thoughts while preparing for the late afternoon service. For the moment he had his back turned toward her, so she approached him quietly, stopping a few feet away just to watch, uneasy about piercing his peace.

He turned and startled at the sight of her. "Catherine," he said happily, then immediately noticed her tear-stained face.

"No, oh, no," he said and promptly moved toward her with open arms. She didn't have to tell him, he instinctively knew. And as he embraced her with all his tender strength, she fell apart in his arms and cried like she'd never cried before; an aching, grieving sob over what might have been. He held her close for some time, feeling pinched by the same grief. He had to admit to himself that as uncertain as the insemination was, he'd gotten caught up in the daydream of parenting as well, and had prayed hard for success. He gently kissed Catherine's forehead as her sobs began to wane, then escorted her to one of the pews.

"Oh, honey, I'm so sorry, I'm so sorry."

"I know," she finally spoke, "I'm sorry for you too."

"Will you join me in a prayer?" he asked. Catherine nodded her head yes, and the two of them knelt together and bowed their heads. Catherine tried hard to focus on a thoughtful and meaningful prayer, but began crying all over again. Michael meditated a moment longer, then gently took her hand.

"Catherine, I know this is not what you want to hear,

but we knew this was a possibility. If the disappointment is going to affect you this deeply, then maybe we ought to rethink what we're doing."

"I can't."

Michael let out an uncharacteristic sigh of impatience.

"Michael, I can't give up."

"Catherine, I thought we agreed we're not going to get carried away by this."

"I know that, and believe me, I'm not going to become obsessed with trying again and again and again, whether it's the insemination or in vitro. But I want a fair chance at having a baby; our baby."

"Look, I want a family as badly as you do. But it's like I said before: our money may be better spent adopting a child, which is probably a more realistic option anyway."

"I know what you're saying," she said, her calm somewhat restored. "But I feel almost like it's now or never to have one of our own. Wherever we go next, we won't have a world-class fertility center like the one we're going to. Or someone with Dr. Webster's reputation. It's worth it, Michael, especially since we're already in the program. If we backed out now it could end up taking another year to see him if we later changed our minds."

Michael remained quiet for a moment. Seeing Catherine this chapfallen truly had him concerned. Despite her claims that she wouldn't want to take the infertility treatment to an extreme, he worried otherwise, her behavior today being evidence of that concern.

"Honey, I know you're hurting. Believe me, it makes me sad too. But you have to promise me that we will stick to our agreement. One more insemination and one stab at the in vitro. If it doesn't work, then that's it. In my conscience, I simply can't agree to spend untold money just to see that this isn't going to work for us. Do you agree?"

Though Catherine softly shook her head yes, her heart strongly said no.

Nowell closed his eyes that night and tried hard to sleep, but his mind would not rest. It had been a little more than a month since he'd returned from England, and Catherine remained as aloof as ever. She seemed preoccupied and intent on keeping her distance from him, which tormented him.

He'd invited her to lunch on several occasions, but each time she'd rejected him, claiming to have something important to do. He asked her to come along on a variety of business matters, just to have her near. And while she always obliged his request where work was concerned, she consistently begged out of anything even remotely social.

He missed her so dreadfully and needed so badly to hold her again that it was almost unbearable to be near her. In his mind, a thousand times, he plotted Michael's demise. But then he'd think of Dresden, and remind himself he'd gotten off lucky, as the police remained clueless over who murdered him. He might not be so fortunate with Michael.

Nowell rolled over, and did as he had every night for the past few months, and looked at Catherine. There she was, in all her elegance and beauty, gracefully realized in a life-sized portrait on his bedroom wall, a piece of work commissioned by a famed artist back home in England. Nowell had provided the man with pictures taken of Catherine during the Christmas party, then told the man exactly what he wanted done besides.

Her blond hair fell full and loose around her shoulders, and her skin was absolutely flawless, seemingly porcelain. Her eyes cast a luminescent glow, and her well-sculpted cheekbones had just the right blush to them, nearly matching in color her perfect rosebud mouth.

But instead of her dark green velvet and taffeta dress, the artist had portrayed Catherine lying seductively on a chaise lounge, with a sheet draped loosely over her torso; one long leg and one breast, fully exposed. Nowell had provided the man with as much as he could on the details of her body, remembering quite well all that he'd seen under her hospital gown, and again as she popped up half-naked in bed after discovering him beside her. The likeness of her in the man's work was stunning, and each night it was as though she came to him through the portrait, fulfilling their destiny—alone at last and secure in their love for each other.

Chapter Thirty-eight

Catherine unlocked the door to Nowell's town house, then flicked on the lights. He was obviously still upstairs, for which she was grateful. It would give her an opportunity to privately call Dr. Webster's office and learn the results of her blood pregnancy test taken earlier that morning.

This third time she'd tried keeping her hopes in check. And though her period was just a couple of days late this month, she repeatedly reminded herself not to get excited. Since beginning her treatment with Dr. Webster, the past two months had seemed like the longest in her life. In some ways, working for Nowell helped, since he always kept her busy. And gratefully, he'd kept his word as well, careful not to push her in any inappropriate way. But things were not the same as they'd once been. In fact, to Catherine, something much deeper seemed to have changed in him. He was just not the same person.

He was still chatty and witty with her, which she enjoyed. But there was a new defensiveness about him. In addition to seeming skittish, he claimed for security reasons that no one enter the gallery without first making an appointment. Catherine attributed this nervousness to Wilton Dresden's murder, believing Nowell perceived they were both at risk until the crime was solved. She had similar concerns herself, but not to the same extent as Nowell. She was always cautious about who entered, but this new appointment policy was a hassle. It seemed to be the least of his concerns.

As Catherine sat down at her desk that morning, the first thing she did was dial Dr. Webster's phone number for the results of her third insemination.

"Manhattan Reproductive Center," came a pleasant voice over the line.

"Hi, this is Catherine Harrison," she said in a near whisper, as though expecting Nowell to pop in at any instant. "I'm calling for the results of my pregnancy test."

"Just a minute, please," the woman said, putting the call on hold and forcing Catherine to listen to a Muzak version of Eric Clapton's "If I Call Your Name."

"Corso," said the next person impatiently.

"Hi, this is Catherine Harrison. I was in this morning for a pregnancy test. Do you have the results yet?"

"I don't know why they transferred you to me," she said with frustration, "hold on." A couple of minutes later she picked up the phone again.

"Negative," she said with clinical detachment.

"Negative?"

"Yup."

"Are you sure?"

"Yup."

Catherine let out a long sigh. "Can I speak to Dr. Webster, please?"

"I'll give you back to the operator," Corso said without further ado. The pleasant voice came back on line, informing her that Dr. Webster was on another call.

"I'll wait, if it's okay," Catherine said, realizing she'd better employ her privacy before Nowell showed up. It was nearly ten minutes before the physician picked up.

"Catherine, good morning," he said. She instantly began to cry. "Uh-oh. Did you just get the lab results?"

"Yeah," she said, sniffling.

"I'm so sorry. Are you okay?"

"No, not really."

"Hmmm. You know there are no guarantees," he said. She let out another sigh, thinking he probably said that to everyone after sucking large sums of cash from them.

"Now what do we do?"

"In vitro," was his simple response. "As you know, you'll have to continue with the blood workups, and ultrasound scans, only now we have to pump you full of drugs at the same time to get the hormones going, and make sure we can retrieve as many ripe eggs as possible from your ovary. I believe we've gone over all this with you and Michael, so he should know what to expect in terms of helping to administer the shots of Pergonal."

"Yeah," she said, sniffling again. "I'll tell Michael, and I'll guess we'll see you soon." She hung up without saying good-bye.

Nowell waited for the dial tone before hanging up the phone in his study, then retreated downstairs as quickly as possible in an attempt to catch her in a raw emotional state. He found her standing at the French doors looking out at the courtyard, a used and rumpled tissue in her hand. Though she wasn't still crying, her smeared makeup revealed the results of her unhappy phone conversation.

"Good morning," Nowell chirped.

"Hi," she responded sadly, turning to find him looking sharp and handsome as ever in one of his navy-blue pinstriped suits, his eyes sparkling.

"My goodness, why so glum?"

"Oh, it's nothing, really. I'm just tired, that's all," she said, then continued to stare outside. She let out a big sigh, prompting Nowell to ask if she would care to step into the garden for a breath of the still chilly, but fresh spring air. It was now the beginning of April, and crocuses had begun poking their playful heads out of the sleepy ground, seeming to beckon them outdoors.

"No, no thanks," she said, then plopped down in a chair. The temptation was there to tell him all about her travails, but she knew better than to get him involved in her personal life. She was feeling so deceived at the moment—by her body, by the medical world. She didn't know how she would summon the courage to continue going through these highly invasive procedures. But she knew, as the woman on the bus with the baby had told her last year, it was her best hope of having a biological child.

"Nowell, I know this is short notice. But would you mind terribly if I took the rest of the day off?"

"By all means. Are you sure you're all right?"

"I'm going to be okay, really. And I'll be in tomorrow, I promise." She smiled affectionately at him as she gathered her purse and coat, then left.

Nowell opened the doors to the courtyard afterward and sat down on a bench, closing his eyes and breathing in the scent of thawing air; seeing everything in the garden now budding with possibility.

Impoverished and barren, that's what her whole life with Michael will be like. How could she stand the thought of it? Nowell wondered, when a bolt of unbelievable possibility shot through his mind. He wasted no time going into the office, then hitting the redial button on Catherine's telephone.

"Manhattan Reproductive Center," said the pleasant voice.

"Yes," said Nowell, "I need to send something over to the lab, to a Ms. Corso. Could you kindly give me her first name."

"Oh, certainly. It's Sharon. Sharon Corso," she answered.

"And what is her exact title, please."

"I'm not sure, let me check. I know she's one of the senior embryologists in the lab."

"Oh, that's all right, please don't go to any trouble. What time does she leave? I don't know if we'll have everything ready to send her by the end of the day."

"Let's see, she usually leaves at three-thirty," the woman said.

"Oh, heavens, we'll have to work fast. Well thank you," he said, "thank you very much. Oh, and one last thing, what is your exact address there?"

Jotting down the address, he thanked her once again, then hung up the phone. He looked at his watch, it was ten o'clock; five and a half hours till Sharon Corso left for the day.

Chapter Thirty-nine

Nowell customarily traveled by hired car when he wanted to get around town. But today he took a taxi to the Manhattan Reproductive Center on the Upper West Side. It was in a nondescript building, not far from Westside General Hospital. He checked out the center first before entering, looking for an employee entrance. It appeared there was only one entrance, which was the front lobby. He walked in with confidence and felt relieved to find the waiting room fairly full, then sat down in a chair and began nonchalantly thumbing through magazines. He looked like any of the other yuppie men in the room—mostly mid-thirties to forties, professional and healthy-looking—except he was the only single man there.

A receptionist, and not the same one with the pleasant voice, didn't even notice him because he blended in so well with the others. After sitting for a few minutes, he casually approached her.

"Uh-hmm," he cleared his throat. She glanced up from a computer she was working on.

"Has Sharon Corso left yet?"

"No, I don't think so. She usually doesn't leave until three-thirty. Do you need to see her?"

"Well, yes and no," he said with a grin. The combination of his good looks, British accent, and refined manners always worked like a charm on woman, and he knew he'd already gained her full attention.

"Actually, an employee of mine told me and my wife about the Center. Sharon Corso is his good friend, and he said she highly recommends this place."

"It is one of the best," she responded.

"Anyway, while I'm waiting for my wife, I thought I'd

say hello to her. Can you tell me what she looks like so perhaps I can have a word with her as she leaves?"

"Oh, sure. I think today she's wearing a red dress, and she has blond hair, kinda shoulder length, and," she whispered, leaning in toward him, "don't tell that I told ya, but bad roots. You won't miss her, if ya know what I mean."

Nowell chuckled. It was amazing to him how catty and indiscreet Americans could be.

"Well, I suppose she should be fairly easy to spot, then," he whispered back. "And don't worry, I won't say anything." He winked at her, then went and sat back down in his seat for a few more minutes. When the receptionist wasn't looking he slipped outside to await Sharon Corso's exit.

At 3:35 P.M. a woman matching her description left the center. She might have been in her late thirties or so, it was difficult to tell since her gaunt face made her appear older. Her dress was short but conservative—more burgundy than red—and as she walked out the door the first thing she did was light up a cigarette, take a couple of long drags off it, then head toward the subway stop at Columbus Circle.

Nowell stayed a few paces behind her, entering the subway station as she did. Though he had never boarded a New York City subway train, he proceeded with confidence to buy a token while keeping a steady eye on the woman. To the dismay of some people also waiting for a train, she lit up another cigarette and began to smoke again on the platform, this time taking deep and repeated drags from her cigarette. She seemed preoccupied to Nowell, and oblivious to the nonsmokers.

She hadn't noticed Nowell either. And he carefully avoided getting too close until after he was in the car with her and the train was moving up the track. He made it a point to stand right in front of her, hanging on to the strap above her head. He smiled at her once, but mostly appeared to look vacantly ahead. Two stops later the man sitting beside her exited the train, and Nowell quickly filled his seat, intentionally bumping her leg as he did.

"Oh, so sorry," he poured on the charm.

"No problem," she said. Her teeth were straight but

yellow from tobacco stains, and creases in her thin face made her look considerably older up close. He glanced at her left hand and didn't see a wedding band, but knew that was not entirely revealing. Inwardly he laughed about the receptionist's observation—her roots definitely needed touching up and the rest of her hair was too blond for her age and complexion.

"I say, I'm much more accustomed to the London tube. This seems a bit rough by comparison."

"I wouldn't know," she said matter-of-factly. "I've never been to London."

"Oh, pity. It's a wonderful place. Must you take this blasted subway often?" he asked her politely.

"Twice a day. Five days a week. Back and forth to work."

"Oh, really." He smiled, then deliberately paused. "Do you work in midtown?" he finally asked over the din of the train's rumble, casting a flattering grin at her.

"Upper West Side," she replied without a smile, but the look in her eyes indicated an increased level of interest in him.

"What do you do?" Nowell boldly asked.

"Lab tech."

"You're a scientist?" he said enthusiastically.

"Well, yeah," she responded more brightly.

"What exactly do you do?"

"I run the lab at the Manhattan Reproductive Center."

"My goodness, what a coincidence. I was just there."

"Oh, yeah," she said with a proud and surprised grin, "I've worked there ten years now." She wasn't interested in probing into his personal affairs, obviously knowing why he would have been there.

"Yes, in fact my wife and I are here from London to see Dr. Webster," he added, but almost in a whisper as though conveying a confidence.

"He's one of the best," she said. "Probably a better success rate for what you're trying to do than any other doctor in the country, maybe even in the world."

"So I understand. It's reassuring to hear it from someone who works there. What exactly do you do in the lab, Miss . . . ?"

"Corso," she politely replied. "I do a little bit of everything. But mostly I'm the senior embryologist."

"So, in other words, it might actually be you who gets us pregnant?"

"Well, to tell you the truth, the doctor does all the manipulating of hormones and then the placement of the embryos. But I have primary responsibility for overseeing the fertilization process—joining egg and sperm together."

Nowell could feel his whole body go tense with excitement. This was an amazing stroke of good luck for him, and if all went according to his unfolding plans, Sharon Corso would be the one quite literally to bring him and Catherine together.

"Well, Ms. Corso, perhaps my wife and I will be seeing you soon. Or at least we know you'll be seeing a part of us!"

She smiled back. "Good luck with everything."

"Thanks." He nodded at her. "Well, this looks like my stop," he said, smiling as he stood, then tipped his hand good-bye. He walked off the train, and turned to see if she was watching. She was not, and with that Nowell quickly leaped aboard the next car just as the doors were closing shut.

He watched carefully to see when Sharon Corso exited the train, which was several stops later and out in the Bronx. Nowell carefully followed her off the train and out onto the street. She walked a good half mile or so, into a fairly decent area, and turned on a street with neat little row houses. Unlike other parts of the Bronx where graffiti and trash were pervasive, the neighborhood appeared clean and orderly.

From the street corner Nowell observed Corso walk up the steps of a small two-story house with security bars on the windows. He wondered if she had any family or if she lived alone. And not wanting to take the risk of being noticed, Nowell waited awhile before quickly passing by her house so that he could write down the correct address. He then cut his way back to the subway station as fast as he could, then climbed into a taxi after exiting at Columbus Circle on the Upper West Side. As soon as he got home, he put in a call to his lawyer, Vincent Gambrielli.

"Nowell, good to hear from you. How are you?" the man asked jovially.

"Fine, Vince, just fine," Nowell responded to his greeting. "How are Sophia and the girls?"

"They're great. Lindsey's going to college next year. Can you believe it?"

"No. The last time I saw her she was just entering high school. Where does the time go?"

"What can I do for you?" Vince asked.

"This is nothing big, Vince, but something that needs to be handled discreetly."

"I'm listening."

"I need a background check on someone."

"What do you want?"

"The basics, really. A credit rating, mortgage, education, marital status, children, any trouble with the law, that sort of thing."

"When do you need it?"

"As soon as possible."

"I'll get right on it. Give me the name and whatever you know already."

"Sharon Corso, her name is Sharon Corso. She works at the Manhattan Reproductive Center, and she lives in the Bronx—135 W. 256th Street."

"Anything else?" Vince inquired.

"That's it."

"I'll get right on it," said Vince, anxious as always to rack up the billable hours.

"Excellent. Please give Sophia my best."

"Will do," said Vince, then hung up the phone. Nowell leaned back into his office chair and stared with confidence at the ceiling. What he was planning was a serious risk, but one worth any price for the remarkable payoff it promised. He could not stop grinning as he reveled in the idea of Catherine, his beloved Catherine, bringing their child into the world.

Chapter Forty

"This is Vincent Gambrielli, may I speak with Nowell?"

"Could you hold just a minute, please?" Catherine asked politely, then put him on hold. "Nowell," she called out to him. He was in the adjoining room with clients showing them some antique silver pieces.

"Excuse me," he said, "I'll be right back." He went into the office. "Yes," he asked somewhat impatiently, "what is it?"

"Vincent Gambrielli's on the phone. Do you want to talk with him, or do you want me to take a message?" Nowell's face flushed as he reached for the phone.

"Vince, how are you?" he asked, then raised his eyebrows at Catherine as if to say "thanks" for seeing to it he got the call. Catherine knew how proud Nowell was to share confidences with one of New York's most well-known and feared lawyers.

"Uh-hmm," Nowell responded. "Uh-hmmm. Listen, I have some clients with me at the moment. May I call you back in a few minutes, I'd like to hear more about it." Vince thought he was being unusually vague with him considering how urgent he'd made his business seem just the other day.

"As long as you call me back within five minutes," Vince chided him, "otherwise I'll be gone all day." Nowell would call him back in less time than that—as soon as he got to a private line.

"Absolutely," said Nowell, smiling at the receiver. "Talk with you soon." He hung up the phone and wasted no time getting back to his clients.

"Something has come up, and I need to take care of some urgent business. This won't take me long. If you have any questions in the meantime, please speak with my assistant, Catherine Harrison." He then excused himself and headed to his private quarters via the elevator. Within minutes he was back on the line with Vince.

"So sorry. I wasn't in a place where I could have a candid discussion with you. What did you learn? Anything good?"

"Well, that all depends on what you consider good. Here's what we know. She's forty-one years old, graduated from Columbia University with a Bachelor of Science degree in biology in 1974. She worked for a little while at a blood lab at Columbia-Presbyterian Hospital, then got her Master's Degree in microbiology at Columbia in 1981, which is also the year she married her soon-to-be ex-husband—a cardiologist by the name of Dr. Patrick Corso. He's been sleeping with one of the cardiology residents."

Nowell sat back in his desk chair, thrilled at what he'd heard so far. He was impressed with Vince's efforts. "Go on," he said.

"From their credit report, they had some money problems a few years ago, which forced them to sell their half-million-dollar house in Larchmont. Right now there's a bitter custody battle going on for their eight-year-old kid, a boy who right now lives with his dad. The father claims Sharon has a drinking problem; she claims, among other things, he's setting a bad example for the boy by bringing strange women home to sleep with him. You know how that kind of thing goes."

"I suppose," said Nowell, who felt like he'd just struck pay dirt.

"Anything else?"

"She's been at the Manhattan Reproductive Center for ten years. She's a senior embryologist and a staff supervisor, apparently very competent at what she does, and makes an honest living. No arrests, no points on her driver's license, or anything like that. Did I answer all your questions?" asked Vince.

"This is splendid, Vince. You did an excellent job. I'll let you know if I need anything else. And remember, this is a matter of absolute discretion."

"You got it. *Ciao.*"

"*Ciao,*" said Nowell, smiling broadly as he hung up with Vince, then promptly dialed the Manhattan Reproductive Center. The woman with the pleasant voice answered the phone.

"May I speak with Sharon Corso, please?"

"May I tell her who's calling?"

"Yes"—he paused for a second—"my name is Phillip Stevenson. Tell her I'm the one she talked to on the subway yesterday."

"Thank you," said the woman, then put him on hold, forcing him to endure the same Muzak rendition of the Eric Clapton song he'd heard a few days before while sharing the phone line with Catherine. He began nervously tapping his fingers on the desk while waiting for Sharon Corso to pick up.

"Hello," she said, sounding somewhat upbeat.

"Ms. Corso, hello," said Nowell warmly. "Thank you for taking my call. You do remember me, don't you?"

"Of course I do. How can I help you, Mr. Stevenson?"

"Well, I know this may sound a bit odd. But my wife and I are rather nervous about our upcoming procedure. And we were wondering if you wouldn't be willing to meet with us to discuss the technical side of what it is we're about to go through."

"Didn't Dr. Webster go over all of it with you?"

"Well, yes and no. He's rather busy, and we got the impression that he wasn't able to spend as much time with us as we would have liked. I also got the impression from you yesterday that you're a very competent woman, and I believe my wife would feel immensely reassured if she met you and knew that you were part of the team that was helping us to achieve our long-time wish of having a baby."

"I see," she replied, obviously flattered by his compliment. "Well, I suppose I could meet with you. Why don't you stop by the lab on your next trip in to see Dr. Webster?"

"We could do that, but don't you think he might be a bit offended if he saw that we were consulting with you and not him? We would love to take you to lunch, or even dinner to discuss it with you."

Sharon Corso had never dealt with one of their patients on this personal a level before, and her first instinct was to say no. But her life, both in and out of the lab, was the same thing, day in and day out, and she couldn't see any real harm in sharing an hour of her time with this nice man and his wife.

"Well, I suppose that would be okay," she told him. "When did you have in mind?"

"We have plans today, but it looks like tomorrow evening is free. Would you care to join us for dinner in the Oak Room at the Plaza?"

She grinned at the prospect of an evening out and a meal at one of New York's finest restaurants. "Sure, what time?"

"Would six o'clock be too early for you?"

"No, that's perfect. I'll look for you then."

"Splendid. We shall see you at six o'clock tomorrow."

"Good-bye," she said as though talking to an old friend. She looked forward to her social meeting with the Stevensons, a nice change of pace from her usual humdrum life.

"Good-bye," said Nowell, then gingerly put down the receiver and leaned back proudly in his chair.

"Catherine," he said while positively beaming, "I think you and I are going to have a baby."

Chapter Forty-one

Nowell slipped into the most expensive suit he owned; double-breasted and hand-tailored with fine chalk pin-stripes. His multicolored tie provided just the dash of color he needed against his starched-white shirt. He needed to look his absolute best for Sharon Corso, and even slapped on his favorite cologne, the one Catherine loved so much.

He couldn't help but feel a little sorry for Corso. She wasn't so unattractive that people would make fun of her looks, but she was not attractive or young enough anymore to draw the attention of potential suitors. Tonight he was going to make her feel like a million.

His chauffeur-driven car was waiting for him at five-thirty, and dressed and ready to go, Nowell jumped in for the short ride to the hotel. He told the driver he would be a couple of hours in the Oak Room, and that he should expect to drive another passenger out to the Bronx afterward. The chauffeur acknowledged him, and Nowell strode into the opulent hotel and directly to the heavily paneled Oak Room. He scanned the restaurant for Sharon first, and not seeing her, approached the maître d'.

"Stevenson, party of three at six o'clock," he told the young man.

"You're early," the maître d' replied in a tone bordering on criticism.

"Indeed. Would you prefer that I wait at the bar, or can you go ahead and seat me now?"

The man looked about the room, which was only beginning to fill up with diners for the evening. "No problem," he concluded, "I can seat you now."

"Thank you," said Nowell, "I appreciate it." The man gathered up three menus, then escorted Nowell to a less-

than-desirable table in the center of the room. Nowell
stopped him before he set the menus down.

"If you don't mind, we could really use some privacy.
I'd prefer that table over there in the smoking section,"
he said, nodding in the direction of a corner table.

"That table is reserved," came the maître d's cool response. Nowell felt irritated by the man's smugness, but
decided to part company with a one-hundred-dollar bill
to get some privacy with Ms. Corso.

"Perhaps I didn't make myself clear; we could *really*
use some privacy," he intoned sharply, then looked at
the maître d' with darkened eyes as he flashed a bill
at him.

"Right this way," the man said, then discreetly ex-
changed the menus for the cash as Nowell sat down at
his preferred table. "Would you care for anything from
the bar, sir?" he asked with newfound respect. "It's on
the house."

"Thank you, that would be lovely. I'll have a gin and
tonic. Make it a Beefeater's, please."

"Yes, sir," the man replied, then sauntered over to
the bar while slipping his hand with the bill into his coat
pocket. He returned a few minutes later with the drink,
smiling warmly at Nowell as he placed it before him.

"One more thing," Nowell said.

"Certainly, whatever you need."

"At approximately six-thirty, I need you to come over
here and tell me that my wife called and she isn't going
to make it. Nothing more, nothing less. Got it?"

"Got it, Mr. Stevenson." The maître d' winked at him,
which irritated Nowell.

Nowell wasn't surprised that the man became easily
persuaded with a meager one hundred bucks. It was
something that amazed him about most people—they
could be had for just about any price, and often a modest one. He remembered his father teaching him a rather
vulgar but accurate lesson about life: "Money talks and
shit walks," he'd said. For all his prim and proper reserve, the old man knew how to grease a palm. He always got the best tables and the best seats in the theater.
His baggage always arrived on time and doors opened
faster for him than anyone else. Through him Nowell
learned to appreciate the value of healthy tipping, and

though he considered this maître d' unworthy, he thought it more important not to be seated center stage in a high-profile restaurant during this essential meeting.

He had downed his first drink, and was halfway through a second one when he saw Sharon enter the restaurant. He politely stood up at the same time she approached the annoying little maître d', who smiled respectfully at Nowell, then escorted her to his table.

"Nice to see you, Mr. Stevenson," she said and extended her hand in a friendly shake. He placed both of his hands over hers and gently shook back. "It's a pleasure to see you too, Sharon. And please, call me Phillip," he said. "Here, sit down." He gestured, pulling out her seat for her. "My wife will be joining us shortly. Would you care for a drink while we wait?"

"You know, I would love a drink," she said and turned to the attentive maître d'. "I'll have a gin and tonic." She looked slightly more attractive to him today, as she wore fresh makeup and her hair was nicely styled. In fact, even her hair color didn't seem so harsh next to the soft aqua-blue suit she was wearing—a nice change from the burgundy dress she'd worn when Nowell first saw her.

"Funny, that's what I'm drinking. Make it with Beefeater's," he instructed the man once again. Nowell smiled at her as he spoke, happy to have some common ground with her, if only in their choice of drink.

She appeared a bit fidgety, looking around the room and then back at Nowell. He saw she had her hands on her purse as though she were going to reach for something, then hesitated. He'd anticipated what she wanted, and reached inside his suit jacket for his cigarette case.

"Mind if I smoke?" he asked.

"Oh, thank God, no," she said with relief, then reached inside her purse for her own pack of filterless Camels. She stuck one in her mouth while Nowell moved to light it. He then pulled out one of his own and lit it up as well.

"We had a rather grueling day, today," he said through a smirk while taking a drag off his cigarette. "First it was Bergdorf Goodman's, followed by Saks, Bloomingdale's, and then Barney's."

Sharon laughed, immediately easing up in his company. He seemed just as likable as he had when she'd first met him on the train. She took a long, satisfying drag off her cigarette, followed by a sip of her gin and tonic. He could see her whole countenance begin to relax as she did, as if someone had just injected a shot of morphine into her arm.

"We love shopping in New York," he went on. "Or rather, I should say, my wife does. We get over here at least once a year so she can get her fill of American fashion and miscellaneous merchandise. We usually come at Christmas, but since we knew we'd be here for Dr. Webster's treatment about now, we put it off till spring."

"There's no place like midtown Manhattan during Christmas," Sharon said with a smile.

"I suppose you've never been to London during the holidays then?" he asked playfully. "Did you grow up in New York City?"

"No, I come from Cleveland. I did go to school here though."

"Oh, really, and where was that? No, don't tell me, let me guess. Columbia University, right?"

"Good guess. How'd you know?"

"I don't know, something about you just seems like the Ivy League type. It's obvious you're a very bright woman. You don't strike me as the type who would move all the way from Cleveland to attend a city college."

"Thank you." She grinned proudly. "I fact, I received both of my degrees from Columbia."

"Very impressive," he said, then glanced at his watch. "I wonder where Evelyn is. I haven't heard from her since I left her at Barney's a couple of hours ago. I'm sure she'll be here any minute."

Sharon smiled at him, stubbed her cigarette out, then nearly finished her gin and tonic with one long gulp.

"Would you care for another?" Nowell asked, anxious to see if Vince Gambrielli's intelligence about her drinking problem was accurate.

"Sure," she said. Nowell motioned for the maître d', who quickly glanced at his watch, then hurried over to the table. It was a few minutes past 6:30.

"Mr. Stevenson, your wife just called and asked me to give you a message."

"She did?" said Nowell with feigned curiosity.

"She said she was sorry but won't be able to make it."

"Did she say why not?" Nowell asked with rising indignation.

"No, sir. Will there be anything else?"

"Yes, I believe the lady would like another drink."

"Yes, sir. And how about you, would you like another too?"

"Oh, why not?" he said with forced resignation. As the maître d' disappeared, Nowell let out a long sigh. "I can't believe she did this to me. Again."

"I'm sorry," Sharon said, a bit surprised but not entirely unhappy with the turn in events. She was beginning to enjoy her time alone with Phillip Stevenson. "We don't have to stay for dinner, you know."

"Oh, no, no. Please stay. I like your company." He shook his head in contempt at his fictitious wife. "She does this to me all the time. We make plans and at the last minute she just decides to do something else and everyone else be damned. Very headstrong woman," he said, looking down at the table, still shaking his head. He reached into his coat pocket for another cigarette, tapping it on the table a few times before popping it into his mouth. "And this is the woman who wants to have my baby. You don't suppose she'll change her mind at the last minute with that, do you?"

"I wouldn't know," said Sharon, not wanting to be critical of someone she'd yet to meet.

"No, of course you wouldn't," he replied. "I apologize, I shouldn't be sharing my marital woes with you. But sometimes it truly gets to me. Being married isn't the easiest thing, you know," he said, then began nervously flicking the flame of his sterling silver lighter off and on before finally lighting up his second cigarette.

"Yeah, I have a little experience in that department, myself," she said caustically, then lit up another cigarette herself.

"Oh, I'm sorry," Nowell said, trying to turn the tide of her sympathy. He didn't say anything else, deliberately allowing an uncomfortable silence.

"Actually, I'm going through a divorce," she said, taking up the slack, "and it's a pretty nasty business."

"That's rough," he replied, still playing it cool in anticipation that she would fully open up. She immediately took the bait, and it wasn't long before she was spilling her guts about everything that had happened in her relationship, and how betrayed she'd felt by her husband, especially where their only child was concerned. She told Nowell all about the bitter custody battle in which they were engaged, and how, at the moment at least, it appeared as though her husband might win.

They went ahead and ordered dinner together, enjoying a choice bottle of wine with their meal, and chatted endlessly about their respective marriages. Nowell claimed to have ambivalent feelings about the in vitro fertilization program, only because his wife was so fickle. He did confess, however, to a deep interest in how the whole process worked, and questioned her intensely about all the technicalities involved. She became increasingly animated the more she had to drink, and very enthusiastic when describing the details of her job. Nowell listened raptly, since it was important to him to know everything that Catherine was going through.

They had an after-dinner drink and a couple more cigarettes, and then three hours after she'd arrived, Nowell finally offered to take her home.

"Oh, no please," she slurred. "I can manage."

"Nonsense," he insisted, "I have a limo right out front."

"A limo?" She seemed impressed.

"Yes. None of that subway business for me anymore. And I'd be delighted to give you a ride home. Where do you live?"

"I live in the Bronx."

"Well, then we're off to the Bronx," he said while standing up and helping her out of her chair.

"Thanks," she said, smiling at him. It had been a long time since anyone had treated her like such a lady. She thought it a shame that he was married, especially since his wife sounded like such a bitch, and had to admit to herself that she found Phillip Stevenson very attractive.

He escorted Sharon outside to the car, opening the

door for her and waiting patiently as she got settled before climbing in.

Sharon Corso felt an unexpected well of sexual tension build in her body as Nowell sat close beside her.
She could smell his cologne—a rich sexy scent—and
wondered if he ever cheated on his wife. An odd thought
struck her, and she briefly wondered if he was even really married.

No, why would he go to all the trouble of lying to me,
she thought, then sighed. It was just her luck that he
was really married. They chatted about unimportant and
lighthearted things all the way to her row house, and as
each mile passed Sharon found herself becoming increasingly anxious about the evening's end, becoming sorely
tempted to invite him in for a drink, but deciding she
was just asking for trouble if she did. Instead, as the
limo pulled up in front of her address, she thanked him
for a lovely evening, then extended an offer to again
meet with him and his wife if she were willing.

"That's very kind of you," he said with a smile. "I
may take you up on that offer. In fact, would you care
to join me for lunch tomorrow?"

"With your wife?" she asked in a sloppy voice.

"Actually, no. Just me." He smiled sheepishly.

She acted like she was surprised by the offer, but was
greatly pleased instead.

"Well, I suppose I could get away for a short lunch,"
she said. "How would you like to do this?"

"We could meet at a restaurant near you. Or better
yet, I understand it is supposed to be rather warm tomorrow. Why don't we have a picnic in Central Park?"

Her eyes grew bright at the prospect. "Phillip, that
sounds wonderful."

"Excellent. I'll arrange everything, you just be ready
to go at, say, eleven-thirty. I'll pick you up outside the
Center."

"Great, I'll see you then." She gently shut the door,
playfully sliding her hand across it as she did. She didn't
want the night to end, she didn't want the car to pull
away. She wanted her time with Phillip Stevenson to
linger on. She waved good-bye through the window, then
headed up her walkway, feeling rejuvenated about herself and her ability to attract a good-looking man. She

hadn't been out on a single date since breaking up with
her husband, and though she knew her encounter with
Phillip the following day might be asking for trouble,
she looked forward to more time alone with him.

As the limo turned away from her block and headed
out to the highway, Nowell slid down in the seat and
ran his hand through his dark hair. It had been an incredibly long night for him, and the combination of the
alcohol buzz and stench of cigarette smoke was beginning to give him a headache. He rolled down the window
for some fresh air, and began to think through all that
had been said and done that evening. He'd played her
like a fiddle, and if everything went according to his
plan, what came next would be sweet music to his ears.

Chapter Forty-two

Catherine heard the front doorbell ring, then looked at the video monitor to see who was trying to enter the gallery. A delivery man with a large picnic basket stood on the stoop, and impatiently rang the door again.

"May I help you?" she asked curiously, not expecting a delivery of any sort.

"Nueman and Bogdonoff," he replied. "I have a delivery for a Mr. Nowell Stuart."

"Wait for the buzz," she said, then hit the appropriate button that would allow him to push the front door open. She left her desk and went out to the front hall to meet him.

"Could you sign here, please?" he said.

"Sure," Catherine answered, then signed as instructed. "Wow, this is some picnic basket!" She simply couldn't imagine what Nowell was up to, since the basket was brimming with an incredible array of goodies, including crisp linens and a chilled bottle of champagne. "Did he say what this was for?" she asked of the delivery man.

"No, none of my business," he answered. He loitered long enough for Catherine to realize he was expecting some kind of tip.

"Just a minute, please, I'll be right back." She went into her office and from her own wallet pulled out a five-dollar bill, then headed back to the hall where she handed it off to him.

"Thanks," he said with a smile, "and enjoy."

"Sure." She smiled back, still not knowing whether she was intended to partake of the picnic or not. Nowell hadn't mentioned anything to her, and from the looks of it, he was expecting it to be some kind of special occasion. Somehow she doubted it was for them to share and couldn't help but feel a pang of jealousy over whomever he was planning on sharing it with. She took the basket back to her office and then buzzed him on the intercom. "Nowell, you just received a rather large picnic basket down here. What do you want me to do with it?"

"Oh, splendid. Let's see, there should be a bottle of champagne in there. Is it chilled?"

"Yes."

"Excellent. Keep it right there. I'll be down shortly." She turned the intercom off and stared at the basket, and full of curiosity, she began poking at its contents. She found chilled asparagus wrapped in prosciutto, an array of delicate sandwiches on mini-baguettes, fresh fruit artfully cut up and ready-to-eat, a small variety of cheeses and crackers, and then a couple of hazelnut tortes, not to mention the bottle of champagne and two flutes.

"Wow!" she exclaimed.

"Does it meet with your approval?" asked Nowell from behind her. She felt her heart nearly stop with embarrassment.

"This is some feast you're having," she said, trying to keep her cool. He could see the curiosity in her eyes.

"Yes, well you can always count on Nueman and Bogdonoff," he said, grinning. Catherine looked up at him and could not believe her eyes. Nowell was wearing casual clothes—including the pair of jeans they'd purchased together in London, now slightly faded from washing. He wore a white button-down shirt with his sleeves rolled up to three-quarter length, along with tassel loafers and no socks. And he had on a pair of dark aviator sunglasses that made him look more handsome than ever. She could smell the scent of his signature cologne from at least six feet away, and a fleeting sense of attraction came over her. At that moment he looked incredibly sexy to her and she couldn't help but feel a bit wistful that she wasn't the one joining him for the picnic.

"What's the occasion?" she asked.

"Oh, nothing, really. Just a picnic lunch with a special gal that I met."

"She must be pretty damned special." Catherine smiled as she playfully poked around inside the basket once more. "Save the leftovers for me, would ya?" she joked. Nowell was thoroughly amused by her keen interest, and loved the irony of the situation, since the impressiveness of the picnic basket was designed as part of a ruse to get to her.

"Well, if you approve, I'm sure she will too. Listen, I have to run. Don't expect me back." He smiled mischievously. "I'm sure you can manage without me."

"You betcha." She smiled, still brimming with curiosity. "Hey, will I get to meet the lucky lady?"

You already have, Nowell thought to himself, then said, "Oh, maybe. We'll see how things go today. You never know, she may not like me enough to go out again."

"I find that hard to believe. Go get 'em, tiger." She giggled, then purred like a cat.

A limo was waiting for him out front, and within ten minutes they pulled up to the Manhattan Reproductive Center where Sharon stood waiting, smoking a cigarette. She grinned as the impressive arrived, then stomped out her cigarette as she walked briskly toward him. Nowell lowered the window as she approached.

"Good morning," he said with a smile. "Glad to see they unlocked the chain to your microscope."

"Yeah, but the hour glass is running." She smiled in return, hastily climbing into the car beside him. Nowell told the chauffeur exactly where he wanted to go, and within no time they were being let off near the Sheep Meadow in Central Park. It was an absolutely splendid day outside, sunny and seventy-seven degrees. Sharon was wearing a pair of navy-blue slacks with a cotton sweater, and took off her flat shoes as soon as they were walking on the grass.

"My God, what a day!" Nowell exclaimed. "I'm so glad you could join me."

"Me too," she said, then hesitated before asking. "Phillip, whatever happened to your wife last night?"

"Oh, dear. You know what she did. At the last minute she went to the Elizabeth Arden Salon on Madison Avenue for a body wrap and massage and didn't get out of there until well past our scheduled dinner. You know what is so maddening? She didn't seem the slightest bit fazed that she'd put you out like that."

"It was no trouble for me at all. To tell you the truth," she added tentatively, "I enjoyed our time together."

"Me too," he said, then briefly and affectionately stroked her arm. She smiled coyly at him, and for a moment Nowell actually thought she could have potential to be attractive.

"How about here, is this a good spot?" he asked.

"I don't see why not. Here, let me help you," she offered, then joined in the task of spreading out their lunch.

"Phillip," she exclaimed as she spotted the bottle of champagne, "I really appreciate all this, but I have to tell you something. In all honesty, I really can't have anything to drink right now. I need to be lucid when I get back to the lab."

"Oh, come on, Sharon, one little glass of champagne won't hurt you." She didn't want to argue with him, and neither did she want to tell him that she was incapable of stopping at one drink—that even one sip would make her determined to polish off the bottle.

"Where's your wife today?" she asked, trying to change the subject.

"Where else?" He sighed. "Back on Madison Avenue. Today she's hitting some designer boutiques. I think all this infertility treatment has her depressed, and shopping seems to be her mode of therapy."

Sharon couldn't believe what a foolish wife he had, thinking if she were married to someone as handsome, kind, and obviously rich as Phillip Stevenson, she would never let him out of her sight.

"Well, I guess I have nothing to complain about," she said. Nowell smiled at her as he opened up the bottle of champagne and poured two glasses full.

"You don't have to drink it," he said, "but at least join me in a little toast."

"Okay, okay," she relented, then raised her glass alongside his.

"To warm weather," he said, then lightly tapped his glass on hers. She didn't say anything in response, instead she carefully twirled her champagne flute in her hand while staring intently at its contents. "And to even warmer friends," he added, clinking her glass once more.

"Yeah," she said, smiling, "to warm friends," then

without hesitation took a sip from her glass. She immediately took a follow-up swig, and then another until her glass was completely drained.

"Oh, my." Nowell laughed as he poured her another glass full. "Now don't blame it on me if later on you see twins where there is only one."

"Poor taste," she said with a laugh, then took another sip of her champagne. Nowell started to offer her some food, but decided to wait until she'd finished her second flute on an empty stomach. It didn't take her long.

"Now," he said, "with what would you like to start? We've got just about anything your heart could desire in this basket." He began picking around at the food, then pulled out an asparagus with prosciutto and offered it to her. As she reached for it he pulled back, then placed it close to her mouth in a gesture to feed her. When she opened her mouth, he ran the asparagus stalk along her tongue in a wildly suggestive manner, stopping only when she caught the tip of it in her mouth and began to suck. She stared at him with devilish eyes as she did, then finally took a bite.

"Ouch," he said with a grimace. She licked her lips, then stuck out her tongue for more. He playfully fed her two more stalks, making sure her champagne flute remained full. It wasn't long before Sharon Corso was buzzed. She took half bites out of a sandwich and ate a few crackers with cheese. The combination of sexual tension, a champagne high, and the noonday sun quickly wore her out, and before long she was lying back on the linen tablecloth. It didn't take her any time to fall fast asleep. With any luck, Nowell thought, she'd stay that way for a while.

He finished off the rest of the champagne, ate a couple of sandwiches, then removed his sunglasses and lay down beside her to soak up the early spring rays. He dozed off himself, and about an hour and a half later woke up with Sharon still asleep beside him. Rather than wake her up, he folded his arms beneath his head and relaxed, basking in the sun and enjoying the slight buzz he still had.

"Oh, my God!" she suddenly shrieked. "Shit, shit, shit! What have I done?"

"What, what is it?" He bolted upright, as though startled and surprised.

"Look what time it is?" she cried. "Oh, God, I have
stuff back at the lab that's being timed. This is a total
disaster. What the fuck am I going to do?" He was not
charmed by her profanity.

"There's a pay phone right down that walkway," he
said. "Quick, go call and tell them that you got held
up." She promptly stood up, nearly falling over from
dizziness. She was clearly drunk and now agitated. "Oh,
fuck me," she shrieked.

"Indeed." Nowell smiled.

"I'm sorry. It's just that this has never happened before. This is unthinkable." She grabbed her purse and
quickly rummaged for a quarter, then bolted away
toward the phone. Nowell sat up unflinchingly and
watched, supremely confident that he was going to have
his way today. She returned a short while later with a
happy and relieved expression on her face.

"Today must be my lucky day," she said, grinning.
"One of my lab partners had been keeping an eye on
my work, so everything is okay."

"What did you say?"

"That I had a doctor's appointment and it was taking
me longer than I thought."

"Do you have to go right back?"

"No." She grinned sloppily, then plunked back down
beside him. "In fact, I'm not going back at all."

"Really!" he replied with genuine delight. "That's terrific. So we can have the afternoon to ourselves?"

"I guess," she said, trying once again to be coy. "I
mean if that's what you want."

"I couldn't think of anything better. Say listen, I have
an idea. Why don't we go back to the car, pick up another bottle of champagne, then tour Manhattan in
style? We can open the sun roof and enjoy the weather
from the backseat comfort of a chauffeur-driven limo."

Sharon lay back down on the grass, this time her eyes
wide open and her mouth forming a broad grin.

"How 'bout another asparagus stalk first?" she asked.

Chapter Forty-three

Nowell and Sharon carried on all afternoon like two giddy teenagers—the world was their oyster, and they were out to conquer it with a bottle of champagne and two crystal flutes. They laughed and carried on till sunset, touring all of Manhattan's major sights, and then for the fun of it headed out to JFK International Airport to watch the planes take off and land. Finally, drunk and full of themselves, they turned in the direction of the Bronx where Sharon was certain she would not let Phillip Stevenson see the light of day until she'd screwed his brains out.

She hadn't had this much fun with anyone, at any time in her whole life. She realized what had been so desperately missing from her own marriage to Patrick, and wondered if Phillip's wife knew what fun she could really have with her husband. *Evelyn be damned,* she thought to herself, then reached over and began rubbing Nowell's thigh. He leaned back deep into the seat and let out a demonstrative sigh of contentment. She continued rubbing the top of his thigh for a few minutes longer, then moved her hand inward and upward until she could feel the hardness in between his legs. He moaned in encouragement, and before she knew it he pushed the button that electronically sealed the window between them and the chauffeur. Unable to control herself, she unzipped his pants and reached longingly inside with her hand, then began probing with her mouth, mimicking with pleasure what she'd done to the stalk of asparagus earlier in the day. The gesture wasn't lost on Nowell, who laughed and warned her please not to bite off the tip.

He was big and hard, creating uncontrollable spasms of sexual joy in Sharon as she manipulated him to the point of ejaculation. Nowell looked down at the blond head on his lap, nearly laughing aloud at the sight of her roots. He wondered what the catty receptionist might say if she could see Sharon now.

The limo eventually pulled up in front of her row house, causing Sharon to cast a longing look at him. "Do you want to come inside?" she asked softly, prompting Nowell to burst out in laughter. "I'll come wherever you want me to," he said roguishly. They both laughed, then moved to get out of the vehicle. Nowell glanced at the driver as if to say "please wait," which the driver intuitively understood. As they exited the vehicle, Nowell asked the chauffeur if he could pop the trunk, and as it opened he retrieved a small, black leather duffel bag.

"What, are you planning on spending the night?" she asked playfully.

"Only if you want me to," he answered, then kissed her lightly on her forehead. "Actually, I wish I could. The truth is, I have some important things in this bag I don't want lost. You know, if anything should happen . . ."

"I understand," she said. "This is not the best neighborhood in the world." He raised his eyebrows at her in appreciation of her understanding, then accompanied her inside her small home. It was a clean but drab place, with a small L-shaped living/dining room and a tiny kitchen on the first floor. She immediately went into the kitchen and returned with a cheap bottle of chilled white wine along with two dime-store glasses, then grabbed him by the hand and led him upstairs. There were two bedrooms up there, one of which was an office/library, full of textbooks and research papers, and the other her bedroom that was slightly cluttered with clothes and other personal belongings. She regretted not having made her bed that morning, but decided that it didn't matter anyway because they'd soon tear it apart.

She wasted no time pouring them the wine, which Nowell nearly spit out at the first sip of the cheap stuff. She also wasted no time unzipping his jeans, drawing his pants down around his knees as she hastily began doing him again. He leaned up against the wall, closing his eyes and thinking of Catherine as she worked him over. And just as he was about to come again, he picked her up and carried her to the bed where he unfastened and pulled off her pants, then climbed on top of her, taking her hard and fast as he did. Whether she truly felt good or not, she moaned as if deeply pleased, lying there quiet and exhausted when he was finished. It was simply an exercise for him.

"Oh, Sharon," he said softly as he stroked her hair. "What a day. What a night. I haven't had this much fun, since . . . since I don't know when."

She grinned up at him in the fashion of so many women he'd known and easily taken before—a bit of coquettishness and a whole lot of wonder. He knew she was thinking, *What next? What happens between us next?*

He took that opportunity to glance at his watch. "It's late. I'd better go."

"Please don't," she begged him. "Can't you stay awhile longer?"

"Not if I don't want to become another John Wayne Bobbitt," he joked. "Evelyn's got quite the temper!"

"Good God, by all means then, go." She laughed, then let out a sad and longing sigh.

"Phillip, when will I see you again?" Nowell could have almost scripted their conversation himself, thinking: *First she asks when we'll get together again; I say I'm uncertain but hope it's soon; she'll ask me to call; we kiss, then maybe kiss again; I leave and if she's lucky I'll call her again. Only this is one woman who will definitely hear from me.*

"I'm not sure. We're only supposed to be here through Friday. Maybe we can see each other again before then." That at least was true; especially after she discovered what he'd left behind.

"At least call me, would you?" she implored.

"I wouldn't think of leaving the country without doing so," he said, adding a meaningful pause. "I wish I could stay longer." He kissed her as tenderly as he could, then jumped up and began pulling himself together. He glanced at his watch once more, then hastened to leave, deliberately leaving the black bag on the floor beside her bed.

She didn't bother to move out of the bed right away, instead she propped herself up on an elbow as she watched him leave, then flopped back down on the mat-

tress as she heard the front door shut and the car pull
away.

"Dammit," she said, feeling cheap and cheated. "Why
did I do this?" she wondered aloud, "I am not the kind
of woman he thinks I am." But as she reflected on their
raucous behavior all afternoon, she smiled. It had been
a magical afternoon for her, and even if Phillip Stevenson never entered her life again, she had gained a valuable insight into herself—that she still knew how to have
fun. She pulled herself up to go to the bathroom, and
as she swung her legs over the side of the bed and
stepped down, her left foot went right into Phillip's black
duffel bag. She threw her head back in sheer delight.
"Now he'll have to see me again." She smiled, wondering if he hadn't left it on purpose.

She also couldn't help but wonder what the hell was
in the bag, since he'd been concerned enough not to
leave it even under the watchful eye of the chauffeur.
She ran her foot along the top of it, trying to discern its
contents. It certainly wasn't a change of clothes. It felt
like several small books stacked one upon the other. She
reached down for the zipper, then hesitated, knowing it
was none of her business. *Who cares,* she thought. *He
doesn't have to know.*

With that she picked up the bag, which was surprisingly heavy, and unzipped the top. What she saw inside
nearly made her throw up in shock. "Is this some kind
of a fucking joke?" she said as her jaw dropped and her
eyes popped. There, neatly bound together and completely filling the bag, were stacks and stacks of one-
hundred-dollar bills. She sat gaping at the sight on her
lap, unable to move.

"Who in the hell is this guy?" she asked, then began
to tremble. She had never seen that much money in one
place in all her life. She picked up a couple of stacks
and began fanning herself with them, closing her eyes
and taking in the smell and heft of that much money in
her hand at one time. Next she counted the bills in one
stack: fifty. And then the number of stacks: twenty.

"This is un-fucking-believable!" she shrieked, picking
up the bottle of wine and guzzling from it. "The guy
just happens to leave one hundred thousand dollars in
my bedroom!"

For a moment she felt incredibly dirty, as though he'd left it as payoff for their romantic interlude, then quickly concluded no one was worth that much money. No, this was some horrible mistake. And she was suddenly afraid that he wasn't who he claimed to be, or that he was in some serious trouble. She started to tremble again, then took another slug of the wine, running her hands along the money again.

God, what I wouldn't do to keep this, she thought wistfully, realizing that it could mean the end to the drawn-out custody battle with her husband. She could fire her half-assed attorney and hire the best one money could buy. She could afford a down payment on a decent place to live, and once and for all bring her little boy home to live with her. Was it too good to be true, she thought, that he would leave this much money and not come to retrieve it.

She got up off the bed and carried the satchel into the bathroom with her. He might have been careless with his money, but she certainly wasn't going to let it out of her sight. Not until she learned who Phillip Stevenson truly was and why he would leave one hundred thousand dollars sitting on her bedroom floor.

Chapter Forty-four

Nowell waited until well past noon to call the Manhattan Reproductive Center. He knew that the longer Sharon Corso had one hundred thousand dollars in her possession, the more she would feel like it belonged to her. He also knew there was no way she could reach him, and that she'd have to live with her wild curiosity until he called. He finally picked up the phone at 3:10 P.M., knowing that she was soon to leave for the day.

"Sharon Corso, please," he asked.

"Just a moment please," said the receptionist. "May I tell her who's calling?"

"Yes, Phillip Stevenson," he said calmly. A few seconds later he could hear that the phone had been picked up, but no one spoke.

"Hello," he inquired, followed by another few seconds of silence.

"Yes," she finally said, her voice terse and edgy.

"Sharon, this is Phillip." There was another long pause. "Are you there?"

"I'm here."

"Well, I'm calling because . . ."

"I know why you're calling," she said angrily. "The real question is, who the hell are you?"

"What are you talking about?"

"We have no record of a Phillip or Evelyn Stevenson having *ever* been a patient of this center."

"Oh, I see." She was talking in a low, strained voice, obviously not wanting to be overheard.

"That was some gratuity you left me last night."

"Well, you see, that's why I'm calling. I wanted to explain."

"I can hardly wait."

"Where's the money? Do you still have it?"

"No, I tossed it off the Brooklyn Bridge. What do you think?"

"I need to see you."

"I'm sure you do," she said, growing more irate by the minute over what she'd gotten herself into.

"When can I see you again?"

"What for?"

"What do you mean, 'what for'?"

"Tell me first who you are."

"I'll tell you when I see you."

"Tell me now."

"I can't."

"Why?"

"Sharon, please be reasonable with me. I can explain. Can I come by your house tonight?"

"Absolutely not. I'll meet you where I feel it's safe."

"Fine." Nowell let out a cynical laugh. "Where would you like to meet?"

She let out a nervous sigh. "Back at the Plaza Hotel."

"Fine. What time?"

"Three forty-five," she said flatly. Nowell glanced at his watch.

"I don't know if I can make it by then," he warned her.

"Three forty-five," she said, "and that's it. I'll see you at the bar."

"I'll be there," he said, playing her silly game, then hung up the phone. It was laughable to him that she was being this aggressive with him—after all, did she expect that somehow he wouldn't come after his cash?

He rushed downstairs, barely telling Catherine where he was headed, then dashed out the door and hailed a taxi on Fifth Avenue. The afternoon traffic was beginning to thicken up, and he kept a close vigil on his watch, fearful that Corso might slip away before he got a chance to talk with her. He knew how to find her, but it would be better overall if he could stick to his plan and see her under what she considered her terms.

The taxi arrived at the Plaza with moments to spare, and for a six-dollar fare Nowell threw twenty bucks at the driver and told him to keep the change. He dashed inside, past the crowds of tourists and onlookers in the hotel lobby and then moved more calmly into the bar.

Sharon was there already, and halfway through a gin and tonic while dragging on a cigarette. She stared at him coldly, and appeared more gaunt and repulsive than he'd remembered—an entirely different person from when he last saw her, still drunk with lust for him.

They didn't say anything to each other as he sat down. He ordered a drink, and then folded his hands on top of the bar. He was a different person to her too. Today he was all business, and she too found this stranger repulsive. They stared each other down for a brief moment, before Nowell finally spoke.

"Did you enjoy yourself last night?" Nowell asked, somewhat lightheartedly.

"You've got to be kidding," she said, digging her heel into the tip of the duffel bag beneath her bar stool.

"Well then, tell me what you are thinking."

"What am I supposed to think?" she snapped back.

"Have you ever held that much money at one time in your life?" he asked, his mouth forming a half smile.

"Can't say that I have."

"How'd it feel? Good, huh?"

"What are you getting at?"

"Quite simply, that that money could be yours."

Sharon's curiosity grew along with her tension. The situation could quickly move beyond her control, as this man, Phillip Stevenson, or whoever he was, seemed quite capable of getting his way.

"What if I don't want it?"

"Why wouldn't you?"

"What if I don't like the strings attached to it?"

"Who said there were any strings attached?"

"You mean to tell me that I was that good in bed?" Nowell laughed. "Well," he said matter-of-factly.

"How flattering. What else?"

Nowell looked around to see if anyone was listening. Except for the two of them and a bartender, they had the room to themselves.

"I need you to do me a small favor."

"What in the hell could I possibly do for you?" she asked, unable to imagine her expected complicity in his scheme.

"More than you could ever imagine," he said, smiling.

"I'm all ears."

He took a deep breath, still absolutely composed. "There is a couple currently seeking treatment from Dr. Webster. I need you to do a little scientific manipulation for me," he said, hoping she would catch his drift, "that's all."

"What exactly do you have in mind?"

"It's quite simple. When it comes time to unite sperm and egg, I want it to be my sperm you use instead."

Sharon tried not to show her shock. What he was asking was not only a deep ethical violation, but she'd be breaking the law as well.

"I could go to jail over something like that," she said in a low, barely audible voice, her eyes growing narrow.

"Well, let me put it to you this way," Nowell said with a sneer, a black-hearted look in his eyes. For a moment, Corso looked away, then leaned back in her chair.

"Let me get this straight," she said. "I do what you ask me to and the one hundred thousand dollars is all mine—I can spend it as I see fit, and I never have to deal with you again."

"I see your Ivy League education is paying off."

"And all I have to do in exchange for this money is to use your sperm instead of someone else's during an in vitro process?"

"Go on," he said, a look of malevolent joy in his eyes.

"And if I don't, then what? I'm dead?" she said, her voice raising a notch as she half laughed.

"I never said that," replied Nowell cynically.

"And what if I say, I don't want the money and I don't want to be dead? Suppose I just called out for the police right here, right now, and told them everything."

"You could, I suppose. But you won't."

"And why not?"

"Because you need the money. Think about it. You do what I ask you to, no one will ever know the better, and you'll never hear from me again. In return, you get to keep one hundred thousand tax-free dollars. I imagine it would go a considerable way in terms of dealing with your custody battle, don't you?"

Sharon began slowly shaking her head, and then wringing her hands. She wanted to smoke a cigarette, but was too nervous even for that. "Why me? Why are you doing this to *me*?"

"You stupid woman," Nowell said harshly. "This is a chance of a lifetime, and you know it. No one, and I mean no one, has to know what you've done except you and me. That's it. You get your one hundred thousand dollars, and I get my baby."

"What if the in vitro doesn't work?"

"We'll see then."

"No, I want to know now, what if it doesn't work? I've done my job. Do I still get to keep the money?"

"Getting greedy on me?"

"If I'm greedy about anything," she said, "it's my life."

"Well, how will I know you did what you were supposed to if it doesn't work?"

"Because it sounds from what you're telling me as if I don't have much of a choice. So why wouldn't I do it?"

She barely listened to his response. *But who would ever know?* she began asking herself. It would be less painful to live with the guilt than to live apart from her son every day. Besides, she thought, she would love nothing more than to stick it to her son-of-a-bitch husband. She'd used donor sperm countless times before during in vitro fertilization, so there was no reason she couldn't just look at this task objectively. She didn't want to know his reasons for doing this and dreaded finding out who the unlucky recipient would be. But she'd get over it.

"Is your mind made up?" he asked tersely.

"Yeah. I've made up my mind." She smiled at him. "I've made up my mind."

"Then you'll do it?"

"Why not?" she asked, her countenance lightening up a bit.

"You really are a bright woman." He smiled back. "Now, what do we do?"

"You give me a semen sample," she said, "and I'll freeze it. When your friend comes in for in vitro, I'll personally take care of it, and make sure your sperm gets used instead. It's as easy as that."

"I want to do it now."

"Right here?" She looked at him incredulously. Her feet were now planted firmly on top of the duffel bag, and as she spoke the realization sank in that the money would soon be hers, all hers.

"Can't we go back to the clinic?"

"No, too risky. I will, however, need to go by there and get a sterile cup for you. You can jerk off wherever you want and then give me the sample. I'll take it right in and start the process."

He cast a wicked and satisfied smile at her. "I have just the plan," he said. He tossed several bills on the table, then escorted her out of the bar, holding her by the arm the whole time. Once outside he hailed a taxi, giving the address of the Manhattan Reproductive Center.

"I'll hold on to this, you go inside and get what you need," he said, placing his hand on the money bag.

"I'll be back in a minute," she snapped.

Nowell watched as she walked back inside the Center, using a key of her own to get into the now closed building. The meter continued running as the driver waited silently for her to return. Nowell stared blankly out the window at the cars passing by. It was an amazing fact of life, he kept reminding himself, how easily people could be bought. He was certain now he could have offered Sharon Corso a lot less than one hundred thousand dollars and still gotten the job done, but he wanted to make his offer irresistible.

She returned as promised, opening up the car door and thrusting a sterile specimen cup in his face. "Here," she said. "I'll wait for you by the front door. Just make sure you get it back to me within a half hour, otherwise it's no good."

"No, no." He smiled shrewdly while grabbing her arm. "You come with me." He pulled her back into the car, then told the driver to head over to Central Park, and stop in the far corner of the lot at Tavern on the Green. He pulled out a wad of cash and flashed it at the driver. "Can you give us ten minutes of peace and quiet?" he asked. "You can even take the keys if you're worried."

The young Russian grabbed the cash and the keys and was out of the car in seconds. Nowell turned to Sharon as he unzipped his pants.

"You're a sick fuck, you know that, don't you?" she said as he grabbed her hand, then placed it on his hardened penis. Their eyes locked together and for a moment she could only stare at him, feeling nothing but contempt. She'd felt used by her husband, but that was nothing by comparison to her present circumstances.

"We have about eight minutes left, I suggest you get busy," he said icily. She closed her eyes, and then with great fury began the task. Nowell leaned back in the seat and closed his eyes, a kaleidoscope of images crossing his mind. First there was Catherine, beautiful and naked beneath the hospital sheet. There was the memory of their embraces and her sweet, tender mouth on his; and then as Corso became more aggressive, even hurtful, he seemed to hear Wilton Dresden's muffled cry for help. It aroused him even more, forcing him to climax well before his self-imposed deadline. "Get the cup," he demanded, "get the cup."

Grateful to have this disgusting ordeal nearly over with, Corso removed her hand, then slapped the cup on top of him as he held his penis tight and ejaculated. She immediately removed the receptacle, then slipped a cap on top of it, careful not to spill any of its contents.

"You do that like a pro," he said, putting himself back together, then glancing around for the cabdriver. He didn't want her to waste any time getting his specimen back to the lab. Sharon remained speechless, slipping the cup into her handbag, then turning away from him and staring out the window.

She used to think that discovering her husband in bed with another woman was the worst thing she'd ever endured—until now. She simply couldn't imagine sinking lower than she had today. The only comfort was the bag of money, once again held tightly between her feet.

The cabdriver returned and tentatively tapped on the window to see if it was okay to resume driving. Nowell nodded yes at him, asking that he head back to the same address where they'd previously waited. They each rode in a heavy silence, broken only when they arrived at the clinic.

"Aren't you forgetting something?" Nowell asked.

"Yeah," she replied sarcastically, "what's your name?"

"Oh, women," he muttered, "one date and they think

they own you. My name doesn't matter. What matters is the name for whom this is intended."

"Well."

"I'll let you know who, when the time is right. In the meantime, that's one precious dish you're carrying. I suggest you handle it with care." She cast a wicked glance at him, grabbed her purse and then the duffel bag, and left the car without another word. She would do as she was asked, and immediately headed into the lab to freeze this stranger's sperm.

Chapter Forty-five

Catherine's abdomen was distended and achy from all the hormones she'd taken to stimulate her ovaries into ripening as many eggs as possible. In addition, her thighs hurt from the daily shots of Pergonal, the high-dosage fertility drug that Michael painstakingly injected into her each morning. She was extremely crabby, but more eager than ever to get on with the actual in vitro process.

She'd been to the Center every morning during the past two weeks for ultrasound scans of her ovaries, and as best as the doctors could tell they'd be able to retrieve at least ten eggs. And though not that many would be planted in her uterus, it increased the odds that she'd have a multiple pregnancy if indeed the in vitro worked.

While Catherine was at work, Dr. Webster's assistant called to say the test results that morning showed she was ripe for the retrieval, and that they wanted her in the next morning for the procedure. Nowell showed up in her office shortly after she'd hung up the phone.

"Good morning," he said cheerfully. He'd been so self-absorbed lately that it was comforting to hear the old Nowell again. Catherine wondered if perhaps he hadn't become serious about the woman he took on a picnic in Central Park. He never talked about her, and when Catherine once inquired, he sloughed off the question without providing much detail. She never called, and he never brought her to the gallery.

He seemed particularly lighthearted today. Perhaps, she thought, it was because she seemed so blue. The drugs were really taking a toll on her emotionally, and it was a daily struggle to keep a smile on her face. Hearing from Dr. Webster's office was the best boost she'd had in weeks.

"Nowell," she started, "I know this is last minute and all. But I have to go to the doctor's tomorrow, and I don't think I'll be in at all. Is that okay with you?"

"That's fine," he said with a smile. He already knew why, as he'd just hung up the phone with Sharon Corso before entering Catherine's office. "Michael and Catherine Harrison," he had told Corso, adding only, "they will be in tomorrow. Do you follow me?"

"Yes," was all she said back, then hung up the phone. He could tell from the tone in her voice that she meant what she said, and he could hardly stand his elation over what he knew was about to happen. He'd kept tabs on Sharon Corso since their encounter, and knew that she'd already begun to spend his money on her custody battle. He also knew that he would make her life miserable if she didn't come through.

Nowell studied Catherine's face for her reaction to the news that tomorrow was her big day. Though still beautiful, she looked tired and he could tell the ordeal of getting up earlier than usual each morning for the daily round of testing was wearing her down.

"Listen, things are kind of slow around here right now. Why don't you take Friday off too. Take it easy for a change."

"Are you sure?" She smiled warmly at his kind gesture.

"Absolutely. You should catch up on your sleep. You've been looking a bit peaked lately. I hope you don't mind my asking, but is everything all right?" He was greatly concerned that she get the appropriate amount of rest, especially after the implantation. He wanted to make sure she got everything she needed, and had no unnecessary stress added to her life.

"I'm fine, just some minor stuff I need to take care of."

"Well, I hope everything is okay for you here. I mean, you aren't nervous about me anymore, are you?"

"Of course not, why would you even ask?"

"Only because we've avoided the issue. You have to admit, don't you, that I've kept my word. I've been a very good boy, haven't I?"

"You know, Nowell, you have. And I really appreciate it. I think we've both handled it well, and I'm grateful to still be working with you. To tell you the truth, I simply cannot imagine another employer treating me better than you have."

Chapter Forty-six

Catherine knew she was pregnant well before taking a blood test. Just a few days following the in vitro fertilization her breasts grew larger and more tender, exactly how they'd felt the month after she and Michael returned from eloping and discovered they were having a baby.

She could hardly contain her elation and tried hard not to get her hopes up until after the doctor confirmed her suspicions. She hadn't said anything to Michael yet, wanting to reveal it only when she was certain, and neither had she breathed a word of it to Nowell. But her mind was fixated on it. She couldn't wait to find out how many of the embryos remained—excited yet again over the possibility of having a multiple birth, but constantly reminding herself to be happy with only one.

She took it extra careful following the in vitro process. And though the doctor had said after a couple of days they could safely have sex, she and Michael had agreed to hold off until they knew for sure of the results. Michael had been joking with her anyway, saying the sex at Dr. Webster's office was the best he'd had in a long time.

"Fine," she teased him back, "then don't come looking to me for any favors."

He'd ask first thing every morning how she felt, fearing that a lack of morning sickness was an indication the in vitro had failed. "No, Michael, that doesn't mean a thing," she would say. "Not everyone gets morning sickness, and besides it doesn't always happen in the morning." Regardless, he looked for symptoms as an indication that they'd accomplished their goal.

Two weeks following her implantation, Catherine went in for the blood test. For some reason, her mood was one of serenity instead of nervousness, as though her body were telling her to be calm for her child. When she got to work later that morning, she waited until Nowell left on some business before calling Dr. Webster. She wanted to hear the news directly from him instead of the rude lab technician she'd spoken to the first time. It took only a short time for him to pick up the phone.

"Hello, Mom," he said teasingly. Catherine, knowing he would not joke about something so serious, was unable to contain her joy and jumped clear out of her seat while squealing into the phone. "Oh, my God, oh, my God, it's true," she shouted at him. "I knew it, it's true. Tell me you're not joking," she demanded. "No, say it again, say it again!"

"Hello, Mom," he repeated once more. "We did it. What do you think about that?"

"I think I love you," she screamed. "I can't believe this. I can't believe this. I can't wait to tell Michael. Oh, my God. Wait till he hears the news."

"Catherine," he said more seriously, "would you please stop shouting in my ear?"

"Oh, I'm sorry," she said breathlessly, "I just can't help myself. Dr. Webster, you have made me the happiest woman on the face of the earth. I can't say thanks enough. Thank you, thank you, thank you."

"It is pretty exciting, isn't it? Now listen up, we still have some work to do. We're going to have to administer progesterone in you until we see a heartbeat—do you understand?"

"Absolutely," she said, already knowing this might be forthcoming. "Dr. Webster," she added, "how soon can we find out how many there are?"

"Well, don't get ahead of yourself here. When we do a sonogram for the heartbeat we'll be able to tell if there's more than one. In the meantime, I want you to take it very easy. No bungee jumping off the TriBorough Bridge to celebrate. You got it?"

"I promise, I promise, I'll be very careful. When do we get to see the heartbeat?"

"Not for another two weeks at least."

The wait till then would seem far more unbearable than anticipating the results of the pregnancy test. Catherine thanked Dr. Webster once again, then hung up the phone, virtually unable to contain her joy. Though she'd thought a thousand times before how she'd cleverly break the news to Michael, there was only way to do it now—just the facts and in person. It was hell waiting for Nowell to return, and even worse trying to tame her behavior so he wouldn't suspect anything. She decided not to break the news to him until after she'd seen the baby's heartbeat.

But he knew the moment he saw her. He hadn't talked with Sharon Corso, he didn't have to. The radiance in Catherine's face revealed the truth, and he nearly fell to the ground with astonishment when he saw her. She came bursting out of her office to tell him she was off to run a quick errand—her face was flushed with excitement.

An unexpected wave of emotion nearly consumed him, and he felt desperate to share the joy with her. *You and I are having a baby!* he thought to himself, looking at her with sweet passion. He felt an instant need to protect her; to protect his family—and wanted to be with her every step of the way. She left almost immediately, carrying herself entirely differently than when he'd last seen her. There was both pride and concern in her motion, balanced by a sense of utter joy. He escorted her to the front door, then gently shut it behind her and immediately headed to his upstairs study.

The first thing he did was dial the Manhattan Reproductive Center. A strange woman, whose voice was not so pleasant as the other receptionist, answered the phone.

"Sharon Corso, please."

"I'm sorry, she's out to lunch." The thought of her being gone precisely when he called made him want to strangle her. "Would you like to leave her a message, sir."

"When do you expect her back?"

"I'm not sure. Do you have a message?"

"No, I'll call back." He hung up the phone and headed straight for his liquor cabinet, needing a drink to calm his jittery nerves. "This is unbelievable." He smiled as a wave of happy disbelief consumed him. It had worked. It had actually worked. He guzzled a stiff brandy, then poured himself another.

This was going to be the hardest nine months of his

life. He wanted to be a part of Catherine's pregnancy every step of the way. He wanted to feel his child's tiny feet kick beneath her skin; he wanted to cuddle with Catherine as she grew round and large and share her pain as she delivered his child into the world. He downed his second brandy, then headed back to the phone. This time Sharon Corso was there.

"Hello," she said. He could almost hear her smile over the phone.

"What are the results?" he asked calmly, managing to contain his emotion.

"Positive. Definitely positive. You have unbelievable sperm."

Nowell basked in the compliment and the opportunity to share the good news with someone, even if it was Sharon Corso.

"You're one lucky lady."

"Does this mean we're finished with each other?"

"Can't we still be friends?" he asked cynically. She wanted to tell him to go straight to hell, but thought better of it. There was no doubt in her mind that Phillip Stevenson was a dangerous man and the less she crossed him the better.

"Sure," she answered, "I don't see why not."

"I'll see you around then."

"Sure, I'll be seeing you," she said, then placed the receiver back, foolishly believing that she was done with him forever.

Chapter Forty-seven

It was one of the most crime-infested neighborhoods in Harlem. Michael was manning a soup kitchen there, and had just opened the doors for lunch to the small crowd of waiting men and women.

The onset of warmer weather usually slowed his business down, but the homeless were still hungry and the need to feed them had to be met, so Michael made it a part of his daily mission to help do the job. He'd become friendly with the regulars—a fairly crusty and raucous group of characters who were relatively harmless, aside from the occasional lapse into threatening psychosis for some. Michael always kept his guard up, but had learned to enjoy his time with the folks whose needs were so great. He'd learned a lot from them, and loved the chance to share God's bounty. After the last meal had been dished out, he grabbed a plate for himself and joined a few of the regulars at one of the tables.

"Hey, Rusty, how ya doin'? Mind if I join ya?" Michael asked. Occasionally Rusty would ask some imaginary friend or enemy "to make room for the damned priest," then scoot over to accommodate Michael.

"Good to see you, Father," he would say, then cross himself. Michael tried to correct him once by telling him that he wasn't a "Father," just an Episcopal priest in training, but the lesson never took. The nickname however ever did, and every one of the regulars referred to him as "Father."

He would customarily lead them in a short prayer of thanks, and then commence eating while listening to a litany of complaints that sometimes amused him, and other times nearly made him cry. These were people whose lives had been shattered by any multitude of sins or illnesses, forcing them into shelters, but mostly onto the streets. Their stories of being homeless were incredible. And Michael often thought that more than half of them could do just fine if they only rechanneled the energy used to survive on the streets into something more productive. He tried hard to get them to focus on managing their needs, and to his frustration discovered that many of them were quite content with the lives they led. They'd staked out a piece of property for themselves—whether it was a park bench or a box over a sewer grate—and they knew where to find meals and for the most part how to avoid trouble.

"Hey, Victor," said Michael to the man across the table. "How are Kayla and Gordon doing?"

"Well, thank you. Gordon made all A's and one B on his last report card. But that little Kayla, well, she has to work a little harder at it, you know, but she made pretty decent grades last time too."

"That's terrific. Would you please tell them both I said hello."

Victor nodded his head while taking a bite of his tuna sandwich.

"I see you got a new shirt, there, pal," Michael said to one downtrodden guest beside him. Compared to his usual garb, the man was wearing a clean shirt that looked like it had never been worn before.

"Yeah, some yuppie from the Upper East Side with a guilty conscience dropped off a whole box of clothes at the shelter the other day," he remarked cynically. "Not bad, is it?" he asked the other guys while tugging proudly at his collar. "Brooks Brothers," he added.

The other guys laughed because they'd seen it happen before and always appreciated such gifts of atonement. They were making so much noise at their own table that Michael hadn't noticed that the rest of the room had gone silent. They were watching Catherine.

It was not a usual sight for them to see such a beautiful, classy woman visit their neighborhood, let alone this soup kitchen. One of the men in the room let out a long, low cat call that finally got Michael's attention. He looked at the men doing the whistling first, and then turned to see the object of their fancy. His heart nearly stopped when he saw Catherine, and he slowly rose from the table as he did.

The look on her face said it all, she was absolutely beaming. She walked toward him in a confident, almost sultry manner, her eyes fixed directly on his, her smile unchanging. He threw his napkin down on the table and got up off the bench, but was so filled with emotion that he could barely make a move toward her. Though still about ten feet away he could read her lips with perfect precision: "We're having a baby," she mouthed at him through her brilliant smile. By now the room was dead silent, with every pair of eyes drawn into the drama unfolding before them. Michael began shaking his head no, while the most enormous grin ever consumed his face.

Though the doctor might admonish him for jolting her so, Michael let out a giant whoop and a holler, then swept Catherine off her feet and swirled her around twice in a giant circle before finally letting her down, but still not letting go. They both began to cry, then held each other tight.

"Hey, everyone," Michael screamed out, "we're having a baby. My wife, Catherine, and I are having a baby."

There could not have been a more festive place to make such an announcement. The twenty or so people dining in the church hall that afternoon stood to clap and cheer for the handsome, young couple. It wasn't often that announcements of good news occurred for them here, or anywhere, but not a one of them missed a chance to congratulate and encourage the smiling couple.

"Hey, can I be the godfather?" asked Rusty. Michael and Catherine laughed as Rusty became deluged with dirty, crumpled napkins tossed by his table mates. Michael hugged and kissed Catherine, then hugged her again. "We'll think about it, Russ," he shouted at the old man.

"Oh, Catherine, this is unbelievable. Unbelievable!" He wiped the moisture from his eyes, then kissed her again. "Our prayers have been answered," he said. "Praise the Lord."

Chapter Forty-eight

Michael sat in a chair along the wall of the dimly lit examining room as Dr. Grace Collins, the obstetrician now responsible for Catherine's care, turned on the ultrasound scanner. It was time for Catherine's twenty-week sonogram, and it would be the first time they'd seen the twins in utero since week five of her pregnancy.

They'd both cried that day, watching in amazement as Dr. Collins pointed out two barely perceptible, flickering hearts on the screen, the first visible sign of their little family taking shape deep inside Catherine.

The mood was vastly different between them today than it had been four months ago. This morning Catherine had barely spoken to Michael.

"It's so ironic, don't you think," she'd cried last night, "that you of all people would force me to continue working for Nowell."

"Catherine, don't be ridiculous. You can't just think of yourself anymore. We have a family to take care of now. And it's your income that's providing our nest egg. The next four months will go by like this," he said adamantly, snapping his fingers, "and there's no telling how long it's going to take me to find a parish after I graduate in May. We'll need every penny of your income stored away for the babies and that transition time before I start working."

"I can't believe it's you who is suddenly worried about money!" she cried. "Michael, he is so strange, I can't stand working for him anymore."

And she meant it. Ever since revealing to Nowell that she was indeed pregnant, and pregnant with twins at that, he'd become practically manic and more intrusive than ever. When, out of her annoyance over his persistent calls, Catherine had told him she no longer wanted to carry her cellular phone, he'd absolutely insisted otherwise, saying she needed it in the event of an emergency. She'd asked Nowell not to bother her so much at home, as she needed her rest, but he didn't seem capable of appreciating that, saying it was far too important that he be able to reach her.

She couldn't understand why, either. He never traveled abroad anymore, and though the New York gallery was still functioning, he barely let anyone in the doors, except his best and oldest customers. He never left Catherine alone with clients anymore, and for that matter he barely left Catherine alone. She spent much of the time at work feeling trapped and frustrated.

Plus, he'd taken an almost obsessive interest in her pregnancy. He wanted to know every detail possible and was keen on offering advice.

"God, Nowell," she grumbled at him one day, "you'd think it was you who was having these babies." He merely laughed at her, but nothing changed. He'd lavished her with expensive gifts already—two silver rattles from Tiffany's; miniature jean jackets from The Gap—and more. Catherine begged him to stop, but he simply couldn't help himself, he'd told her.

He'd also gone to great lengths providing Catherine with the best nutrition, stocking the kitchen with expensive bottled water and an abundance of fresh fruits and vegetables. He also kept a supply of calcium tablets on hand, in addition to an array of other vitamins. And then he insisted that she take naps.

"The guest room is entirely yours," he said. "No one else shall sleep there besides yourself. Whenever you feel the urge, you must go right on upstairs and take a nap."

Indeed, every afternoon he prodded her into going upstairs and lying down, whether she felt tired or not. He claimed he didn't want to be responsible for adding more stress to her life with on-the-job pressures; but the truth was his officious behavior had left Catherine feeling more stressed out than ever and she wanted out of her job. And now, of all things, Michael was the one discouraging her from leaving.

Michael seemed dismissive about her concerns, at one point claiming the worries were nothing more than the product of raging hormones, this last point causing her to go practically crazy with rage. And so, on a day that would normally be full of happy anticipation, they sat in the same room, though worlds apart emotionally.

"Please remain quiet as I go about this procedure," Dr. Collins requested. "We'll discuss everything afterward, but for now I want total silence."

Catherine and Michael easily complied. As Dr. Collins positioned the scanning device on Catherine's protruding belly, Michael edged up in his seat. It wasn't long before he saw a tiny hand on the monitor, watching as it tightened into a clenched fist and then opened again. Michael's face broke into a broad grin, and he looked up at Catherine who remained stoic, her eyes fixed steadfastly on the screen.

He could see the curvature of the first baby's spine, perfectly shaped, only miniature in proportion. Michael was overwhelmed by the miracle unfolding before his eyes, and blinked back tears of pride and joy. Dr. Collins skillfully directed the instrument at the baby's face, and there, its tiny head turning toward them, they could see the shape of two eyes and the form of a hand in the creature's mouth.

"Oh, my God," Catherine finally spoke and then began to softly cry, "the baby, my baby, is sucking its thumb!"

Dr. Collins smiled appreciatively at Catherine, but continued with her quiet analysis of what was on the screen before her. To her trained eye, she could see more than either Michael or Catherine could ever possibly imagine, and carefully scanned the in utero horizon for signs of birth defects or life-threatening illnesses.

It wasn't long before a vision appeared of the other child who, unlike its sibling, was sound asleep. By now, Catherine's body was shaking from the happy sobs. She wanted so desperately to touch her children, to hold them, and tell them how much she loved them. Michael, unable to control his own tears, moved beside her and took her hand, and for the next twenty minutes, they watched, as mother and father, the sight of their peaceful little family within.

This was more than a glimpse at her children, it was a look at her future. As the picture on the screen unfolded, so did clarity in Catherine's mind. Michael was absolutely right. She needed to do everything possible now to make a better future for these babies, which included enduring Nowell's odd behavior. Reassuring herself that she only had a few short months left to work for him, she squeezed Michael's hand in a gesture of love and support.

When it was apparent Dr. Collins was almost finished she looked up at them earnestly and said, "Congratulations. It appears as though we have two perfectly healthy babies. Now, would you care to know the sex of each child?"

Catherine and Michael looked at each other and nervously laughed. They thought they'd resolved this matter before, each claiming they didn't want to know. But the temptation this moment was steep. Catherine finally spoke.

"We already know the twins are fraternal, so let's be surprised by the rest."

Michael nodded in agreement, unable to imagine the surprises this pregnancy would bring.

Chapter Forty-nine

Catherine never thought she'd complain about being pregnant, but the pressure created by the twins made it feel as if her stomach was practically in her throat and like her bladder was twisted in a wrench. She had terrible acid indigestion, making it seem that everything she ate she tasted twice. And she could barely get enough sleep because of the frequent need to urinate each night.

Yet overall it had been a relatively easy pregnancy, and now well into her eighth month, with only thirty-three days to go until her January due date, Catherine had done everything she could to prepare for the birth of the twins. Since Michael would soon be finished with school, they didn't even bother to get an apartment with a second bedroom, instead converting the living room into a nursery.

Michael confessed to being more excited about becoming a father than anything before in his life—including being on Duke's championship basketball team.

Catherine, for her part, was more nervous than excited. She fully expected to go through a normal delivery, and despite the drugs available to diminish the pains of labor, she was scared of the whole ordeal.

"There's nothing to be afraid of," Michael would reassure her whenever she brought up her concerns. "Dr. Collins is going to take great care of you, and I'll be with you every step of the way."

"I know, I know. Still, I'm entitled to be a little nervous, don't you think?"

"I think you think too much," he would tell her, then teasingly ordered her to "breathe, breathe."

"You drive me crazy," she would say, feigning anger at him. But in her heart, she couldn't have adored him more, and couldn't think of anyone's children she would rather have. "We are so blessed," she said repeatedly throughout the pregnancy.

It had come time for Michael to start interviewing at different parishes where he might work following his May graduation. With General Theological Seminary's fine reputation, and Michael's excellent academic achievement, he had become a leading candidate at several desirable churches. And on that thirty-third day before she was due to go into labor, Michael had flown to Atlanta to interview at two separate parishes.

Catherine had bid him an early farewell, but was a bit slower than usual getting out of bed that morning. Despite the fact that she was working reduced hours, she was still going to be late getting in. She called Nowell to let him know she wouldn't be arriving until just after eleven.

"I'm sending a car for you. I don't want you wandering around trying to get a taxi in this wintry weather."

"Nowell, really, I'm fine. I'll see you in a couple of hours."

"Catherine, don't do this to me. I'm sending you a car, and that's final. I'll have it pick you up at noon, how's that? And if you're even later, fine. Just don't push it."

"Okay, okay," she acquiesced.

The car arrived promptly at noon and within fifteen minutes delivered her to Nowell's gallery. He was anxiously waiting for her arrival, and quickly rushed to the car door to help escort her up the steps when she arrived. She was practically breathless by the time she'd landed on the stoop.

"Whew! This is good breathing practice," she told Nowell whose face was etched in concern.

"Are you sure you're all right?"

"I'm fine. Let me just get inside and sit down."

She waddled her way into her office, and almost immediately began sifting through some leftover paperwork from the previous day, then began returning calls.

"Catherine," her designer friend Judy responded happily upon receiving her call, "haven't you had those babies yet?"

"No, not yet," Catherine answered somewhat wearily, tired of hearing that question.

"Why are you even at work? Shouldn't you be taking it easy?"

"This is my way of taking it easy. I'm fine, really."

Judy, always the town crier when it came to good gossip, kept Catherine on the phone for a better part of an hour, filling her in on many lurid details of New York's high society. When they finally hung up, Nowell, who had managed to make himself comfortable in her office, begged for all the scoop.

"First, let me go to the kitchen for a glass of ice water. Would you like some?"

"You stay put"—he smiled—"I'll be happy to get it."

"Nowell, it's bad enough having Michael breathing down my neck. Don't worry, I can take care of myself."

Nowell raised a teasing eyebrow at her, then watched with amusement as she maneuvered awkwardly around the furniture and disappeared into the hallway. Full of happy sentiment, he stood up and looked out the French doors, listening peaceably to the crackling fire behind him. He loved having his family near.

He felt overcome by contentment. In a matter of weeks his children were going to be born, and his plans to have his family permanently together would begin to unfold. He had already discussed what needed to be done with Vince Gambrielli, who was prepared to move ahead at a moment's notice.

Nowell couldn't believe his own stroke of good luck when he learned that Dee, his ever glib housekeeper, had told other members of his staff that she'd seen Nowell and Catherine sleep together. Then there was Stephen's nephew, the unlucky servant who dropped the tray after catching them in a lover's embrace. There would be no denying that they'd had an affair, not with so many eyewitnesses. And then no denying that the twins were his. If Catherine was as smart as he knew her to be, she would one day be forever grateful that he'd engineered a new life for her.

Life is good, Nowell mused to himself. He let out a deep, pleasurable sigh, then thought once more how it would be only a matter of weeks till his daydreams turned to reality. *And it is about to become so much sweeter,* he thought, plopping back down in the chair, then stretching his legs out.

But his calm was not to last. He had almost begun to doze off when his blissful thoughts were shattered by a blood-chilling cry. It was Catherine, and he could hear the utter panic in her voice as she desperately screamed for help.

Nowell leaped up and dashed into the hallway, his heart racing wildly, where he discovered her—white as a sheet and leaning against the wall as a torrent of blood gushed down her leg. She was shaking uncontrollably, standing amid two broken glasses that once contained their ice water. At first Nowell thought she'd cut herself, then promptly realized she was bleeding vaginally.

"Nowell," she wailed, reaching out to him with a look of utmost terror in her eyes. "Help me, please," she was crying. "Oh, God, help me. Help me. Something is terribly wrong." The blood was beginning to form a small pool around her feet as she stood there, unwilling or unable to move; like a shipwreck victim.

"Oh, dear God," he shouted back, as he noticed a trail of blood coming from the kitchen to where she stood. There was no one else in the gallery today, as the cleaning woman had gone for the day, and Nowell felt completely stupid and uncertain of what to do. He was no stranger to the sight of gushing blood, but he knew nothing of how to contain it.

"Call an ambulance," she screamed, and began slowly sinking down the wall. "My babies," she sobbed violently. "Please don't let anything happen to my babies."

It was torture for him to watch. His first instinct was to stay with her, to protect her and his children. But he remembered how quickly Wilton Dresden had died once the blood started flowing, and knew that whatever was happening to her might be as swift and deadly. He couldn't stay to comfort her, he had to get help and rushed to the nearest phone.

"Police or rescue?" the 911 dispatcher asked calmly.

"RESCUE," he screamed into the phone. "I NEED AN AMBULANCE, NOW!"

"Can you tell me the nature of the problem, sir?"

"Go to hell," Nowell bellowed impatiently. "Just get

an ambulance over here, now!" he demanded, shouting his address into the phone.

"Sir, I need to know the nature of the emergency so I can tell the paramedics what to expect."

"It's my wife! We're expecting twins and she's hemorrhaging to death. Get someone over here, now."

He heard several clicks on a computer keyboard. "Someone is on the way now, sir. Is there an apartment number? Will you be there to let them in?"

"For chrissakes, I'll leave the front door open," Nowell shrieked.

"Sir, can you stay on the line with me until someone gets there?"

"No," Nowell screamed back, and leaving the phone dangling he ran back to Catherine, who had slunk all the way down to the floor, lying on her side in the blood and broken glass. She was crying hysterically while clutching her belly. Nowell was at an absolute loss over what to do, then remembered he was supposed to leave the front door open, which he promptly did, then returned and knelt by her side, clearing away whatever glass shards he could.

"Oh, God, Catherine, what is happening here? What do you want me to do? I'll do anything."

"Nowell," she cried, "I'm so scared."

"Don't worry, someone will be here any minute." He grabbed her hands and held them tight.

"I need Michael, please call him. I have the number where you can reach him in my purse."

"Catherine, don't be ridiculous. I'm not leaving you again. Here, rest your feet on my knees," he offered, believing it would help staunch the flow of blood. He helped her turn on to her back so that he could raise her legs, but had no idea what to expect—whether one of the babies was about to be born right into his hands, or if she would die right there in his arms first. He knew that whatever was happening, it was the threshold of tragedy, and that there was nothing he could do to prevent it.

"Where in the hell are they?" he screamed impatiently. Her eyes were open and staring at him, but the terror was beginning to fade, as though she had gone into a state of shock. He heard the sirens wail a few blocks away, and moments later heard the commotion of an EMS team climbing the steps.

"Hello," someone shouted in earnest.

"Here!" Nowell screamed. "We're over here." A man appeared seconds later, telling Nowell to get out of the way so he could assess Catherine's condition.

"How pregnant is she?" he asserted.

"Eight months, and we're expecting twins." Catherine by now had faded, and remained oblivious to the conversation.

The man immediately began giving orders to the other paramedics, and with his walkie-talkie began speaking to the dispatcher, providing an overview of what was happening.

"We're taking her to Eastside Medical Center," he told the dispatcher as the team worked hurriedly around him to stabilize Catherine and then get her on the stretcher.

"That's not where she's supposed to deliver," Nowell snapped.

"No, but it's the closest hospital here. She could be dead by the time we got her to another hospital."

A shudder of horror, then panic went through Nowell. "You cannot let her die," he told the man forcibly. "I'm telling you, whatever you do, do not let her die."

The paramedic ignored Nowell. "Let's go," he barked at his team after they'd inserted an IV in her arm. "Let's get her out of here."

In fewer than five minutes from the time help had arrived, Catherine was bundled up and out the door into the waiting ambulance and on her way to Eastside Medical Center.

"Are you coming?" the chief paramedic shouted at Nowell. Nowell wasted no time running behind them, failing to lock the door as he did, then climbing into the back of the van with the emergency team.

"We're losing pressure," one of them shouted.

"What the hell is happening?" Nowell demanded. "I want to know what is happening to my wife and my children!"

No one paid attention to him, they all focused instead on Catherine's vital signs and in providing any care that they could. In what seemed like an eternity, but was less than five minutes more, they were at the emergency entrance to the private hospital.

Nowell could hear the chief paramedic giving information to the medical team awaiting her arrival. There was discussion of preparation for an emergency C-section, and no sooner did they arrive than she was whisked away from Nowell's sight and fast into surgery. Despite his pleas otherwise, he was not allowed to join her in the operating room. Instead he was ignored and forced to wait alone for news of her fate and that of his innocent children.

Chapter Fifty

Eastside Medical Center, living up to its fine reputation for obstetrical care, had wasted no time after the first emergency call readying itself for the unknown patient. There were at least twenty professionals waiting in the operating suite for Catherine: two teams of pediatric specialists, two anesthesiologists, and the senior staff obstetrician, along with a host of residents and nurses.

Dr. Alberta Juarez was the attending obstetrician. Upon seeing Catherine she immediately suspected one of two things: either the placenta had ruptured, or, worse, the umbilical cord had done so, which meant that one or both of the babies was bleeding to death, if not dead already.

Catherine's case was complicated by the fact that the hospital had no history of prenatal care with her, and Dr. Juarez didn't know all that she was faced with. She had no idea if the twins were identical or fraternal; whether Catherine had a prior history of bleeding; or her exact week of gestation. But there was no time to find out, and to optimize the babies' chance of survival, Dr. Juarez knew she must operate fast.

The unconscious Catherine was swiftly prepped for the surgery, her stylish maternity clothes furiously cut away. The anesthesiologist rapidly put her under a general anesthetic, while the nurses scrubbed her abdomen in preparation for an emergency incision. An EKG was slapped on her, as well as monitors on her abdomen to determine the fetal heart rates, while a resident utilized a sonogram to determine the position of the babies. "They're fraternal," she indicated to Dr. Juarez. "We have a cephalic presentation on the first and breech on number two."

"We're showing acute fetal bradycardia," said another

doctor, describing the first baby's heartbeat. "And distress in the other."

Dr. Juarez began making the incision. Within minutes Catherine's abdomen was open, and with skilled but speedy hands the doctor was able to retrieve the first baby, a boy. Despite his unresponsiveness and gray-blue pallor, the team of pediatricians made valiant attempts at resuscitation, including a massive blood transfusion. But it was too late. The boy was dead. Meantime, Dr. Juarez moved swiftly to deliver the second baby.

It was a girl, who proved to be more pink and vital than her brother, but who needed emergency care nonetheless from the trauma forced on her in the once placid womb. Another team of pediatric specialists hustled her away, and while Dr. Juarez worked feverishly on Catherine, they did everything possible to stabilize the baby girl.

Deliveries were always a bloody mess, but it became apparent to Dr. Juarez that the one ruptured umbilical cord was not the only site of hemorrhaging. Catherine's uterus refused to contract as would normally happen and a steady flow of blood continued pouring out of it. Dr. Juarez called out for emergency blood tests and then a variety of drugs to contract the uterus, but all attempts through IV drugs failed.

"I need a shot of Hemobate," she shouted. "Now!"

In less than a minute the circulating nurse handed her a syringe full of the drug, which she promptly shot right into Catherine's uterine muscle. She watched and waited impatiently, but nothing happened.

"Shit," she said, continuing to massage the uterus to encourage it down to a smaller size. Nothing seemed to work. With over twenty-five years of obstetrical practice to her name, it took a lot to unnerve Juarez. But the nonstop flow of blood from the patient, along with the stubborn condition of her uterus, caused a slight wave of panic to fall over the usually calm physician. It had never taken her this long to stabilize a patient. One of the residents hurried back into the room with discouraging results on blood tests.

"She's got DIC, Dr. Juarez. Her PT/PTT and Fibrogen are abnormally low—her clotting factor is only twenty."

"Jesus Christ," she said. "This woman is bleeding to

death. I need more blood products, stat," she ordered. "Get me some plasma, now." The doctor attempted to control the bleeding by tying off a major artery, but it didn't work, Catherine continued her profusive bleeding.

"We're losing pressure," said the anesthesiologist, "she's down to seventy over forty, and her heart rate is up to one-twenty-five." As Catherine's body began to lose blood pressure, her heart started working overtime to compensate for the loss—a dangerous and deadly combination requiring a last-ditch decision by Dr. Juarez.

"I'm going to have to do a hysterectomy," Dr. Juarez finally concluded. She knew it was the only possibility left to save Catherine's life.

Chapter Fifty-one

Nowell could do nothing to calm himself. Catherine had been in surgery for over two hours, and so far no one had reported back to him. Certainly by now the babies had been delivered, he told himself, incredulous at how insensitive the hospital staff was for not keeping him updated. He'd asked several times about her condition, and each time he got the same response: "She's still in surgery. The doctor will be out to speak to you when it's over."

In his highly agitated state, he'd smoked nearly a pack of cigarettes and was in a pavilion adjacent to the waiting area doing so when he saw an older, but strikingly handsome female doctor heading his way. Her hair was short and thick in varying shades of gray and white, and her olive skin defied her age, showing barely a wrinkle or crease. As she got closer, he could see beneath her stylish glasses a tired and apprehensive look.

"Hi," she said tenderly, while extending her hand. "I'm Dr. Alberta Juarez. I understand you're the father." Nowell stubbed out his cigarette, and turned his head to exhale while keeping his eyes fixed on her. He could tell by the look in her eyes that it wasn't good news.

"How is she?"

The doctor pursed her lips. "Why don't we have a seat over there?" she asked him softly, pointing to a nearby bench. He shook his head no.

"Just tell me, is she okay?"

"It was pretty rough in there, and your wife is in critical shape, but she's expected to make a full recovery. I'm sorry though, you lost one of your babies. A boy. It's an extremely rare thing to have happen, but his umbilical cord ruptured, and his blood supply literally drained right out of his body. It's a condition known as vasa praevia. I'm really sorry. The other doctors tried everything, but there was nothing we could do for him."

Sudden memories of the news over his parents' plane crash flooded Nowell's mind. He remembered Nigel waking him up in the middle of the night to tell him, and how it felt like he'd been hit by a freight train. It had seemed impossible. He was happy to get rid of Elizabeth; but to lose his beloved parents had been more than he could handle, and he'd never been the same since. It wasn't until Catherine entered his life that he'd felt so alive again.

"But my wife," Nowell said earnestly, his eyes becoming moist, "she's going to be okay?"

"Well, yes. But I have to be honest with you, we nearly lost her too." Dr. Juarez looked down at the ground before breaking the rest of the news to him. "I'm afraid your wife won't be able to have any more children. In order to save her life we had to do a complete hysterectomy."

"Where is she? Can I see her?"

"She's in recovery right now, and will be headed to the intensive care unit after that. She's in pretty bad shape, and I'd expect her to stay there for at least three to four days before going to the maternity ward. You can see her as soon as she's settled in." She then looked at him with a rather quirky smile. "There is some good news, you know. Would you like to see your daughter?"

In shock over Catherine's serious condition, compounded by the tragic news of his son's death, he'd somehow failed to realize that the other baby had survived.

"My what? No! No!" he said with rising joy. "This is truly unreal. I have a daughter?"

"Yes." Dr. Juarez smiled, gently removing his hands from her lapels. "She's in the neonatal intensive care unit right now, since she suffered some fetal distress. But she weighed in at five pounds three ounces, which is great, and she's expected to thrive."

"Can I see my baby? Please?"

"Sure, follow me," she said kindly, patting him softly on the arm and then leading the way to the neonatal unit. And there, inside an incubator, with an array of tubes protruding from her body, was the tiniest human creature Nowell had ever laid eyes on. He was completely unprepared for the raw emotion that would be drawn out of him at the sight of his daughter—their daughter—the product of his great love for Catherine. He had never felt like this before in his life; it was a love different from the one he possessed for Catherine; or even that for his late parents. He placed his hand upon the viewing window and pressed hard, trying in vain to suppress his tears.

"Daddy's here, my sweet love," he cried softly. "Your daddy is here."

Chapter Fifty-two

A sudden change in Atlanta's weather forced a delay in Michael's flight back to New York. He would have called Catherine to let her know, but his plane had already taxied out on the tarmac and was waiting for take-off when word came in of wind shear conditions.

It was an older plane he'd boarded, one without the phones built right into the seats. He would just have to explain what had happened once he got home. It took about an hour and a half before his flight was finally airborne, which would put him back in New York after midnight. He was certain Catherine would be up for her second or third trip to the bathroom by then, and would enjoy hearing all about his interviews.

He really liked Atlanta, and considered it a strong possibility as the place they might next move. The pending birth of his children made him look at everything in an entirely different light—what were the church neighborhoods like? Were the schools any good? What about parks and playgrounds? He always thought he'd end up in the poorest section of town as a matter of choice, but now his concerns had shifted for his children's safety. He looked at a woman across the aisle from him, who appeared to be about five months pregnant, and then smiled sympathetically at her as she got up to go to the bathroom. He almost felt sorry for her, thinking how few the days were now before his children would be born, and how much longer that woman had to wait.

Michael's plane finally touched down at La Guardia shortly after midnight. Despite the late hour, it was a hustle to get a taxi, so it took him a while longer to get home to their Chelsea apartment. All the lights were out when he arrived, and the peaceful quiet in the apartment made Michael assume Catherine was fast asleep. Knowing how difficult it had been for her to get a good night's rest lately, he decided not to go into the bedroom and stir things up until he heard her get up to go to the bathroom.

He went to the refrigerator and pulled out a Heineken, then sat down on the sofa, barely able to see the television through the two cribs, the changing table, and other infant paraphernalia. He plunked his feet up on the well-worn coffee table, then told himself he'd better get used to lots of long nights like this.

He channel-surfed for a while, drank another beer, and then slipped into a sound sleep still sitting up in his best suit. He startled himself half to death when he awoke to find sunshine filling the apartment. He was slightly disoriented, but recovered his bearings and was immediately struck by the fact that the TV was still on. Why hadn't Catherine roused him? he wondered. Surely she would have been up at least once by now.

"Catherine," he shouted out, but was met by an eerie silence. He jumped off the sofa—nearly tripping over a package of diapers—and headed fast into the bedroom.

"Shit!" he screamed and began to panic. The bed had not been slept in and there was no sign of her. "Oh, shit!" he began to scream again. "She's at the hospital! She must be at the hospital!"

Suddenly feeling all thumbs, Michael tried to pull himself together and find the phone number for Westside General. But in his determination to get to her as quickly as possible he abandoned the phone, jumped into his shoes, and headed out the door, hailing the first taxi he could find.

Running madly into the hospital, he grabbed the first person to cross his path.

"How do I get to the maternity ward?" he shouted at a nurse passing him on her way to work. She explained, but in his excited state it only confused him, so she suggested that he follow her.

"I can't believe this," Michael lamented on the elevator, "I should have been here. I can't believe this!"

"Did your wife just have a baby?"

"I don't know, but I think so. I just got back from a business trip and she wasn't home and there wasn't a note. She's eight months pregnant with twins."

"Hmmm, well good luck." The nurse smiled at him as she bid farewell on the seventh-floor maternity hall. Michael made a dash to the nurse's station.

"My wife," he said breathlessly. "I think my wife is here. Catherine Harrison, we're expecting twins. Where is she?"

Two nurses on duty looked at each other quizzically, then back at Michael. "I don't think there's anyone here by that name, but I'll check," said one of them. She looked at all the charts while shaking her head.

"No, I'm sorry, there's no Harrison on this floor."

"I don't know what to make of this," he said. "Where could she be?"

"Kinda hard to lose someone who's pregnant with twins," the other nurse said with a giggle. Michael didn't laugh, and neither did the other nurse. He let out an exasperated sigh, then ran a hand over his unshaven face. "I was gone on a business trip last night and didn't find out till this morning that she wasn't at home. There was no note. I don't know what to do."

"Who's her doctor?" asked the more serious one.

"Collins. Dr. Grace Collins."

"Tell you what. Why don't I page her for you. She may know something."

"Great," said Michael as he nervously tapped his fingers on the station desk while waiting to hear back from the doctor. It took about seven minutes, but finally the phone rang.

"Maternity," answered the nurse. "Yeah, hi, Dr. Collins," she said. "We have a man here by the name of . . ." She paused, then spoke to Michael. "I'm sorry, what's your first name?"

"Michael."

"Michael Harrison," she went on. "He can't find his wife, Catherine, and thought she might have come here, but we have no one on the ward by that name. Do you know anything about where she might be?" She paused to listen. "Uh-huh, uh-huh," she said slowly. "Okay, hold on." She handed Michael the phone. "She'd like to talk with you."

Michael eagerly grabbed the receiver. "Dr. Collins, hello. Listen, sorry to bother you so early in the morning."

"It's all right, Michael, I'm always up at this hour. Tell me what's going on."

"I know it sounds funny, but I really don't know. I came home from Atlanta around one-thirty this morning, and instead of bursting into the bedroom and waking Catherine up, I fell asleep on the sofa. When I woke up a little while ago I realized that she hadn't been home the whole time. She didn't leave a note or anything, so I thought she might have gone into labor and headed over here."

"Were there any messages on your answering machine?"

"Oh, no"—he rubbed his hand down his face again—"I forgot to check the machine."

"Listen, why don't you go back home and do that first. Maybe she spent the night at a friend's, although she's supposed to have slowed down by now," Dr. Collins added somewhat critically. "Listen, either way, please get in touch with me and have her do the same, would you?"

"Sure, and thanks for your help." He handed the phone back to the more serious nurse.

"Well, I suppose you could consider it a dry run." She smiled at him.

"Yeah, I suppose," he said sheepishly. "I guess I'll be seeing you back here soon. Hey, and thanks for your help too," he said, then headed for the elevator.

This just isn't like her, he said to himself. *Something just isn't right.*

Chapter Fifty-three

At around 4:30 A.M. Nowell took advantage of a lull in the activity around Catherine to sit down in a bedside chair and take a nap. She'd been out of it all night long, constantly tended to by a team of highly skilled nurses and doctors. In addition to the traumatic delivery and surgery, she was suffering from respiratory trouble. There were as many tubes coming from her as he'd seen on their newborn daughter.

His nap was short-lived though, as Dr. Juarez appeared and began talking with an ICU physician about the kind of night it had been for Catherine. Dr. Juarez smiled at Nowell as he woke up.

"Good morning," she said. "I'm not sure who had it worse—your wife or you, sleeping in that chair."

"I think I could have slept standing up," he said, smiling back. "How is she?"

"Critical but stable."

Nowell was checking his watch when it suddenly dawned on him that Michael should have arrived back from Atlanta by now and was probably frantic trying to find his beloved wife.

"Dr. Juarez, have any other family members stopped by?"

"No, not that I know of. Visiting hours are restricted here, and aren't until much later besides. Incidentally, may I have a word with you outside, please," she politely asked.

"Why certainly," he said, scratching the stubble on his firm chin and then stretching his face in a large yawn. He had thoroughly convinced the hospital staff that Catherine was his wife, and by the time he and Vince Gambrielli got finished with Michael, he was certain she would be. He stepped into the hallway with Dr. Juarez like any concerned husband would.

"Listen, I suggest you don't say anything to her right away about what happened with your son or the hysterectomy. When she comes around just keep things to yourself until I'm there with you. Okay?"

"I understand. How's my other girl?" he said, beaming. "Have you seen her yet this morning?"

"Yes, and she's doing remarkably well. In fact, I won't be surprised if she's removed from the neonatal intensive care unit later today and put into the regular maternity ward. You'll get a chance to hold her then." Dr. Juarez paused, then added, "Are you doing all right? We've focused so much of our attention on your wife and baby that we haven't talked about your loss. We have counselors trained in this sort of thing, if you'd like some help."

"No, no thank you. There is a sense of sadness, indeed," Nowell responded. "But it is replaced by an overwhelming sense of joy over the birth of my daughter and the fact that my wife is going to be all right. We will deal with the death of our son in our own private way when it's appropriate."

"I like your attitude." Dr. Juarez smiled. "Oh, by the way, what's her name?" The question took Nowell completely by surprise.

"Do you have a name for the baby?" she inquired again. "At some point you'll need to sign her birth certificate."

Nowell couldn't believe the opportunity at hand. Of course he had a name picked out, he would name the baby after his mother. He always thought it was ironic that his mother and Catherine shared the same maiden name, so he couldn't imagine why Catherine would object to naming their baby as such. "Yes"—he smiled at Dr. Juarez—"her name is Cornelia Howard Stuart."

"That's a big name for such a little girl," she said.

"Only because there are big things ahead in this little girl's future," he said, smiling back.

"Damn," said Michael as he slipped back into the apartment and saw there were no messages on the answering machine. "Where is she? Does she know I'm going out of my mind?" he said aloud, then checked the bedroom once more to see if Catherine had come home. His mind raced with the possibilities over where she might be, and his only conclusion was that she must have spent the night at Nowell's town house. He knew she was accustomed to taking short naps there during the day and that Nowell had turned one of his guest rooms over to her so that she could sleep whenever she wanted.

He picked up the phone and dialed Nowell's gallery, but it just rang. "I'm sure that's where she is," he said calmly, trying to reassure himself. "Where else could she have gone?"

Michael tried hard not to imagine the worst—that she might have been a victim of some crime on the way home and that not even Nowell knew where she was. "No, she's gotta be up at his town house," he concluded, then promptly left the apartment and caught a taxi in that direction.

He paid the driver and hopped out. Though it was still early in the morning, he rang the bell repeatedly, while continuing to glance nervously at the security monitor overhead. His frustration and anger began to mount with each empty ring, resurrecting the bad feelings he'd had toward Nowell when Catherine first started working for him. The thought that she might have spent the night here without notifying him left him unnerved.

Michael had worked hard to put aside his jealousy toward Nowell, and had even come to accept his generosity and his patience with Catherine's needs during her pregnancy. But Michael was also a shrewd judge of character. And though he'd learned to keep negative feelings to himself, his gut reaction was always the same—to watch it. He sensed Nowell was a cunning and manipulative man, someone accustomed to getting his way through his seeming "goodwill," or, really, his money. He now felt remorse for pushing Catherine into staying with Nowell when she'd wanted to leave.

And now, standing on Nowell's doorstep that particular day, with no answer to his persistent knocks and rings, Michael felt his dislike toward the man resurfacing. *Surely he knows where she is, and should have called me,* he thought angrily. He pounded heavily and then turned the handle on the door, which to his astonishment opened. It gave him an eerie feeling, knowing from Catherine what airtight security Nowell normally had. Nervous about entering, he called out both Catherine's and Nowell's names several times from the threshold before finally walking inside.

It was dark in the stately entrance hall, so Michael left the door open while searching around for some light. He finally found a table lamp halfway from the door and switched it on. He kept hoping for the best—that he'd find Catherine sleeping soundly in a large, downy bed upstairs, so deeply asleep that she forgot to call him. His head quickened as he made his way farther into the town house and back toward what appeared to be Catherine's office. He saw her coat and purse, then shuddered.

He felt then that something was terribly wrong, but it wasn't until making his way back out into the hall that his deepest fears were confirmed and he realized something truly dreadful had happened to his wife.

It was a horrifying discovery, almost like coming upon a brutal crime scene, as he first heard the crunch of shattered glass beneath his feet, then noticed the pool of dried blood and the blood smeared on the wall beside it. Though he stared at the blood coldly, the sight of so much of it caused a flash of fear to race down his spine, and he instinctively screamed out her name, which drew only a hollow echo for a response.

A further wave of panic set in as he saw the trail of blood leading into a kitchen, and the chilling realization set upon him that some terrible end had come to her pregnancy, or that she and Nowell might be the victims of some vicious crime. He wanted to run out of there and get help; he wanted to call the police. But his instincts told him he'd better check first to see if they were there and in need of help. He hit the elevator button, and with no idea where this trail would lead, he bravely entered the car and rode to the second floor of the gallery. He quickly scanned the rooms, but found nothing out of order, and no other blood. So he got back into the elevator and conducted the same fruitless search on the third floor, and then rode up to the fourth floor that he knew contained Nowell's private living quarters.

Michael saw no further traces of blood in the hall, but still began opening the doors. Behind the first door was a richly decorated guest room that he assumed was the one Catherine used, but there were no signs of disturbance or of anyone having slept there. Next was a lavish bathroom, and again, everything seemed in order.

What am I doing? he questioned himself again and again, unsure of how he would react if he did come upon some gruesome discovery. He thought to stop at this point and just leave, but the compelling need to protect Catherine moved him on. He tapped on the set of double doors that he presumed led to Nowell's master bedroom suite, but there was no answer.

"Catherine," he yelled out. "Nowell?" But again his cries were met with an eerie silence. He tentatively opened the doors to the bedroom, and what he saw next hit him in the chest like a Patriot missile. Across the room, as large as life and situated between two oversized windows, was a stunning oil portrait of his wife. Michael felt as though his senses had been knocked clean out of his head not only by the mere discovery of it, but also because it showed Catherine practically nude.

Michael walked in a trancelike state up to the portrait, unable to believe the striking resemblance to her. He felt as though he might become physically ill at the sight of it—why in the world would Catherine have posed for this? The artist had managed to capture both her innocence and sultriness, but the portrait nonetheless was tawdry to him as a satin sheet was draped over her lower torso, and her right breast was exposed, bearing an uncanny resemblance to the real thing—its fullness and even the color of her nipple. There was simply no way that a portrait this accurate could have been painted without reference to the real thing, Michael concluded. He felt as if he might actually throw up, then moved over to the edge of the bed to sit down while staring fixedly at Catherine's alluring eyes.

How could she have done this to me? he asked himself, trying in vain to regain his composure. It was impossible to comprehend. Had he been so blinded by his love for her and his abiding faith in God that he'd failed to see an affair flourishing between her and Nowell?

No, this simply can't be. She wouldn't do this to me, he tried to rationalize, but there seemed no other explanation for what was staring down at him.

"Oh, Catherine," he cried out loud at the portrait, "don't do this to me."

He didn't know what to think, he didn't know what to make of anything. All he knew was that the discovery before him was as upsetting as the trail of blood that had initially led him to it.

"Dammit," he cried at the picture. "Where are you? Where are you?"

He knew he needed to call the police, to try to find out if they knew something that had happened. But as he left Nowell's bedroom he noticed two more doors down the hall that he'd yet to open. The first led to Nowell's study, which revealed no more surprises. But what he discovered in the next room was like being hit by another high-velocity missile—it was a nursery, complete with two of everything: two ornate white cribs draped with heavy white canopies; two white wicker rocking chairs; two changing tables stuffed with diapers, ointments, and other assorted goods; two armoires brimming with expensive infants' clothing and an array of stuffed animals that made it look like F.A.O. Schwarz had been cleaned out.

"Oh, God, God help me," cried Michael in utter anguish as he crumpled to his knees and clutched his chest. There was no thirst, no hunger nor pain that he'd ever felt in his life to match the suffering he felt at that moment. It was simply unbearable.

"Why are they doing this to me?" he cried in a soft whisper, while feeling as though he would nearly explode with anger and frustration. His mind raced fervently with questions and possibilities. Of course Catherine had fallen in love with Nowell. Michael had sensed that danger from the beginning. She was wildly impressed with his wealth and his connections—with everything he was and that Michael was not. But why the charade? Why would she claim she wanted to stop working for Nowell? Was she simply waiting until their children were born before she broke the news to Michael that she was leaving and taking them to live with Nowell?

Everything and nothing made sense to him. Why would she even bother to go through all the trouble to have his children if she was in love with another man?

Michael began to feel helpless. He closed his eyes in agony, while a passage from the Book of Job ran through his mind: *"When I looked for good, then evil came unto me: And when I waited for light, there came darkness."*

"Oh, my beloved Lord," Michael prayed aloud, "please do not forsake me."

Chapter Fifty-four

Michel headed slowly down the stairs, unable to quell sickening feelings that Catherine was in danger while at the same time fighting the sense that she had been unfaithful all this time. If there had been an emergency, Michael thought, she'd have been transported to the closest hospital; most likely Eastside Medical Center. He picked up the phone in Catherine's office, got the number from directory assistance, then called the hospital.

"Eastside Medical Center."

"Patient Information, please," Michael asked.

"Just a moment," said the woman.

"Patient Information," another female voice said.

"Yes, I'm calling to see if you have a patient by the name of Catherine Harrison."

"Checking." The few seconds that she took to check seemed like an eternity to Michael.

"Sorry, sir. No one by that name."

"Thank you for checking, ma'am." Michael placed the receiver back down and tried to think of other hospitals in the area, when Dr. Collins's plea to call him when he learned something came to mind. He quickly called her.

"I'm sorry, sir, but she's with a patient right now," said the receptionist. "May I have her return the call."

"No. This is an emergency. Tell her Michael Harrison is on the phone and that I need to speak with her now."

What were only a few minutes felt like an eternity until Dr. Collins picked up the line.

"Michael," she said, "what's going on? Have you found Catherine?"

"No," he said emphatically, then went on to describe the gruesome blood he discovered in the hallway, adding that Catherine's coat and purse had been left behind.

"I called Eastside Medical, and they don't have anyone there under her name. What I'm wondering," said Michael, "is if you wouldn't mind using your clout as a doctor to call the police, even 911, and find out if any emergency was registered at this address, and where she might have been taken."

"That's a good idea, Michael, I'll get right on it. Give me the number where I can reach you."

Michael did as instructed, but could not sit still. He felt like he needed to be doing something—looking for clues—anything that might lead him to Catherine. He began rummaging through her purse, but found nothing out of the ordinary. He even checked her coat pockets, but with the exception of a rumpled Kleenex came up empty. Even her desk was void of anything telling. He sat down in her chair and fidgeted with the phone cord when suddenly it rang. He barely let it go half a ring.

"Hello," he said, anxiously gripping the receiver. It was Dr. Collins.

"Michael, I've got both bad and perplexing news. Catherine was picked up by a team of medics at that address yesterday and taken to Eastside Medical Center. But what's been reported back to me is that she's registered under the name Stuart. She's in the intensive care unit."

"The intensive care unit!" said Michael, letting slip for a moment the name formality. "Good God. What has happened?"

"I don't have all the details yet. If you can wait a few minutes longer I can get back to you on that . . ."

He wasn't about to wait and impatiently dropped the phone and departed the town house, leaving it exactly as he found it, then jogged the ten blocks to the hospital. Breathless when he arrived, he sought out information about where the ICU was located, then jumped on the elevator and headed up there.

There was a wide set of swinging double doors at the far end of one hall, with INTENSIVE CARE UNIT spelled out above them. Michael hurried into the ward, but was immediately stopped by a nurse who regarded him with steely eyes.

"Excuse me, but where are you going?" she asked tersely.

"I'm looking for my wife, Catherine Harrison." He was met by a suspicious look.

"My wife is Catherine Harrison, and I understand she's here in ICU. I need to see her now," he demanded.

She looked at him somewhat vaguely, then answered him matter-of-factly.

"We don't have any patient by that name."

"Could she have been moved?"

"No, we've never had any patient under that name."

"Wait, wait," he said. "She may be registered under the name Stuart. I'm her husband, Michael," he offered, hoping a simple introduction would ease his way toward his wife.

"Would you come with me, please?" she asked, and instead of delivering him to Catherine's room, she introduced him to the head nurse.

"This man says he's Catherine Stuart's husband," she said matter-of-factly. "Do you want to talk with him?" Michael felt his heart quicken, as though Catherine had died and they wanted to break the news to him gently. What the head nurse said next nearly made him pass out.

"Sir, I'm sorry. But we have very strict guidelines here. The patient is with her husband right now, and I'm afraid you'll have to leave."

"That's impossible," Michael shouted. "I am her husband. Do you want some kind of proof?" He reached for his wallet, but the head nurse wasn't interested in seeing his evidence.

"I'm going to have to ask you to leave," she said firmly, "or else I'll have to call security."

"You can't call security on me," he said, roiling with anger. "I'm her husband. And I can prove it. I demand to know who is in the room with her," knowing full well who it was.

"Sir, once more, I'm going to have to ask you to leave," she said as she picked up the phone and dialed security.

"This is unbelievable, absolutely unbelievable," said Michael to the uppity nurse. "Don't waste your time with security, I'm leaving. But I'll be back, trust me," he said with furious eyes, storming out of ICU, then heading fast for the first pay phone he could find.

"Dr. Collins," he asked bluntly of the receptionist.

"I'm sorry, she's with a patient right now."

"Tell her Michael Harrison is on the phone."

"Just a moment," she said, then put him on hold. It didn't take long for Dr. Collins to pick up.

"Michael, where are you? Have you found Catherine?"

"They won't let me in to see her. They claim that her husband is already in the room with her. It's her boss, I'm sure, but they won't even listen to me. Can you help me?"

"Absolutely, this may take a minute, but don't go, stay on the line, would you?"

"Yeah, I'm not going anywhere," he said, sighing, then leaned his back up against the wall and waited. In his emotionally agitated state he could hardly stand to watch the people passing by, but neither could he close his eyes since when he did all he saw was Catherine's portrait hanging in Nowell's bedroom. He tried to say a prayer to calm his nerves, but he couldn't focus. All he knew was that his wife was in the ICU; that Nowell Stuart was claiming to be her husband; and that a nursery was ready and waiting for a set of twins at Nowell's town house.

"Michael," Dr. Collins finally interrupted his torrent of bad thoughts. "A friend of mine that works at the hospital is going to meet you wherever you are and escort you up to ICU. Tell me where you're at?"

"I'm near the front entrance."

"Stay put, she'll be there in just a few minutes."

"Would you mind telling me what's going on? What the hell has happened to my wife?"

"Michael, I'm afraid it's quite serious."

"BELIEVE ME—THERE IS NOTHING YOU COULD TELL ME THAT WOULD SURPRISE ME NOW. JUST TELL ME!"

Dr. Collins let out a tentative sigh, and then began rather slowly. "Michael, yesterday afternoon your twins were delivered by an emergency C-section."

"Oh, my God," he said, his voice barely audible now. Her reference to "your twins" stirred different emotions. She was talking about his children; his own flesh and blood. "Are they okay?" he asked.

"Well, I'm afraid one of them didn't make it. A boy.

But your little girl is okay. She's in the neonatal intensive care unit, but is expected to be released from there today. Catherine, however, is not in very good shape. They had to do a complete hysterectomy on her in order to save her life."

It was a highly unusual situation Dr. Collins found herself in, explaining tragic news like this over the phone. But she wanted Michael to know what he was getting himself into before he headed up to the ICU. She could hear the chatter of people around him, but nothing from Michael. She listened more closely, then heard quiet sobs coming from the other end of the phone, and felt miserable that she wasn't with him. Overall it was a frustrating situation for her since she didn't have privileges at Eastside Medical Center and couldn't tend to her patient there. But her friend and former colleague who worked there would be a tremendous help. She could suddenly hear Dr. Theresa Remy introducing herself to Michael.

"Michael, are you still with me?" Dr. Collins asked into the phone.

"Yeah," he said softly.

"Good. Let Dr. Remy take you upstairs. She can help to get everything straightened out."

"There's a lot more to be straightened out than I think either of us bargained for."

"What do you mean?"

"Nothing. I'll call you later. Thanks for your help," he said, then hung up the phone.

The information Dr. Collins had received on Catherine was sketchy, so after hanging up with Michael she immediately put in a call to Dr. Juarez for a detailed report on the surgery. She felt heavy-hearted for Michael and Catherine, both of whom she knew had been beyond themselves with anticipation over expecting twins. The loss of the son was tragic, and then the loss of Catherine's reproductive system as well made it seem downright cruel. She needed to know from Dr. Juarez exactly what went wrong and if every measure possible had been taken to save the baby's life and Catherine's ability to have children.

As a courtesy, she also placed a call to Dr. Stan Webster to let him know that one of his patients had delivered. He was always good about visiting his former charges in the hospital; always anxious to see the fruits of his in vitro magic.

Meanwhile, Dr. Remy, a young woman with a warm, friendly face and intelligent eyes, chatted with Michael briefly about his situation.

"Listen, before we go up to ICU," she said, "would you like to see your daughter?"

"Oh," he said with a sigh, "absolutely." He then followed her to the elevator, neither of them saying a word on the crowded ride upstairs or even in the hallway of the neonatal unit. Dr. Remy disappeared inside the nursery, where four fragile-looking babies were all hooked to life-support measures of varying degrees, then rejoined him as a nurse went inside the sterile room and pointed proudly to the largest baby of them all.

Michael thought he'd felt every raw emotion possible that day until he laid eyes on his daughter; her tiny hands reaching, then retracting; her rosebud mouth opening and closing as though eager to taste everything joyful in life. She had a little knit cap on her head, so he couldn't see her hair color, but her delicate face bore a striking resemblance to her beautiful mother.

"Oh, this can't be," he began to cry softly. "She's beautiful." Dr. Remy gave him a gentle, congratulatory pat on the back.

"It's really something, isn't it?" She smiled softly.

"You have no idea," he replied as he looked longingly at his daughter, wanting desperately to cradle her and let her know that no matter what happened he would always be there for her. He missed Catherine terribly at that moment, needing desperately to see her as well and to resolve the mystery over what he'd discovered at Nowell's.

"I'll see you later, sweetheart," he said, then gently kissed the glass windowpane. He and Dr. Remy traveled on up to the intensive care unit, where she made Michael wait at the nurse's station while she located the head nurse, who came back looking at Michael rather quizzically.

"I'm sorry," she apologized. "Something like this has never happened on the floor before. Who is the man in there with her, then?"

"I'm sure it's her boss. I was gone on a business trip yesterday when she went into the hospital. She was at work," was all Michael offered.

"Well, let me get him out of the room first. We really don't want the two of you in there together. Your wife's situation is very delicate right now."

Michael drew in a deep breath, attempting to fight off more tears. How could he have not been there for her, he began asking himself. But despite his remorse, the deeply disturbing thought continued nagging him—what if Catherine had carried on an affair with Nowell? It seemed that ever since he'd awoken that morning he was living in another world—a world made real only by the piercing pain in his heart.

A few minutes later a weary, but confident-looking Nowell Stuart emerged from Catherine's room. He had almost a serene look about himself, as though he were in perfect control of the situation and that his being with Catherine during the most traumatic time of her life was perfectly just.

"Michael," he said casually as he faced him in the hallway. Just the sight of him made Michael feel ill. Michael said nothing, instead casting a fierce, angry look as he passed Nowell, only to change his mind a few paces later, then stop and turn.

"Did it ever once occur to you to get in touch with me?" Michael asked as calmly as he could manage, though his voice cracked with emotion. "She is *my* wife after all."

Nowell smirked, but said nothing.

"Why in the hell didn't you call me?" Michael demanded.

Nowell looked at him coldly, and answered in a firm, measured voice, "Did it ever occur to *you* that your wife wanted it this way?"

An uncontrollable rage clouded all Michael's better senses as he lunged at Nowell, swinging wildly and striking him with coldhearted force in his jaw. Nowell fell back and watched as Michael wound up again, deliberately not bothering to block the second blow. Dr. Remy gasped and with the assistance of the head nurse tried to grab Michael from behind, while Nowell took a step backward, holding on to his jaw as if in wrenching pain.

"What's the matter, choirboy," Nowell sneered, "is the truth a little too hard to handle?"

"Get him out of here," Michael belted out. "I want him out of here, now!"

"Don't worry, I was just leaving," said Nowell, then looked at the nurse and the doctor with understanding eyes. "I'm sorry about my friend's behavior. He's just beginning to realize his true loss."

Michael took a deep breath and tried hard to hide his trembling lip. If ever he had to call upon his faith to restore himself, it was at that moment. Regardless of what he was to learn, he was determined not to hear it from Nowell, and proceeded on into Catherine's room with whatever dignity he had left.

Chapter Fifty-five

Catherine had never felt such excruciating pain in her entire life, both physically and emotionally. She had awakened briefly during recovery, but her doped-up condition, along with the tubes in her mouth and nose, made it impossible to react fully. She'd heard snippets of conversation related to her, but which she chose not to believe. One nurse said something about a hysterectomy, another said something about the poor babies. Another kept calling her Mrs. Stuart.

Catherine felt certain of only one thing—that she'd had her children. She'd experienced an overwhelming sense of grief during that brief time she'd woken up, and she felt that if she didn't die from the physical pain she would surely die of a broken heart.

Lying in the intensive care unit, all hooked up to myriad monitors and tubes, she'd come around again in the morning, only to catch a glimpse of Nowell sleeping in the chair beside her. Obviously Michael hadn't made it here yet, and she didn't want to share her anguish with anyone but him. *He's got to find me,* she told herself dreamily. *He's got to come and get me,* she thought, then drifted back off into a deep sleep.

When she opened her eyes next, it seemed at first as if nothing had changed. She was still hooked up to countless tubes and wires; still unable to speak due to the respirator in her mouth; the room was still dark and her body still wracked in pain. Assuming Nowell remained in the chair beside her, she turned her head slightly only to discover he wasn't there after all. That it was Michael who was now keeping a bedside vigil. His head was bowed and his hands folded in prayer.

With the tube down her throat she was incapable of making even the slightest noise to attract his attention.

Michael, she screamed with her eyes, *Michael, I'm here. I'm awake. Look at me, please!*

Moments later he rubbed his hands up and down his face. He looked tired and worn, as though he hadn't slept in days. The usual sparkle in his eyes was dulled by an unfamiliar look of pain, prompting Catherine to believe it was all true—they'd lost their precious babies. In her own anguish and frustration, tears welled up in her eyes, the emotion causing her to choke on the tube in her throat.

"Catherine, my God, Catherine," Michael startled, then jumped up out of his seat and leaned down beside her. He immediately hit the call button to summon a doctor or nurse, uncertain whether she was choking to death and not knowing the first thing to do. Michael screamed for someone to come help; his cry was immediately met by the head nurse who dashed past him and to her side. She promptly scanned the monitors and the connections, while placing a firm but reassuring hand on Catherine's forehead as she struggled to raise herself in a desperate attempt to communicate.

"It's okay, Mrs. Stuart," she said, "it's okay."

Catherine's eyes grew large and even more imploring.

"Just relax," she told Catherine, "everything is going to be all right. Please let the machine breathe for you. You're in the intensive care unit. Everything is okay."

"Her name is not Mrs. Stuart," Michael said firmly. "Her name is Catherine Harrison, and she is my wife.

"Does she know what happened?" he went on. The nurse cast him a frustrated look, then shook her head no.

"I need to get the doctor," she reported, then spoke directly to Catherine. "Mrs. Stuart, I need you to take it easy. The doctor will be in here shortly. I know this tube down your throat is uncomfortable, but it will have to stay there for another day or so." She promptly left the room, leaving the two of them alone once more.

Catherine looked hard at Michael, and with whatever strength she could muster, reached over to a pen on the bedside table and waved it feebly at him.

"What?" he asked. "What do you want?" She made a gesture that she wanted to write. Michael quickly looked around for a scrap of paper, then pulled the boarding pass from his trip to Atlanta out of his rumpled shirt pocket and handed it to her. In shaky and delicate hand-writing she simply wrote two words: "Know what?" She wanted to know what Michael was referring to with the nurse.

"Catherine, I think you should wait for the doctor to come and see you."

"NO!" she screamed at him with her eyes, then weakly jabbed the pen in his direction as if to say "I want to hear it from you."

Michael knew that sooner or later she would have to learn the truth about what had happened, though the issue with Nowell was an entirely separate matter to be handled later and in a much different manner. Michael sat down on the edge of the bed, removing the pen, and then held her hand tenderly in his own.

"Catherine, I don't know everything that has happened," he began softly. "I'm still waiting to find out myself. But I do know this," he said as he looked thoughtfully into her moist eyes. "We have the most beautiful baby girl you ever saw in the whole wide world, and she looks just like her mama." He squeezed her hand and could feel her faintly squeeze back as tears welled up in her eyes again, then spilled down her pale cheeks. It was like a radiant burst of sunshine had cut through the darkness in her soul to learn that one of their babies had survived. She wished so desperately she could see her daughter, to hold her and let her know how special she truly was.

Michael gave her hand another little squeeze before beginning again. "I'm afraid, however, that the Good Lord took her baby brother," he said, then stopped, choking hard on tears of his own. Catherine nodded her head, as though she already knew, then squeezed his hand again as if to reassure him. They looked at each other, a look that only two people deeply in love can share, as if to say "we still have each other, we will survive." And for that moment Michael could forget about all that he'd seen at Nowell's; all that had happened with him in the hallway; and all that was yet to occur. All he knew was that Catherine had survived; their daughter had survived; and that God willing their love would prevail.

But his joy was short-lived. When a knock came on

the door, Michael didn't even bother to turn around, assuming it was the doctor. But the fresh wave of terror consuming Catherine's face prompted him to look. The nurse indeed had returned, only she was escorted by two New York City police officers.

"Mr. Harrison, would you come with us, please?" asked one of them, a rather large imposing man, made even more ominous by his midnight-blue uniform.

"Why? What is this?" asked Michael incredulously.

"Mr. Harrison, I think you should leave the room," the nurse advised seriously.

"What is going on?" asked Michael again, now seeming resistant.

"You're under arrest, Mr. Harrison, for the assault and battery of a Mr. Nowell Stuart," said the second officer, a young woman who quickly moved to slap on a pair of handcuffs. She began reciting Miranda rights to him. "Do you understand?" she concluded.

"I don't believe this," he said gruffly.

"Do you understand?" she repeated.

"Yes, yes," he said, then glanced over at Catherine who had begun to cry again. The nurse ran an affectionate hand over Catherine's head as the male cop made a quick search on Michael for any concealed weapons.

"How can you do this to me here?" he asked fiercely as he was escorted away. "Especially with my wife in the condition she's in?"

His questions were immediately answered in the smug face of Nowell Stuart, who'd watched the entire arrest from right outside Catherine's room.

"You son of a . . ." Michael's voice trailed off as Nowell raised his eyebrows and cast an innocent look at the arresting officers. Michael knew that regardless of whatever ruse Nowell had concocted, the man would use anything against him now and that he'd better use utmost caution. Nowell smirked in response, then waved good-bye while disappearing into Catherine's room.

Chapter Fifty-six

Michael had never felt so humiliated in his entire life. Despite scores of youthful pranks and a penchant for fast driving, he'd never been in trouble with the law. And now, five months before becoming an ordained priest, he was posing for a mug shot in Manhattan's Central Booking Division. He felt his career vanish in the pop of a single flashbulb.

Compounding his frustration was that he knew what he'd done was wrong—he'd simply become fed up and struck another man—a mark of Cain according to Christian doctrine, and proof of his inner weakness to the man he struck.

Oh, and of all people, thought Michael ruefully. *If ever there was a time I need to be strong—for myself, for Catherine, and for that tiny baby—it's now.*

He was fingerprinted and frisked once more, then asked to relinquish any sharp objects he might have in his possession, including a ballpoint pen and a paper clip holding together some personal notes from his trip to Atlanta.

Michael tried to think of it as a learning experience. After all, he told himself, he was trained to minister to inmates and this was certainly a way of gaining perspective on what they went through. But it was utterly disgraceful to him, and whatever perspective he was about to gain on the other side of jail bars would be clouded by his intensely burning anger at Nowell Stuart.

"Do you have an attorney, Mr. Harrison?" asked the arresting officer, who'd accompanied Michael to Central Booking to process him.

"No," Michael said meekly. "I've never needed one."

"Well, there will be a public defender at your arraignment unless you plan to make other arrangements."

"I understand."

"Your arraignment is scheduled for nine-thirty a.m. tomorrow."

"Tomorrow?! You've got to be joking. Am I free to go until then?"

She snorted in an attempt to smother her laughter. "Yeah, right," she said. "Actually, you're the grand prize winner of a round trip to Rikers Island."

"Rikers Island!" said Michael with sheer panic in his voice. He knew all too well what it was like out there— a modern-day lion's den. His head began reeling with renewed anger at Nowell Stuart; and each time he thought of him he recalled Catherine's portrait. He simply couldn't make sense out of anything that was happening to him, and knew there was only one thing he could do. He began to pray. He clasped his handcuffed hands, bowed his head, and closed his eyes, silently asking the Lord to give him the strength to get through. His meditation was abruptly interrupted by the cop.

"Did you reach someone yet to bail you out?"

Michael looked up at her, and thought to say he had just summoned the only one that could truly do the job. "No," he finally answered. He'd tried to reach Jack Whitlock while at the Nineteenth Precinct where he was first taken after the arrest. But his secretary, Ruth, told him he was gone on a faculty retreat all day. Michael dared not leave a message with her because it was a surefire way to spread the news of his arrest around the campus.

"What happens if I can't reach anybody?"

"You get an extended vacation at Rikers Island," she said sarcastically.

"How much will bail be, anyway?"

"First time offender like you, probably a thousand."

"A thousand dollars! What kind of *punishment* could a first and *only* time offender expect to receive?"

"On a misdemeanor assault in the third degree, up to a year. In reality, it depends on the mood of the judge and the ambition of the prosecutor."

"What's your guess?"

"They might go easy on you, seeing as how you've never been in trouble before, and you're almost a mem-

ber of the clergy. Maybe a fine, maybe some community
service or something."

Piece of cake, thought Michael.

"But," she went on, "we got a lotta moody judges
and a lot of ambitious prosecutors, if you know what
I mean."

Michael groaned. "Listen," he asked, "may I make
another phone call?"

"You got a quarter?" she asked, in other words telling
him he had to pay for the call himself.

"In fact, I don't. May I use the phone here, please."

She finally cast a slight smile at him. "Sure," she said,
"what's the number, I'll dial it for you."

Michael gave her Jack Whitlock's home phone number, then listened as the phone rang several times. It was
finally picked up by the answering machine.

"Jack, this is Michael," he said with some relief. "I'm
afraid I have some good news, some bad news, and some
very unfortunate news. The good news first. Catherine
and I are the proud parents of a beautiful baby girl. But
it was a very traumatic day for Catherine yesterday, and
I'm sad to report the other baby didn't make it." Michael paused for a moment trying to collect himself.
"Anyway, Catherine's in the intensive care unit at Eastside Medical Center, and I am in jail and in need of bail
money. It's embarrassing beyond belief to confess this
to you, but I belted Nowell Stuart in the jaw today. He's
decided to press charges, and I need you to help get me
out of here. I'm downtown at Central Booking, and my
arraignment is tom . . ." The machine bleeped at him
telling him that his time was up. He could only hope
that Jack would know what to do next. Michael looked
at his watch, which amazingly showed it was just 10:30
A.M. "This has been the longest day of my life," he said
with a sigh as he hung up the phone, "and it's only
just begun."

The cop looked at him sympathetically as he handed
her the phone to hang up. "I don't know whether to say
sorry or congratulations," she said.

"Either one will do," he replied.

By three o'clock in the afternoon Michael was still in
the holding cell at Central Booking awaiting his trip over

to Rikers Island. After making acquaintances with two drunks, a drug dealer, a shoplifter, and an accused murderer with bloodstains on his jeans, Michael staked out some space in the cell to take a nap. It didn't last long.

"Harrison," shouted an officer.

"That's me," said Michael as he jumped off the bench and went to the bars.

"Your attorney's here to see you." Michael looked at the officer with confusion. *Was there some misunderstanding?* he asked himself *I told the cop I didn't have one. Maybe Jack Whitlock hired one for me.*

He was led in handcuffs out of the holding area and into a room where he was met by a suave-looking Italian man, impeccably dressed with thick dark hair slicked back and tortoiseshell glasses perched perfectly atop a classic Roman nose.

"See ya, Vinny," said the cop with a wink, leaving the room.

"Thanks, Tony," Vince Gambrielli said with a smile. Michael just stared at him. It was obvious from his trimly tailored suit and designer shoes that this was no public defender, nor anyone he could imagine Jack Whitlock sending.

"So, you got yourself in a little hot water, heh?" he asked in a rich baritone voice.

"Who are you?" asked Michael suspiciously.

"Oh, sorry. Name's Vince Gambrielli. I'm an attorney."

"I figured that. But who are you? I mean, what do you want from me?"

"Nothing. I'm just here to give you a little friendly advice."

"Why do I get the feeling it's from someone who's not so friendly?"

"Hey, I'm a nice guy."

"You know what I mean. What do you want from me?"

"I just wanted to give you a heads up on something. Try to save you a little bit of trouble down the road."

"Do I need my own attorney before I listen?"

Gambrielli looked at his watch. "I'm a busy man," he said. "How soon can your attorney get here?" Michael sensed correctly that Vince Gambrielli was an expensive

puppet of Nowell Stuart's and that sooner or later he'd
have to listen to what the man had to say. He decided
he'd rather it be sooner. He slumped back in his chair
and stared Vince Gambrielli directly in the eye.

"Should I proceed?" Gambrielli asked politely.

"Be my guest," said Michael.

"My client tells me you assaulted and battered him
with no reason or provocation in the hall at Eastside
Medical Center today. Is that correct?"

"I said I would listen, not answer any questions," Michael replied.

"Just wanted to let you know that not only is Mr.
Stuart prepared to press full charges, but the prosecutor
will also request a temporary restraining order to prevent you from coming anywhere near him, his family, or
place of business."

"Twist my arm," Michael said, smirking.

"You think this is funny, Mr. Harrison? Perhaps you
missed something. I said the restraining order will prevent you from going anywhere near his family, which
includes his newborn daughter."

Michael felt as though he could have been knocked
over by a feather—that what he had just been told was
possibly the craziest thing he'd ever heard. But the
image of the well-adorned nursery in Nowell's town
house popped into his mind. "What do you mean, 'his
newborn daughter'?" he asked bitingly while leaning
into the table.

"Well, that's primarily what I've come to tell you
about. You see, my client, Mr. Nowell Stuart, is the father of the child your wife just delivered. We can prove
it too, and the truth will come out in the paternity suit
we are about to file."

What the hell is he talking about? he thought. It was
like being part of some big practical joke that had snow-
balled out of control. Only looking at Vince Gambrielli's
designer clothes and designer demeanor, he knew that
what was happening to him was no joke. His life, everything he'd worked for, everything he'd believed in, was
hanging in the balance, and he knew Nowell had the
resources and wherewithal to influence the outcome in
either direction. *Why would Catherine do this to me?
This is ludicrous. It simply can't be his baby, she could*

barely get pregnant with me, how could she get pregnant with him? Or could she? This is just downright evil—this is not Catherine's doing, he concluded in silence.

"I don't care what your client thinks, or says, or whatever," said Michael. "I'm not afraid of him, and I'm not afraid of a paternity test. That baby is mine. And what the hell does he think he's doing, posing as Catherine's husband? It must be illegal, if not a bit strange, don't you think?"

"Well, say what you will, Mr. Harrison. Not only has your wife been having a long-time affair with my client, but we have eyewitnesses who can corroborate the facts. You might be interested to know," he said, his voice lowering and sounding more sinister, "that one of Mr. Stuart's staff members actually saw the two of them sleeping together at Stuart Hall."

Michael felt physically ill. How could any of this have happened without his knowledge? Were his instincts painfully correct to begin with? Should he have forced Catherine out of that job long ago to protect her from Nowell? No, he decided, it wouldn't have made a difference. If she loved him, and wanted him, she would have found a way to get to him. Images of that beautiful baby girl he'd seen today came popping into his mind. Why would he have felt such a powerful emotional surge toward her if she were not his child? he wondered. *He should have seen this coming,* he kept thinking. But in reality, he didn't know what to think.

"Are you getting the picture here, Mr. Harrison?"

"What exactly is it you want from me?"

Vince Gambrielli reached inside his briefcase for a two-page document and a pen.

"What I want is not as important as what you need. You know as well as I that your career will be over if news of your arrest and the unfortunate circumstances involving this birth spreads. My client is willing to drop the charges if you are willing to sign this document stating you acknowledge you are not the father of that child."

Does he think I'm mad? That I would just sign my life away like that? He would love nothing more than for me to wither under his pressure, thought Michael defensively. *I won't do it; I won't go down without a fight. At*

*least not until I've talked with Catherine and learned the
truth from her.*

"Are you finished, Mr. Gambrielli?"

"You get the picture, don't you, Michael?"

"Are you finished?"

"My work has just begun." He smiled, then stood up,
offering his hand to Michael as he prepared to leave.
Michael thought first not to touch it, as though it was
evil incarnate. But then he wanted to know—he wanted
to know for the purpose of his own God-loving soul—
what it felt like. It was a warm, gentleman's handshake.

"One more detail, Mr. Harrison. As far as Eastside
Medical Center is concerned, Mr. Stuart is the girl's fa-
ther. He even signed her birth certificate this morning.
Cornelia Howard Stuart—nice name, don't you think?"

Chapter Fifty-seven

When Michael awoke the next morning, his first thought was that he was on a bench in the Atlanta airport, waiting for the weather to clear before he could board his plane. *No,* he painfully realized, *this is New York, and I'm in Rikers Island.* He looked at his watch, which read 7:45 A.M. *Whatever happened to Whitlock?* he thought as he ran his hand over the stubble on his face. It had been over forty-eight hours since he'd taken a shower or shaved; forty-eight hours since his life jumped the track. He looked around him—the shoplifter was gone, and so were the drunks who had been with him in the cell at Central Booking. But the murderer and about a dozen other accused ne'er-do-wells were crammed in there with him.

He started the morning as he would any other—with the Lord's Prayer. And then, forcing himself into deep meditation, he began praying in earnest over all that was happening, including a prayer for Nowell Stuart, that he would somehow come to see the glory of God in his own life.

A short while later he was handcuffed again, then returned to the District Courthouse for his arraignment. His public defender was a short, stocky man who tried to defy his baldness with a long but skimpy rattail that ran down the back of his cheap suit.

"Marty Johnson," the man introduced himself, then shook Michael's hand. Marty's hand was as sweaty as his forehead, as though he'd jogged several miles to the courthouse. He pulled a well-used handkerchief from his pocket and wiped his brow with it.

"Listen, how you wanna plead? Guilty, not guilty, what?"

Is insanity an option at this point? thought Michael. *Should I tell him I feel like I'm going insane?*

"Have you heard anything from a guy named Jack Whitlock?" Michael asked instead.

"Nope. What about him?"

"I called him to bail me out. Has he tried to reach anyone yet?"

"Nope, sorry. Anyone else we can get in touch with?"

Michael tried to think if there was anyone he could trust with this matter, but there simply was no one other than Jack. He knew Jack would help him eventually, and until then he'd simply have to endure. He quickly scanned the room to see who all was there, spotting the dark beady eyes of Vince Gambrielli staring right at him. Gambrielli was seated quietly in the rear, prepared to take it all in and report each detail back to his client. Michael's eyes narrowed as he stared fiercely back at the man, refusing to back down in the face of such intimidation.

"No, there's no one else I can call right now," Michael told Marty. "But it's okay. I know my friend Jack will make it sooner or later."

"How do you want to plead?"

"I suppose not guilty."

"Yes or no, guilty or not?"

"Not."

As the proceeding began, Michael turned to look at Gambrielli, who had now trained his attention on the judge. It didn't take the judge long to cut to the quick of the matter, or for the prosecutor to press full charges and ask for the restraining order. A trial date was set for three weeks later, and bail was set at one thousand dollars—cash on the barrel. And still no sign of Jack.

The judge was about to dismiss the whole group and send Michael back to Rikers Island when a court officer approached the bench and began speaking to the judge. Michael turned around and discovered that Gambrielli had slipped away, and that Jack Whitlock was miraculously standing in the back of the room instead. Michael heaved a huge sigh of relief.

"Marty, my friend is in the back of the room. He's here to bail me out."

Marty quickly turned at the same time that the judge spoke to Jack.

"Are you here to post Mr. Harrison's bail?"

"Yes, sir," said Jack.

"All right," said the judge, an elderly man with a stern face and no-nonsense demeanor. "Trial is still set for three weeks from today. Mr. Johnson, I believe you know what to do from here."

"Yes, sir," replied Michael's attorney.

It took another hour to process the final paperwork and release Michael into Jack's custody.

"Jack," said Michael contritely as soon as they were out of the courthouse. "I cannot thank you enough."

"Sorry I didn't get here sooner. After yesterday's retreat I stopped to visit my mother just outside of Fairfield and ended up spending the night. Meredith finally reached me, but it was too late to take a train into the city. Are you all right? Did they treat you okay?"

"I'm fine. Let's just get out of here."

"Listen, Meredith is worried sick about you. She wants to know if you'll come over for a late breakfast."

"What I really need is to get back to Catherine," said Michael, despite feeling emotionally exhausted and famished.

"Son, I suggest you take a short break. You've been through a big ordeal, and it might not hurt to get your thoughts into perspective on this matter."

Thirty minutes later they were inside the warm, cheerful apartment of Jack and Meredith Whitlock, sort of a second home to Michael since he'd been at school. He now felt grateful for accepting the offer.

Over pancakes, bacon, and two pots of coffee among the three of them, Michael explained every last detail of what had happened since returning from Atlanta—including the discovery of Catherine's portrait in Nowell's bedroom and the nursery set up for two. Meredith gasped at the news, particularly when hearing about Nowell's paternity challenge.

Michael even shared the intimate details over Catherine's pregnancy through in vitro fertilization, finally explaining to Jack why she'd been so upset that day he'd seen her on campus not long ago. "The second insemina-

tion had failed and she thought she'd never have a
baby," he told them.

"I don't know what to do," Michael continued
gravely. "One day I'm living my life to the fullest, happy
about serving the Lord and excited about the birth of
my new baby. And the next day my family is
wrenched apart."

"Remember, Michael, loving your enemies doesn't always mean offering the other cheek. It can mean not
setting your agenda to match their agenda. Do what you
must without bringing yourself down to his level. And
then pray for him," said Jack.

"I have," said Michael, somewhat defensively. "But I
have to confess, I never realized how hard this would
be. We preach this gospel so easily, but if you were in
my shoes, do you think you could be so forgiving?"

The couple remained fixed and quiet, until Meredith
reached over and stroked Jack's arm.

"You know," Michael finally said while standing up.
"It's been a long couple of days. I'm going to go home,
take a long shower, and perhaps nap, and when I can
think a little more clearly I'll decide what to do."

Jack rose as he did. "Meredith and I are here for you.
Anything we can do to help, please let us know."

Michael shook his head somberly, then headed out the
door, deliberately walking slowly as he made his way
home. He dreaded going into the apartment and seeing
all that baby paraphernalia, and bypassed it as quickly
as he could once he walked in the door. True to his
word, he took a long hot shower and then fell into bed,
where sleep easily overcame him for the next four hours.

Chapter Fifty-eight

When Michael finally awoke it was midafternoon, though he was far from refreshed. He felt lethargic from all the emotion of the past few days, but managed to swing his feet over the side of the bed anyway. He needed to get down to the hospital and see Catherine, hoping that he could at least spend some private time with her and try to sort out what was happening in their lives. Was it really over, he wanted to know. Was it at all possible that she intended to leave him for Nowell? He didn't believe she was capable of such deceit; of living such a vicious lie.

He didn't know what bothered him more; all the unanswered questions or the fact that he missed his wife terribly. He missed her swollen belly beside him in the morning. He missed her sensitive touch. He missed her sweet smell. All he could do as he tried to think it through was pick up her pillow and hold it tight. And then he thought about the baby—the sweet, precious baby waiting to receive him in the nursery. And about her brother, a child none of them would ever come to know. Michael remembered the visions on the screen during Catherine's sonogram, of the one sucking its tiny thumb and the other sleeping peaceably.

And then he began to cry. Hard sobs racked his body, along with an intense feeling of guilt. He'd pushed Catherine into remaining with Nowell, despite her protests. And worse—it was only for the money.

He finally managed to pull himself together, and as he was about to head out the door for Eastside Medical Center he noticed a flashing light on the answering machine. He really didn't have the energy to return anyone's calls, but decided to find out who it was nonetheless. He played back the tape and advanced it to each new message, but at each interval all he heard was a click. Someone had hung up the phone after each of three attempted calls.

Michael tried to put aside the nagging thought that it was Nowell playing mind games with him, but as he was about to leave the apartment the phone rang. He promptly answered it, expecting to hear another click or perhaps prolonged silence as Nowell tried to torture him some more.

"Hello," said an unfamiliar voice on the other end of the line. "Hello?" said the caller again, as Michael only listened at first.

"Who is this?"

"Is this Michael Harrison?" she asked back.

"Who's asking?" he snapped.

"I don't want to tell you that right now. But I do need to tell you something," the person on the other end continued nervously. "I think your life may be in danger."

"Who is this?" he demanded a third time. "If you don't tell me who this is I'll hang up."

"No," the caller begged, "don't go. I've been trying to reach you half the day. I'm in trouble too, and I think we can help each other."

"What do you mean? How do you know me?"

"Just trust me, that's all I'm going to tell you right now. Can you meet me at the Lexington Luncheonette on 83rd and Lex in about an hour?" she asked.

"How will I know you? How do I know *you* aren't trying to hurt me?" he asked skeptically.

"I suppose you *don't* know that, but you must trust me," the caller said, "I'm wearing black, and I'll be sitting in a phone booth beside the restaurant's window facing 83rd Street. I know what you look like, I'll be watching for you."

"I'll see you in an hour," said Michael, then hung up the phone. He locked the apartment behind him and reluctantly headed for the subway that would take him north on Lexington Avenue.

Michael walked the few blocks from the subway to the Lexington Luncheonette. It was an authentic diner first opened in 1925, a place where you could still get a cup of coffee and the day's gossip for under one dollar. He sat on the stairs of a nearby building just kitty-corner to the restaurant and observed the comings and goings, keeping a watchful eye on the phone booth the entire time.

There were actually two phone booths—one occupied by an elderly man who fumbled twice with his change before making his call. And then a teenage girl picked up the phone in the adjacent booth, gabbing animatedly for at least fifteen minutes before finally hanging up in a tiff.

He was so focused on the teenager that he almost hadn't noticed a blond-haired woman with roots as dark as her black cotton sweater enter the opposite phone booth. She wore dark glasses and was smoking a cigarette. *She couldn't be more obvious about being inconspicuous,* thought Michael as he watched her for several moments more before crossing the street. He deliberately brushed against the windowpane outside the phone booth on his way inside the restaurant to alert the woman he was there, which startled her so badly she dropped her cigarette and grabbed her chest in what looked like mortal fear.

Michael was stopped by a waitress on his way in, but informed her that his party was already inside. The woman exited the phone booth, and without removing her glasses had slipped into a booth in the back of the restaurant just ahead of him. She didn't utter a sound as Michael slid across from her.

"You are expecting me, aren't you?" he asked her.

"Hello, Michael." Her voice was gravelly and her demeanor jittery. Beneath the glasses Michael could see dark circles and fear in her eyes, though it was obvious in her face as well. He couldn't tell how old she was, early forties maybe, possibly younger. The smoking had robbed the vitality from her skin, but it was clear that something else had robbed it from her life.

They stared at each other a few moments longer while the woman proceeded to light up a cigarette. "You don't mind if I smoke, do you?" she asked. Michael knew her need to smoke was greater than his distaste for it. "Go right ahead," he said. Both her face and voice were familiar to him, but he couldn't place her.

"I feel like I know you," he said. "How would that be?"

She let out a low, throaty laugh. "Well, your sperm count is exceptionally good," she said, "if that rings any bells."

"Oh, my God"—he fidgeted in his seat—"of course, you're the one I handed my, my . . ." He felt too embarrassed to say it.

"Semen specimen to," she finished the sentence for him. "My name is Sharon Corso, I'm the senior embryologist at the Manhattan Reproductive Center."

Michael had seen her for less than a minute during Catherine's in vitro fertilization process. He'd been instructed to take his specimen directly to the lab, and was specifically told to deliver it to Sharon Corso. She received the plastic jar from him, made him sign a log sheet, then jokingly asked him if he wanted a boy or a girl.

"Both," he'd said with a laugh at the time. It didn't seem so funny anymore.

"Why are you here right now? What do you want from me?" he asked impatiently.

She took a long drag off her cigarette and was about to speak when an older but perky waitress interrupted her. "Would ya care for some coffee?" she asked, a freshly brewed pot in her hand. "Sure," they both answered. She filled two cups already on the table. "How 'bout a menu? You gonna have something to eat?" Sharon said no, Michael felt it necessary to oblige the waitress. "Sure, I'll look at a menu," he said.

"Be right back." She smiled, then took off only to become distracted by new customers. Corso took a sip of her coffee, then looked at him over her cup as though she were hiding behind it.

"My life is in danger because of you," she said slowly. At any other time those words might have been laughable to him. But not today.

"You don't believe me, do you?" she went on anxiously.

"I'm sorry," Michael said. "It's just that if you knew what I'd been through lately you could tell me the sky was falling and I wouldn't be surprised."

"Does the name Phillip Stevenson ring any bells with you?"

"You sure are into ringing bells, aren't you?"

"Listen, believe it or not, I'm here to help you. If you don't want to hear what I have to say I'll throw a buck on the table for my cup of coffee and be out of your life forever. Otherwise, I believe I can make a big difference in your life."

"I'm sorry, really," Michael said. "No, I don't know a guy by the name of Philip Stevenson."

"Well he sure knows you. In fact," she said, finally removing her glasses to reveal swollen, red-rimmed eyes, "he called and threatened to kill me if I did or said anything to hurt him or his new baby over at Eastside Medical Center."

"What? Who is this man? Why would he try to kill you and what has this got to do with me? Do the police know about this?"

Sharon Corso tried to speak and could only shake her head no at his last question. For the moment she was completely overcome by emotion, and choked on her own words each time she tried to speak.

"I did a horrible thing," she finally said, then began to cry again. Michael grabbed a handful of napkins from the canister at the end of the table. "Here," he said, trying to comfort her, "just take your time. I'm not going anywhere." He was a thoroughly captive audience and at this point would have stayed all day to hear her out.

"When you and your wife Catherine were going through the in vitro fertilization process, this guy . . ." She sniffled, trying to compose herself. She stopped and lit up another cigarette. "This guy," she went on, "Phillip Stevenson, sort of came into my life. I thought at first he and his wife were patients at the Center. At least, that's what he told me. Anyway, it turns out he wasn't a patient there after all." She stopped, wondering how much detail she should reveal of her sexual involvement with the man, then decided only to allude to it. "I became totally attracted to him," she went on, hoping that Michael would catch the innuendo, "if you know what I mean."

"I think so," said Michael, nodding his head.

She took a long drag, then heaved a big sigh as she

exhaled. "Anyway, after he left my house this one night, he conveniently left a bag with one hundred thousand dollars in it beside my bed. It turned out to be a bribe." Michael felt a growing knot in his stomach, his intuition telling him loud and clear what happened next. It wasn't Phillip Stevenson who'd "conveniently" left one hundred grand at her disposal, it was Nowell Stuart. He felt certain of it, but didn't say anything, waiting to hear the woman out, encouraging her with the look in his eyes.

"I didn't know what he meant by it, I didn't even know who he really was because the next day when I got to work and checked the records there was no patient by the name of Phillip Stevenson. Anyway, this guy comes around again and basically here's the deal he gave me. I get to keep the one hundred thousand dollars in exchange for using his sperm in your wife's in vitro process."

Michael felt as though he could have leaped over the table and strangled the woman. It made him physically ill to think Catherine had actually carried Nowell's babies. He had never experienced such intense feelings of hatred for anyone as he did that moment for Nowell Stuart or this woman sitting across from him.

Don't bring yourself down to his level, Jack Whitlock's admonition to him rang through his head. He took a deep breath and started thinking through all he'd heard the previous day.

Then what Vince Gambrielli had said was true. Or was it? he thought. *Suppose this woman is a setup. A way of putting pressure on me to believe it is so. No,* he thought. *In my training I've seen too many down and out people, and this woman is truly distraught. She is clearly telling the truth, and now it all makes sense. Whether Catherine is a witting partner or not, Nowell plotted this all along and I only abetted him by belting him in the mouth yesterday. I just gave him a trump card he probably wasn't even expecting.*

"Let me ask you a question," Michael started very slowly, "is this Phillip Stevenson by any chance British? A good-looking guy?"

"Yeah, so you do know him?"

Michael let out a slight guffaw. "I just want to know

one thing," he said with a mixture of sadness and anger. "How could you have done this to us?"

"I needed the money," she defended herself.

Michael shook his head in utter disbelief.

"If you're so afraid for your life, then why don't you just go to the police?"

"You don't understand. I'd lose everything. My job, my future, and most importantly—my son. I'm in a wicked custody battle for him, which is why the money was so much easier to accept."

"You're telling *me* you have everything to lose?" Michael snapped. "My wife, who I love and adore, just gave birth to another man's children because of you and you're telling me *you* have everything to lose. I'm outta here," he said fiercely. He started to slide out of the booth when she forcibly grabbed him by his forearm.

"Wait, wait," she implored him. "There's something else. Which is the real reason why I'm here. I can help you."

Catherine sputtered and choked as the doctor removed the respiratory tube from her throat. "I want my baby," she cried faintly with the first free breath she could get. "I need my baby."

"Take it easy, hon," said Gail, one of the nurses who'd been tending to her for the past two days. "Let the doctor finish up here."

"My husband," she then whispered painfully, her throat sore and irritated, her mouth absolutely parched from two days on the breathing apparatus. Gail began checking her blood pressure while the doctor proceeded with listening to her breathing.

She was desperate to get moved out of the ICU, which would be at least one more day she'd been told. Her whole body felt stiff and achy, and the pain in her abdomen was intense, causing shooting pain each time she shifted her weight. But still, she was that much closer to holding her daughter, and being rejoined by Michael, together as a family at last. And just as importantly, breaking away from Nowell Stuart once and for all.

He'd barely left her bedside since the incident with Michael. He offered no information as to what had happened, or over Michael's whereabouts. Instead, he focused all his attention on her, constantly stroking her hair, holding her hand, and telling her how much he loved her and their baby daughter, and how he couldn't wait to have them all home, safe and protected, where they belonged.

Chapter Fifty-nine

Nowell decided he wasn't taking any chances. As long as the hospital recognized him as Cornelia's rightful father, then he would bring her home the first chance allowed. He'd planned for round-the-clock nurses to tend to Cornelia once she'd arrived, and the same for Catherine. He felt certain that she wouldn't want to be apart from their daughter for one second, and would happily move into the town house once she fully understood the opportunity he'd provided for her. At last, she could fulfill her love for him.

Smiling, he shut the nursery door in his town house, as everything was in perfect order now. He'd had the second crib dismantled and put away, rearranging the room to receive one child only. There was no need to remind Catherine of their loss. In addition, he'd quietly made arrangements for the body of their infant son to be flown to Stuart Hall, where he was to receive a proper burial in the family cemetery. When Catherine took over as lady of the house, she would appreciate knowing what lengths he had gone to to keep their family together.

Turning on the security monitors, then securely locking the front door, he headed out of the town house on foot to the hospital. Despite the bone-chilling December temperature, a cheerfulness resonated in Nowell. He wanted so badly to tell each and every one of them how he'd just become a father to the most beautiful baby girl in the world. He smiled broadly at each person instead.

Arriving at the prestigious Upper East Side hospital, Nowell nodded at the security guard, the same man he'd tipped off to look out for Michael Harrison. Michael's restraining order was in effect already, and there was no way he could come near Cornelia without getting into trouble with the law. The security guard nodded reassuringly back at Nowell, as if to say everything was A-OK. Nowell stopped in the hospital's flower shop and purchased the largest arrangement of flowers available as a gift for Catherine, then proceeded toward the elevator and on up to ICU.

But knowing that Cornelia had been moved into the regular nursery after he left early this morning to shower and change, he decided first to stop by and see how his precious daughter was doing. He wanted to provide Catherine with a full report on her progress, as he knew she would be anxious for details.

Nowell got off on the fourth-floor maternity and nursery ward, then lightheartedly marched over to the viewing window. There were at least seven babies in there, all tightly swaddled and each with a tiny cotton cap on its head. It was difficult at first discerning which one was Cornelia, as at first glance all the babies seemed to look the same.

He took to reading the name placards outside each bassinet bearing the last name of each child, preceded by BOY or GIRL: GIRL STUART was not among them. Feeling slightly disappointed that she hadn't been moved out of the neonatal intensive care unit yet, he stopped a nurse as she made her way out of the enclosed and locked nursery.

"Pardon me," he said warmly. "But I believe my daughter, Cornelia Stuart, was scheduled to be brought down here this morning. Do you happen to know when that might be?"

"Oh, she's been moved here already," she answered sweetly.

"Indeed? I didn't see her in the nursery just now."

"Well that's because she's now on her way up to her mother. I understand they finally took her mom off the respirator this morning, and the first thing she asked for was her baby. The doctor consented to allowing your wife to see the baby for a very brief visit."

Nowell could feel his jaw go tense with anger. He'd specifically asked to be the one to do the honors of presenting Cornelia to Catherine.

"When did the baby leave?" he snapped.

"Just a few seconds ago. You can probably catch the

nurse right up ahead through those double doors, she's pushing Cornelia in the bassinet. The elevators take forever around here, you know."

Nowell turned on his heel without so much as a word of thanks and wasted no time pursuing the nurse. He came up on the elevator bank and saw no one—instead, way down the hallway he spotted a nurse pushing a bassinet. He was struck by the fact that she was moving rather quickly, but even more struck by something oddly familiar about her—the dark roots of her blond hair.

"You fucking whore," he shouted from thirty feet down the hall, thrusting his flower arrangement to the floor. Corso didn't even turn around, instead scooped the tiny baby from the shelter of her bassinet and made a quick turn down another corridor. Nowell was at the hallway intersection in seconds flat, but Corso and his daughter had vanished. He began thrusting open each and every door down the hallway, only to find startled patients or empty rooms. Suddenly he began to hear the pitched wail of an infant.

He listened carefully for a moment to determine where it was coming from—a room halfway down on the opposite side of the hallway. Without warning he burst into the room, only Corso was nowhere in sight. Instead, to his great surprise, he discovered his daughter, alone, frightened and wailing on a big, empty bed. He moved quickly toward her.

"I will kill that fucking bitch when I get my hands on her," he growled under his breath. *"I will kill her."*

Rather than picking his daughter right up, Nowell stopped, as he had never handled an infant before, especially one that was wailing so. It was during that brief hesitation that he received a glancing blow to the back of his head. Whatever hit him hurt, but did not wound. Startled, he turned around, but this time got whacked rather forcefully on the side of the head by Sharon Corso, who had yanked the phone out of the wall and was using the metal base of it to smash him. The second hit grew blood from his temple, and as Nowell worked to regain his bearings, the woman once more scooped up the baby and disappeared.

Though stunned and now working to stop the bleeding with a handkerchief, Nowell stumbled out of the room

in time to see Corso enter a nearby stairwell while clinging fast to Cornelia.

Quickly and wildly Nowell began taking the stairs.
Turning up one flight and then another, he ran hard and
fast into a young lab technician, knocking over the
woman and forcing a wire basket full of blood samples
out of her hands. The vials crashed to the floor, each
breaking and spilling their contents all over the two of
them.

"Get out of my way," Nowell screamed, picking up a
broken vial with a long, jagged edge and pointing it at
the woman. The woman screamed and skirted back as
far as she could. The commotion and her scream were
enough to alert Corso up above that Nowell was close
on her heels.

She exited onto the next floor, trying as best as she
could to muffle the child's cries by bringing the baby
close into her chest. Fortunately the floor on which she
landed was the same as the ICU, and she knew that
Michael would be waiting for her around the corner. She
dashed as fast as she could down the corridor, knowing
any second Nowell would bear down on them, when she
ran almost headlong into Michael.

"We gotta get outta here," she said, breathless and
terrified.

Michael barely had a chance to respond as he saw
Nowell, blood on his face and clothes, had turned the
corner and was heading fast toward them. Michael could
not imagine what Corso had done to him, yet wasted
not a precious moment tearing away with her and the
baby, then exiting through another stairwell, taking the
steps two at a time as far as they could. When they
arrived at the first floor Corso tried the door, but it was
locked. The only set of stairs left was cordoned off, with
a warning sign posted that it was a restricted construction site beyond. Holding the baby tightly, Corso and
Michael stepped beyond the stanchion and down the
stairs, landing next to the middle of an entry hall leading
into a new wing being built for the hospital.

Since it was a Saturday, the construction site was vacant of workers, and the sounds of the infant's wails
echoed loudly throughout. It seemed there was no place
to hide, as Michael and Corso made their way past elec-

trical cable, concrete wire framing, workhorses, and exposed beams.

As if by God's grace, the baby's cries turned to whimpers and then stopped. Corso pulled the infant up close and stroked her tiny body in a gesture of reassurance. Michael, however, knew their danger was more imminent than ever, as they were now stuck in a place with no one around to protect them.

He immediately moved Corso out of the main hallway with its dangling wires and concrete floor and into an unfinished, yet adjacent room. He didn't know what to do otherwise, as he knew of no other means of escape and figured that surely Nowell was right behind them. He prayed that the baby would remain quiet, particularly considering the bone-chilling temperature inside this unfinished building.

Michael and Corso sat still and terrified, hovering in a corner as the baby seemed to drift off to sleep. Michael collected his breath, and as he looked down at the baby, a strange calm seemed to come over him.

"There's something else," Corso had said at the Lexington Luncheonette, *"which is the real reason why I'm here. I want to help you.*

"You asked me how I could do this to you?" she said, *her eyes growing clear and innocent as she stared right at him. "I didn't do it,"* she said softly.

"Didn't do what?" asked Michael as he was just about to leave.

"I didn't use his sperm. The baby is yours. She is definitely your child."

Michael slumped down, truly unable to believe what she'd just said, but hoping against hope it was true. "What are you telling me?" he said in a slow whisper.

"What he did to me, and the way he made me go about it, it was like he raped me. I hate that man. I hate him for what he did to me and what he wanted to do to you and your wife. Besides, it might have been easy to take the money from that bastard, but my conscience wouldn't allow me to go through with what he wanted. If you don't believe me, take a test. Take every test there is. That baby girl is yours, I swear to it."

As her words ran through his mind, a well of emotion sprang up in Michael, and he tapped Corso on the shoulder and gestured for her to pass the infant along—his very first chance to hold his daughter.

He was overwhelmed with emotion as he cradled the sweet, tiny child in his arms, and for the very first time got to see her face up close.

"Lucky you," he whispered, "you look just like your mama." And then he drew the child in as tightly as possible. Corso smiled at him, but was nonetheless vigilant for sounds of Nowell. It seemed that at least five minutes had passed without any sign of him, and then five minutes more before Corso spoke.

"I think we lost him. We gotta get that baby out of this hospital, now. Regardless of the fact that she *is* your daughter, that restraining order still stands and we'll both be arrested until we can sort this out through science. I've got an idea," she said matter-of-factly, not allowing Michael's emotion to interfere with their dangerous predicament.

"You stay here and let me check to make sure the coast is clear. There may be another way to get outta here, besides the way we came in. I'll take a quick look, then be back in about two minutes."

"No," Michael said emphatically. "You stay with the baby, I'll go. I've a much better chance of standing up to him than you."

"I am not afraid of that man anymore," said Corso firmly. "Besides, what's more important is who is capable of protecting the baby."

"You've got a point," Michael said, sighing. "Please make it fast."

Corso moved cautiously at first, glancing out the doorway. Seeing no sign of Nowell, she nodded at Michael and then disappeared. Michael could hear her footsteps echoing down the corridor in one direction, and then back in the other. She seemed to move quite a distance away from him, and then there was nothing but silence.

The wait for her return seemed interminable, and the silence thick and unnerving.

"Where could she be?" Michael whispered nervously in the baby's ear. He wondered if perhaps she hadn't gone through a door that was locked from the outside, only to find she was trapped on some other set of stairs. He waited a good ten minutes longer before finally deciding to move; he needed to find Corso, but more importantly he needed to escape the hospital with his daughter.

Gingerly he rose from his position, holding the dozing child carefully so as not to disturb her fragile sleep. He peered outside the door frame, and seeing no sign of Corso or Nowell, he proceeded out into the corridor. He walked down to the entrance from which they came, but discovered it was locked. He moved back down the corridor, past the construction debris and toward what appeared to be a new hallway. As he turned the corner he gasped—there in front of him was Nowell Stuart, holding a gagged Corso tightly in front of him with a large, jagged piece of glass at her throat.

"Hello, choirboy," he said, smiling. The petrified look in Corso's eyes told Michael to get the hell out of there as fast as he could. Michael, however, remained frozen.

"Out taking the baby for a walk, I see." Michael still did not respond.

"How utterly sweet. Well I tell you what else will be a sweet sight to behold—the blood of our friend here, if you don't just put my baby down right at my feet and then back away."

"Not a chance," Michael finally spoke with furious conviction, "she is not your baby."

"No, of course not," Nowell said, laughing. "What else would I expect you to say? Except that I know better, as does our friend, Ms. Corso. Don't you, my dear," he asked while lightly running the shattered end of the glass vial along her neck. It drew a tiny amount of blood, forcing Corso to pull away from him. Nowell held steadfast though, trapping her tightly in his grip.

Michael knew at that moment that Nowell was more than willing to murder the woman. He had never felt such anguish in his life, knowing that either way he could never live with himself—giving up his daughter to this crazed lunatic or watching this woman be killed by his failure to act. Nowell ran the glass a little deeper a second time, drawing yet more blood from Corso's throat.

"Put my child down, choirboy, or else I promise you and your friend will both die."

Michael moved forward a few paces as though he might comply, but the look in Corso's eyes told him

again to run. But he couldn't. As never before he felt
his faith being tested, then did what to another man
might have been unconscionable—he laid the baby down
on the cold concrete floor between them. Nowell did not
loosen his grip.

"Step back," said Nowell.

"Let her go now," said Michael, stepping tentatively
backward.

"Not on your life, choirboy," snarled Nowell, then
plunged the glass dagger deep into Corso's neck, causing
blood to fatally gush and then spurt forth. At that instant
Michael leaped forward to gather the baby, but not before Nowell had released Corso's limp body and was
directly on top of him, attempting to stab Michael with
the sharp vial.

With all his might, Michael managed to fend off what
surely would have been a fatal blow to his own neck,
and knock the makeshift weapon clean out of Nowell's
hands. Fighting each other fiercely, precariously close to
the infant, Michael managed to land a clean punch to
Nowell's nose, immediately breaking it and drawing
blood besides. Startled and in pain, Nowell temporarily
relaxed his grip, allowing Michael to stand and forcibly
kick the man in the head. The blow dazed Nowell just
enough to give Michael an opportunity to try scooping
up the baby and run. But as he reached for the child,
Nowell regained himself, catching Michael by the ankle.
As Michael stumbled, Nowell stood, bending down for
the shard of glass. Michael managed to kick himself free,
then straighten up, kicking the glass shard away just as
Nowell's hand reached it.

In a rage and with insane strength, Nowell pummeled
Michael, beating him repeatedly about the face and
chest, forcing him away from the baby and out into the
main corridor as he did. Though his adrenaline ran high,
and his fear for Catherine and their baby ran deep, he
simply couldn't manage to get a good blow back. With
nothing to brace himself, his efforts to resist were in
vain, and with one mighty kick in the groin from Nowell,
Michael staggered back toward the wall, from which extended several yards of exposed steel rebar used to rein-
force concrete. With one more kick from Nowell,

Michael was slammed into the wall, screaming madly as two sharp stakes impaled him.

Despite the searing pain, Michael tried to step forward but could not. He was literally stuck to the wall, his blood running along the rebar and dripping onto the ground.

Nowell took a step back and laughed.

"Good-bye, choirboy." He smiled, then swiftly departed with the baby girl.

Chapter Sixty

"Gail," Catherine managed to whisper, "my baby, I need my baby."

"I promise you, it won't be long," the stout and cheerful nurse said as she fluffed up Catherine's pillows. "But first, you need your rest."

"Where is Michael?" Catherine uttered, but before she could say another word, a blaring cry came from down the hall. "Code Blue, room four," shouted one of the nurses. Catherine had seen this happen once before, as a Code Blue turned into an all-hands experience in this ward. Gail quickly abandoned Catherine, rushing from the room and leaving her alone and depressed.

Where in the hell is Michael? she cried to herself. All that had happened to her these past few days had been more devastating than anything ever before. The staff barely acknowledged his arrest and offered no follow-up information on his whereabouts. She needed Michael badly, and she needed him now. Instead, what she got was Nowell and his manic behavior, and a ward full of doctors and nurses who knew little or nothing about the true dilemma she or her husband faced.

Gratefully, she dozed off, but her calm was not to last. Somewhat confused and agitated by being shaken awake, Catherine looked up and then gasped.

"My baby," she managed to whisper dryly, her face breaking into a nervous smile.

"Our baby." Nowell smiled back, while clutching the tiny girl in one arm, his free hand rubbing Catherine's leg. His appearance was extremely disheveled, and though he smiled serenely, there was a detached and wild look in his eyes. Worse was what appeared to be bloodstains on his hands. Catherine looked closely at the infant, and released a faint sigh of relief as the child moved its tiny hand.

Nowell inched slightly closer, and as he did his overcoat shifted open revealing larger bloodstains on his white cotton shirt. Catherine gasped again. She had never felt such distilled terror. This man before her, the same man who had been her friend, her employer, and nearly her lover, was now an absolute stranger and she knew that her life—and that of her newborn daughter—were in grave danger. Feebly she reached out her arms for the child, but Nowell stepped back.

"Catherine, my love," he said, his smile fixed, his hand still touching her leg. "We did it. We finally have our baby. Isn't she beautiful. Just like her mother."

My God, she thought, *he's gone completely mad.*

She tried reaching for the call button, but Nowell cut her off.

"Catherine, don't," he commanded sharply, moving closer toward her. Then his voice quickly softened. "Don't you want to hold our daughter?"

"Our daughter," she whispered faintly, reaching out yet again. He stepped back.

"I'm here to take you home. Take you back to the town house. You'll have everything you possibly need. Just imagine, the three of us alone together at last."

"Together?" she asked coarsely, her voice barely audible. She forced a smile at him wondering how she was going to get the baby out of his hands. She glanced out the doorway hoping she could summon help from someone passing by, but the hallway remained empty.

He moved closer toward her, this time stroking her face, then running a hand through her hair. "Together, at last, my love," he continued in his strange possessed manner.

"Nowell," she said imploringly, her eyes looking longingly at her child, and then up at him. "They won't let me go yet. I can't go."

"Nonsense," he said, unexpectedly throwing back the covers.

"Stop!" Catherine cried. "What are you doing?"

With his free hand Nowell jerked her up into a sitting position. Catherine tried to scream as the pain was that bad. But it was in vain, her voice failed her, and the staff, immersed in their Code Blue emergency, remained oblivious to her plight.

"Nowell, stop, you're hurting me," she cried. He firmly gripped her arm, pulling her even harder yet.

"The sooner we're home, the better," he said through his fixed smile. He pulled Catherine up even farther, causing excruciating pain to rush through her abdomen, then swung her feet over to the floor. Yanking the IV out of her arm, he next put his arm around her waist and hoisted her up, causing tears of anguish to run down Catherine's face. Standing for the first time made her nearly faint, but he held tight, forcing her to shuffle her way toward the door.

"I can't go out in the cold like this," she cried, clinging to him for support.

"Nonsense," he said as he angrily forced her out into the hallway. Catherine could hear the clatter of instruments and doctor's orders being shouted, yet still, no one noticed them. Desperately weak and again feeling faint, Catherine suddenly pitched forward.

Unable to balance holding her and the infant at the same time, Nowell lost his grip on Catherine causing her to fall headlong into an abandoned crash cart, and then to the floor. The crash cart bounced precariously against the wall and nearly tipped over, some of its contents spilling on the floor around her. Catherine prayed someone would hear the commotion and come running, but the staff remained absorbed in the resuscitation of the dying patient. Feeling as though she might die herself from the pain radiating throughout her body, Catherine lay prostrate on the floor amid the spilled emergency medical supplies.

"What are you doing?" Nowell snapped at her anxiously. "Get up. We have to get out of here—NOW!" he demanded.

Grabbing madly at Catherine while still maintaining a grip on the baby, Nowell tried yanking her back to her feet.

"Nowell, I can't," she cried, "the pain. I'm in so much pain."

"Stop it," he said fiercely, "stop it. You're fine. And you'll be even better once I get you home."

"Michael," she cried faintly. "I want Michael."

Nowell bent down, clutching the baby tightly to his chest.

"Michael," he said calmly as a bizarre smile consumed his face, "will *never* bother you, or me, or our baby again." Catherine managed to turn slightly, her eyes being met by his glazed look. *Oh, my God,* she thought wildly, looking at the blood on Nowell's hands and shirt. Her own blood began to turn cold thinking what might have possibly happened to Michael.

Suddenly the baby began to whimper. Nowell clumsily attempted to soothe her, but it was in vain as her cries grew louder and more demanding. He looked around nervously to see if anyone had noticed, then grabbed at Catherine's arm again.

"Get up!" he said, his countenance cruelly snapping again, "we're wasting time."

Every wail the child let out increased his edginess. Catherine prayed one of the staff members would hear the baby and come running, but it was hopeless. Nowell attempted quieting the baby once more, and Catherine, though desperate to take her child away from him, was grateful for his distraction. Among the strewn medical supplies on the floor around her, and within her grasp, was a full syringe of epinepherine. Catherine knew it was a dangerous gamble but she felt it might be her only weapon against his madness. While Nowell worked to smother the baby's cries, Catherine cautiously reached over and slid the syringe beneath her gown.

Slowly and painfully forcing herself into an upright position, then supporting her weight with her hands while maintaining a fixed lock on him, Catherine began to speak.

"Nowell, I can't tell you how much I've missed you," she whispered dryly.

He appeared baffled by her statement, and instead of immediately jumping to her bait, he backed away.

"Would you please just hold me," she asked sweetly.

"Don't be ridiculous," he said tensely. "There will be plenty of time for that once we're home."

"But I need you now," she cried. "So does your daughter. Just hold us, together, please."

Nowell looked around nervously, tentatively drew her in, then abruptly pushed her back. Catherine's heart raced, fearing he would see the syringe concealed in her trembling hand.

"Come on," he insisted, grabbing her arm yet again.

"I will," she replied, "but, please, please just hold me. Hold me and the baby together." She smiled faintly at him.

Exasperated, but unable to resist pleasing his beloved Catherine, Nowell moved in and wrapped his free arm around her. But it wasn't a tender embrace. Instead he attempted pulling Catherine into an upright position. The awkwardness of handling her and the child at the same time proved too awkward for him, but provided Catherine with the first clear opportunity.

Nowell never saw it coming, and as swiftly as she could manage, Catherine reached up and jammed the syringe into his chest quickly forcing every last drop of the drug right into his heart.

Nowell arched back as a searing pain from the epinephrine began to burn through his heart, then grabbed at his chest, trying desperately to remove the syringe. But it was futile, and in seconds he keeled over, gasping for air as he fell. And as he did, his stricken eyes looked curiously at Catherine, as though he simply couldn't believe she'd betray him.

But there was nothing Catherine could do, and with every last ounce of strength she could muster, she did the only thing she wanted to do—snatch her child from his dying grip.

Chapter Sixty-one

"Thank you, that will be all," said Catherine, watching as Stephen closed the study door, leaving a steaming pot of tea behind. Even in May it could be unusually cold and drafty in Stuart Hall, and she welcomed the chance to warm up over the hot drink while finishing her correspondence. She could hear Rags outside whoofing for attention, but she knew he was in good hands and was receiving plenty of it. She smiled, wishing at the moment she were outside with them.

She finished the letter, then inserted the check, when the study door unexpectedly burst open. Her eighteen-month-old daughter came bounding in the room, with Rags fast behind. The girl's father, seeming somewhat breathless, stood leaning on the door handle, but smiling proudly.

"I've written a letter you might like to read before I send it off," Catherine said, smiling genuinely at him as she handed it over. He sat down in one of the well-worn leather club chairs and began reading, then smiled again.

Dear Jack,

I am hoping this letter finds you and Meredith in good health. I understand that you have tendered your resignation from General; what a loss to that fine institution.

I know this $250,000 check won't make up for the departure of such a fine professor, but I want you to tell the Endowment Committee to get used to it, as it is our intention to send an equal amount each year and ask that a scholarship fund be set up in your name.

As you can imagine, Michael and I are still in awe that Nowell Stuart willed his vast estate to Julie Anne while she was still in utero—he was so confident she was his child. As executrix of the estate, I've been given ultimate discretion over how the funds are spent. And I feel this is only one measure for saying thanks to you and Meredith for opening your hearts and home to us last year during Michael's prolonged recuperation from those nearly fatal wounds.

I am delighted to report that Michael is fully recovered and more tireless than ever (though I believe he's met his match in Julie Anne!). We have so much to be grateful for. When I think of the events that shaped our lives over the past two years, I cannot help but think of the verse from Matthew: "Ye are the salt of the earth; but if the salt have lost its savour, wherewith shall it be salted?"—a lesson lost on our departed and tormented friend, Nowell. Money was the salt of his life, but it brought him none of what he craved the most—love.

Michael says he will never forget the look on Nowell's face during what might have been the final seconds of his own life. He knew that the man was a lost soul—as though his life had no purpose; no savour.

We are reminded about God's savour, His goodness, and His rich love in our own lives—lives that were spared and deeply enriched by the gift of Julie Anne. And though now rich beyond our imagination otherwise, we've decided to spend a good deal of money adding savour to the lives of those who are in need.

To that extent we've made a decision about Stuart Hall. It is far more house than we ever desire, and so we'd like to turn it into a retreat for seminarian students and professors where they can go to study, write, and meditate. Michael and I would like to know if you'd care to retire here as sort of a professor emeritus. Our offer is firm and stands if ever you should decide to take it up.

Please give my love to Meredith, and our regards to those on the Endowment Committee.

> *Best regards,*
> *Catherine Harrison*

"If you don't mind, I have one small addition to make," said Michael, a mischievous smile consuming his face as he reached for a pen.

P.S. There is one last note, and hopefully an enticing one: Here at Stuart Hall, Julie Anne has inherited one of the finest collections of wine in the world—one which I'm sure she'd want her official wine steward (her Daddy!) to share with her Godfather Jack!

Very fondly,
Michael Harrison

SIGNET ONYX   (0451)

SPELLBINDING PSYCHOLOGICAL
SUSPENSE

☐ **NIGHT CRIES by Stephen Kimball.** David McAdam, along with his wife and son, have become a killer's target. While David's arsenal is a breathtaking command of computers and nerves of steel, he is plotting against an enemy whose methods are equally high-tech—and whose weapon is primal terror.   (186222—$4.99)

☐ **THE RED DAYS by Stephen Kimball.** A brilliant mix of high-tech suspense and old-fashioned gut-churning action, this dazzling thriller will keep you riveted until its final provocative twist. "A tense story of eerie terror."—Ronald Munson
(176839—$4.99)

☐ **SIDESHOW by Anne D. LeClaire.** Soleil Browne cannot understand why she is dreaming of a little girl who lived sixty years before. Soleil watches helplessly as this 12-year-old orphan is forced into a life of abuse and threatened by even worse. Soleil knows she can save the child, if only she can find a way to reach her. "A remarkable and intriguing thriller."—*Philadelphia Inquirer*
(406109—$5.99)

☐ **GRACE POINT by Anne D. LeClaire.** When Zoe Barlow moves to the coastal town of Grace Point to make a new start of her marriage, she never dreamed of what was to await her. Her son suddenly disappears, and there is no one to trust as Zoe searches desperately, stumbling through a generation-old legacy. Chilling erotic suspense.... "A gripping novel of love, lust, ancient sins and deadly secrets."—Judith Kelman   (403959—$5.99)

Price slightly higher in Canada

Buy them at your local bookstore or use this convenient coupon for ordering.

PENGUIN USA
P.O. Box 999 — Dept. #17109
Bergenfield, New Jersey 07621

Please send me the books I have checked above.
I am enclosing $_____ (please add $2.00 to cover postage and handling). Send check or money order (no cash or C.O.D.'s) or charge by Mastercard or VISA (with a $15.00 minimum). Prices and numbers are subject to change without notice.

Card #_____ Exp. Date _____
Signature_____
Name_____
Address_____
City _____ State _____ Zip Code _____

For faster service when ordering by credit card call **1-800-253-6476**

Allow a minimum of 4-6 weeks for delivery. This offer is subject to change without notice.